HAMMER
TO
FALL

Uncommon Bonds - 2

A Novel by
WILLIAM E. NOLAND

HAMMER TO FALL
Uncommon Bonds – Book 2
Copyright © 2022 William E. Noland

FIRST EDITION SOFTCOVER
ISBN: 1622537173
ISBN-13: 978-1-62253-717-4

Editor: Lane Diamond
Cover Artist: Kris Norris
Interior Designer: Lane Diamond

EVOLVED PUBLISHING™

www.EvolvedPub.com
Evolved Publishing LLC
Butler, Wisconsin, USA

Printed in Book Antiqua font.

BOOKS BY WILLIAM E. NOLAND

UNCOMMON BONDS
Book 1: *Playing with Fire*
Book 2: *Hammer to Fall*
Book 3: *From the Beginning*
Book 4: *Day of Judgment* [Fall 2023]

DEDICATION

For my parents.

CHAPTER 1

Central Etruria, 593 BC

Just the faintest sound woke Rika, a stowaway on the honeysuckle breeze that drifted through her small, unshuttered window.

Below, her parents slept on, the distant and muffled cry insufficient to rouse them from the exhaustion of long and seemingly endless labors. Until recently, she had shared with them the cramped space that dutifully served her family in various capacities day and night. As fortune would have it, her sister, Sethra, had been married at harvest time last year. This granted access to the tiny but coveted loft, meant originally for storage, where formerly her two older brothers had bunked before they too moved out.

The space gave a modicum of privacy in the otherwise unrelenting scrutiny that characterized their confined and insular village. With Rika's transition to womanhood underway, she valued this prize of solitude above all others. The small window presented an unfettered vista down the hill and over the treetops of the woods below. She spent much of her precious and insufficient free time gazing into this tranquil panorama, which existed oblivious to and uncaring of the toils of the forge, or the loom.

Their cottage sat at the edge of the settlement, so few others were likely to have heard the noise. If they had, like her, they would know in their hearts what it meant. Unlike her, however, they would surely have pulled their blanket tighter and thanked Tinia for sparing them, or Calu for passing them over in favor of another. Even their anger and mounting frustration would not impel them to rise and investigate.

What purpose would it serve? The answers they sought were shrouded by the secrecy of that part of the temple where only the priests, those of noble blood, or a small cadre of elite household guards were allowed. Furthermore, making their displeasure known would surely bring the wrath of their lord and his soldiers.

She, however, knew better, or thought she did. So, despite the risk, she softly padded to the little window and looked out. From the road that led past her village and up the hill, torchlight winked and danced between the branches of trees still shy of their full complement of leaves.

Many small settlements sat dotted around the periphery of the prosperous and opulent plateau. Some contributed labor to the workshop. Farther west, they extracted ore from the hills for local use or, increasingly, for export to Fufluna near the coast. Mostly, these people eked out their existence by hunting or trapping game, or plucking fish from the ponds and streams around the hill. A portion of this bounty they ceded to the noble family in exchange for protection, meager allocations of grain from the fields in the east, and access to the annual festivals and feasts conducted outside the temple, which cemented all these far-flung communities into some semblance of a unified whole.

In a turbulent world, life here had long seemed safe and bucolic, but that began to change when the fortunes of the noble family mysteriously waned several years ago. Now, ever more hands were needed to mine and transport ore, and despite the importation of slaves for the most odious tasks, many who once hunted, fished, or augmented the craftspeople in the workshop were sent west.

It meant increased work for Rika's family and those in villages like hers, whose proximity to the plateau dictated residents labor almost exclusively in the workshop, or directly serve the noble family. More importantly, however, this left many of these small outlying settlements nearly empty. Those who remained, largely the elderly, for whom such grueling work was now impossible, made easy targets for the guards who came to collect them.

It could be days or even weeks before word spread that, yet again, another two had gone "missing," the euphemism used for what everyone knew—that they'd been taken, never to return. The question was, taken where, and why?

Where wasn't difficult to envision: the temple presented the logical location. Most believed a blood sacrifice took place, the likes of which the cultured Rasenna had abandoned for many generations. Verification of this, however, had proven elusive. With its stone floors and timber construction, the structure was unsuited for either burying or burning human remains. No bodies, or evidence of pyres or burial grounds, had ever been found outside, almost inconceivable in a settlement so small and ever full of prying eyes and gossip.

So, while the location appeared evident, exactly what periodically happened in the temple on late nights such as this one remained unknown, at least for now. She felt certain she'd discovered a way to solve this mystery. Thus, she alone rose, while others slumbered on or turned a deaf ear to what they might, or might not, have heard.

Southby, Massachusetts, Friday, July 26, 2013

Eric watched as Margot bit her lip.

She gazed from the paper on her desk to her computer screen, back and forth. Suddenly, a spark of inspiration appeared to strike. She let her lip free from the clutches of her front teeth, typed in some numbers on her keyboard, and hit return.

Again, a quick glance from paper to computer screen, but with a dissatisfied and puzzled look, she leaned back in her chair and resumed torturing her defenseless gums.

Eric snickered.

She shot a quick glance in his direction, but he was too fast for her. His eyes had already returned to his own computer screen, and the selection of hybrid bikes it currently displayed. He'd wanted a new one, so he'd been conducting a little surreptitious comparison shopping on this quiet Friday morning.

Well, not quiet for poor Margot, he reflected.

He knew she had the Peterman's invoice in front of her. Peterman's was one of Schneider Industrial Flooring's largest suppliers of cleaning chemicals and raw ingredients for certain types of heavy-duty flooring. They billed quarterly, and to get the best pricing, you had to order in certain quantities, but these were specialized products, and Peterman's didn't always have the amount a customer might want in stock. So, they'd honor the discount and ship portions of the various products over time. Clients had to keep track of what had been shipped versus their own inventory, as that represented what was being invoiced each quarter. Making matters even worse, Schneider typically placed multiple orders for the same product, and all that had to be tied out against various lot numbers.

Freaking nightmare.

Eric knew all about it, because he'd struggled through this process not long after he started in the Business Office. Now, he watched Margot as she got her first taste of this particular little ray of sunshine. It reminded him that it had been the Peterman's invoice that put him in the chair he now occupied: Business Manager.

That hadn't been his goal when he'd started. It was an accident, really. He'd been working for his dad's company since his semi-aborted freshman year of college, a year he tried hard not to think about. He turned from it even now while he recalled that unusual period.

Eric worked hard, borderline fanatically — for reasons of his own — trying to put that miserable first semester behind him. At first, he worked with the flooring crews, meaning he schlepped their equipment, fetched their coffee at Dunkin', and helped mop up when things were done. All shit jobs, but he did them well, and he kept at it during breaks when he made a second stab at school.

The following summer, the guys started showing him some of the flooring processes. By the time he graduated with a History degree from UMass in the spring of 2012 — on time, remarkably — he'd performed just about every job function in the Schneider crew repertoire. He had absolutely no idea what he wanted to do after graduation, so, he just stayed on at Schneider. He never intended to remain long-term, but then the receptionist in the Business Office left, yet again.

His dad asked him to fill the spot for a while. He'd get a chance to learn the business side of the operation, and it would be a little break from the physical grind of working with the crews. Having no compelling alternatives, Eric accepted.

Judy Denoff served as Business Manager. She'd been around since Grandpa had run the place, and she had her files and her processes pretty much tied up with a silver bow.

Eric had known her since he was little, and things started off fine. She had him answer the phones, open and send the mail, make endless streams of photocopies, and file almost equally endless streams of paperwork. None were exactly taxing exercises, and he mastered most of these in the first two weeks. By early July, he started to get a little bored.

He offered to help Judy convert some of her manual ledgers to Excel, but she refused. Not shocking, as she hadn't grown up using computers. It frustrated him, though, because Schneider always seemed to be behind in payments. He knew it would be so much easier if they tracked things electronically to figure out why. So, he decided to fiddle around with it a bit on his own, using copies of the invoices he opened in the mail.

For a while, he worked quietly on the recent June 30th Peterman's invoice, discovering how devilish it was. Then, one day, Judy asked him to address and mail some recent invoice checks. Seeing the Peterman's invoice and check together for the first time, he noticed the check was written out for less than the basic invoice amount, and didn't include the arrears amount at all.

He asked her about it.

She said it was due to Peterman's stupid way of invoicing, and that she had the correct figures in her files. He supposed that was possible — the whole thing really did seem to be a disaster — but then she also told him to stop messing with the invoices and to just pass them to her.

That surprised him. He was supposed to be learning. No wonder receptionists quit all the time if they had so little to do. He started to feel that perhaps more was going on here than met the eye.

When Judy went to lunch one day, he copied ten years of Peterman's invoices, which only amounted to forty bills. It took him a couple of weeks working covertly, but in the end, he realized that Schneider owed Peterman's thousands of dollars. He even discovered that four years ago, the vendor had written off several large lots of product in good faith just to try to clarify the process and "start from scratch," but Schneider had again quickly fallen behind.

Reluctantly, Eric brought the information to his father, and by August first, Judy was gone.

She'd apparently been underpaying vendors, and siphoning off the difference, for years. She'd put it an account she created when Grandpa had been sick and probably didn't know what he was signing for.

With few great short-term options, his dad asked him to step up into the Business Manager role. In some ways, it was a tall order, but after what had happened, his father expressed full faith in his abilities, and promised to pitch in personally during the transition.

Eric quickly got his arms around the basics; it wasn't exactly "rocket surgery." He knew, however, that many things remained that could be improved, and that everything would need long-term care and maintenance. He didn't consider this kind of work to especially be his calling. He also knew, or at least hoped, that he wasn't going to stay at Schneider forever. So, he developed a better idea.

The company needs a new receptionist, so why not bring in someone I can train, who can step in when I leave?

When presented with the plan, Eric's dad begrudgingly agreed. He didn't want to lose Eric, but he recognized this would be the best path forward if it came to that. He even let Eric conduct the initial interviews, but reserved final say on who was hired.

About ten months had passed since then. As he sat at his desk, Eric remembered the first time he met Margot Hall, whom he continued to clandestinely monitor as she struggled with the Peterman's invoice. She'd reminded him a bit of someone else—not so much her looks, though there were similarities, but more that confidence, that poise. Then, as now, he danced lightly across this memory, his feet barely brushing the floor... hardly remembering at all.

He guessed she was near his age, twenty-two, or possibly a little older. Margot's black hair sported a boy's cut. Her clothes were just on this side of business acceptable, betraying a slight bohemian flair. She smiled impishly when they shook hands, but underneath, her demeanor seemed more serious, more deliberate. She didn't appear nervous at all, almost as if success, or failure, was a *fait accompli*. Her eyes flashed with a keen intelligence he hadn't seen in the other candidates he'd interviewed.

"So, what attracts you to this position?" he asked, as always.

"Well... I mean... industrial flooring.... What's not to like, right?"

It took him a few seconds, but finally he laughed.

"But seriously," she went on, "my partner is a new teacher in the high school, and I moved here with her. I need a job. I'm smart, I'm a hard worker, I'm detail oriented, and I don't really care what my day job is like. I'm a musician, and that's my passion, but I'm not stupid, and I know that'll never pay the bills. This looks like a position with growth potential, and it beats waiting tables. What more would you like to know?"

Jeez, stop beating around the bush and tell me what you really think!

In truth, she impressed him. After thirty seconds, he felt as though he knew more about Margot than he did about most other candidates after an hour. As they talked further, he learned she even had some relevant experience—albeit volunteer at a cat shelter during college, answering phones and helping run the office. She closed the interview by telling him she had a gig at a local coffee house that weekend and hoped he could come.

This seemed to him like a weird thing to say in an interview, but it definitely piqued his curiosity. Margot stood out. She was different. With their interview completed, he brought her in to meet his dad. They all spoke for a bit, then his father asked her to wait in the reception area.

"Well, she's certainly smart," his dad said. "I think with you training her, she could do the job. I'd still hate losing you. I also wonder about turning it over to someone so young who doesn't have the experience you've developed with the business."

Eric laughed. "I'm young too, Dad. Seriously, though, I know what you're saying about business experience. I'm just not sure how critical that is for most of this job. Knowing what the flooring crews do is helpful, but it's not essential. I can teach her the basics. I just think she's more suited to this kind of back-office, detail work. That's not my thing. I like a little more variety in what I do, and like working with people, as long as there aren't too many of them. I think she's what you need. She'll bring some energy and make a long-term commitment, and she'll do way better in the long-run than I ever would."

His dad took that in. "You think she's a good... well... fit?"

Fair question.

Southby had gradually dragged itself, kicking and screaming, into some semblance of modernity. The employees of Schneider Industrial Flooring, and their clients, were a different breed though.

Or maybe they're the same breed, and it's everyone else who's different.

The question remained: would they accept Margot?

"I think it'll depend on you, Dad," he replied. "I'll get her trained. Her competence won't be questioned, but you'll have to fully support it. You'll have to make people understand it's not a point of debate. She's no shit. I think she can handle some occasional crap from the guys. My sense is she's dealt with stuff like that before. If it gets any more serious, though, you'll have to step in. It's your call."

Eric went to the gig and had a great time. Margot's spirits were high after getting the call from his dad on Friday. Eric met her partner, Jessica, and Margot sang and played guitar beautifully. Her songs about love and relationships came from the heart. It made him remember, despite his efforts not to.

As usual, he failed.

Margot got up and walked to the file cabinet.

Hilarious. She's doing exactly what I did.

Eric knew he had a spreadsheet that already logged all the invoice information she was about to go through. The problem was, if you didn't really understand the Peterman's invoices, the spreadsheet was only good until something went wrong, which it often did. Then you were screwed.

He wanted her to struggle through the process of tracking everything. It would only be four quarters worth of data, as Schneider had paid their balance due and asked Peterman's to reissue the past years' worth of invoices so they could all start fresh. She'd have some work to do, but not that much, and the struggle would be worth it.

Someone had taught him that once, and he considered it largely true, though he had yet to fully comprehend what value certain struggles imparted.

Whatever.

He quickly looked down at the bicycles on his screen as she scurried back to her desk, Peterman's file folder in hand. He'd positioned his computer so he could keep an eye on her, even though it meant the sun made his screen difficult to read when it shone through the window. He didn't do it to spy on her, at least not in a bad way. He just wanted to make sure she was cool, and that people were treating her okay.

She'd been very cool. She was doing fine.

Credit Margot? Credit Southby? I don't really care.

All he knew was that she seemed ready. Only payroll and working directly with the guys preparing the purchasing lists remained for her to learn. The big test would be purchasing, which Eric still did himself, but he planned to start involving her soon. When she'd mastered these two things, he could go. Where to, he had absolutely no idea, but he'd be free.

Whatever that means.

The phone rang and she picked it up.

"Schneider Industrial Flooring, how can I help you?" Margot was good on the phone, smooth and clear. "Umm, hold on, let me see if he's here. What did you say your name was again? Okay, just a second."

She put the call on hold and leaned toward his door. "Hey, Eric, it's for you... unless you want me to tell them you're out. You want it in there?"

He glanced at the time. 9:23. *Could be anybody, probably not Erica, though. She'd call on my cell phone.* "Nah, I'm going for coffee. I'll take it at your desk on my way out." He hauled himself out of his chair and walked toward the door. "Did they say who it was?"

"Umm... Alotta Swars, I think she said. I didn't quite catch it. She's got some kind of accent."

Eric froze.

Time froze.

Kicked in the gut, he couldn't breathe. Dizziness washed over him. He grabbed the door frame for support.

"Eric, you okay?" Margot said with alarm. She got up and ran to him.

He opened his mouth, sucked in air, then blew it out slowly and rhythmically. As always, the sound of his breath calmed him, though this time it returned him to a reality he didn't really want to experience.

"Eric?" she repeated. "You in there?"

He couldn't answer her right now. He had no breath to spare, no thought to waste on anything other than taking this call. He stumbled to the reception desk, placed his left hand on the top for support, picked up the receiver, and poked the hold button with his pinkie.

He put the phone to his ear.

Oh, God.

"Hello?" he said, as if in a trance.

"Eric!"

Lotte!

"Eric, can you hear me?" He heard street noise behind her, and the phone seemed to cut in and out. "Eric, are you there? This stupid phone. *Verdammt!*"

The German word hit him like smelling salts, activating the stunned portions of his brain and hurtling him into the here-and-now while simultaneously drowning him in an ocean of the distant past.

"I'm here, Lotte. I'm here. I hear you."

"Ah, excellent! Eric, it's so good to hear your voice. Listen, I'm downstairs, right outside your building. Can you come down?"

Downstairs? Here? Now?

He reeled.

Margot came up beside him with a worried, but also curious, look on her face. "You okay?" she silently mouthed.

He nodded numbly and returned to the call.

"Umm... do you want to come up? We're on, like, umm... the second floor."

"No, I have all my luggage here. I just got in from the airport. I don't want to drag it all up there. Please, can you just come down?"

"Hold on." He laid the receiver on the desk and walked out of the reception area.

Margot followed.

He crossed the hall to his father's office; he was out this morning playing golf at the club and wouldn't be back until after lunch. Eric made for the window behind his dad's desk, which had a view of the front of the building.

There she was.

Lotte!

Her ultra-straight uber-black hair almost touched her shoulders, a little longer than he remembered. She wore black jeans and sported her near signature black Euro-style Adidas sneakers with red stripes.

Do those ever go out of style?

Surprisingly, she had on a multi-colored short-sleeve knit top, with a low crew neck and holes where her shoulders poked through. She wore oversized sunglasses, had a black leather purse around her arm, and held her phone in her hand.

A suitcase on rollers and a smallish duffel bag sat on the ground beside her. She jumped slightly and waved with excitement when she saw him in the window.

"Oh, my God!" Margot said over his shoulder. "Who is that? Eric, she's totally hot!" Despite the situation, he found that kind of funny and it served to ground him somewhat.

Glad I'm not the only one who thinks so.

He gave a feeble wave to Lotte, then turned to Margot and gave her a chastening look. "Easy there, tiger. She's an old friend of mine. I haven't seen her for... like... shit. I don't even know. Five years? She wants me to go down. Can you go back and tell her I'm headed her way? I'll fill you in later."

"Yeah, for sure, but I'm holding you to that!" She gave a sassy wink and ran back to the reception area.

He staggered down the hall toward the stairs, feeling like a death row prisoner marching to his inevitable execution. This would undo years of his carefully cultivated program of DeLottefication. What could she possibly want from him at this point? Had he not asked her for time? Did she not understand that *time*, in this case, might actually mean *forever*?

This is not how I expected my day to go.

Despite the relatively early hour, it was already hot outside, and humid... typical for New England in late July. August would be worse.

He didn't give a shit.

She stood on the sidewalk and waved when he came out.

He walked toward her, trying to remember to breathe, and trying to refrain from crying... or screaming.

"*Alter!* Eric," she gushed when he got close. "You look amazing!"

That took him aback.

He knew he'd changed physically since the last time he'd seen her. He'd grown until almost eighteen, topping out at just under six feet tall, and since freshman year, or really since the time he started at Schneider, he'd had a lot of physical activity. He'd started going to the gym after being severely out of shape. He still didn't consider himself "jacked" by any means, but he was lean and vastly more muscular. It made him feel a little better that she'd noticed.

He couldn't stop her from throwing herself into his arms, and despite his improved physique, she still challenged his spine with one of her super-hugs.

For a long moment, they stood in each other's embrace.

Eventually, he began to feel his circuits frying and stepped back. "What are you doing here, Lotte?"

"Oh, it's complicated," she said in a weary voice. "I'm so tired. I just got in from Germany, and then a long Uber ride here from Logan. Thankfully, they have that now in Boston. A cab would have cost a fortune!"

"Why did you take an Uber *here* from Logan? Why didn't you go to your dad's?"

Mr. Schwarz had moved to Boston about a year and a half ago, right before Eric had graduated from UMass. The house on Holton Hill Road belonged to someone else now. He couldn't fathom what she wanted in Southby.

"It's a long story. I actually don't want my father to know I'm here. I have something I need to do, and I want your help. What I'd really like now, though, is to take a nap and have a shower. Can I crash at your place for a bit, then take you to lunch?"

This was too much for him to process.

Lotte is here. Lotte wants help. Lotte wants to crash at my place. What the hell is next?

Yet as always, saying "no" to Lotte came hard for him, even though he knew that "yes" came with a steep price.

"Umm, okay," he said, dazed. "My car's over here. My place is nothing special, though, I'm warning you."

She laughed. "You should see some of the places *I've* slept in over the past few years! I'm sure yours will be fine."

Having no imaginable response to that, he picked up her bags and they walked to the side of the building where the parking lot sat. Eric drove a red 2008 Mazda 3 hatchback that his parents had bought him for his high school graduation and birthday present that year.

Lotte had seen it, briefly, before she left.

Indeed, sitting behind the seat of that car was the last place he'd seen her as he dropped her off that final night and watched her walk to the front door of 246 Holton Hill Road. She turned to wave. He waved back, and then drove away. He'd managed to get partway down the steep incline before his sobs of misery clouded his eyes and forced him to pull over.

All neither here nor there now, of course.

It was only a ten-minute drive between the little Southby office park in which Schneider Industrial Flooring had their office and Eric's downtown apartment, not far from the building where his grandma still lived at eighty-eight years old. Lotte commented on the changes in Southby, which seemed incremental to him, but probably far more noticeable to someone who hadn't been there for a while. He just nodded or said, "Yep." He needed processing time.

This is beyond surreal. I still can't believe this is actually happening.

Soon, they reached his building, a rather faceless brick tenement from the post-war period, though Eric wasn't sure to which war that referred. Given the state of the building, it might have been the Second Punic war. Hannibal himself might have lived in his apartment. It certainly smelled like elephant droppings.

The building had no elevator, so he hefted her bags to the fourth and top floor, down the somewhat narrow hallway, and finally to his door. He opened up and ushered her through. He wasn't kidding when he told her his place wasn't anything special, and he'd almost gone out of his way to make it even less enticing.

The small entrance foyer had a closet stuffed with coats and shoes. To the right, the kitchen had a two-seat table for "dining," if you could call it that. The living area to the left housed a futon couch, a black coffee table of indiscriminate material construction, a gray bean bag chair, and a small TV on an even smaller stand. His now venerable Xbox sat on the floor next to the television, gathering dust.

Straight ahead, a hall led to the bathroom and, off to the right and mercifully out of Lotte's sight, the sole bedroom. There, a futon mattress sat on the floor among the plastic bins that stored clothes not yet hung — or that didn't fit — in the closet. No pictures graced the walls, and the shades — sans curtains — were wide open. The sun streamed in through the kitchen window.

Lotte took it all in through her oversized sunglasses. "Wow, Eric, love what you've done with the place."

Oh, har har har. I don't need this shit. What does she care how I live? What business is it of hers? "Yeah, well, it's just temporary."

"Oh, but look, you have a turtle!"

On the wall to the right, toward the kitchen, sat a fairly large terrarium, and in it sat a turtle.

"What's his name?" she said excitedly.

"Her name, actually." He picked up the roughly eight-inch-long creature in his hand. "Females have a flat or slightly convex bottom half of the shell. See... here. Also, short, thin tails... and she has dark red eyes. Female for sure. Eastern Box Turtle. I figure she's about ten, but maybe younger or older. Hard to say."

"So?" she asked, prompting him with her outstretched palm.

"So, what?"

"So, what's her *name, Dummkopf*?"

"Oh, right," he said, shaking his head. "Langsam. Her name is Langsam."

She covered her mouth and tried to contain a hoot of laughter... and failed. "You named your turtle, 'slowly?'" The look of glee on her face was irrepressible.

"Yes," he curtly replied, replacing Langsam in her terrarium.

She continued giggling.

"Look," he said. "Help me move this coffee table. I'll fold out the couch. You'll like it better than the mattress in my room, which is just on the floor."

"You sleep on the floor?" She seemed incredulous.

At least it stopped her from giggling.

"On a futon mattress on the floor, yes. It's fine. I'm fine. Everything's fine. Help me get this set up, and I'll get you some sheets and a pillow. Bathroom's there. Let's get this done. I have to get back to work."

She seemed to sense his anxiety, not such a great feat, given that it was likely triggering seismic readings in Siberia about now. She quietly helped him set up the couch-futon. When the sheets were on and the pillow had been produced, he made for the door.

"Pick me up at twelve-thirty, *ja*?" she said, finally removing her sunglasses.

He stared at her, stunned. "Wow. Eyebrows. Like... real ones."

They were black, like her hair, and her name, and sometimes, he thought, her heart. They slanted inward toward her nose, giving her a slightly devilish look. Despite his frustration with the situation, he found himself mesmerized. It wasn't just her eyebrows. In defiance of his will and his common sense, the whole amalgam of Lotte, who now inexplicably stood in his apartment, captivated him utterly.

She laughed. "Yes, well, you figure out pretty quickly that mascara eyebrows don't work so well when you're doing fieldwork in *38 Grad*!"

38 didn't seem so hot to him, but he still had no clue about Celsius.

"Okay," he finally mustered. "Twelve-thirty it is. See you then."

"Thank you, Eric, you're amazing. I'm so glad to see you. I've missed you so much."

I missed you too, Lotte. So much.

He gently closed the door, and bit his lip as he lumbered back to the car.

CHAPTER 2

Central Etruria, 593 BC

Rika's tiny loft window looked out onto a crooked, thatched eave in the rear of the structure. A child could slip through and then climb carefully down, along the central beam, where the rough daubed walls had flaked away and revealed handholds in the wooden wattling underneath. She'd played this game many times with her brothers, when they were all much younger and smaller. Sometimes, they might daringly attempt the feat in the opposite direction, until her sister Sethra, or their parents, scolded her to stop, citing dangers to youngsters and, evidently of even greater importance, the fragile façade and roof of the somewhat venerable house.

The building had not gotten any younger, and she'd grown considerably since the ebullient siblings once frolicked in the seemingly endless sunshine of youth, but, alas, this route provided the only exit that wouldn't awaken her parents. She didn't bother to don her sandals. Carefully and quietly, she squeezed through the opening and onto the thatched roof. Though familiar, anxiety assaulted her as she shimmied toward the ground... partly because of the darkness, and partly because of the height, which intimidated her far more than when she'd been a little girl and had given no credence to the possibility that anything could threaten her mortality.

Perhaps Sethra and my parents had a point.

The glow of the torches again caught her attention. They walked on the path that led to the plateau, and the complex of buildings there, which sat at the heart of this region's prosperity. She knew the way from a lifetime of experience. Even without light, she could follow at a discrete distance. To avoid detection, she diverted onto the side path that led to the workshop. Normally bustling with enterprise, it struck her as strange to see the gigantic building dark and void of activity.

Her entire family worked here from dawn until dusk. Her mother operated a loom when she wasn't carding or dyeing wool. Her father and brothers created and fired various ceramics, or smelted bronze... a labor they pursued well into the evening back at the village, with blessings from the noble family. At only twelve summers, she spent most of her time spinning wool, though her training on the loom was nearly complete. By next harvest, that activity would likely dominate the remainder of her life. The prospect of this numbed her mind, but few options existed for women born to her station.

Rika quietly crossed the small bridge spanning the creek that separated the workshop from the other two structures of the complex. As anticipated, torchlight streamed from the central of the three great doors of the temple, giving a view of the middle chamber... the only part of the interior of the building she'd ever seen. As always, the outer entrances to either side stood closed, but dim illumination snuck under the thresholds of the doors.

I think those areas are lit as well. Perfect!

The spaces to the left and right of the tripartite structure were unknown to any from the village. Sturdy inner doors provided entry into these areas, but they were typically kept locked, and blocked off by colorfully painted earthenware statues of the ancient patriarchs of the noble family, adorned with their square beards and wide-brimmed hats. From the little bridge, she could see that the statues on the left had been moved, and the inner door to the western enclosure now stood open.

Some of the party with the torches had gathered in the central space, while others milled about outside, their task apparently complete. They stood near the three great pits where libations were poured into the earth in tribute to the gods during festivals.

She would have to swing wide to avoid detection, but her destination, the far west wall, was still shrouded in darkness. As quietly as she could, she skirted the bank of the stream, and then cut northward along the edge of the woods.

Recently, on the first truly gorgeous day of spring, she'd been called upon to help clear this area of leaves and underbrush. When the weather turned dry, this detritus could create a fire hazard, which might threaten the temple and the noble residence. The work, though taxing, had been a wonderful respite, an opportunity to be outdoors, and free for a time from the endless spinning of wool.

The shade of the temple had drawn her. Once, this building had been truly grand, and of far greater importance to the noble family than the copper mines. Her father told stories about when he'd been young and dignitaries would come to visit from important cities like Velch, Cisra, Fufluna, and even as far away as Felsina, when it eventually became part of the league of the Rasenna. They came bearing tribute and gifts, including many beautifully decorated drinking vessels that carried the inscriptions of the donors. The conical-based cups and other items now covered the floor near the walls of the central chamber, and surrounded the statues of the ancestors. Her father didn't know why grandees might send such valuable tribute, or travel so far to such a remote place, but come they did, and the activity always centered on the temple.

All this began to change when Lukius Tarquinius Priscus came to dominate the boisterous and uncouth Latini to the south. Slowly, the visits decreased, and by the time she was about five, they had ceased completely. The focus of activity in the complex shifted from the temple to the extraction and export of ore, as well as the production in the workshop of colorful and high-quality ribbons and cloth to decorate the hems of clothing. According to her father, the disappearances began at around this time as well. Whether or not these events were connected remained a matter of speculation.

With diminished attention, the temple had fallen in need of many repairs. In truth, despite its sturdy foundations, the building always seemed to require far more care than the other structures that had been built near the same time. Indeed, plans were already in place for a new building. Some preliminary work had started, but the shortage of labor slowed progress, and at the same time prevented completion of repairs on the current structure.

As Rika drank from her waterskin in the cool of the temple's shade that fine spring day, she'd spotted a crack in the plastered façade, obscured behind a small bush. The wattle that held the clay in place lay exposed, and some of it was broken. She realized that if the inner layer were likewise cracked, she could look in on the westmost area where no villager had ever set eyes.

She'd surrendered to her ever-curious nature that glorious spring day, and surreptitiously bent over. To disguise her actions from those who worked nearby, she'd held out her wicker basket as if gathering leaves and scrub, and cautiously peeked inside. Dim slices of light interrupted the pervasive darkness as they streamed in from the crack in the wall and under the large outer door. If the room had been lit, she could have seen inside that day.

This was now precisely what she intended to do.

<hr />

Southby, Massachusetts, Friday, July 26, 2013

"I come bearing coffee," Eric announced as he walked through the door to the reception area.

Margot looked up from her computer and smiled broadly. Peterman's papers were scattered all over her desk.

Oops, maybe it wasn't so obvious she only needed to go back four quarters. I'll deal with that later.

"You want iced or hot? I got one of each, and I'll take either, so it's your call."

Her eyes danced between the Dunkin' coffees he held in each hand. "Iced," she finally declared. "Thanks, but this isn't gonna bribe me out of hearing about that girl."

Crap, my plan is foiled. He didn't really believe a simple coffee would slake Margot's curiosity. *It's always good to have a dream, though, right? Well, okay... maybe not always.*

"All right," he reluctantly conceded. "It seems quiet, and I'm too rattled to do much work right now anyway. Patch the phone into my office and we'll sit in there."

Eric had only talked to one other person about Lotte, and that was Jennifer, his one true friend from college. In a sense, she was his only friend in the world, if you didn't count Lotte... and for the most part, Eric didn't count Lotte—anymore.

He wasn't sure why he was going to talk with Margot. He certainly didn't have to. He just found that, for whatever reason, he felt comfortable with her, as he did with Jennifer. Neither of them seemed to want or expect much of him, other than fulfilling the role of boss in Margot's case. At the same time, he sensed they each received something special from his friendship, as he did from theirs. What exactly created and sustained these special bonds remained unspoken, perhaps even unknown, but he felt it with Jennifer and Margot in ways he didn't with any of his other friends.

Margot sat on the little two-seater couch in his office.

He swung his chair around to face her. "So where do I begin? I met Lotte in tenth grade when she became my German tutor. At the time, she was going through some incredibly tough stuff. Her mother had committed suicide two years before, they'd just moved from Germany, and she was having these awful dreams."

She was being haunted by a creature from the Elemental Plane of Fire.

He left that one out.

"Anyway, we got to be friends, and it was incredible... like a fantasy. We rode bikes, went on hikes, just walked everywhere together. We were in each other's house all the time."

Eric, Lotte, and her father would all pick a book to read and discuss. She always finished first and jumped on to read other things while she waited for the slowpokes, but it didn't matter. He learned more from their discussions than he did from all his high school classes combined. They read a book by Brian Greene about physics, and he wished this was what his stupid geometry class could have been like. Mostly, they read a lot of history, and he started to consider that as a potential college major.

He and Lotte did fun things too. They played cribbage and board games like *Trivial Pursuit* and its various offshoots. She usually won. He could never get her into video games, though. She said they were "too violent." He cracked up at the irony of that after what they'd been through together. She still loved to visit with Grandma, and he actually joined in when they spoke in German, as long as they kept things pretty simple.

For the most part, Lotte always wanted to be learning. They spent huge amounts of time together reading, watching PBS, or listening to podcasts which had started to get really popular. It felt to Eric like a paradise. He experienced the dual joys of being with Lotte, and seeing through her eyes the excitement of unfettered intellectual curiosity.

"When we started back to school in the eleventh grade," he went on, "we were inseparable. Lotte worked so hard, and when I was around her, I just worked too. My grades improved. My German improved. My whole outlook on life was just... different."

Margot interrupted. "So, I'm confused. Were you just, like, friends, or was there more?"

Oh, there was more. Much more.

Just after his seventeenth birthday in July 2006, or maybe early August, they went for a walk on the trails behind Holton Hill Road. They visited the pond where the frogs sunned themselves, but there weren't any frogs out that afternoon.

Lotte had always been a touchy person. Kisses goodnight had become a regular feature of their relationship the year before. Sometimes, when it was late and Mr. Schwarz had gone to bed, there was a little more. Eric went along with whatever she wanted, and let her lead because... well... that's what Lotte did.

That day at the pond, she led... and he followed.

She touched, and he touched back.

She said, "Take me," but he let her take him instead.

She took all of him: his heart, his soul, his body.

He let her have them. He gave them to her willingly, and for what he thought would be forever.

"Eric? You okay?" Margot looked at him with worry.

He shook his head. "Sorry, what was the question?"

"Never mind. You answered it. So, what happened?"

"What happened. Wow." He prepared for the onslaught of emotions that always accompanied these memories. "Senior year, Lotte got early acceptance to UMass. That's where I wanted to go too. Everything was cool."

Kuuuul.

"One day near the end of the school year, we were sitting in her living room, doing homework, probably, when her dad brought in the mail and dropped a big envelope on the coffee table. She grabbed it."

She opened the bulging package of materials with trembling fingers. A paper clip secured a cover letter to top of the pile. She read it, and her eyes went wide.

"I got in," she whispered.

"Got in where?" he asked.

"Oxford."

"I didn't know there was a college in Oxford, Mass."

"Oxford, England, Eric."

Oh.

"Okay," Margot said after he'd finished. "So, she went away to college. Is that what this is about?"

He had to admit, in a sense, it was... but there was more to it than that. "We kind of limped through the rest of June and July. In the middle of August, she left for England. That's the last time I saw her until this morning."

"Why? Didn't she want to still be friends?"

"Oh, yeah, that was the plan. Friends. We were gonna communicate by Facebook, which was starting to be all the rage. We planned to call or text periodically, too. Then she'd be home on holidays and stuff."

Eric went to UMass in August 2008. It rapidly became clear that he and big changes were not exactly on speaking terms. If Lotte had been there, he'd have made it. She would have led, and he would have followed. Unfortunately, she was far, far away doing new things—learning, exploring... being Lotte.

Her Facebook site displayed all the people that had friended her, and all the cool things they did together. Eric only had three friends, one of whom was his mother, who thought it would be neat to try Facebook too. He talked to Lotte by Messenger occasionally, but the time difference and her busy schedule didn't make that easy. Plus, he didn't want to drag her down with his adjustment issues. She couldn't really help him unless she were there with him, anyway.

So, added to the confusion of his new environment, he missed her terribly—her smell, the feel of her skin, her laugh... which, now that the dreams were gone, was almost always full and hearty, with teeth and everything.

He ached for her—a physical, palpable pain.

His was a ship without a captain, without a rudder, without rigging and sails to catch the wind, and seemingly without a lifeboat. His ship basically needed a new ship.

He was lost at sea... until he found a new captain.

Parties were ubiquitous at UMass. He largely tried to avoid them, but his roommate was a big partier who often cajoled him into coming along. Mostly, Eric just stood in the corner with a Coke.

"Cocaine?" Margot asked with alarm.

"No!" Eric groaned, doing a facepalm and shaking his head. "Coca-Cola, but that turned out to be just as bad. I was at a party and somebody said, 'You should try some rum in that Coke, man!'"

What the hell, right? A little rum won't kill anybody.

Turns out, it didn't. It actually made things better. The painful hole in the pit of his stomach that Lotte could have filled didn't hurt quite as much after the second drink. His ship had its new captain.

Captain Morgan.

The parties he once avoided, he now embraced. One party a week became two... became three. Two drinks became three... became four... became....

Then, just after Thanksgiving break, Lotte called. She wouldn't be home for Christmas. She'd been selected to go to the upper Midlands to intern on a recently discovered Viking dig site through January.

"Eric, it's just incredible!" she gushed. "It's what I've always wanted! It's such an amazing opportunity. I'll see you probably in the summer, *ja?*"

Eric took his hands from his eyes. The pain of that memory always made him cover them. After a moment, he continued. "That was the last time I spoke to her. I said screw the parties. I just bought a bottle. I didn't even mess with the Coke anymore. It just made me burp."

Margot folded her hands and leaned back on the two-seater, but didn't take her eyes from him.

"Needless to say, I flamed out. By the skin of my teeth, I didn't flunk anything, but it was a fucking debacle. When I got home, I knew I had a problem. I was wicked out of shape, and I thought about drinking all the time. I was so incredibly hurt. It had been so amazingly good with Lotte, and it felt like all that had just been *ripped* away, like it had never really ended, it just... stopped... right at the moment of near perfection. How can you go from the top to the bottom like that? How do you cope with that kind of change?"

Margot sat silently.

"I deferred. UMass let me take the spring off and come back in the fall to try again. I knew that if I was gonna make that deadline, I'd need to do something different, and that started with Lotte. I couldn't wait for her. I'm just not built for that. I needed clarity, not this weird twilight world of, 'Maybe I'll see you next summer.' I also wasn't ready to be friends. We were lovers. I wasn't willing to settle for less."

"What did you do?"

"I deleted my Facebook account. I got a new cell phone and number. I asked my dad if I could work flooring... just shit work... something where I'd have simple things to do and clear direction, and where I'd have some time to think. I joined the gym. I quit drinking." He took a deep breath. "I quit Lotte."

"She never tried to call you?"

"Oh, she did. She called here. The receptionist at the time gave her to my dad. He told her to give me some space, that I was going through a tough time. I didn't find out about that call until about two years ago, when my mom let it slip. Whatever. It was the right thing. Space was exactly what I needed — time and space. Lotte has a way of warping those. If I wasn't gonna be hyper-driving around the galaxy with her, I needed to get back to my own world — the planet dull."

Margot laughed. "You're funny."

You should have seen me in my prime, bwa ha ha ha!

"Okay," she said. "So, what now? What are you planning to do?"

"I'm gonna go to lunch with Lotte, see what she wants."

"Why, Eric? Why would you do that? What happened to, 'I quit Lotte.'"

Eric had worked his ass off at Schneider that spring and summer. He went to the gym diligently, and found out he actually liked it. He bought a new bike too, though he didn't have much time to ride. By the end of the summer, he felt ready to go back to school, but he needed to do one more thing.

Mr. Schwarz seemed thrilled to see him standing on the familiar porch of 246 Holton Hill Road. "Eric, my boy! So wonderful to see you. Come in, come in! To what do I owe this pleasure? My goodness, you look so healthy. How are your parents? How is your *oma*? Oh, I'm so happy to see you!"

Effusive as ever, Mr. Schwarz led him to the kitchen after a visit to the giant mudroom that Eric had always fancied the "Mud *Château*," to remove his shoes.

"Can I get you a drink?" Mr. Schwarz asked. "I recall Coca Cola is your favorite, *ja*?"

"Oh, just water, thanks. I wanted to say 'hi' before I left for college. I'm trying again."

He smiled warmly. "This is good, Eric. I'm glad to hear this."

"Mr. Schwarz, can I ask you a question?"

"Of course, Eric, anything."

"How did you know when you wanted to be an architect?"

He beamed, as always. "From the time I was a young boy, I knew I wanted to design things. I was always tinkering, constructing models. I thought about engineering, but I found I also have an artistic eye, and grand ideas! When I discovered architecture, I knew I'd found my calling."

Eric pondered this. "I don't think I have that... *calling* thing. I have no idea what I want to do. I can always work for my dad. Jeez, I could probably run the place, but I don't know if that's what I want to be. What would you do if you were like me?"

"Oh, Eric, you'll find where you belong. For you, it will be a bit harder and it will take more time, but it will happen. If I were you, I would cast a wide net. Try many things. Don't be afraid to fail or turn away if something is not for you. Soon, you will learn what fits and what doesn't. Be patient with yourself. Go slowly. *Langsam.*"

"That's incredibly good advice, Mr. Schwarz. I can do that. I can do the slow thing, and I can explore by taking different kinds of classes, and I know for sure I can do the 'fail' thing!"

They both laughed, then spent time talking about Eric's family. He noted how Mr. Schwarz carefully avoided any mention of Lotte.

When it was time to go, Eric made one more request. "Will you please give this to Lotte?" He held out a sealed envelope with her name written in tiny letters.

"I'll make sure she gets it," Mr. Schwarz solemnly replied.

"Thank you. Thank you for everything you've done for me."

"Oh, Eric," he said with uncommon seriousness. "I've never told you this. I have no idea how, but I genuinely believe you saved my daughter's life."

Umm, bingo.

"For this, my boy, I'll forever be in your debt. I believe that terrible dream I had when I fell was an expression of my fears for Lotte at that time. Her mother's wardrobe was in the background. The terrible blackness was coming out of the mirror, hovering above her head. I think this showed I feared the loss of her mother might destroy her. That it *was* destroying her!"

Nice try, but don't quit your day job.

"It all changed when you came into her life. I know things are not so good with you two right now, but who knows what the future may bring, or what possibilities might come with a new day?"

"*Möglichkeit.*"

"Yes, Eric, *möglichkeit!* Possibility! Take the time you need, but don't give up on that. Lotte cares for you deeply, but as you know, Lotte is Lotte. Just don't give up on *Möglichkeit!*"

"Möglichkeit," Eric said.

"Gesundheit!" Margot responded. "What the hell is that supposed to mean?"

"It means 'possibility.' You asked why I would go to lunch with Lotte and see what she wants. Well, that's my answer. There's still that *possibility*, and a part of me just can't let that go. I don't really like it, but I can't deny that it drives me."

She leaned forward in the two-seater and took the final sip of her Dunkin' iced coffee.

Eric's had gone cold. He was shaking enough, though, and didn't need any more caffeine.

"Eric," she said in a serious but sympathetic tone. "You're my boss and I really respect you, but you're also my friend, so I'm just gonna say this. You're weird! Part of me wants to tell you that broken hearts are for assholes and to get over it, and part of me wants to hug you because you're so hopeless... but so lovably hopeless. What does Lotte want? What does Lotte want? What does Lotte want? Who gives a shit? What do *you* want, Eric? And don't say, 'I want what Lotte wants,' because I *will* hit you. You know it. And it *will* hurt!"

It was the classic old question for Eric. Sometimes it seemed he'd never figure it out. Forget Lotte; he couldn't figure out what he wanted to do with his life even if she wasn't in it. Would it be Schneider, or was he going to move? If he moved, what would he do? He really didn't know, and seemed to have no internal compass to guide him in answering that question.

As far as Lotte, what do *I want?* "I want Lotte to want me," he ventured, preparing to be hit, but maybe not so hard.

"Then *make* her want you, Eric. Make yourself so irresistible she can't live without you. Or make her *choose. Make... her... choose.* In or out? If it's out, cut bait and stop wishing for 'moldy kites' or whatever the fuck it was you said."

"Möglichkeit."

"Whatever. This is I-T, it! You're stuck, and you've got to get yourself unstuck, one way or another, and for good."

Ouch. True, but ouch. "Couldn't you have just hit me really hard?"

She got up. "I did, Eric. I just did. I've gotta pee. That coffee is going right through me."

"Oh, Margot, don't do anything with that Peterman's stuff. Let me show you something that'll save you a ton of time. We'll do it after lunch."

"Okay, thanks." She turned to go, but then stopped. "Hey, Eric? I love you, man."

"I love you too, Margot."

I love you too.

CHAPTER 3

Central Etruria, 593 BC

Rika held her breath and stepped lightly over the scraggly brush and grass that separated the trees from the temple. Wondrously, no one appeared to notice. She carefully parted the branches of the small bush and pressed her forehead to the cool, daubed façade of the wall.

Torchlight illuminated the space within, visible through the narrow crack she'd discovered. On the far wall, she could see the inner door had now been closed. This side bore a painted figure, but she could see only strange, claw-like feet, and what appeared to be the bottom tips of wings... likely the representation of a god, but she wasn't sure which one.

The walls to either side of the doorway were likewise painted. She could barely see the leftmost, which depicted a traditional funerary procession, while the right presented a familiar celebration or banquet in honor of the dead. A web of fractures and chips scarred the plaster. It gave her hope that the crack in the wall she now peered through hadn't been noticed, and would continue to go undetected.

Several people stood near the inner door, one a burly guard who steadied a fair-sized pig, secured by a rope around its neck. Two other guards stood watch over two older men who were shackled together, miserably hunched down on their knees. To their left, just barely in view through her peephole, two other robed and hooded figures chanted in unison before a stone altar. From their voices, one appeared to be male, the other female.

"... beseech your blessings and raise our voices in thanks for your guidance and beneficence. That you might share in our prosperity, we offer this sacrifice to Tinia, Lord of Thunder, bringer of the nourishing rains. That you might share in our prosperity, we offer this sacrifice to Uni, Queen of the Heavens, Mistress of the Animals, bringer of love and wisdom. May your hands guide us as ever they have. Praise be unto you!"

With that, the man who grasped the pig stepped forth and led the beast up a wooden ramp to stand above the altar. The ancient stone bore the stains of blood from countless sacrifices, and the creature snorted nervously. Without warning, the robed man produced a long, curved, ceremonial blade and skillfully slit the animal's throat. The beast's handler held fast as the swine's lifeblood drenched the fearsome rock and cascaded into a sandstone trough below.

Rika had seen it many times. The slaughter of animals occurred regularly in the village and at the workshop, and she knew the gods would look favorably on this sacrifice, as the pig hardly struggled at all. Something, however, in the drama of this moment overtook her. She unwittingly let out a little gasp.

Instantly, she covered her mouth and silently whispered a prayer to Athrpa not to cut short the thread of her life. Could they have heard her over the din of the dying swine? No one in the room appeared to have noticed. When the creature finally lay still, she again began to breathe, hoping her momentary lapse had not been detected.

"Is this to be our fate?" one of the prisoners asserted in an angry voice. "To die like an animal to suit the pleasure of the gods? Is this the pact you make to ensure the continued prosperity of your *noble* house? What of those who toiled their whole lives for you? Many of the very tiles of your ever-so-regal roof were made by *my* hand! This is the thanks I receive?"

To Rika's tremendous surprise, the answer emanated from a spot almost directly next to her inside the chamber. A woman's voice came from her left, where she had been sitting or standing just out of sight. Now, this mysterious robed and hooded female strode gracefully into the center of the room as she spoke.

"No, Vel. You'll not be sacrificed on an altar. Well do we know what you've done for us in your lifetime. We honor your service by employing your offspring and keeping them safe from barbarous incursions, as we have for generations. Now, in death, you'll receive the honor of traveling to the underworld accompanied by the Gatekeeper. He will be your guide. Look not on this as a punishment. Rather, it's a gift we give you, and know it or not, you give a gift in return. You'll be part of all of us forever. Rejoice."

"Ha! Rejoice indeed! If this be such an honor, why do *you* not go in my stead? You're nearly as old as I, Thana Zalthu! Well do I remember you playing carefree as a child while we worked to support your family. We took joy in watching you, as we did in our service to your father, rest his spirit. You always treated us well, until these last half-dozen years. Why, Thana? What's happened that this must be the way of things?"

Her shoulders slumped as she faced him. "I also remember, Vel. Those were indeed fine times... but times change, and as ever, we must change with them. The gods and their servants must be appeased, or we Rasenna may be swept aside by the endless tide of newcomers. Without their aid, we may have fallen to the invading Latini hordes hundreds of years ago. Now the Hellenes threaten from the south. The peace we've created through our recent alliances and pacts of truce may not last forever. The power of this temple will be called upon again, so to us falls the burden of seeing that its might is undiminished. When my time comes, I assure you, I'll undergo the same journey on which you are about to embark, but I yet have work to complete, so that time must wait."

Vel began to speak again, but a swiftly outstretched palm from Thana Zalthu silenced him. "Enough! All here is prepared. Cutu, you know what to do. Separate our honored guests, and I will accompany that one to the other chamber. Vel, I bid you farewell and hope your passage brings you peace."

With that, the guards forced the prisoners to their feet and untied the ropes that bound them together. Thana rapped smartly on the painted door, which swung open. She and one guard escorted the other captive into the middle chamber of the temple, followed closely by the pig's handler, and finally the other robed and hooded woman.

The massive portal closed behind them with a hollow thud.

Southby, Massachusetts, Friday, July 26, 2013

Margot's words rang in Eric's ears as he drove toward his apartment. She was right, of course; if holding onto the possibility of having Lotte in his life was what kept him from moving forward, the matter needed to be settled once and for all... and this was the time to do it.

He harbored no misconceptions about Lotte being the *entire* problem; she wasn't. There was more to it... other *possibilities* that weighed on his mind. These other considerations, when combined with his natural tendencies to fall into ruts, be fearful of change, and experience difficulty getting started, were enough to cause a major conundrum.

In his heart, though, he felt increasingly certain that Lotte was still the *major* underlying factor, as evidenced by the intense emotional chaos he'd experienced the second she reappeared. Like Soviet Seven Year Plans, DeLottefication had failed. It had only postponed what now appeared to be the inevitable collapse of the Berlin Wall he'd built around his love for this girl.

Well, young woman, now, and quite a comely one at that. Whatever.

He turned over in his mind how he'd really approach the issue. Margot had laid it out pretty well: confront her and make her choose, or try to win her back. For the most part, he'd never confronted Lotte about anything. She played to win, and no argument he could make would hold water with her. Had he ever confronted her about anything, it would have been destroying the wardrobe, but he'd known at the time what a disaster that would have been for their relationship, not to mention being an exercise in futility.

So, it looks like win her back *will be the strategy. She needs my help, so I'll help her. I'll be what she needs right now, which appears to be a friend. I can do that. As long as she's here, with me, I can do the friend thing. If that's a path to what I want and what I need, then I'll do my damndest.*

He pulled into the parking lot. With a deep sigh, he dragged himself upstairs, and took another calming breath as he inserted the key and unlocked his door.

This is the first day of the rest of my life... possibly.

"Knock, knock," he called, in case she was still asleep.

"In here!" she sang out from his bedroom. "I'm just getting dressed."

Well, so much for sparing her the wonders of the plastic boxes and futon on the floor. In truth, the futon was darned comfortable. *Nice and firm. Who needs a frame?*

He checked on Langsam, making sure she had food and water. For now, it was just grass and some berries along with her pellets, but he'd get some worms or insects this weekend. He'd also take her for a walk. She liked the morning sunshine before it got too hot, when dew still dappled the grass.

"Okay, ready," she said as she came out of the bedroom. She wore the same jeans, but now sported black sandals with a medium heel and a different multicolor knit top. She still used black toenail polish — *shocker*.

"Honestly, Eric, how long have you been here? It looks like you never unpacked."

"Umm... a little more than a year," he sheepishly replied. *How time flies.*

She just shook her head as she grabbed her purse and sunglasses from the dislocated coffee table. She'd done a respectable job of straightening the sheets on the still unfolded futon-couch in the living room.

"So, where are we going?" she asked as they locked up and headed back to the car.

"I'm taking you to Peaches. It's fairly new. I think you'll like it. My co-worker recommended it to me. They do lunch, dinner, and have music at night as well. She plays there occasionally."

He went to Peaches a lot. The waitstaff knew him, and he knew a lot of folks who went to Margot's shows as well. It was a funky crowd. It reminded him of being with Jennifer at UMass, when they hung out with her friends or went to cast parties.

"Sounds great!" Lotte happily replied.

They reached the car and, out of habitual politeness, he went around to open her door. When he got there, he paused and turned to face her. "Hey, Lotte? I'm sorry if I was a little weird this morning. I was just super-surprised to see you. Actually, I was in total freaking shock. Still am, really, but I just want you to know how glad I am that you're here."

She fell into his arms. "Oh, Eric, I'm so relieved. I thought about calling but... well... I don't know. I was afraid it would be too easy to say you didn't want to talk to me on the phone. I figured this way, at least I'd see you, even if you turned me away. I'm so happy to hear this. Thank you!"

Well, that went reasonably well. Maybe I've got a shot at this after all.

Peaches, not a big place to begin with, was crowded, this being Friday at peak hour. Fortunately, Nicole, the hostess, hooked Eric up with a two-top near the door to the kitchen—not perfect, but it would save a thirty-minute wait. He ordered a flat-bread pizza, and Lotte got a half chicken avocado sandwich and a salad.

"No Coca-Cola?" she asked, noticing that he stuck with water.

"No, I'm kind of off the Coke thing. Makes me burp. Not really very healthy either. I usually just drink water."

"Well, you look *extremely* healthy! I've never seen you look so good. You must go to the gym."

"Yeah, gym, run, bike, whatever. I even do some yoga a friend of mine showed me." He left out the challenging ballet stretch routines Jennifer had taught him, feeling he'd been taunted enough by Lotte for today.

"Well, you look incredible," she said.

He felt himself blushing.

"Me? I never have time for the gym. Far too busy. I do have my bike, and in Berlin, you walk everywhere unless you take the U-Bahn. So, I stay fit. You like?" She raised her arms in a "V," hands outstretched at her shoulders, head cocked, flashing a movie-star smile.

He considered asking Nicole to call for an ambulance, feeling cardiac arrest was surely imminent. "Yeah, I like," he numbly replied. *I double ultra-uber like!*

She broke the spell by crossing her eyes and sticking her tongue out sideways at him. In truth, that didn't totally break the spell, but it made him laugh, and brought him at least a little closer to *terra firma*.

"So, what are you doing in Berlin?" he asked, finally finding his breath that had so enticingly been taken away.

"I'm at the Pergamon Museum. I'm an intern at the Werner Institut, which is housed there. They're pioneering advanced electonic data collection methods, and using computer modeling and analytics to assess that information in conjunction with geologic and seismic data. With these tools, they can locate ancient ruins, find the best places to dig, and how to excavate in the least intrusive manner, or just create 3D computer models of what's buried. It's cutting edge work. I'm very lucky to be there, even though the position's unpaid."

"Wow. That sounds like nothing I'd be good at. I'm sure you are, though." She laughed.

"What do you hope to do with all this? It's an unpaid position. How do you live?"

"I'm in a small flat. I have two stupid roommates who bring in boys all the time. It's like a zoo, but I can't really complain. My father is paying, and I don't want to waste any more of his money than I have to right now. I'm applying for graduate school. I'll waste his money when I get accepted somewhere."

He chuckled. "Do you know where you're going?"

"Oh, I have applications out to several places. My interests are hard to categorize, so I'm applying to anywhere there's a professor who might take on my thesis. I'm trying to integrate classics, archaeological field work, geology, geography, computer programming, and the data collection and analytical methods that I'm learning at the Werner Institut."

Wow, rocket surgery. Now I know what it looks like.

"Jeez, Lotte, I always knew you were smart, but... like... wow! How did you get into all this?"

"At Trinity, I studied Classics. That's often where archaeology is now housed, and that's what interested me. You remember I did the Viking dig in the midlands in my first year?"

He remembered, though not fondly. He nodded.

"I went back that summer, and started getting exposed to more fieldwork, doing excavation and data collection, archaeological survey and drawing, objects conservation, illustration, photography, cataloging... all the basics. It was incredible to actually touch artifacts buried in the ground for twelve-hundred years!"

He recalled the artifacts being uncovered in Dr. Esfahani's conservation room. It looked like tedious and painstaking work to him, but to each their own.

"The next summer, I went to Poggio Civitate, an Etruscan dig site in Tuscany. It was a wonderful place, but what a shitshow that was for me! *Pfui!* A story for another time. I went back the following year and it went much better. I learned so much. That's where I first started seeing the power of the computer modeling. When I went back to Oxford, I started taking technology classes, and geology. Oh, Eric, have you been to Tuscany? It's simply *amazing!*"

He couldn't remember the last time he'd been out of Massachusetts. His family never made that trip to Germany with Grandma. She just never seemed comfortable enough to do it. "No, never been there — never been overseas at all." *It wouldn't have been any fun without you, anyway.*

"Well, you must go. It's absolutely incredible. After two years there, though, I wanted something different. During my senior year, I went to Turkey. I spent time in Istanbul before heading to Ankara, and then to a Hittite dig site near Cappadocia. They were actually using Werner Institut technology, so I got familiar with that. When I graduated, I applied for the internship. It all just sort of *happened.*"

Yeah, shit like that happens to me all the time. Why, just the other day, I was walking down the street, and someone offered me my dream job doing, doing, umm... I don't know what. He started to think maybe that's why nobody offered him his dream job.

The food came and Lotte ate for a time in silence. She was obviously hungry. "Mmmm... this is good. Can I have a piece of that pizza?" she asked, her mouth full of chicken avocado sandwich.

"Sure," he replied. He wasn't that hungry anyway.

When she'd largely finished, he ventured a question. "So, what are you doing here, and what do you need my help with?"

She licked her fingers and had a sip of iced tea. "I need you to drive me somewhere to meet someone."

Well, that's not too cryptic. "Where, and who?"

She probed her teeth with her tongue. "It's about four hours from here. I have the directions. I need to meet a... well... friend of mine."

"Why didn't you just rent a car and drive there yourself? You'd be there by now."

"Well, two reasons. First, I can't drive."

"Lotte, you took driver's ed! My mom let you drive her Civic. You can drive."

"Oh, Eric," she said, sounding like her father. "That was ages ago. I didn't drive at all in England. I wouldn't have lasted five minutes on the wrong side of the road. Stupid English!"

"Hey, aren't you *English?*"

"Takes one to know one," she said, making a silly face. "Anyway, at Poggio Civitate, they let me drive the jeep once. I landed it in a ditch. I was so embarrassed, and on top of everything else that summer! *Alter!* That was the last time I was behind the wheel. You don't need a car in Berlin at all. So, let's say I can't drive *anymore, ja?*"

"So, you need a chauffeur," he said with not so mild annoyance.

"True, but second, if I'd driven myself, I wouldn't have gotten to see you!" She flashed another movie star smile, and his annoyance melted like the ice had in her glass of tea.

Well played, Mr. Bond.

He admitted defeat. "Okay, four hours isn't so bad. What's the plan, there and back?"

"I'm not sure. I may need more time. Could we plan to stay overnight? My friend has a house, a summer home that belongs to his parents. I think he can put us up."

"What do you mean that you may need 'more time?'" he asked, getting suspicious. "What is this about?"

She glanced around the room. "Not here, Eric. I'll tell you more when we're driving up there. Honestly, I'm not exactly certain *what* it is. I have to see for myself. There's some sort of trouble, but Mason wasn't clear what it was."

"Who's Mason?"

"He's my friend. I'll tell you more tomorrow when we're alone and we can talk. Can you do it, Eric? Will you do this for me?"

He didn't really like the circumstances, but of all the things Lotte could have asked, this wasn't that bad. And in the new spirit of winning over the hearts and minds of all ex-girlfriends in a ten-mile radius, it was a no-brainer. "Sure. Absolutely. We'll leave tomorrow. Back Sunday. No problem."

"Oh, Eric, thank you! I don't know what I'd have done if you'd said no."

Just as he was about to bask in the glory of her gratitude, his phone rang. "Hold on a sec." He glanced down to see who was calling. "Oh, shit! Hold on... uh... I mean... can you give me a second? I need to take this."

She just waived her hand, not appearing to care.

He turned in his chair so he didn't face her. "Hello?"

"Hi, Eric!" a cheerful voice responded. It was Erica, probably confirming tonight.

Shit, shit, shit! "Hey, how ya' doing?" he said, trying to play it cool.

"Great! Whatcha up to?"

"Just finishing lunch. Have to head back to work soon. What's up?"

"I just wanted to make sure we were still on for tonight. Reservation is at six. Can you pick me up at five-thirty?"

"Umm... uh... hold on just a second. I just need a minute. I'm putting you on hold, okay?"

"Okay," Erica replied, cheerful as ever.

"Hey, Lotte?" he squeamishly asked. "What were your... like... plans for tonight? Do you know where you're staying?"

"Well," she hesitantly replied. "I was hoping I could stay with you. I'm perfectly happy on the couch thingy you have."

Umm, think, stupid. Yeah, that could work. Couch thingy, that's fine. No issues with that.

"Yeah, sure, that's cool. No problem. What were you thinking of doing, like... uh... before then? Like, for dinner and stuff."

"Oh, I don't care. Maybe we could just get takeout and watch TV. I'll crash early. I'm jet lagged. Why, do you have something you need to do?"

Umm, yeah, kind of. "Umm, yeah, kind of. I'd forgotten I had plans for... uh... dinner with a, like... a friend. This is her on the phone... I mean them... I mean her. Umm... her. She's just... like... confirming... and stuff."

Lotte stared wide-eyed. "Eric, you have a date."

Why fight it? The turtle has left the terrarium. "Yeah, I had a date. I mean I *have* a date. I mean, I forgot I had a date. It's just been a crazy day, Lotte. I'm sorry."

"You don't have to be sorry. I barged into your life with no warning. You're dropping everything over your weekend to help me. Go on your date. I'll be fine, unless you need your place for privacy? Is it *that* kind of date?"

There were supposedly 666 layers of the abyss of Hell. Eric felt certain he'd just discovered the 667th.

"No, Lotte," he replied, trying to repress the exquisite agony of that question. "It's not *that* kind of date. Dinner. That's all. Sometimes we watch a movie at her place after, but I'll bail on that for tonight. I'll be home around nine-ish. This okay with you?"

"Absolutely," she said, still wide-eyed.

"Okay, hold on." He went back to his call. "Hey, sorry about that. Yeah, I'm good for tonight. See you at five-thirty, but no movie after. I've got some things to do tomorrow and I need an early start. See you later. Okay, bye."

He returned his attention to Lotte, who still stared at him.

Finally, she spoke. "So, what's her name?"

Oh, God, let the taunting commence once again. "Her name is, umm... Erica."

She slapped her left hand to her mouth and choked back laughter. "You have a turtle named Langsam and a girlfriend named Erica? Oh, this is priceless!"

"She's not my *girlfriend!*" he said, perhaps a bit more emphatically than he'd intended. "We're just friends. We go out. We do stuff. We haven't known each other that long."

"How long?"

"Oh, jeez, I don't know. I've known her since I took over in the business office. She works at the bank. I met her there. She asked me out in... umm... I don't know... July or August. So, like a year. Something like that."

She shook her head. "She asked *you. Alter!* You're still timid little Eric, aren't you? Then you say you've been going out for a bloody year, and you're still 'just friends'? No wonder I took matters into my own hands! Quite literally, *ja?*"

It had been many years since he'd had felt the sting of the scalpels. He'd long ago lost his suit of protective armor, and now assumed he'd need to change his shirt for the multiple blood stains. He had no reply to her onslaught.

"Oh, Eric," she said, her features softening a bit. "Don't look that way. I'm sorry, I don't mean it. You have many good qualities. Assertiveness simply isn't among them. It never really bothered me. It's just always so hard to know what you want."

Welcome to the club.

"Umm, I need to get back to work," he finally said, trying to end the discomfort of this conversation.

"Of course. Let me get the check," she politely replied.

He let her pay. *It's the least she can do.*

"All right, shall we go?" she said, almost as if nothing had happened.

"Sure. Thanks for lunch. What are you gonna do this afternoon?"

"Actually, I was hoping to visit your grandmother. Will you take me there?"

That surprised him. "Really? Umm, yeah, I guess. Let me call her to make sure she's there... and awake."

"Great, thanks. Look, I'm sorry if I hurt your feelings. Sometimes I'm too rough. I don't mean to upset you."

"It's okay. I'll be fine."

It's not okay. I'll never be fine.

"So," she asked as they left the restaurant and headed for the car, "where are you going on your date?"

Will the torment never cease?

"Ironically," he reluctantly and painfully replied, "to a restaurant called *Tuscany*."

She could barely contain herself.

CHAPTER 4

Central Etruria, 593 BC

Rika again held her breath as the man who stood by the now-bloody altar stepped carefully around the body of the motionless swine and disappeared to her left, toward the northern wall and out of view. The guard holding Vel began to push him forward, but with unexpected quickness, the old man whirled around and grabbed the sword from the soldier's sheath.

"I'll not go without a fight!" His wrists were still bound together, so he held the weapon in both hands.

The guard backed off, drew his dagger, and smiled. "What will you do, old man? Run me through? I have armor, and training. You can't hurt me."

"And I have desperation!" Vel shouted as he lunged forward.

The thrust dealt the soldier's haughty confidence a blow as it found its mark. The point of the sword tore into the man's leg, just above where his greaves stopped at the knee. Before the guard could counter with his dagger, Rika watched with nervous excitement as Vel drove his forehead directly into his opponent's face and smashed his nose.

The hapless soldier toppled backward. Blood streamed from beneath his hand as he grasped at the clearly excruciating injury. Before he could gain his bearings, the old man swung the sword directly into the soldier's other hand, which still clutched the dagger. He screamed in renewed agony as two fingers flew into the air, severed at the knuckle. The weapon fell innocuously to the floor.

As the guard collapsed to his knees, Vel kicked him in the shoulder. The wounded man crumpled against the wall, utterly incapacitated.

"Now," the old man breathlessly exclaimed as he turned, "set me free, or his fate will most surely be yours!"

Rika couldn't see the face of the hooded man who replied from where he stood behind the blood-soaked altar. "You know I can't do that. Even if I called for the door to be opened, there are many guards still in the temple and outside. You'll not get far. Besides, all is now ready."

At this, she felt something—a vibration, a rumbling, a disturbance.

Her forehead registered the faint movement as she pressed against the rough daub, as did her bare feet nestled in the grassy soil that rippled in a manner she'd never thought possible. At first, she presumed it an earthquake, but then her ears picked up the sound.

Low. So low at first as to be virtually inaudible—felt, not heard. As the tremors increased, however, so too did the noise. It pulsed and cycled, and the air around her felt charged with an incomprehensible energy. Though the mighty foundations of the temple seemed to absorb much of the vibration, her body still quivered in sympathy with a rhythm she felt certain came not from this world. Small wonder the temple constantly needed repairs, if this sinister and baleful ceremony were a regular occurrence.

Terror only began to describe how she felt. She considered running, but even in her stupefied state, she knew that a lifetime of flight could never distance her from this experience. She knew this wasn't right, that it wasn't natural, and that it would haunt her to the end of her days.

She'd abandoned any hope of escape when a bright light suddenly shone through the crack in the wall that had now so comprehensively changed the course of her life. It looked like lightning, an impossible bluish-white in color, but no more impossible than the sound and vibrations that now permeated the air around her. It radiated from the northern wall, so she couldn't see its source, but it filled the space with its iridescent and unearthly glow.

Paralyzed with fear, she watched as Vel madly dashed to the door. He pounded on it and screamed to be let out. "What madness is this? Have you all lost your minds? Let me free, I beg you! Please, save me from this horror!"

The man called Cutu came back into sight. When he rounded the altar, he turned and beckoned to someone—or something. A menacing form began to emerge from the intense bluish-white light. Given the dreadful shadow it cast across the floor, it clearly wasn't human. Great wings adorned the creature's back.

Terror seized her, and she covered her eyes with shaking hands as Vel's frantic screams intensified, until they transformed into wordless sobs of dumbfounded woe. Now she knew what occurred here. Now she had the answer that she and all the villagers had sought. It seemed pointless to stay and watch the brutal and horrifying end.

She finally found the strength to back away... but something blocked her that hadn't been there before. As her backside made contact, she felt arms enfold her, one around her neck, the other across her mouth. The grip tightened as she struggled and madly kicked out with her bare feet, trying to gain purchase. Her captor, however, proved to be too strong, and clearly seemed motivated to keep her from escaping or making noise.

"Quiet, child!" said the voice of the woman who had left the room, Thana Zalthu, High Priestess of the temple. "If anyone else hears you, your life is forfeit. Cease your resistance and finish what you came here to do. Show me you have the courage to see this to its end, and perhaps I'll spare you. I assure you, this is your one and only chance."

Rika could sense the truth of the woman's words, and knowing she had little choice, she surrendered and let Thana Zalthu guide her terrified gaze back to the ominously glowing crack in the temple's well-worn wall.

Southby, Massachusetts, Friday, July 26, 2013

"Eric, you woke me!" Grandma sounded groggy.

He assumed she must have been sleeping in the TV room to have reached the phone in the kitchen so quickly. She slept a lot these days.

"Sorry, Grandma," he said into his phone from behind the wheel of the Mazda, "but I have a surprise for you. Are you feeling up for a little company?"

"Well, I got a small nap so I suppose I can manage. What is this *surprise* that you have for me?" Her thick German accent seemed to grow even more pronounced as the years went by.

He laughed. "It wouldn't be a surprise if I told you now, would it?"

"Eric, I'm old. I don't like surprises. Don't tease your *oma*!"

"You'll like this one, Grandma, trust me. Buzz me up when I get there."

When they arrived, Grandma buzzed them in and they boarded the elevator. He remembered carrying the heavy vase Lotte and her father had given Grandma the first time she'd visited—he couldn't see anything past the flowers, save Lotte's legs flowing out from her blue and white dress.

Was that the day my feelings for her started to change? Was that the beginning of all this?

He put that thought away as they approached Grandma's door and knocked. He stepped aside as she opened it, so only Lotte could be seen.

It took her a second, but then came the deluge. "Oh, *Gott im Himmel*, you've brought me my Liselotte from Berlin!"

Grandma was probably the only person on Earth who could use that name. He'd never even heard her father use it, and Eric would never have dared.

They hugged, and kissed, and Grandma wiped away tears.

See, I told you you'd like this surprise.

"I'm so sorry. Come in, come in," Grandma finally said. "I don't mean to make you stand in the hallway!"

"I can't, Grandma, I've got to get back to work. I'm gonna leave you two so you can have fun." Turning to Lotte, he said, "When you're done, my building is just a few blocks down the street, 680 East Main. You'll see it on the left. Here's my key." He handed it to her. "Just leave the door unlocked in case you take another nap. I'm cutting out a little early, so I'll be home around quarter to five. Call me on my cell if you need anything, okay?"

"Well," she replied. "That might be difficult as I don't have your cell number. Remember?"

Riiiiiiight.

"Yeah, okay. I guess we better fix that. Give me your number and I'll text you mine."

She did. It was one of those weirdo foreign configurations and his phone had issues with it, but he finally got it to work.

He suddenly smiled. "Hey, what's your last name so I can enter your contact information?"

She crossed her eyes and stuck her tongue out sideways at him. Then she too smiled and touched his arm. "I still remember that day. Whatever happened to Colton West?"

"Fuck if I know."

"Eric!" his grandmother exclaimed. "Don't speak that way around Lotte!"

Oops!

"Sorry, Grandma, my bad. Okay, I've gotta run. Call me if you need anything. See you this evening."

"Eric," Grandma said. "Thank you, this is a wonderful surprise!"

He beamed. *You're welcome, Grandma.*

Eric got back to Schneider around 2:30, far later than he'd wanted. He walked toward the reception area that led to his office, but saw that his dad had returned from golf and changed direction. Margot waved and flashed her eyebrows as he went by.

I'll fill her in later.

His dad sat at his desk.

Eric gave a quick knock on the open door. "Hey, you busy?"

"Hey, kiddo!" his dad replied, smiling. "No, come on in."

Eric was fairly sure he'd never be anything but "kiddo" to his dad, but that wasn't so terrible. "How was golf?"

"Oh, not bad. Shot an eighty-eight. It started getting too hot for me, but it was fine. Where have you been?"

Where have I been? Purgatory, maybe? "You're not gonna believe it. Guess who showed up here today?"

His father just shrugged.

"Lotte."

At this, his dad leaned back in his chair and folded his hands across his chest. "Lotte, huh? How is she?"

"Well, she's still *Lotte*. She needs my help with something. I have to drive her somewhere over the weekend. I'll be back Sunday."

His father pursed his lips and his brow furrowed. "You sure that's a good idea, kiddo?"

That was a tremendously complicated question. To Eric, is seemed both a great and terrifying idea, with the potential for wonderful or horrifying results. In theory, though, it presented a path to finality — one way or the other — and that felt like the most important thing to him right now.

"Yeah, I know, Dad. It opens up a lot of old stuff, but I think something like this was bound to happen, eventually. Lotte wouldn't have let me hide forever, so I'm gonna take this chance to... to... well, I'm not sure. To put a period at the end of the sentence, I guess, if that makes any sense."

His father flexed his interlocked fingers. "It makes some sense, but I don't know. I don't know if there's a nice clean end to this for you. One way or another, I'm afraid you're going to struggle with this girl for the rest of your life, whether she's in it or not. I do think you need to find peace with the situation, but I'm not certain you're going to find it through her. You have to find it in yourself, like you did when you got back on track after that awful first semester. I don't want to see you in that place again."

Eric didn't ever want to be in that place again, but in some sense, he was, and really had been since that time, despite creating the impression that he'd "gotten back on track." It was a question of degree. He'd righted the ship in some ways, but still languished in others. He knew he had to do something, and felt certain that dealing with his relationship with Lotte was central to that "something." Still, his father's words troubled him.

"What do you mean I'll struggle one way or another? If Lotte came back today — I mean, like, back to *me*, not just back in town — I'd be okay. Don't you think so?"

His father's lips and fists tightened. "You need to think about what you really want. Do you want Lotte as she is today, traveling the world, pursuing her goals, meeting new people all the time? Or do you want what you had with her in high school? You're you, Eric. Change hasn't come easy in your life. So, no, I'm not sure you'd be okay. I think you'd struggle, even if you two were a couple. You'd have to accept that life isn't ever going to be simple, or safe and predictable with her. She's going to go where she goes and do what she does, and I think you'd find that challenging. There would be great moments, but it would never be clean — not for you, anyway."

This shocked Eric, in part because it seemed his dad knew quite a bit about what Lotte had been up to.

Come to think of it, Grandma mentioned Berlin. How did she know that's where Lotte lives?

What threw him the most, however, was the idea that getting Lotte back might not be the paradise he anticipated. If that were true, perhaps they really might be better off as friends.

Friends that only see each other when she deems it possible, *or when she wants something from me.*

In his heart, he knew this would prove to be problematic. He'd still be left with feelings for her... intense attraction that would be rekindled every time he saw her, like it had been today. Plus, it felt like a one-way street. She'd get what she wanted, but did he really want to call her twice a year and ask about the weather in Berlin, or wherever?

Margot was right: it had to be "in or out," and if he couldn't win her back, he'd have to cut things off once and for all, even though he'd probably regret it for the rest of his life. What his dad said just added a new wrinkle. Despite the depth of his feelings, what if she wasn't really the right match for him? It began to feel like a lose-lose proposition.

Playing with fire, Grandma once said. How true that turned out to be, in every sense of the word.

"I hear you," he finally replied. "I'll have to think about what you said. It's just so... *complicated.* I have to help her. I told her I would. She's here, and I feel like I need to take the chance to work through some stuff. You're right, it may never get totally resolved, but it may get more resolved than it is now. Two days' investment doesn't seem unreasonable."

His dad was silent for a bit before responding. "Okay, kiddo. You know you have my support in anything you want. I like Lotte, and I hope you two can work things out, but my number one priority is *you.* I'm not going to lie and say I don't think you risk getting hurt."

"I wouldn't want you to lie, Dad. I appreciate what you said. I'll keep it in mind. Honestly, that possibility had already been in my mind, but you saying it definitely brings it home. I'll try to be careful."

"Well, that's all I can ask... besides getting back to work, that is."

Eric laughed, and he felt his mood lighten. "Point taken! I have to work with Margot on the Peterman's stuff. She's doing great. I'm gonna start bringing her with me on my site meetings next week with the guys for the purchasing lists, too. We'll patch the phones to her cell so there's coverage."

"That's fine. You've done a really wonderful job with her. You're a natural teacher. You guide people but let them figure things out on their own. That's a gift. I sure don't have it. I'm a tyrant! The guys are happy I've backed away from on-site supervision and shifted more to sales, that's for damned sure."

"Well, I had a great role model. Lotte taught me how to learn, and in the process taught me how to teach. Actually, I had two great role models, if I count you showing me what *not* to do."

"Get the hell out of here!"

They both laughed as Eric skedaddled.

"You look distracted."

"Sorry, what?" Eric said as he lifted his head from his plate of *Gnocchi alla Sorrentina*.

"I said you look distracted," Erica repeated with mild frustration. "Is the food not good?"

"No, no, it's fine." It wasn't Boston's North end, but for the Southby area, he found it quite good. "I'm sorry, just a busy day. A lot on my mind."

"Does it have anything to do with this weekend?"

"I'm sorry, what?"

The usually unflappable Erica was beginning to flap slightly. "Eric! You told me something came up that you had to do this weekend. Is that why you're distracted? What are you doing?"

"Oh, right! I'm really sorry." He *was* really sorry. This wasn't fair, having dinner with Erica and thinking about nothing but Lotte. He thought back to when he'd gotten home from work.

He found Lotte stretched out on the futon, back propped up by a pillow against the wall, box fan pointed directly at her and blowing on high. She had the TV on with no sound while she played with her phone. She wore shorts and her feet were bare, legs groping toward the mute television. She also wore one of her signature weirdo black band t-shirts. Eric recognized the ugly guy with the mole, smoking a cigarette.

She smiled weakly. "Hi. *Verdammt*! It's so hot. Don't you have air conditioning?"

"Sorry, just a couple of fans. I told you not to expect much."

She pouted and shook her head. "Whatever. Hey, do you have any books? I was a *Dummkopf* and left mine in Berlin."

"Yeah, they're all packed in the boxes over by Langsam's terrarium. Help yourself. Sure nice to see what's his name again. Lemming, right?"

She looked down, as if she'd forgotten what she was wearing. "It's Lemmy! Little shit."

"Right, Lemmy, how could I have possibly forgotten that? I guess I got confused because Lemmy probably drives the lemmings over the cliff because they're all running away from that mole."

"Oh, ha ha ha. So funny. Anyway, the other thing is... do you know a good Chinese restaurant that delivers?"

"I don't really like Chinese food. Too greasy. Hold on." He went to the kitchen and rummaged in a drawer. "Here." He handed her a takeout menu. "The Bow Thai delivers. I eat there a lot. Try the Lemongrass Chicken. It's awesome."

"Thanks." She smiled again.

He gazed at her sprawled on the futon. Something about her utterly electrified him. He wondered how he could ever put that feeling aside. It seemed the opposite of possible. *Unmöglich*... impossible. He shook his head and went to change.

When he emerged from his room, she popped up from where she sat. "Eric, you look so good! I still can't believe it. Here, hold on, it'll look better with one more button." She fastened the second to last button of his polo shirt.

He could almost feel sparks from her fingertips.

"There. Very handsome. Erica's a lucky girl!"

Eric stared across at Erica with the sick feeling he was supposed to say something, but he'd completely lost track of their conversation.

Not so lucky right now, he disquietly thought. *She's a truly nice person, and she deserves better than this.*

Eric met Erica at the bank when he first started in the Business Office. She often went to the teller window when he came in to make deposits. With the disaster surrounding Judy, Schneider decided to take no chances and opened all new accounts. Eric worked with Erica, who was the bank's Assistant Manager, to get all that set up. They got to be friends.

One day, they left the bank at the same time, and she asked if he wanted to go for coffee. She was a Starbucks girl, and he was more of a Dunkin' guy, but he went along, and paid for her half-skinny-double-caf-latte-skim-whatever thing she ordered. He ordered a medium coffee, which turned out to be far more difficult than it should have been. It took the cashier a few moments to understand what he wanted. Apparently, he was supposed to have said, "Grande," which he found pretentious beyond words. Compared to Dunkin' coffee, it was like drinking a combination of motor oil and rocket fuel.

It turned out Erica had gone to Southby High. She'd been a year ahead of him, and went to college at UMass Lowell, studying Business and Accounting. Blonde and pretty, with soft features and a gentle smile, she was easy to talk with, and always cheerful. They laughed about their similar names. They hit it off and planned to do dinner some time.

That was that.

He enjoyed being with her, and as time went by, he came to recognize in her that dreaded word: *possibility*. This, however, would be a different sort of possibility compared with Lotte — much different. Erica's possibility constituted a house in Southby, in a neighborhood like Rolling Meadows, or its moral equivalent. It would be two-point-five children and an SUV to truck them around to all their various activities, the ones Eric had avoided in high school. Life with her promised to be safe and secure.

He hated to admit it, but dating Erica felt to him like dating his mom.

Is that bad? Well, obviously, it's bad in, like, an Oedipal *kind of way. Eeewww.*

He just sensed that she'd let him coast. He could stay at Schneider. He'd let Margot be the Business Manager, and he'd get into project management like his dad had done for years, then sales. Eventually, he'd slide into his father's role when Dad retired. He'd have plenty of money, plenty of security, golf on Friday mornings....

Actually, I hate golf, and the whole parade of country clubbers that surround it. I'd go to the gym, ride my bike, whatever I want. What's not to like about this scenario? No Lotte? Seriously? That's it? Am I nuts?

Apparently, he was, because he just couldn't seem to take the next step with Erica. They "dated," but he didn't really consider her his girlfriend. To him, they were just good friends that did stuff together. He didn't want to take things further until he'd figured some things out. His ambivalence toward continuing to work for his father represented a major hurdle.

At a deeper level, though, it came down to commitment, and he'd never felt an overriding passion for anyone or anything... other than Lotte. Much as Erica might be a great match for him, and much as a job at Schneider offered financial security, Eric couldn't shake the sense he'd had since meeting Lotte that life offered more compelling options. Until he resolved that, it would be unfair to Erica to get more serious.

What he hadn't, perhaps, appreciated, was the extent to which Lotte still lurked at the heart of his troubles. Her sudden reappearance drove that home in his mind, and made him understand why he persistently kicked all these Coke cans down the road, never far enough to be truly out of sight, but distant enough that he didn't have to deal with them. At some level, everything tied back to his suppressed, but essentially unresolved, feelings for her, and until he confronted that, progress would continue to prove elusive.

"Eric," Erica said, derailing his train of thought. "You were saying?"

"Right, sorry! I'm just taking somebody somewhere to visit a friend. We'll be back Sunday, no big deal."

"Who is it?" she asked, seeming happy he'd finally rallied to provide a response.

"An old friend of mine from high school."

"Oh, do I know him?"

Shit.

"Umm, well, it's not a him. It's a her. I don't know if you knew her or not. I hung out with her in junior year when you were a senior."

She squinted. "Oh, my God. Is it that girl? What was her name... Lisa, Laura?"

"Lotte," he said, kicking himself for having mentioned high school at all. His mind was really not in the game right now.

"Lotte! That's it! Oh, I remember her. *Everybody* remembers her! Actually, after that first year when she was such a bitc... er, well, I mean, so *grouchy*... she was pretty cool—after she started hanging out with you. You guys were quite an item. I remember that."

He was surprised. "I didn't realize you knew that. You never asked me about her before. Why not?"

"Eric, I asked you on, like, our first date if you were still in touch with anyone from high school. You didn't mention her at all. I assumed it ended badly and that you didn't want to talk about it. I wasn't going to push it."

"Gotcha." It made sense. Erica definitely had a practical streak.

"So, what does she want?"

"Like I said, she wants me to drive her somewhere to meet this friend. I don't know where exactly. We'll probably stay with this friend of hers overnight, be back Sunday. That's it."

Basically.

"How long is she in town?"

"I have no idea. She's just here to see this friend. She'll probably leave Monday."

"Where's she staying?"

Oh, God. Will this day never end?

"Umm, she's staying with me."

She did a double take. "In your crappy little apartment? Where's she sleeping, with the turtle... or with *you*?"

Ouch. He'd never seen Erica mad. *This is not going well.*

"No, not with *me*... or the turtle. On the couch. It's just one night, maybe two. She'll be gone next week." This was probably true, he thought, with no small amount of dismay.

She silently poked at her food. Eventually, she took a sip of wine and started eating again. "I'm not mad. I just wish you'd told me, Eric. Finding out this way just makes me think you're hiding something. If this is going to work with us, that can't be the way it is. You've got to be honest. We have to trust each other. Right?"

She was right, of course: he *was* hiding something, as much from himself as from her. Suddenly and unexpectedly, the decisions he'd been procrastinating about for ages all felt like they needed to be made at once. There was only one way to approach it: one issue at a time. It started with Lotte.

"I'm sorry, Erica. You're right. Lotte surprised me today. I wasn't expecting this at all, and I think I got a little rattled, but that's really no excuse. Let me help her out, get that squared away, and that'll be that. I won't do this again. Promise."

That seemed to cheer her up. "Okay, I understand. It's fine. I really like you, you know?"

She took his hand and smiled.

He smiled back... and again, immediately began to think about Lotte.

Eric quietly opened the door to his dark and silent apartment. He smelled the hint of Lemongrass Chicken in the air.

Good choice, Lotte.

Gingerly, he closed the door and tiptoed toward his room.

"How was your date?" she asked, voice thick with sleep.

"I'm sorry. I tried not to wake you."

"It's okay. How was it?"

It was kind of a horror show. He wasn't going to get into that with her. All he wanted right now was to go to sleep and get this insane day over with. "It was fine. How was your visit with Grandma?

"Mmmmm," she said, stretching. "Wonderful. It was so nice to see her. Thanks for taking me."

"Don't mention it. It was great to see her so happy. She really likes you. Hey, how did she know you lived in Berlin?"

She was quiet for a moment, then she yawned. "Postcards. I send them to her on occasion. She told me she loves them."

Hmmmm. He suspected there was more to it, but she seemed tired, and the stress of the day had exhausted him as well. He didn't feel like dealing with anything right now. "Okay, I'm pooped, and I know you are too. I'm going to bed. See you in the morning."

She mumbled goodnight and he retreated to his room. He undressed, threw on some sweats and a t-shirt, and went as quietly as possible to the bathroom to brush his teeth and pee. Then he slipped back into his room, closed the door, lost the sweatpants, turned on his little fan, jumped onto his futon, and clicked off the goose-neck lamp on the floor beside him.

Whew! Schlafen. To be sleeping and get this ridiculous day behind me. That's all I want. The sound of the fan and its cool breeze calmed him.

Just as the first glimmer of slumber started to envelop him, he heard the door open.

"Lotte?" he called over his shoulder.

"*Shhhhh!*" she replied.

He heard something thump behind him. *Her pillow?*

"Lotte, what are you—"

"*Shhhhh!*" she again shushed him as he felt her climb onto the futon beside him.

Visions of a past, horrible nightmare cascaded into his mind. He tried to turn to face her, but she pushed against his shoulder. He felt her slip her arm around his chest and pull her body close.

"Lotte?"

"Eric, hush! Go to sleep. You say barely anything all day, then when someone asks you to be quiet, you want to talk. I just want to feel you next to me again. For this moment, just be happy. Forget everything else that's always circling endlessly in your little brain. Just *shhhhh*, and go to sleep."

This would be hard to do when ninety-nine percent of what circled in his little brain was currently plastered to his back. He felt her warmth. It had been a long time since he'd felt anyone's warmth, but hers burned with far greater intensity. Only the fire the Afrit summoned came close, but that was a terrible fire.

This was Lotte. Hers was the fire he wanted, like a black sun—a fire that could burn, but could also heal. This was no nightmare. In a sense, it was his dream, his wish fulfilled. He let out a deep breath and basked in her warmth, content at the end of a stressful day to touch a small piece of the paradise for which he'd so long yearned.

As he drifted toward sleep, he hoped for good dreams... and maybe some healing.

CHAPTER 5

Central Etruria, 593 BC

The trees of the orchard grew on the relatively gentle slope to the east of the building complex. Farther down the hill lay the rich agricultural flatlands, and eventually the river.

Rika had never been this way. It wasn't strictly off limits, but everyone knew the apples, figs, and especially the rare and prized lemons, were the property of the noble family. To be caught amongst the trees would bring suspicion of theft, so most simply avoided the area, save those conscripted to pick the ripened fruit.

Under different circumstances, she would have reveled in the beauty and sweet smells of the area coming to life. Sadly, her racing heart and sense of impending doom at the inevitable punishment rendered these pleasantries irrelevant and nearly invisible.

Three days had passed since that fateful night, and all had proceeded as if nothing had happened — at least by outward appearances. Inside, she still shook as if from the tremors that had rocked the walls of the great temple during the terrible ceremony. Her appetite had been minimal, and sleep had come only fitfully, interrupted by visions made even more horrible by the embellishments of nightmares.

She had tried to make herself very small this morning as Thana Zalthu crossed the wooden bridge and walked up to the group of girls who spun wool onto wooden spindles with ceramic whorls by the stream near the workshop. The woman made a show of inspecting each girl's work, nodding with satisfaction, or offering advice on how to create a tight and orderly spool.

Finally, she had spoken. "I have need of assistance with my weaving. You... join me after mealtime in the orchard. If your work pleases me, you may become my assistant."

Clever cover for what the youngster sensed would have little to do with the production of textiles. Surely, this would be the time she would pay for her nighttime exploration. Rika left her midday meal uneaten, and now walked with resignation to the appointed spot to meet her fate.

Thana Zalthu sat on a finely woven blanket at the base of a fragrant tree, the remnants of her meal strewn on an elegant tray, silver with beautiful gold highlights, which rested beside her. With age, her hair now contained more gray than black, but alert and piercing eyes gazed out with a mixture of curiosity and disapproval from behind her hawklike nose.

"Be seated," the imposing woman directed.

The girl sat cross-legged, just barely on the corner of the blanket.

"What is your name, child?"

"Rika," she replied, after taking a moment to find the breath to speak. "My name is Rika."

"A beautiful name. Do you have your letters?"

"No. None of my family can read or write."

"That will need to change. I see you brought your things. I assume you've nearly completed your training in making the ribbons. Do you have a tablet weaving weight?"

Rika reached into her bag and pulled out one of the tubular ceramic objects, fluted and domed at each end, and made in the dark and burnished style so favored these days, as it resembled expensive cast iron. She handed the item over.

Thana briefly looked it over, then removed a bronze pin from her hair. With the sharp point, she began to carefully etch something into the center of the shaft as she spoke. "How do you feel about what you saw, Rika?"

"I... I saw very little. I had covered my eyes and was about to leave. By the time you bid me look, whatever *it* was had vanished back into the strange light... along with Vel—or so I imagine."

"Listen carefully to my question," Thana sternly retorted. "I did not ask you *what* you saw, I asked how you *felt* about it. So?"

Chastened, Rika quickly concluded she had no reason to lie. "I feel... troubled, and scared. The world suddenly makes no sense to me, and I fear it never will."

Thana continued to scratch at the weight with her hairpin. "I understand. Once, I was young like you, and the first time I saw, I too felt scared. I had been prepared, or as prepared as one can be to face the incomprehensible, and the circumstances were different then. It had been an encroaching enemy whom the beast escorted to the afterlife, not an old and trusted servant. The shock, however, is similar. With time, it lessens, though I've found that repeated experience, and the comprehension that brings, is by far the greatest balm. Do you understand what I'm saying?"

"That... that the more you see what... *happened*... and the more you know about it, the easier it becomes, and the less you fear. Does this mean you want me to bear witness to the ceremony once again? If so, why? Simply to ease my mind?"

"In part, but you already surmise there may be other reasons. What you did, Rika, showed courage."

"I was a fool!" she interjected, unable to contain her consuming remorse. She quickly realized she had inadvertently interrupted Thana, and lowered her head in apology and deference.

"What you did was imprudent," the woman responded, appearing to ignore the breach of protocol, "but sometimes courage cannot wait for all facts to be known. Nor can curiosity always be satisfied by standing aside to let others take the risks. Why did you not tell another in the village of the crack you found in the wall?"

She frantically searched her mind for an answer. To do as Thana suggested would have been far more sensible, but to investigate herself had seemed so much more exciting. She wanted to feel special, having solved once and for all the puzzle of the disappearances. "I... I wanted to see for myself. I wanted to *know*. I thought it would make things... well... *different*, somehow, for the village, and also for me."

Thana smiled as she picked away at the little ceramic weight. "Precisely, and this is why I feel you might be useful. Priorities in the family are shifting. No longer are priestly duties sufficient for the younger generation. Already, our lord's son, Marce, commits his time to Cisra, negotiating trade with Sidon, Tyre, and Carthage. His father worries about his increased dealings with noble houses in Tarchuna, but that is beside the point. Pevtha and Semini were married off to cement relations with other nearby noble households. Economically, these are wise undertakings, but the temple must be properly tended. I'm fortunate to have Hathli, my niece's eldest daughter, and her husband Cutu, but rumors circulate that they might be sent to Cisra. I won't live forever, and there's no one else in the family to take my place. I need someone with potential, someone who has courage and curiosity, someone who wants something... *different*."

Even in the warmth of the day, Rika felt a chill in her spine. She hadn't expected this, and realized the entire course of her life might be about to change yet again. Without question, it presented an opportunity, but at what cost? Might she become the very thing her fellow villagers despised and dreaded, due simply to one night of reckless exploration and daydreams of not spending her life tending a loom?

Or could there be more to it than that? Could Thana actually be right that I have this potential? Could this be my calling, and might I be able to help the villagers if I agree to assist her?

"What is it?" Rika asked. "What creature or god do you call who takes lives in this fearsome manner?"

Thana looked up from her work with resolve. "All in good time, my dear. Even though you have joined us in the middle, we must start at the beginning. Here... your first lesson."

The woman handed her the weight, on which she had scratched some characters.

А𝚼𝟷𝟿

"It spells your name, from right to left. You must learn to read and write so you can understand and answer the missives from the nobles and rulers of the cities. They don't always come here. Sometimes they send messages via a courier, and sometimes we must travel to them — far away. All has been quiet for some time, but they will call again, and when they do, we must be ready. The fate of our people hangs in the balance. All this, you will come to understand. For now, you will stay with your parents until you are a bit older, until it would be proper for you to move into the residence. I will summon you on days I can make time. Our arrangement must remain a secret, as must all you learn from me. On this point, there are no exceptions, and no second chances. For now, you are simply to be known as my weaving assistant. Are we agreed?"

Rika met the woman's severe but knowing gaze and nodded. Unexpectedly, she found herself far more settled, and infinitely hungrier, than she'd felt for days.

Southby, Massachusetts, Saturday, July 27, 2013

Eric smelled coffee.

He reached behind him. Unsurprisingly, Lotte wasn't there, but her pillow lay in mute testimony to her former presence in his bed.

Well, futon. Whatever.

He glanced at the clock. *Holy crap! 8:17 a.m.!* He'd been asleep for over ten hours, and felt refreshed. The sun shone through his window's flimsy shade. A new day called, and he and Lotte were about to go on a road trip.

Life is good.

He threw on his sweats and padded into the kitchen. Lotte sat at the little two-seat dining room table, reading a book and drinking coffee, or perhaps tea, as he saw a teabag and a spoon on a little plate beside her. She'd already dressed and seemed ready to go. Mercifully, the Lemmy shirt was gone, though the replacement wasn't much of an improvement.

The black — *naturally* — shirt sported the face of some weirdo goth-looking dude, though Eric wasn't totally certain about the person's gender. The guy, presumably, cupped his chin in his hands, fingers near his ears. His black hair was a complete mess, and his lips were bright red... the only color aside from the white background, and the lettering which read:

"THECURE."

"Moin!" Lotte smiled as he walked toward her. "I made you coffee. I hope I did it okay. I only drink tea."

"Well, let's find out." He strolled to the coffee machine. It looked like coffee to him. He started pouring a cup for himself.

"Do you have anything for breakfast?" she asked. "I'm *staaaaaarving!*"

"Yeah, sure. I usually have Greek yogurt with Alpen and honey. If you want something else, I may need to run out and get it."

"*Alter!* So healthy. It actually sounds wonderful. I'll have that."

He made breakfast while he drank his coffee.

She silently read the book she'd found in one of his boxes.

"Coffee's great!" he said over his shoulder. "Better than I make it."

I could get used to this. He sat in the other chair at the table and laid down the bowls and some spoons.

She pushed the book aside. "Oh, it looks yummy!" She dug in.

"I didn't mean to sleep so late. Don't we need to get to... umm.... Actually, where is it we're going, exactly?"

"It's all right. I knew you were tired. You were fast asleep all night. I hope I didn't wake you tossing and turning from the heat and the new time zone."

"Not at all. You're right. I slept like a stone." *An incredibly happy stone.* "So, you ever gonna tell me where we're going?"

"Ah," she said over a mouthful of yogurt and Alpen. "New Hampshire. It's past the White Mountains, near the Maine border. A little town called Bailey, just past Berlin, of all things!" She laughed and swallowed her food. "It's a pretty straight shot until you get to the end, then I have directions written down, because we'll lose the cell signal."

"Okay, sounds fine. Should be nice up there. Do we need anything?"

"I shouldn't think so." She took another spoonful of yogurt. "We won't be camping, at least I hope not. I hate camping."

"Well, then I'll shower, get some things together, and we can go. Oh, shit! I forgot I was gonna walk Langsam. Could I take her out for a bit before we go?"

She giggled. "You walk your turtle? Do you have a little turtle leash?"

"Very funny. She likes sunshine, needs it really. I have a UVB light, but as much as possible, I give her real sunlight. That's why I keep the blinds open during the day."

"Well, let's go walk your turtle. This I want to see!"

Eric called his mom while they were outside and asked her to feed Langsam on Sunday. "Any way you could stop at the pet store and get some worms or insects?"

"Eric, you know I hate doing that!" His mom loved his turtle, but disliked some of the icky stuff she ate. "Can't it wait until you're back?"

"Yeah, I guess. Just give her the berries in the fridge and you can grab some grass from outside. There's pellet food too, but she doesn't like that as much. Thanks for doing this. Sorry for the short notice."

"It's fine, honey. Say 'hi' to Lotte for me!"

He did.

By 10:15, they were underway, and by close to noon cruised on Interstate 93 in New Hampshire, somewhere between Manchester and Concord. Lotte had been quiet, gazing out the window for most of the trip. She seemed happy, but thoughtful.

"Are you thinking about why we're going up here?" he asked, hoping to get a little more information about what was going on.

"Mmmmm... sort of. Truthfully, I don't know that much. Mason contacted me the day before yesterday. He sent me an encrypted email with a link to some sort of protected website. He's really advanced with computers. Actually, I think he sent the link to several people, but the other addresses were blind copied, so I don't know who else got it. He wanted to know if anyone could help him... well... identify something. The protected site had some photos on it. I had a look. It was hard to tell, but I'm pretty certain I recognized what he was asking about."

"Can I see the photos?"

"The site wouldn't let me download them. He's being very hush-hush about all this. I took some crappy pictures with my phone, but I don't want to show you while you're driving. It's very hard to see anything in them. Anyway, we'll be there soon and can see the items for ourselves."

He ruminated on that. "So, identifying this stuff is important enough that you had to fly out immediately?" *If this is true, I'm sure I could send her a slew of oddball photos and have her on Lufthansa from Berlin to Logan every week for the next sixty years!*

"When I replied to Mason that I thought I might know what he had, he called me a few hours later. He begged me to come out right away. I asked why repeatedly, but he wouldn't say. I've never seen Mason like this. It's very odd, and based on what I saw in the photos, I decided to do what he wanted. I told my supervisor at Werner that I had a family emergency, and I got on the next flight."

Most curious. "Is that why you don't want your father to know you're here?"

She gazed out the window for a few moments before answering. "Not exactly. In truth, I just didn't feel like dealing with him on this trip. He's got a new girlfriend."

"Really! Wow, I didn't see that coming, though I guess I shouldn't be surprised. It has been a while. Are you okay with this? Do you like her?"

She tossed her head back and shook her hair. "Yes, I'm perfectly okay with it, and normally I'd like her very much."

"So, what's the problem?"

"*Alter!* Of all the people he has to meet! When my father moved to Boston, he got involved again with the Museum of Fine Arts. His new girlfriend works in the Development Office. Fundraising. Her specialty is the Arts of Islamic Cultures. She worked closely with Dr. Esfahani."

"Oh, my God." He hadn't heard that name for a while, happily.

She moaned. "Exactly. The few times I've seen her, she always tells me I'm one of the last people to have talked with Dr. Esfahani. She knows everything about the case and the investigation. She follows it, and even though it's largely cold at this point, she tries to keep urging the police to maintain the search. It's always, 'Dr. Esfahani' this and 'Dr. Esfahani' that. It's maddening!"

"Ugh, that's awful, but.... You say the case is cold? Do you know the latest?"

She turned to him, a conspiratorial look in her eye. "Apparently, Dr. Esfahani had a boyfriend. He worked in some sort of financial office for a wealthy Boston family that had some kind of horrible scandal — theft of money, fraud. The police thought that somehow this was tied up with her disappearance. It threw them off the trail for years. At this point, it's been...

what... seven, eight years, with no new leads, no real physical evidence. It took them over a year to find the bloody car, and by then some homeless person had been sleeping in it! I have to say, Eric, I think we're in the clear."

That's music to my ears, and not wind ensemble music, mind you! Clearly, though, it sucked for Lotte to have the situation continually thrust in her face like that. *Maybe this is what karma is all about.*

"Wow, that's a huge relief," he said. "What will you do about your father's girlfriend?"

"I have no idea. Thankfully, I don't have to see her that much. Although...." She again gazed out the window.

"Although... what?"

"Oh, nothing. Let's talk about something else, this situation is just so *infuriating.*"

He was fine with that. The idea that the *Sword of Dr. Esfahani* no longer hung over their heads satisfied him. After a suitable pause for Lotte to calm down, he diverted the conversation back to the topic at hand. "So, who is this Mason guy, anyway?"

"Oh, he's quite a piece of work. I met him in my second year, but he was a junior. He went to UMass and did a summer program at Trinity between his second and third years, which he then somehow managed to turn into a full year abroad. Manipulative little shit called it, 'going to Oxford through the back door.'"

Yeah, well, Oxford probably wouldn't have let me in through the delivery entrance.

"Anyway, he was on the same classics track as me, with an interest in archaeology. We started dating, and the following summer — Eric! *What are you doing!*"

He'd slammed on the brakes and now headed for the road's shoulder. The car ground to a halt near a metal guardrail. For a time, they heard only the sound of other cars whooshing by. His little Mazda rocked slightly as they passed.

"Eric?" she cautiously ventured. "What's wrong?"

He still gripped the wheel with both hands, knuckles turning white, and stared straight ahead.

"Eric, is something wrong with the car?"

He sat for a while longer, then pried one hand from the wheel and removed his well-worn Red Sox hat. He wiped sweat from his brow and then returned the hat to his head.

"Yeah, Lotte," he finally said. "There's something wrong with the car. It has *you* in it!"

"Eric, what's wrong? What did I do?"

He stiffly turned his neck enough to meet her worried face.

"Lotte," he said with utter disbelief. "You've got to be fucking kidding me. What do you mean you started *dating*?"

A look of realization spread on her face. "Oh, dating. Well, it means we were... well... how do I put it? Well... dating.... seeing each other... involved."

"So, Mason was your boyfriend?"

"Well, yes, I supposed you'd say so."

"Lotte, I don't give a shit what *I'd* say. I'm asking you! Was he your boyfriend?"

She blanched. "Yes, he was my boyfriend."

"So, you're taking me to see your fucking boyfriend?"

"Well, ex-boyfriend, but yes, that's basically what I'm doing. I didn't think it would matter to you."

We can't be that far from Concord at this point. I wonder what it would cost to call an Uber and send her back to Southby... or Boston... or Hades. He sat and stared ahead, feeling the Mazda gently sway in the turbulence of passing vehicles.

After an indeterminate period of between three minutes and three millennia, he vaguely perceived her typing on her phone.

"Eric," she said, "let's drive a little bit, *ja*? Just up here, let's take Exit 13. It's the next one."

He didn't move.

After a bit, she tried again. "Please, Eric, I don't think they want us parked here. Let's go and take a little break. There's a nice place up here just a short way. We'll get some ice cream and talk."

Ice cream was about the last thing on his mind right now, but something in his petrified brain knew she was probably right about sitting on the shoulder of I-93. The police were bound to show up soon. He put the car in drive.

Lotte directed him to a nice-looking little dairy bar on South Main Street in Concord. They parked on the street. "What do you want? I'll go inside and get it," she said in a sympathetic voice.

He didn't want anything. He wanted to go home, but apparently that wasn't on the menu at this place. He asked for a small dish of vanilla soft serve and waited in the car.

She soon returned with two dishes of ice cream, his dish of vanilla, and some gigantic chocolate thing with Reese's Pieces and multi-colored jimmies. "Come on, let's find a nice place to eat these."

The "nice place" turned out to be a strip of grass and scraggly trees behind the Market Basket about a block away. The area served as a barrier between town and the highway. He sat on an old tree stump while she sat in the grass. Again, the sound of whooshing cars served as backdrop to their grand repartee.

"Eric," she said with unusual tenderness. "I'm going to tell you the whole story. Just listen. Please, give me a chance. I'm not so heartless as you think I am."

He doubted it, but he listened.

"Mason and I ran in the same circles. We had a lot of classes together. He was brilliant and could be incredibly funny and charismatic. Over the course of the year, we got to be friends, and that did evolve into more."

"Why am I listening to this?"

"Because you asked me who Mason is, and this is your answer... and because it's important. Please listen."

He ate a spoonful of his vanilla soft serve that was rapidly melting in the noon heat. He hated to admit it, but it tasted great.

She continued. "In the spring, he applied for the summer dig program at Poggio Civitate in Tuscany. He encouraged me to apply as well. I did, and we both got accepted."

Hooray! He fought against the growing nausea.

"It might make you feel better to know that it turned out to be quite the disaster for me. There was a woman there from the University of Salamanca in Spain, Emilia Reyes. What an incredible bitch she was, but she was gorgeous, and she was on the make. Mason played right into her trap, though the truth is he was always on the make as well. I walked in on them one day in the dormitory. They were in bed together. All Mason could say was, 'Oops,' with a stupid grin on his face."

Oops.

"The worst part of it was: everyone knew. I was the laughingstock of the program. I was so ashamed and embarrassed—people talking behind my back. I haven't felt like that since we fled Bremen. It was awful. I nearly left, but that would have been horrid for my CV. Somehow, I stuck it out, and even did well enough with the field work to be asked back the following summer."

"So, pardon the interruption, but if he did that, what in the name of fuck are you doing helping him now?"

"*Alter!* It sounds so stupid. That second summer in Tuscany, I went with a group of Poggio Civitate students to Sarteano, which is farther to the east, near Umbria. There was an important find there in 2003, The Tomb of the Infernal Chariot, and they've had dig teams there ever since. The group I was with visited the excavations—a little social call, as we often do—and guess who was there?"

"I can't imagine. The King of Tuscany?"

She rolled her eyes, but amazingly kept her cool. "No, Eric. Mason and Emilia. I almost died. Mason had graduated and was working there, and he'd finagled some kind of job for her as well. Incredibly, they were still together. As far as I'm concerned, they deserve each other, but Mason apologized, and Emilia wasn't quite the bitch she'd been the year before. We sort of patched things up, and I gave him my contact information. We've been in touch occasionally since then. He *is* brilliant."

I'm sure. Brilliant and brave and strong and really, fucking... archaeological! Can't wait to meet him!

"He's also a self-centered prick," she slashed with her little scalpel. "So many in academia are. It makes me sick."

"Lotte, I don't need to know any of this, but.... You want to talk about self-centered? How about looking in the mirror?"

At this, they both momentarily froze and stared into each other's eyes.

"Umm, I didn't mean it that way," he backtracked, but then he proceeded, full steam ahead. "What I mean is, I feel like your dog! You need a ride, you need my help, you need a place to crash, you need me to take you to see your fucking ex-boyfriend, you need, you need.... What the hell was last night, Lotte? What was that about? Why are you here, and why am I with you? What the fuck do you need me for?"

Without a doubt, this was the worst argument they'd ever had, but Eric felt like he was the only one in the fight. She seemed totally calm, and had even finished her ice cream, while his had withered to a gooey mess in the bottom of his dish.

Too bad. It deserved a better fate.

She reached for her phone, tapped and swiped for a moment, then held it up for him to see. He looked at a picture, really a picture of a picture, blurred and hard to make out. He saw some sort of formation of stones on a granite boulder, and some objects on the ground.

She swiped the phone again, and another picture of a picture appeared—a painted piece of ceramic, one side of what appeared to be a box. It was badly degraded, and obviously extremely old, or else very poorly treated. The middle of the painting was missing, scraped away by the ravages of time, but the right side depicted some sort of squarish formation, while the left side showed some similarly shaped, smaller objects that appeared to be on the ground.

"Is this supposed to mean something to me?" he asked.

She got up and sat next to him on the stump. It was too small for two, so she crowded next to him, which produced conflicting feelings in his troubled mind.

"It's hard to see," she said, "but look here. On the painted box, look at the shape on the right. It's a rectangle. You can see the bottom and the top. The middle's been all chipped away. Look on the left — three markers: one on the top, one on the bottom, one in the middle. The top and bottom are the edges. The dimensions aren't precise. It forms a sort of fanned-out area that would have been on the ground, which may be marked by these dotted lines, but the middle of the picture is missing, so I can't say for sure."

Now that she pointed it out, he could see it. She flashed back to the other photo.

"Here," she said, pointing at the stones on the boulder. "You see, all these interlocking stones on the wall form a rectangle, and on the ground here, three larger stones on small platforms complete the fanned-out area on the ground."

"What are all those little bumps inside the rectangle on the wall?"

"I can't tell. They appear to be made of the same material as the other stones, but I'd have to see them to be sure. But, Eric, look at the whole picture. What do you see?"

He looked closely but still found himself stumped. "I don't know. Stones on a rock wall, a few bigger stones on the floor on some kind of stands. Similar patterns on the box. Wait a minute! The box is the model. It's a guide. They're the same. Like the papyrus chart was to the mirror, and the semicircular piece of marble, and the bowls. If the rectangle is the mirror, and the three things on the ground are like the black marble slab and the bowls, it looks a lot like the artifacts from the wardrobe. Same basic pattern."

"Exactly! This is what I see as well, and to cap it off, there's this!"

She again swiped her phone and revealed another picture. This one, there could be no mistaking — two silver spiral rings, each tipped with a small black stone at each end. One ring was slightly larger than the other, though not as large as the one intended to fit the Afrit's massive talon.

She put her hand on his left thigh, in the exact spot where he still bore three little scars from his battle with the impish Afrit. "This is why

I'm here, and this is why you're here with me. No one else in the world besides us knows what this might mean, and if something's happened, as I fear it may have, then I need you. Not as my dog, Eric, but as my friend. As my partner."

He stood up and tossed his ice cream dish into a patch of scraggly trees. He then guiltily went to fetch it. *I hate litterbugs.* "I'll be right back. I'm gonna throw this in the Market Basket dumpster."

"Will you take mine too?"

With a deep sigh, he took her dish as well. The walk was really just to clear his head. He did try to calculate whether he could run back to the car and start the engine before Lotte could catch him. She could be really fast when she wanted to be, though, and she hated to lose, so he abandoned the plan. He tossed the ice cream cups in the putrid and reeking dumpster, and returned to her. She'd commandeered his tree stump, so he sat in the grass.

"Honestly," he said, in a tone as free from anger as he could conjure. "How could you not think it would matter to me that we were going to see your ex-boyfriend? Were you planning on telling me this at all?"

For a time, she sat in thoughtful silence. She put her phone in her purse and crossed her legs. "I *was* telling you, Eric. In the car, I was telling you, just as I'd intended. I obviously underestimated how you'd react. Maybe I should have been gentler, but after I got your note all those years ago, the one you gave to my father, I assumed you were done with me. You said you needed to move on, that the distance and separation was just too much, too painful. You asked me to give you time and space and to respect your decision."

He remembered writing the letter. It took him twenty drafts to craft five sentences. If forced to write the letter again today, he wouldn't change a word.

She went on. "After that, and after all this time, I didn't think you'd really care, and that it wouldn't matter to you at all. You didn't even want to stay in touch. That hurt me, Eric. I understood, but it did hurt. In the end, I moved on, just as I imagined you had. I assumed you had girlfriends. You certainly seem to have one now, even though, for some reason, you appear to fight the idea with every fiber of your being. All this I accept. I suppose I thought you'd be equally accepting. I'm genuinely surprised you feel this strongly about it... really, that you have any feelings about me at all."

He put his elbows on his knees and his hands across his forehead. *How can she not know how I feel? How can she not know that, even after all this time, she's still the center of my world?*

One thing he knew for certain: his behavior was not in keeping with "The First Law of Margot." *And thou shalt maketh her want you, irresistible ye shall be, and lo, her heart shall ye winninth; Margot 7:26.* Somehow, he knew he'd have to file this one away and rally the courage to carry on.

And meet Mason... her boyfriend. Well, ex-boyfriend. Whatever.

Now there was also this little matter of what appeared to be another Afrit-summoning device. If she was right, which he assumed she was because... well... Lotte was always right, then there may well trouble, and if there was trouble, especially *that* kind of trouble, she would need him. Despite his anger, his hurt, his frustration, and, when he got right down to it, his jealousy, if Lotte needed him for this, he'd be there.

Slowly, he rose and walked to where Lotte sat on the tree stump, legs still crossed. He extended his hand so he could help her up, and she took it.

"Let's go," he said. "I'm melting out here. We need to drive."

She slung her purse over her shoulder and grabbed his arm with both her hands. This way, they walked together back toward the car.

CHAPTER 6

They drove in silence.

At Exit 35, I-93 gave way to Route 3, which soon disgorged the little red Mazda onto Route 2 headed east toward Berlin. There, they'd pick up Route 16 headed north. Somewhere near Milan, they'd head east into the mountains toward the Maine border. Then Lotte's directions would take over when the cell signals started to get spotty.

Wow, Berlin to Milan in, like, twenty minutes. Who needs Europe?

No longer at full boil, Eric still simmered on low. He wasn't mad at her for having boyfriends. What did he think was going to happen when he cut her out of his life? It was more the idea that now one of them would be put in front of him. He'd be shaking the guy's hand, talking with him, facing the fucking *reality* of him! That's what he dreaded, and despite her rationale, which had served to somewhat patch and placate his bullet-riddled self-confidence, he still resented the nonchalance she'd shown.

Lotte being Lotte. Maybe Dad's right. It appeared that even when things were going well, she could still deliver a body blow from out of the blue. Was this what the future held? Was this what he *really* wanted?

Perturbed as he might be, they had bigger turtles to hatch at the moment. What were they going to do if this was indeed another wardrobe-like situation? He assumed Lotte also ruminated on that question while she wordlessly stared out the window.

The wardrobe... hmmmmm....

"Hey, Lotte?" he asked, making her jump given how hushed the car had been. "What happened to the wardrobe when your father moved? Where is it now?"

The somewhat sad look on her face became even sadder, and despite her oversize sunglasses, he could tell she'd closed her eyes. "It's gone, Eric," she said, her voice tired.

"Gone?"

"Yes, I had to be rid of it. It was a terribly difficult decision, but I couldn't look after it being so far away. Too much worry, too many problems. So, it's gone. I don't really want to talk about it right now."

This stunned him. He didn't think she'd ever come around to destroying the wardrobe. He counted his lucky stars he'd never pushed it with her. Apparently, she'd just needed time to see it his way, that the risk presented by the wardrobe and artifacts outweighed the potential benefits. "Wow. Well, I guess that's that."

She nodded. "Yes, that is indeed that."

They drove on in silence.

As anticipated, once they passed Berlin, the cell signal faded. Nearing Milan, Lotte opened the paper on which she'd written down the directions from Mason.

"Your right is coming up," she directed. "There should be signs to Bailey and New Speck Mountain. Ah, there!"

He banged a right onto a small two-lane road that led upward into the hills. The air began to feel cooler as they ascended. They passed occasional houses or farms, but this appeared to be a remote area.

Eventually, they came to the little town of Bailey, nestled in a gulch at the base of what he assumed was New Speck Mountain to the north. To call Bailey "small" was something of an understatement. It consisted of a few houses, a little grocery, a liquor store, a rather drab-looking bar, what appeared to be a general store — *They still have those?* — and some kind of municipal building with a post office, a weathered sign that read "Police," and a door for a fire truck.

Beyond town to the south, he could see water, probably a lake. "This is just a summer getaway place. Probably very few full-time residents here."

She glanced at her directions. "We just go through the town, then a mile or so up the road. On the left, look for New Speck Lane. Then it gets really quite insane."

Extraordinarily, that was also a bit of an understatement. New Speck Lane was hardly wider than a single-car driveway. It snaked up the mountainside back in the direction of town. A few homes sat nestled here or there, mostly bungalows or summer cottages. They followed the directions off the main street onto a gravely, dirt road, then it was "turn at the tree marked with an orange stripe, up the big hill, right at the fork, left at the next fork," blah, blah, blah.

Just when he was certain they were lost, she cried out, "There it is!"

A twisting dirt driveway led to a somewhat dilapidated two-story cottage perched above on a small slope. A beat-up, old, blue Toyota RAV4 sat near some stone steps that ascended toward the building. He pulled up behind the RAV4 and shut off the Mazda, steeling himself for what would inevitably happen next.

They got out of the car and he opened the hatch to retrieve their luggage. As he was lifting Lotte's duffel bag, he heard a voice singing from the steps above.

"*Du-na du-na, du, da-da du, da-da du! Du-na du-na, du, da-da du, da-da du!*"

"*Alter!*" Lotte groused, rolling her eyes.

The singing continued. "*I've been droolin'! Baby it's been grueling!*"

"Mason, please!" she pleaded.

"*Won't you give me! A dose of your schooling!*"

"You know I hate that fucking band! You just do this to make me angry!"

"What's the matter, sweetheart, don't you like *Whole* Lotte *Love? Neeeeaaaarrrroooowww!* Get it, *Whole* Lotte *Love? Neeeeaaaarrrroooowww!*"

"Oh, I *get* it, Mason. Like there's anything to really *get*. I swear, though, if you don't stop now, I'll get back in the car and drive home."

The singing stopped and Eric beheld a tall, thin man with thick black glasses, scruffy, longish blond hair, and the traces of what was to be — or had once been — a beard. He wore a beat-up pair of jeans, and as best as Eric could tell, nothing else — no shirt, no shoes, no socks, and who knew, or particularly cared, about the underwear.

"Oh, Lotte, baby!" he said walking with his arms outstretched toward her. "I just do it 'cause I missed you so much!" He threw his lanky arms around her, and she rather grudgingly patted his back before pushing him away.

"Yuck, Mason!" she said, shaking her hands vigorously. "You're all sweaty! Go put on a shirt. It's disgusting!"

"Hey!" he cried, suddenly wild-eyed. "Take off yours and I'll put it on! I can sing like I'm on helium with a nasal infection as well as that little wannabe vampire can!"

"Oh, *ha ha ha*, Mason. So funny. Look how I'm laughing. Not. Really, so stupid. Like a six-year-old."

"Fine, whatever. If they're the fucking *Cure*, though, then I'm just gonna keep the disease!" He paused to laugh at his own joke.

She just stared at him.

"Oh well," he finally said, a smug look on his face. "At least you and I can agree that today's music *sucks ass*!"

"Whatever, Mason. Here, there's someone I want you to meet. Eric, this is Mason. Mason, Eric."

Autopilot kicked in as Eric extended his hand. "Pleased to meet you, Mason." *Kill me now, kill me now, kill me now, kill me now.*

Mason began to return the gesture, but then faltered. "Wait a minute! Eric! Not *the* Eric? Eric... Eric... oh, what the hell was it? Eric Schnitzel-something."

"Schneider," Lotte interjected. "Eric Schneider."

"That's it! Eric Schneider! Eric the fucking *Great*! Man, am I honored to meet you! I'm not fuckin' worthy!" He started a series of short bows from the waist, his hands following as his head rocked up and down.

"Mason, stop," she chided. "It's not funny."

He stopped bowing and froze solid for a moment, hands in the air, a silly grin on his face while his eyes shot from left to right.

Too bad. I was sort of enjoying that.

"Man," he said, finally shaking Eric's hand with a powerful grip that belied his gaunt appearance. "I don't know what your secret is, but I hope you share it with me. You're all Lotte could fuckin' talk about when I first met her."

"*Mason!*" she screamed. "I absolutely promise that if you don't shut up this instant, I'll get back in the car right now." For emphasis, she picked up her duffel bag.

"Okay, okay," he said, backing down and finally releasing Eric's hand, which had started to hurt a bit. "*Wooooo*, touchy, touchy. Anyway, seriously, Eric, man, nice to meet you. You here on business with Lotte, or are you just along for the ride?"

Eric was confused until she stepped in. "He means are you also here to look at the artifacts. The answer, Mason, is yes. Eric isn't an archaeologist, but in this situation, he may know some things. In any case, he's someone I trust and need with me. Can we please now go inside? I'd like to 'freshen up.'"

"Oops," he said. "Lotte's gotta pee. We better get movin'."

With that, he and Eric grabbed the bags, and they all trekked up toward the house. As they got closer, Eric could see the building's issues were primarily cosmetic. Paint peeled from the siding, moss grew on the roof, the porch sagged, and the screen door didn't really have the capacity to screen much anymore. The place seemed solid, though, and once they were inside, it was actually quite cozy, with wood paneling and a solid oak floor.

A large kitchen and dining area sat to the left, a living area to the right, and stairs straight ahead led to the second floor. The dining room table was covered with all kinds of computers and other equipment. Boxes littered the floor, and cables trailed everywhere.

"What's powering all these computers?" he asked. "Do you actually get service up here?"

"We have propane and a generator. Sadly, no internet. They tried to get cell service, but there's just not enough year-round demand to support it. It's basically summer homes here, places where wannabee wealthy families do the 'get out of the city getaway' thing."

"So how did you send me that encrypted email?" Lotte asked.

"I prepped it here then went down to Berlin and sent it from my phone. It sucks, but beggars can't be fuckin' choosers. My grandparents bought this place years ago. My dad loved it, but my mother's not really into it, so it's mine to use when I'm not overseas. You guys can dump your bags in the guest room upstairs. It's on the left."

Lotte and Eric hesitantly looked at each other. "Umm, I think I'll be good on the couch down here," he finally offered.

"No, you take the room," she countered. "I don't want to make you come all this way to sleep on a couch."

"Couch is cool by me. It's a big couch. I'll be fine."

Mason stared at them. "So, I take it you two aren't bangin'?"

"*Mason!*" Lotte looked prepared to punch him.

"Hey, I just assumed you were bangin'. My bad. Listen, Eric can have the guest room if you want to sleep with me. What do you say, baby?" He flashed a lopsided smile and batted his eyes.

She shot him a look as withering as any Eric had ever seen. "What happened to Emilia, Mason?" she spat, her scalpels in full deployment. "Did she finally come to her senses and leave you to your infantile prattle? As smart as you are, you act like such a child. Grow up, or else stop pretending to be an intellectual and just live off your trust fund, and be the little playboy you fancy yourself!"

Eric hadn't seen a display like that since Colton West.

Even Mason seemed dumbstruck. With a troubled look, he paced the floor. Finally, he turned, and in a harrowed voice said, "Emilia's gone."

"Well," she replied, somewhat less sharply. "I'm not surprised the way you behave."

"No, it's not that. It has nothing to do with me — well, not directly anyway. I mean she's gone. Like gone, gone. Vanished, gone. I think I know where, but... well, I don't know how to get her back. That's why you're here. That's why I need your help. I guess it's time to tell you what happened, isn't it?"

"Actually, it's time to use the bathroom, if I could."

"Oh, right. Sorry. Yeah, you can use the one upstairs. Eric, there's a half-bath off the kitchen if you need it. I need a fuckin' beer. Anybody else?"

Both new arrivals shook their heads.

"Okay, I'll get you some water."

Once they'd gotten settled, Lotte and Eric sat next to each other on the big couch in the living room. Mason brought them their water, then returned to the kitchen to get his beer. On the way back, he grabbed something on the dining room table near the computers. He flopped into a chair and put the item, something folded in a white handkerchief, on the coffee table.

He took a deep breath. "Okay, you're not gonna like this, but here goes. As you know, Emilia and I have been in Sarteano for the past couple of years. I was a dig supervisor, and she was assisting in archives until she finished up school. Anyway, we had a little break and decided to do some camping. There's this beautiful spot by a river a few miles outside of town. It has this crazy freaking rock outcropping where the water has, like, undermined the bottom of the hill—really remote, really amazing. We were camping there when a small earthquake hit."

"Yes, I remember," Lotte said. "That was just a few weeks ago. They were concerned for the Tomb of the Infernal Chariot."

"Yeah, well, it's fine. It was a really minor earthquake, centered in the hills to the west, and the tomb is deep underground, but the tremors were strong enough to tip part of this damn rock outcropping right into the river. We were on the other side, setting up our camp when the whole thing happened, and we heard the rocks hitting the water. After things settled down, we ran over to check it out. It was incredible. We could see what looked like an opening where the rock had given way, and in that opening, we saw a painted wall."

"A tomb?" she asked.

"No, but we had no idea of that at the time. What we did know was that it looked like what was left of this outcropping was hanging by a fuckin' thread. One aftershock would send the whole freakin' cliff face into the river. So, we waded across. It's only two feet deep—oh, excuse me, point-six fucking meters for the American challenged."

She rolled her eyes.

"We climb up there, yeah? We see the wall, and see that it's part of a room, half of which is gonzo. Near the back, there was an alcove with a painted ceramic box about the size of a big trunk. I've never seen an Etruscan funerary urn or monument that looks like that, and it didn't look Roman to me either. So, this place probably wasn't a tomb—more likely a temple or sanctuary of some type. The box was in rough shape on the outside, but the lid and sides were intact. The entrance to this space had probably been opposite the wall we first saw, but it had been blocked up for eons. There was evidence of an older earthquake that had sealed off the stairway to the surface, and we even found human remains. People got trapped in this place and were either killed by falling debris, or eventually they just starved to death. There wasn't much left of them, just a pile of petrified powder. I wouldn't have even recognized what they were, except for the rings, which I spotted on what was left of one of the bodies."

"Astonishing" she said, wide-eyed.

Haven't heard that word for a while.

"Anyway, this place is creaking. It's gonna go. Emilia gets out her camera, flashes a bunch of pictures, and then we go for the lid. It was pretty solid and heavy, but we managed to get it off. Inside are all these... well... at the time, we thought they were *bucchero*. Just these black pieces of ceramic in various shapes and sizes. On the top, there were a bunch that looked like long, thin, totally smooth dominoes. They were set in ceramic trays, stacked one on top of the other, and each piece had its own little cubby hole. We took those out, and underneath, supporting the trays, were these three clay stands that look like overturned flowerpots with a slit in them. Along the sides at the bottom were three slightly curved, larger pieces, about a foot, foot-and-a-half long. It looked like they were supposed to slot into those stands. Then, at the bottom, there were a ton of these little round balls about the size of marbles with a single spike sticking out of them, and one single piece, about a foot long, that looked like an elongated T."

"Very odd. I've never seen *bucchero* like this."

"No shit, Sherlock. That's because it wasn't *bucchero*. When we tried to pick up some of the round pieces at the bottom, they were all stuck together, and stuck to that T-shaped piece. This stuff is magnetic!"

"Metal?" she asked.

"Well, you tell me." He unwrapped the white handkerchief and revealed a black strip about five inches long and maybe two inches wide. It looked like highly polished stone, and had slightly beveled edges with a triangular point on one end, and a triangular recess the same size on the other. He handed the object to Lotte.

"Amazing! It has no grain at all, almost like a plastic. I've never seen anything like this. It needs a geological analysis. I assume the others are like this, with the points and recesses, so they interlock?" She handed the piece to Eric.

It was surprisingly light but seemed incredibly strong.

"Crackerjack, Lotte," Mason replied. "They go together to make a big rectangle. There were even four specially designed corner pieces set in the ceramic trays. One of the pictures I sent showed it set up against a granite rock face. I assume that's what you recognized. It's like a gigantic picture frame that you can walk through."

Eric and Lotte exchanged a knowing and worried look.

"So, what did you do?" she asked.

"Right. So, I told Emilia to start getting the stuff out of the box, and I ran to get our packs. I dumped all our shit out, hauled ass back, and we loaded all these black stones, or whatever they are, into the packs. We took the stands, but we didn't have room for all those trays. I swear, we were barely back on the ground when that room fell into the river. Damn thing's probably been there twenty-five-hundred years, maybe longer, and it picks that moment to reveal its secret. Almost makes you believe in God, huh?"

Or demons.

"Mason," Lotte said, her tone troubled. "Why do you even have these things? They belong in a museum where they can be studied. Think of what we can learn from them!"

"Oh, Lotte, you should be Catholic. The Pope would love you. He'd make you 'Saint Lotte, Protector of the Holy Artifacts.' All would bow at your fucking feet."

"I am Catholic, you stupid moron! Well, by birth anyway. My father's parents were from Bavaria, but that's beside the point. What right do you think you have taking these, and how the hell did you get them here?"

"Jesus, Lotte, let me fuckin' finish. So, there we are. We have two bags full of this magnetic stuff. Nobody knows we have it, and there's no trace of where it came from. Emilia says, 'We can sell it.'"

"*Tüddelkram!*" she groaned. "You're blaming this on Emilia? She's not even here to defend herself!"

"Hey, I'm not freaking blaming her. I'm giving her credit! She was right, we'd make a fortune! Even if there's no provenance, some rich douchebag collector will pay something for this shit. Emilia isn't like us, Lotte. She doesn't have a trust fund or a rich Santa Claus daddy who buys her every precious fuckin' thing her little heart desires. This was Emilia's chance to cash in. I wasn't gonna say no, and I wasn't about to turn down my cut, either."

"How could I ever have been attracted to you?" she said with disgust.

My thoughts exactly.

"Must have been my sparkling personality and can-do attitude," Mason sarcastically replied. "Anyway, we quit Sarteano. Jose was ready to move up anyway. They didn't really need me."

"Oh, how is Jose? He was always so nice."

"Jose's fine," he replied with annoyance. "Would you like me to tell him you said, 'hi'? Stop interrupting." He shook his head and huffed. "So, this stuff was all stuck together, but with a little piece of wood, we were able to pry things apart. That's probably what the bevels are for, so you can get leverage. I think those ceramic trays were keeping them spaced apart so they wouldn't bond into a big mass."

"What about all those round pieces at the bottom, and that T-shaped piece? Why were they just scattered around and stuck together like that?"

"I think, at one time, they were wrapped in some sort of fabric or kept in bags. I saw traces of it on the T piece and remnants of what was probably cloth at the bottom of the box. Over the centuries, it had decomposed, but that gave us an idea. We figured out that if we wrapped each piece in some cloth and kept them separate, they wouldn't bond. Even when they're in close proximity to each other, the magnetic pull is almost totally negated unless they're actually touching. So, it was amazingly easy to get the stuff out. We just bought some suitcases and put them in checked baggage, simple as that. Nobody batted an eye."

"All right." She sighed with resignation. "So, you got it back here. Why didn't you sell it yet? And what does any of this have to do with Emilia disappearing?"

"Well, I could tell you, but it might be easier just to show you. Wanna' take a little walk?"

What choice do we have? Apparently, this is what we're here to do.

They traipsed after Mason on a steep little path that started behind the house and led up the mountainside. It was rough going, and though it was only quarter to four, Eric was starving.

Should have eaten that ice cream.

Mason wasn't remotely like anything he'd pictured, some dashing guy who wore a lab coat and talked with refined eloquence. He seemed far more rough and ready, better described as "eccentric" than erudite. Not at all what he'd imagined Lotte wanting, but who really knew Lotte's mind?

No one. Rhetorical question.

Anxiety still washed over him when he thought of them together—romantically, that is.

As they climbed, he timed his breathing to labored steps, attempting to assimilate this new dimension of reality into his life. He found it a significant struggle, but all the things that had produced anything of true worth in his life had been hard won. Sadly, experience had shown him that the benefits of certain struggles were at best vague, or, in the end, seemingly nonexistent.

As the ground leveled out, the path ended, and they stood in a clearing on a small plateau. The rock face of the mountain towered above them, against which a fairly large camping tent sat with its back flush against the stone. Several boxes, a table with two folding chairs, and a small propane tank and generator lay scattered outside.

Mason marched over to the tent, unzipped the front, and pulled aside the flap. "Y'all come on in, now," he said in fake southern drawl.

Lotte went first and Eric followed.

Mason clicked on a battery-operated lamp that dispelled the darkness.

"Oh, my!" she said with wonder.

The back side of the tent had been cut away, and the rock face lay exposed. On the stone wall, a black frame large enough to walk through had been assembled, formed by pieces similar to the one Mason had showed them.

"What's holding the frame in place?" she asked.

"There are spikes on those corner pieces, similar to the ones on the little round stones. Honestly, though, it barely freaking needs it. There's enough iron ore in the rock that it basically sticks. These things are *highly* magnetic, especially when you put them all together."

Eric approached the wall and looked at a cascade of perhaps two hundred or more marble-size pieces of the black, stone-like material, stuck to the wall within the confines of the frame. The rock was actually recessed about two inches behind the frame. "The rock face is indented. How the hell did you do this, and what do all these little round stones in the frame do?"

Mason went to the corner of the tent and picked up an electric device that looked a lot like a drill. "Air hammer. It's connected to the generator outside. We've got a drill too, for the holes that the spikes on the round pieces stick into. We started doing it by hand, but fuck that! Took ages. I went down to Berlin and bought these suckers, and we were done in a day or two. As far as the round pieces, give me a minute to get it all set up, and you'll see."

He reached in his pocket, pulled out the white cloth, and removed the stone they'd seen earlier. He walked to the frame, bent down, and placed it in the open space from which he'd apparently removed it. It made a sharp little *click* as it snapped into place. Then he went to the side of the tent, picked up one of the larger curved stones, and set it in its small ceramic stand. He placed this facing the frame at a slight angle near the right side of the tent, then situated another stone in a similar manner on the left.

"Okay, get fuckin' ready!" He fetched one final large piece of stone, secured it to a ceramic stand between the other two, and pointed it directly at the center of the frame.

The instant he did this, a noise began—a low hum that resonated in the earth below their feet—and the stones began to glow. The web of small round stones within the frame coalesced into a solid mass of shimmering, blue-white light, and within the perimeter formed by the frame and the three objects on the ground, the air seemed to dance with a similar radiance.

"Mason, stop!" Lotte cried. "You're opening the portal!"

He shot her a wicked glance. "How the fuck do you know that? How could you possibly know what this is? Anyway, you're totally wrong, at least about opening it!"

To prove his point, he walked directly into the middle of the shining, fan-shaped area between the frame and the other stones. "See? Perfectly safe? I can stand here all damn day and never go anywhere. Wanna' know why? Because we're missing a fuckin' piece, Lotte, that's why! The T-piece is gone, and so is Emilia! She took it in there!"

He pointed to the glowing myriad of small stones within the frame. "She took it with her when she fucking disappeared!"

"All right, Mason," she said, trying to calm him. "You've shown us. You made your point. Now, please, just shut it down and let's talk. I'll explain how we know what this might be, and we'll figure out how to find Emilia. I promise, we'll find her. Just do this now, please?"

He angrily yanked the central stone from the floor, and the hum and glow instantly ceased.

Eric felt a slight perturbation in the air, as if some sort of energy was being released, or was being reabsorbed.

"Happy now?" Mason asked with venom in his voice.

Lotte turned and stormed out of the tent.

Eric looked at Mason, shrugged, and then followed. Outside, he watched as she fell into one of the chairs, slammed her elbows on the table, and cradled her head in her hands.

He cautiously approached. "You okay?" he asked, knowing full well she wasn't.

She raised her head and mimed a scream as she shook her outstretched hands, fingers crooked. Then she sat heavily back in the little foldable chair. "He doesn't know what he's playing with. Neither did Emilia, and soon enough, we'll know what happened with her. Prepare yourself, Eric. It only gets worse from here."

Right on cue, Mason emerged from the tent. *"Ohay,* Lotte," he said in a faux Ricky Ricardo accent. "You got a *lotta esplanin'* to *dooh!"*

She shot right back. "Sit down, Mason! If you want my help, first you answer *my* questions!"

He hovered by the entrance to the tent. After some hesitation, he slowly dragged himself to the other folding chair and collapsed into it. "Ask, and ye shall receive," he said, with a biblical air of diplomacy.

"First off, how did you figure all this out, how to set up the frame, and the stones on the floor, and the small round stones? Go through it with me carefully. The details may be important."

He hesitated, then put his arms on the table and began to speak. "We got the shit here from the airport, and started sourcing buyers. The offers we got were okay, but not what we were hoping for. Then we started thinking: these aren't just 'antiquities,' these things might have properties of their own other than magnetism. Okay, what the hell are those properties, and might they be worth anything? We looked at Emilia's photos, and I realized the pieces inside the box corresponded with the painting on the outside. It was like a little instruction manual of how to set them up. It was stylized, sure, but you could get the idea."

Eric realized Mason had done the same analysis as Lotte, but without benefit of having seen the Afrit artifacts. She'd said he was smart, but he could now see Mason's intelligence in action.

"We decided to give it a shot," Mason continued, "just like the instructions. We had to find a stone wall, so we came up here. At first, we assembled the frame and sort of laid it against the rock, and then placed the three larger pieces on the ground. There was a definite effect. We heard that freakin' humming noise, and the stones seemed to... like, brighten a little. It totally freaked us out, but we knew we were onto something. Then, we affixed the frame to the rock face, drilling holes for the spikes on the corner pieces. This time, it really clicked. The frame and stones on the floor started to glow like you saw. The orientation has to be just right."

"What about the little round pieces, and that T-piece?" Eric asked.

"Those aren't in the picture on the ceramic box. We had no fuckin' idea what those were for, but then we had a little accident. One time, when we had everything going, Emilia had the T-piece in her hand, and she dropped it. It fell into the kind of fan-shaped area between the frame and the other stones, and fuck if it didn't shoot to the center of that space and start spinning. It just started going faster and faster — got to be a goddamn blur after a while. The other pieces started going haywire too, glowing and humming."

"But it wasn't complete," Lotte said from across the table. "You still hadn't accounted for the little round stones."

"Oh, Lotte, that's why I love you," he gushed. "Beautiful *and* smart. The winning combination! Totally, you're right. Nothing on that box indicates where those little stones would go. It probably flaked off over the years, or got damaged in one of the earthquakes. We were hosed, but then Emilia started going through her photos. She noticed one that had something interesting. We'd missed it before because it's basically a moronic picture of me standing in front of the wall we saw first, waiting for her to finish taking her fucking pictures! Behind me, though, on the wall, she saw these little holes, and she also saw that the wall was slightly indented. This would have been the wall right across from the original door, and that's when it came to us! This is the main goddamn altar, not the fucking alcove and the box! That's just a stupid storage box."

Lotte nodded. "And this is what you tried to recreate here, the 'main altar.'"

"Exact-a-mundo! We already knew the orientation and proportions were important, so we figured there also had to be an indentation like we saw on the wall in the sanctuary. So, we started chipping this out using hand tools, then I bought the air hammer and a drill when I realized doing it by hand was a no-go. We had the small emergency generator in the shed out back of the house, along with all this old camping equipment. We set everything up, used the air hammer to make the indentation, used the drill for the holes, and we were set."

"So, what happened?" Eric asked. "If you opened the gate together, why don't you know what happened to Emilia?"

Mason stared at Eric, then Lotte, and then rotated freely between the two. "You're gonna tell me how you two know this fuckin' thing is a gate, or portal, or whatever. Oh, yes, you will. For now, I'll finish answering Queen Lotte's question, but then, it's *my* turn. So, where was I? Oh, yeah, we had everything set to go. Right at that moment — can you actually freakin' believe it? — Thessaloniki."

"Huh?" Eric asked, completely befuddled.

Lotte seemed more in the know. "Oh, you got Thessaloniki. Congratulations."

"Well," he said, with modesty that seemed a little false, because everything about Mason seemed a little false. "I didn't *get* it, but when I went down to Berlin to check my emails one day, I'd received one from them saying they wanted me to interview. This I could *not* turn down. This is major shit... Greek dig sites in a place rife with unexplored areas. So, I had to get on a plane pronto. I only planned to be gone a few days, so we left everything up here so it would be ready, and Emilia said she'd keep an eye on the place. When I got back, the stuff was humming like you just saw it, except no little T-piece, and no Emilia. She didn't fuckin' wait for me to get back. She tried it on her own. Now she's in there, and I don't know how to get her out."

All three were silent for a time.

Finally, Lotte spoke. "Two more questions, Mason. First, where are the rings?"

"The rings?" he said, as if hearing of them for the first time. "Oh, right! Those spiral rings. Totally forgot about them. Typical Etruscan shit, even though they had little bits of this black stone on the tips. We didn't see anything on the box about how to use them, so we figured they were just cosmetic, things the guy in the sanctuary had on him when the ancient earthquake hit. Prime stuff to sell when we had a chance. They're in a drawer down at the house. Why, are they important?"

"Important, Mason? They're only the key to everything."

He looked perplexed. "Umm, okay. So, what's your second question, my avenging savior angel?"

She leaned forward, put her elbows on the table, and rested her chin on her interlaced fingers. "How do you know Emilia went into this 'portal,' as opposed to something coming out?"

CHAPTER 7

Central Etruria, 593 BC

The sun set and brought relief from the day's heat. Rika relished the cool shade of the trees as she walked along the path back toward the compound.

Three months had passed under Thana's tutelage, and as high summer set in on the plateau, the inquisitive youngster reflected on all the things she'd learned, and all that remained as yet unknown. Already, she knew, preparations were underway for another ceremony of sacrifice. She wasn't certain whether she'd be expected to attend, but gradually, Thana had augmented her reading and writing lessons with instruction in the use of the strange device—in truth, devices—that summoned the mysterious otherworldly beings.

In her bag, she carried two ivory writing tablets with beautifully carved frames, along with various spools of wool and loom weights that lent credence to her role as a weaving assistant. On one of the palettes, Thana had impressed the still very simple questions into the soft beeswax with her stencil. She would answer these queries as best she could on the other board, a lesson in both reading and writing. She knew the quiz pertained to the proper placement of the artifacts, the order and correct angles of their arrangement that would initiate the process, and employment of the rings that would bind the creature's actions, as well as those of the summoner.

It still scared her, but Thana had been right. Knowledge had lessened Rika's fear, and had given her a sense of control over her life, in addition to the powerful forces with which she soon might interconnect.

A twig snapped in the underbrush and startled her from deep thought.

"Is someone there?" she called, turning to where the dense trees rapidly descended into darkness.

Without warning, another noise came from behind her, too close to turn and look before she felt strong arms envelop her and drag her roughly off the road. She fought back with all her might, but found herself hopelessly overpowered. Any thought of escape rapidly faded as another figure rushed into the brush from the direction of the path, likely the person she'd heard originally, perhaps as they readied to grab her, or simply to provide a distraction.

In any case, there were two of them at least, and by the time she'd found the wits and breath to scream, the first had covered her mouth with a sweaty palm.

"Grab her legs!" he hissed. "Let's get her on the ground!"

The other complied, and despite her desperate kicks, she felt herself lifted, then forced hard into the earth. Soon, the second attacker clambered on top of her. He used his weight to stifle her legs, and pinned her arms to the ground. She gasped when she saw that her assailant wore a mask. Wild eyes gazed out from crude slashes in the repurposed wicker basket and presented a terrifying visage.

"Stop fighting, you little sow!" he spat.

His voice sounded muffled from his disguise. His was a boy's voice, not a man's. She guessed him to be older than she, but probably not by much, maybe the age of her youngest brother. She had so little contact with the boys, it would be hard to say which of a dozen or so he might be.

They had her trapped, and she couldn't breathe for her mouth being covered. She did as instructed and ceased her struggle.

"That's better," the boy chortled. "Now, let's see what the lovely Rika Matuna has got going on under here, shall we?" With one hand, he began to grope at her tunic.

She thrashed anew in utter and complete panic.

"Stop!" the other boy who held her mouth commanded. "That's not why we're here. We're to question her and go, no more."

"Well, I want more. This is too good to pass up. Hold her down. I just want a little squeeze or two, assuming there's anything there at all."

"I swear by the spear of Laran, if you touch her in that way, you'll have me to contend with!"

"Yeah, we'll settle that score later. Right now, I'm busy."

To Rika's amazement, her mouth was freed as the boy behind her launched at the one holding her down. They tumbled away, arms locked in violent struggle as they fiercely grasped at one another for any potential advantage. The makeshift masks were the first casualties of the conflict, and shock assailed her when she recognized Plecu as her most dangerous aggressor. Her brothers and he were friends. She felt a deep sense of violation at his actions.

"What in the name of the gods is wrong with you?" Plecu screamed as he fought off the other boy's blows. "What do you care about what happens to this traitorous little tramp?"

"Stop calling her that!"

"Ho! Wait a minute! You fancy her, don't you? Brother, why didn't you say so? I'd have let you have the first go!"

Something in the other boy's manner instantly changed. His spine stiffened, and he looked momentarily to the heavens.

Rika then watched in stunned silence as he intently raised his arm, then drove his fist directly into Plecu's face. She could almost feel the impact herself, heralded by a loud crack that marked the end of the contest.

Plecu rolled miserably on the ground, hand to his cheek while the other boy stood and put his foot on his rival's chest.

"Be gone, Plecu. I'll complete what we came here to do. Speak of this to anyone, I swear, I'll finish you."

The injured boy slowly regained his senses. He still held his face as he skulked back toward the road.

For a moment, Rika cursed her stupidity for not having fled during the fight. Then she saw the precious contents of her bag sadly strewn across the leafy ground. She could never leave her things behind. She also felt her legs tremble, and realized they surely could not have carried her far before one, or both, assailants would have tracked her down.

The scrum's victor turned to face her, and she recognized Arte, another of her brother's friends, whose sister was also close with Sethra.

"Are you all right?" he asked, still winded from the fight. "Did he hurt you?"

She suddenly felt anger boil to the surface. "And what if he had? Am I to suddenly feel fortunate you saw fit to spare me? *You* grabbed me first! To me, you're as much a threat as he was!"

He motioned with his hands for calm. "I don't want to hurt you. That wasn't supposed to have happened. We just wanted to talk with you."

"This is how you talk with a girl, by grabbing her from behind? Have you both lost your minds?"

"Well, all right, it's more than that. We need information from you, but it isn't safe to speak openly of such things. The masks were supposed to keep you from knowing who we were."

"Yes, that's normally what they're for, isn't it? Nicely done." The barb clearly landed as Arte grimaced slightly. "So, what is it you're so desperate to know? I assume it's not just the size of my breasts!"

"No, not at all," he whispered, eyes closed, obviously in embarrassed agony. "It's about what you're doing with *her*! Thana Zalthu, High Priestess of the temple, though we never see her preside over any rituals that *we're* allowed to attend. We know you spend days in her presence.

Even now, you return from seeing her, and we know you're not there to assist with weaving! What are the two of you up to?"

Rika gulped. She'd been drawn into a very tricky situation, but she tried to maintain her formidable demeanor. "What business of it is yours? I *do* assist her with weaving! My things are there. See for yourself."

He glanced briefly at the items that littered the ground. "What are those?" He pointed at the ivory tablets, which jutted out slightly from her bag. "She teaches you letters. We know. We watch from afar when we can, in the orchard. Why would she do this? She talks to you for hours on end, and you listen. What does she say? It's everyone's business when folk go missing. These are people's kin, Rika, relatives from villages all around this area, including our own. We need to put an end to it. What do you know about all of this that can help us?"

Her mind spun like wool on the whorl. What did she truly *know?* Yes, she'd seen something, but Thana assured her that as terrifying as that had been, it had an explanation and a rationale. True to her word, they'd gone back to the beginning, to an island called Thera, which long ago had been engulfed in a great volcanic eruption. The woman recounted how, many years thereafter, when the fires had cooled, a man from the east had braved the dead and desolate landscape, and returned with an unusual prize—a strange rock that, when handled in certain ways, could summon beings from the realm of the gods.

Thana told her how, for many generations, the man's apprentices and successors had used this artifact to help great rulers and kings. One who had facility with the mysterious rock was Antenor, advisor to Priam, sovereign of the city of Truwisa. After a fearsome siege, Truwisa had been laid low as the result of a clever trick perpetrated by the ancestors of the Hellenes. Antenor and his family, spared after the city's destruction, fled to the south, where he encountered a secretive society of savants who were adroit at working miraculous objects.

There, the grayish rock, if indeed it were ever truly *rock* in the first place, had further been forged and refined. For reasons unknown, Antenor then sailed with the newly recrafted artifacts into the west, with a group of Paphlagonians called the Enetoi. They had similarly been displaced by recent conflagrations, which swept almost the entire known world of that time.

They arrived on unfamiliar shores and set up life anew, but Antenor and his family didn't remain. Instead, they again traveled south, directly into the bosom of the Rasenna. According to Thana, the creatures he and his descendants summoned helped secure the lands in which their people now lived, notably staving off the incursions of hostile and strange-speaking barbarians who invaded with horse and chariot not a century after Antenor's passing.

What could Rika say? She knew not what had changed that prompted these otherworldly beings to now harvest the lives of vulnerable locals. Thana had implied a reason existed, and Rika sensed that the terrible secret would soon be revealed to her, but until then, how could she judge? How could she betray Thana when the survival of her very culture could hang in the balance?

"I know far less than you imagine, Arte," she finally answered. "Thana speaks to me of the past, of our people, and of faraway lands, like the city the Hellenes now call Ilium. Yes, she teaches me my letters. She does this so, someday, I may be more than yet another weaver, perhaps a scribe for the noble family, keeping the ledgers for their financial dealings. Of the disappearances, or Thana's possible role in them, I can't say anything that might help you understand."

"Can't, or *won't*? Rika, I warn you, anxiety grows as the time yet again approaches when people go... well... *missing*. If something happens, and certain villagers find out you didn't tell us what you know, I can't protect you."

"Protect *me*? Since when did you become *my* champion? When you punched Plecu in the face? I suppose I owe you thanks for that, but now that I know people like *you* are spying on me, I'll surely be more cautious!"

"Rika, I didn't mean it like —"

"Silence! You have the answer to your question, Arte. What more can I do for you before I gather my things and go?"

He again closed his eyes in apparent consternation.

She dusted herself off and began to collect her belongings back into her shoulder bag.

"Is it true?" she asked, considerably relieved as she retrieved the small weight that Thana had engraved with her name. She hadn't seen fit to use the item anymore, save to gaze at it by lamplight in her bed before sleep finally overtook her.

"Is what true?"

"What Plecu said. Do you indeed fancy me?"

He stood silent for a time before he responded. "Would it be so awful if I did? There are limited choices here for both of us. I wouldn't dare approach you until next summer. It would be improper. I'll admit, I've noticed you. I could think of far worse fates that Athrpa could weave for me than a life with us being together."

In spite of herself, she warmed behind a blush. "Perhaps something to anticipate for next summer then, assuming your overture doesn't include another clammy hand over my mouth."

He winced once more, until she saw him notice her sly grin. "No. This I promise. I'll not touch you again unless you permit it. But Rika, mark my words: if something happens, I may not be able to shield you from the worst of it, should anyone find out you were a part of all this. Be ready."

"I appreciate your warning," replied the youngster who suddenly no longer felt so young. "I'll be ready. But, Arte, know this: if something happens and *you're* involved, I may not be able to shield *you* from the worst of it. On this, mark *my* words."

Bailey, New Hampshire, Saturday, July 27, 2013

"Fuck."

Mason took a long swig of beer, thumped it on the coffee table, and sat back in his chair. "So, you're telling me one of those fuckin' Afrit things came out of that doorway and took Emilia, just because she didn't have those stupid rings to make some kind of *deal* with it?"

"I don't know if it's an Afrit, exactly," Lotte replied, "but I suspect something like it. Possibly something that responds to magnetism, as the Afrit did with fire."

"So, what makes you think it's still here? How do you know it didn't just take Emilia back with it through that doorway?"

"Well, I don't with certainty, but that T-piece is missing. All the pieces seem to be required to actually open the gate. This implies that the creature would leave that piece behind when it returned to its own world, allowing the gate to be re-opened in the future. In fact, the T-piece may not be able to pass through the portal at all. It might not be able to return to pure energy like the entity that's passing through."

Mason's gaze drifted away as the implications of the situation seemed to dawn on him. "Fuck, Lotte, so this thing's probably still out there, and it has Emilia. What the hell are we gonna do?"

"I don't know. I'm going to have to consider our options, but right now, I think we should eat dinner. It's been a long day and I need some food and a chance to relax before I can focus on it."

Thank God, Eric thought. *I'm beyond starving!* He'd listened patiently as she recounted their tale of freeing the Afrit from its mirror prison. Like it or not, Mason was now privy to this knowledge, including what happened to Dr. Esfahani. Eric felt uncomfortable with that. He didn't exactly trust Mason to keep his mouth shut, and even had some fear that, down the road, he might try to use what he knew as leverage against them.

Although, maybe that's my heart talking, and not my head.

"Yeah," Mason finally replied, seeming to gather his wits. "I'm hungry too. Problem is, I don't have shit in the house. I haven't been out at all since I got back. I'm gonna have to make a grocery run. Burgers on the grill good?"

They both nodded vigorously in reply.

Mason sprung out of his seat. "Cool, I'll shoot down there, be back in a bit. I'll hit the packie too. Eric, what's your poison?"

This threw him a bit off guard. "Oh, I'm good, thanks. Maybe I'll have a beer or something."

"Oh, come on, man, you can do better than that. Special occasion! We have to toast our new partnership in crime with something nicer than a fuckin' beer. What'll it be, dude?" He looked down with an intent stare, waiting for a reply.

"Eric," Lotte said with concern in her voice. "You don't have to if you don't want. It's all right."

Eric felt the challenge and knew she could sense it too. Stupid as it might be, he realized that failing this test would forever diminish him in Mason's eyes, and this he could not tolerate.

One drink won't kill me.

He locked eyes with Mason. "I'm a rum and Coke guy. I assume they'll have Captain Morgan's. Can I give you some cash for it?"

"Now we're talkin'! No chance, man, my treat all the way. Listen, I haven't said fuckin' 'thank you' yet for dragging up here and saving my sorry ass. So, thank you. Both of you. Seriously. I had no idea what was going on, and I hit the damned jackpot with you. I'm freaking ecstatic you're both here."

With that, he went to put on a shirt, waved, and cruised out the door.

Eric felt good, like he'd made the right call. "So, what *are* we gonna do?" he asked, directing his attention to Lotte, who still sat silently next to him on the couch.

"I'm not exactly sure," she replied, obviously deep in thought, "but I think we're going to have to try to lure whatever this creature is back to its portal, try to get it to go home. We have the rings. Maybe we can bargain with it."

"What is it with these rings? Why do these things *bargain* with us? They're way stronger than we are. Why don't they just kill us and go home."

"I've thought about this question a lot over the years. The best answer I can give is that you have to see it from their perspective. They come through this gateway into another world, a world where they can harvest power that makes them stronger, but the gateway is a fragile and complex thing. Without someone to attend it, to guard it, how do they get home? We could walk up that path right now, remove a piece from the frame and leave with it. The portal might never function again. They strike the deal so that everyone gets what they want."

"Wow, makes sense. It's just incredible there's something else like this besides the Afrit."

"I've long suspected there were. You look at history, the rise and sudden fall of civilizations.... What happened to the Hittites, for example? They had a powerful and successful society for centuries, and it collapsed practically in the blink of an eye. Of course, there are many possible explanations, but based on what you and I know of the expansion of Islam, I don't think it's unreasonable to think a creature like the Afrit *might* have been involved. The Afrit itself is referred to as belonging to a category of entities, the Jinn. So, it's also reasonable to assume there might be more entities of this nature. This is why my course of study is so complex."

"Huh? What do you mean course of study? You mean, like, what you're applying to graduate school for, all that data collecting analytical geo-thermal computerized nuclear literary biblical crap?"

She laughed. "Exactly, you little shit! Don't play dumb with me. I know you heard what I told you. *Alter!* You're just like my father." She gave him a playful shove.

Guilty as charged, he thought, laughing, and fondly remembering Mr. Schwarz' dippy humor. Then it struck him. "Wait a minute! You're studying all that stuff because of the Afrit, and the other freaking things like that you think are out there?"

"Yes." She looked suddenly serious.

"My God, Lotte, you're gonna hunt them!"

The slightest smile creased her lips, a patented "Lotte's Almost Kind-Of-Smile," but unlike before, when the dreams had haunted her, now her eyes blazed like miniature black suns. Her porcelain skin glowed clear and pure. She held her chin high with confidence, and defiance.

"Yes, Eric, I'm going to hunt them, as many as I can. I'm going to find them, track them down, secure them so their power can't tempt the weak-minded fools or the well-meaning saviors alike. This is my calling, Eric. I'm a huntress, and the hunt is on!"

When Mason returned from the store, he dumped the grocery bags at the door and stormed into the living room where Lotte and Eric still sat. "These are all over fucking town!" He slammed two sheets of crumpled paper onto the coffee table.

Lotte spread them out and they both looked. "Missing," one read, with photocopied pictures of a man and a woman, hikers apparently who had been staying at a guest cottage near the lake. They'd vanished about a week ago. "Have You Seen This Man?" captioned the other, a photo of an elderly gentleman who had disappeared three days ago plastered underneath.

"That's Larry Henderson!" Mason angrily said. "He lives at the far end of New Speck Lane. Known him all my fuckin' life. This is too many people to go missing all at once for it to be a goddamned coincidence! This thing is out there preying on people. Emilia's dead. I fucking know it. This is a shitshow!"

"Mason," Lotte said in a soothing voice. "Calm down. We don't know that. You're right, this is probably not a coincidence, but we don't yet know what it means. This changes nothing. We still need to find the creature, and we still need to look for Emilia, whatever might have happened to her. Come on, let's go start the grill and talk about what we might be able to do." She rose, and Eric began to follow, but she put her hand on his shoulder and whispered in his ear, "Let me handle this. Just give us a few moments alone, please?"

A slight pang of jealousy struck him, but he realized he would be of no help with Mason. Plus, this was the fastest path to getting dinner underway, and he was starving. He let them go, and went to set the smaller table in the kitchen so they could eat. By the time they settled in, Mason was far calmer.

She can be quite the diplomat when she wants to be.

Dinner was pretty much 'old home week' for Lotte and Mason. They toasted their new association, rum and Cokes all around.

Eric drank, and the familiar warmth quickly began to course through his body, especially being so famished. It brought that slight numbness that, years ago, had so welcomingly deadened the pain of losing Lotte.

Now it eased the tensions of a trying day. Despite his dread, he'd survived meeting Mason. It still felt super-weird, but he knew that, with time, this wouldn't carry the emotional weight, which even now seemed to be lifting from his shoulders.

Mason re-filled his glass, but Eric didn't intend to have a second drink. Instead, he made himself invisible, listening to their discussion about various digs they'd been on, who of their mutual acquaintances was doing what and where, when might Mason hear about Thessaloniki, whether or not he would go if he got the job, and so forth. Mason sought more details about their ordeal, now nearly eight years past, so the conversation returned to the encounter with the Afrit. Lotte described how Eric had thrown the ash in Dr. Esfahani's face after offering himself to be taken.

"Man," Mason said, "now I know why she always told me you saved her fucking life. Fast thinking, dude."

At that, Eric glanced at Lotte, but she'd buried her face in her burger. "Well," he humbly replied. "Necessity is the mother of dissension."

Mason cracked up. "Ha! Too fuckin' funny! Here's to that, my man!"

They clinked glasses and drank.

When dinner was through, Lotte and Eric cleaned up. He noticed his glass was empty, but didn't really remember drinking it. He did, however, notice she'd barely touched hers, so he picked it up and headed to the living room, where Mason built a fire in the fireplace. They talked some more and digested the massive dinner. Eric had eaten three burgers and some macaroni salad.

"*Alles klar Jungs*," Lotte finally said with a great yawn. "I'm exhausted. I still have a touch of jet lag. Time for bed. Eric, are you sure you're okay on the couch?"

"Yeah, I'm fine. It'll be nice to sleep by the fire."

"Okay then, *Gute Nacht alle zusammen*." She skipped up the stairs.

"Well, big day, huh?" Eric said, hoping Mason would get the hint. "You're probably exhausted."

He yawned. "Yeah. How about a little nightcap first?"

Crap! I've already had three rum and Cokes, or was it four? Did Mason make me another after I finished Lotte's?

He couldn't remember. In any case, he didn't really want one, but things had been going so well with Mason, he hated to spoil it. "Yeah, okay, but just one. I'm pretty tired too."

Mason poured the drinks, more rum than Coke. "So, what's your story, Mr. Eric Schnitzel-Schneider the Great? You don't talk a lot, do you? You barely said two words during dinner."

Do I even have a story? It felt like Mason had already heard the most exciting *thing* that had ever happened in his life, and Mason had his own experience with the greatest *person* that had ever happened in his life. At this thought, Eric took a large sip of his new drink.

"Not much to tell, really," he finally replied. "Went to UMass, studied history. I have no idea why, but I enjoyed learning about all the things I knew nothing about. Now I work for my dad's company in Southby. I'm not sure if that's what I want to do, but I'm not sure what *else* I'd do, so I'm just sort of figuring that out."

"Girlfriend? Or, boyfriend?"

He chuckled. "There's a woman I see. I wouldn't say 'girlfriend,' but it could move in that direction." *By 2038, at the pace I'm going.*

"What about Lotte?"

What about Lotte? "Well, I'm not really sure. We haven't seen each other in a long time. In fact, this is the first time in about five years. She went away. She has her own life now. I'm not sure I really have a place in it. I'm not even sure I'd want one if I did."

"That's a lie," Mason said, taking a swig of his own drink. "You're gonna tell me that if Lotte fuckin' Schwarz came down here right now and told you she loved you and she wanted to spend the rest of her life with you, that you wouldn't do it?"

He gulped. Mason was right. He probably would do it. Would it be the best decision for him? Maybe, maybe not. If she led, however, he would follow. Of this, he had no doubt.

"Oh, I'm just fuckin' with you, man," Mason said, topping up the drinks with the bottle of rum. "Lotte's a catch, no question. The problem is, she's so fuckin' serious. She's like one of those big-ass drill machines they use in mines, or to cut out subway tunnels—so much power just moving head on, cutting through everything in her way. Equipment like that isn't built for peripheral shit like relationships, and parties, and love, and all that crap. For a while, she saw me as, like, a 'kindred spirit,' or whatever. Fellow archaeologist hot shot who could open doors for her, who she could 'study with.' Can you fuckin' believe that? She actually meant it, too!"

Eric remembered studying constantly with Lotte. She always had to be learning, moving forward. He'd loved it, basked in it. By osmosis, he'd gained knowledge, just by being with the person he most enjoyed, doing the thing she most enjoyed. It remained the best time of his life, and it tore him to pieces when it was taken away.

"Anyway," Mason went on. "It was a goddamn miracle I got her out on a date. Others had surely tried. Most of my friends told me not to bother, that she wasn't interested. It took me months to wear her down, and it almost fuckin' killed me. I had to be something I most decidedly am not: *serious*! I could only do that for so long. She blames me for what happened at Poggio Civitate, and I'm not denying what I did was a douchebag move, but truthfully, we were done by then. She'd seen through my game, just like she saw through most of the losers who'd tried with her before."

Interesting, Eric thought as he drained his glass.

Mason divvied up the last of the rum and drank his down. "So, I look at you, and I think about how she talked about you. Man, it was like, 'reverent.' You two certainly went in different directions, but you aren't like anyone who runs in our circles, all the high-flying hot-shot intellectuals who blow their own fuckin' horns all the time. You're quiet, serious. She likes that. The few friends she had were that way, but she never got involved with any of them. She scared all of them to death because she was like their fucking queen! They all looked up to her, and they approached her like they'd approach goddamn Xerxes—on their knees."

Despite increasing lethargy, Eric hung on Mason's words while he drained the last of the rum in his glass.

Mason rose and wobbled slightly. "If one of them had risen up, though, if one of them had taken the chance... well, I don't know. Maybe the 'Little Engine that Could' might have found love after all. That's all I can say, Mister Eric Schnitzel-Schneider the Great, because I am drunk, and I am going to bed."

Recurrent waves of nausea finally wrested Eric from sleep. The embers of the fire burned low. He knew this feeling. He had maybe five minutes, perhaps less. There was a half-bath off the kitchen, but the house was dead silent. He knew the noise would wake at least Lotte, and that would be an embarrassment he could not endure.

So fucking stupid!

He dragged himself into an upright position and, to his mild surprise, found that a blanket covered him, and he no longer wore his shoes, socks, or pants. He didn't remember removing them.

Whatever, no time to ponder that mystery.

He propped his hands on the coffee table and forced himself upright. The room spun. He took stuttering steps toward the kitchen, grabbed a bottle of water, and as quietly as possible exited through the front door. Somehow, in the darkness, he found the steps down the hill, passed by the cars, and stumbled as far as the street. There, he collapsed to his knees in some weeds and violently vomited.

Why, why, why do I do this?

He usually found it so easy to avoid drinking. He had no real compulsion to do so. Time and effort had largely buried the pain of Lotte, which only occasionally surfaced when he woke from sleep and realized yet another day would pass without her. He'd have been perfectly happy with water and maybe one beer tonight, which he never drank in quantity. With the harder stuff, though, once he'd had the first one, it became easy to have a second, and once the perimeter of his normally bristling defensive wall had been breached, the fortress soon fell.

Another swell wracked him, and he heaved into the scrubby grass. His head spun as he retched and spat. That round complete, he reached for the bottle of water to wash out his mouth.

God, please don't let Lotte hear this.

He lay on the dirt road and waited for his stomach to settle. After one more small bout of vomiting, he started to feel slightly better. He was still dizzy, but at least now he could drink water and hold it down.

Man, tomorrow is gonna suck. Wait a minute... tomorrow! Tomorrow is freaking Sunday. We have to leave. I have to get back to work on Monday. How in the world are we gonna lure this... this... whatever the hell it is, back to the portal in one afternoon? Screw it. This is Lotte's department. She's upper management. I just work here.

He planned to talk with her about it in the morning. Slowly, he slogged back to the house to catch what sleep he still could, sickened as much by his behavior as the drink itself.

The birds woke him.

He rustled in his bag and retrieved his phone. Almost 6:00 a.m. Nothing stirred in the house. Lotte and Mason were apparently still asleep. He felt dizzy, but not like he did last night. He knew the incessant chirping and the light would keep him awake, so he went to the bathroom, peed, and brushed his teeth.

Still woozy, he returned to the couch and put on some shorts, a green Celtics t-shirt, and his socks and shoes. Then he re-filled his water bottle at the kitchen sink and went outside. In the scraggly yard by the side of the house, a weathered wooden bench provided a nice view of the woods. He left the bottle on the bench, walked a short way farther, and stood staring into the trees.

He closed his eyes and gently started to sway and stretch, and she was next to him.

"Just hold the barre and raise your arm. Sweep it around. Good. Now, dip your knees, and plié, straight back up. Nice."

Eric did exactly as Jennifer asked.

She nodded in approval. "Just do some more of those. God, Eric, you could have been a dancer. You're muscular but lean."

They enjoyed having the little studio in Totman gymnasium to themselves. He stole a glance in the mirror and caught a glimpse of her wearing her ballet tights and leotard. She held one arm high in the air, arced above her head, and one leg extended behind her as she gracefully floated up and down. She reversed direction and repeated the motion from the other side.

While they worked, it dawned on him how desperate he'd been to connect with someone, anyone, after months of self-isolation. Her tender and patient manner calmed the nervousness of meeting a girl alone for the first time since Lotte. She showed him a variety of ballet warm-ups and yoga stretches — good counterbalances, she explained, to his normal weightlifting, which often left him stiff and sore.

That had been merely the first session of what would become many over the next two years, but it remained the one to which his memory always returned.

Now, he ran through these moves, or his vague approximations of them, with his eyes closed. He pictured Jennifer's warm smile, heard her soothing voice guide him to the proper positions, felt her hands barely brush against him, but still exert a force that reshaped his body — and his soul.

He opened his eyes and the trees re-emerged. Sweat covered his body, and the lurching feeling in his stomach still made itself known, but he knew the routine would help cleanse his body of the toxins he'd so foolishly imbibed the night before.

I'll never let this happen again!

He turned to fetch his water from the bench.

"Moin!"

He practically jumped out of his skin with surprise.

Lotte smiled where she sat on the bench, feet on the seat in front of her, arms wrapped around her knees.

"Jeez! You scared me to death! Quit doing that!"

She laughed. "It's not my fault if you're not paying attention."

He shot her a comically dubious glance. "For real? Man, gotta watch my back around you. I should have learned that ages ago. You're like a mischievous little Ninja."

She giggled, but then in a more serious tone said, "But, Eric Schneider, so full of surprises. What you were doing was so beautiful! Where did you learn to move like a dancer?"

"Oh, a friend of mine from college taught me," he replied, wondering how long she'd been sitting there watching. "It's good for stretching, getting centered. Yoga too. It feels great, helps me calm down."

"Yes, I was wondering how you were feeling. Looks like you boys finished off the rum. Are you okay? Mason is still in a coma." She gave a slight laugh.

Did we actually finish that whole bottle? Yeah, I guess we did. Ouch!

"Oh, I'm okay. I shouldn't have had so much, though. I'm gonna be dragging today, big time. Speaking of today, what are we doing? I have to be back in Southby tomorrow."

She put her hand to her chin and rubbed her lower lip with her finger. "We do need to go back to Southby, but... Eric, you know we'll have to return here. We can't let this thing take more people. Between us, I do think Emilia is dead, as are the others. We have to leave now, and you have to find a way that you can come back immediately, probably later today. Can you do it?"

There used to be a cable station that showed old reruns. Eric's mom had liked to watch it, and from time to time, he'd been sucked in as well. Right now, he pictured himself on Gilligan's Island, thinking he'd been in for a three-hour cruise and finding himself indefinitely marooned.

I'm not the Captain, or the Professor — that would be Lotte — and I'm certainly not the Millionaire. I guess that makes me Gilligan. Great.

In truth, he'd seen this shaping up and had already been thinking about calling his dad and Margot. He hadn't taken any time off since he'd started, and while this was shorter notice than might be optimal, Schneider could cope with his absence for a week or so. It might present a greater challenge to sway Erica to this opinion, especially given who she knew he'd be with, but as Lotte sometimes said with one of her little British colloquialisms, there was "nothing for it."

"Yeah," he reluctantly replied. "I can do it. I'll get some time off. I'm due. But why do we have to go back to Southby? I could just drive down to Berlin, where we can get a signal and call my dad, or there's gotta be a landline phone in town somewhere."

She stared at him, chin resting on her knees. "You know why, Eric."

"Honestly, Lotte, I'm clueless. I have no idea what you'd want back in Southby. You're gonna have to fill me in."

She stretched out her legs, planted her feet on the ground, and placed her elbows on her knees. She looked directly into his eyes and held his curious stare as she spoke. "The artifacts, Eric. We need to get the artifacts."

"But... but... you said the wardrobe was gone, that you had to get rid of it, that it had been destroyed!"

She thought for a moment, then calmly replied, "You asked me about the wardrobe, and I told you I had to be rid of it. That was true. When my father moved, he sold most of the furniture, new and old. His apartment in Boston is far too small for all that. He offered that I could put the wardrobe into storage, but it would have been in one of those outdoor garage things. The temperature and humidity changes would have ruined it, not to mention what damage it might have done to the artifacts and the papers. Who knows how long it would have sat there. Probably years. So, as I told you, I couldn't look after it. Too much worry. Too many problems."

"I thought that meant you'd destroyed it. You seemed so sad about it."

She looked at the ground. "I am sad. Terribly sad. It was my mother's, and her mother's, but it needed to be sold with the rest of the furniture. I'm sorry if you took that to mean I'd destroyed it, or the artifacts, but I wasn't especially in the mood to have a conversation with you about it right then. I was upset about our fight and thinking about other things. You asked me about the wardrobe, and I answered, but that's different to me than the artifacts, which I removed."

"Which are now in Southby?"

"Precisely."

He pursed his lips. "So, what exactly do we need the artifacts for?"

She raised her head and again met his gaze. "Obviously, we're going to summon the Afrit. I need to talk with it."

CHAPTER 8

Central Etruria, 593 BC

The heat of the day hung heavy in the air and made each breath or movement laborious.

The summer had become hot and unusually dry. No rain had graced the plateau for weeks. As harvest time approached, concern mounted for the staple barley and other grains on which so many depended.

It came as no surprise to Rika that Thana had not called her this day. Her mentor likely reclined in the relative comfort of the dark and cool residence, the privilege of her status. Rika toiled with the other girls, weaving or dyeing textiles.

At least in the workshop, I'm out of the sun.

The thought brought her some minor pleasure. Her brothers and father worked in another part of the large building, where they lay out clay on the floor that soon would be shaped into tiles for the roof, gutter sections, and decorative crowning for the new temple. To her, it sounded infinitely more interesting than tablet weaving, churning out the meander-patterned strips of cloth that would surely give someone *else* such great pleasure. The Zalthu imprint carried a reputation for quality known far and wide, and the fine fabrics the women produced were part of the economic lifeblood of the region.

Little did she care. She'd never fully accepted the fate Athrpa had woven for her. Even before she encountered Thana Zalthu, she'd dreamt of finding a way to flee this confining community. Destiny appeared to have steered her in a different direction, one that carried both attractive and unappealing qualities.

Her association with Thana produced jealousy and suspicion. Even her parents, ever loyal to the noble family, and supremely proud for the recognition of their daughter's prowess, harbored hesitations. To stand out in any way always made one a target, and Thana's mysterious reputation only exacerbated matters. Naturally, the extra grains, meat, and fruits the family were awarded did much to assuage their concerns.

Thank the gods they don't know the true reason for Thana's interest in me. They'd never let me leave our cottage again!

For others, Rika's status created a rift of envy and covetousness, intermingled with not a small amount of fear. This had damaged lifelong friendships. As she operated her loom, she sat near the edge of the enclosed space, alone and far from the gathering near the center, where women and girls chatted or sang in languorous unison as they worked.

This represented the price, she realized. She'd wanted something different, and now her *differentness* had ostracized her from the group. Even her mother kept a discrete distance, unwilling to sacrifice relationships that would sustain her well after her fledgling had flown from the nest.

I hope it's worth it.

All this bothered her, but in her heart, she knew she'd never wavered from her choice once it had been made. These people already felt as if they lagged far behind her, part of a life she had little hesitation to abandon.

Some movement distracted her from the work. Several men, or perhaps older boys, crouched low to the ground as they slunk away from the workshop and toward the trees to the south. Had she not been at the perimeter of their area, she would never have seen them. It seemed very odd behavior, especially in this heat. When they'd disappeared into the underbrush, she picked up her shoulder bag and rose.

Something isn't right.

Her mind raced. She couldn't pinpoint any specific danger, or if indeed any danger existed at all, so she feared to unduly raise the alarm. Her gut, however, told her to move and be ready. She sidled through the weaving area to the north side of the building.

"And where do you think you're going, young one?" Alfia, one of the supervisors sternly inquired. "Your work isn't done, and today you have no excuse to avoid your *proper* chores."

Rika noted the slight, but shrugged it off as other matters dominated her attention. "I beg your leave, mistress. It's *that* time for me. I need a moment. I promise, I shall return."

Her forthright answer appeared to mollify the woman, though she heard many giggles from the other girls. It made no difference to her. Once clear of the weaving area, she rushed toward where her father and brothers labored in the eastern end of the building. She didn't get far before she heard panicked shouts and saw men pouring from the structure, their bare feet stained from having run across the still wet and malleable clay.

"Fire!" they shouted, and as if in response, a huge tongue of flame shot forth from under the eaves and into the hazy sky. Those weaving, or tanning hides, or carving tools from animal bones, ceased their activities and ran to investigate the commotion. When the source of the trouble became clear, all began to stream haphazardly from the burning building.

Some water buckets were stacked near the creek, and men quickly formed two lines to pass the sloshing vessels from one to another, until what remained of the contents were thrown onto the fire. She saw her father and brothers at various places in the lines, frantically transporting the pails back and forth.

They struggled in vain.

Whatever had started the blaze had gone unseen for too long, and now the eastern end of the building had become engulfed in flame. She ran back the way she'd come to make sure her mother had gotten out safely. Guards from the residence raced across the little wooden bridge. They directed those manning the buckets to divert their attention to the parts of the workshop that remained intact, in an attempt to save which portion they could. Even their noble lord, Thana's brother Larce, arrived to watch in horror as the tragedy unfolded in front of everyone.

Rika's heart jumped as realization dawned on her. *Not everyone! This is not as it seems!*

A quick glance inside revealed her mother, among other women. They desperately gathered fiber, partly completed items, and what weaving equipment they could carry. Satisfied all her kin were safe for now, Rika determinedly turned and began to approach Larce. She knew full well she might have her tongue cut out for insolence, but this didn't stop her.

People swarmed chaotically as they frantically carried valuable items to safety, away from the flames. She'd barely gotten clear of the building when a burly guard unwittingly crashed into her. She fell hard to the ground, dazed and disoriented, and could only watch in mute dismay as the contents of her bag spilled into the dry earth. The items were trampled by the frenzied crush of the mob.

She suppressed a sob, and painfully dragged herself to her feet. If she didn't reach Larce quickly, all might be lost. She extended her elbows outward to fend off more accidental collisions, and pressed on.

Somehow, she finally reached him. She began to tug on the great man's tunic as she pleaded. "Noble one, hear me, I beg you! You must take your guards from this place!"

He swatted at her with the back of his hand. "Quiet, you little fool! Can you not see what's happening? We have a chance to save part of the workshop, and if not, we need to contain this blaze lest it overcome the entire rain-deprived plateau! What idiocy do you propose? I should have you flogged!"

"Please, you must believe me! I'm Thana's assistant. I'm loyal to you both. I saw men running from the building before the fire started. I fear they set it intentionally, but their target isn't the workshop. It's the temple! You must protect the temple! That's the true threat!"

The bitter anger in his face diminished as her words sunk in. "Where is Thana?" he shouted.

A woman from the residence, whom Rika didn't know, responded. "She feared for the artifacts if the fire spreads. I saw her headed to the temple with Hathli and Cutu."

"Come!" he finally resolved. "There's little we can do here. If this one speaks true, then there may be danger. You men, yes, all of you, follow me, quickly! And you, youngster, you'll come as well. We shall see what value your loyalty brings us."

Bailey, New Hampshire, Sunday, July 28, 2013

Eric had time for a super-fast shower, and that was about it, before Lotte wanted to leave.

Mason's door had remained closed. He never appeared at all after last night's binge.

Mercifully, they stopped for coffee and a muffin in Berlin.

"Does Mason know where we went?" he asked as they drove along Route 3.

"*Ja*," Lotte replied. "I told him yesterday when I tried to calm him down after finding those posters. He's expecting us back tonight, or tomorrow morning. He's fine."

"Why didn't you tell me last night?" he asked, a little annoyed and suddenly a little jealous again.

"Well, I might have, but it seemed as if you weren't entirely... well... focused. I intended to talk with you this morning, when your head was clear, or at least clearer."

Ouch. She said it really diplomatically, but still... ouch!

He gave a deep sigh. "Lotte, I'm so sorry. I really didn't intend to drink that much. I haven't done that in a really, really long time. I feel like an idiot."

Great way to win the hearts and minds of all ex-girlfriends within a ten-mile radius, moron!

"It's all right. I'm not angry. I'm just glad you're okay. You do look a little pale, but I think you actually drank Mason under the table. Serves him right!"

He thanked his lucky stars he'd made it outside last night. It was fine with him if Lotte thought he'd bested Mason. Sadly, he knew the truth, and he repeated his vow that this wouldn't happen again.

She raised her sunglasses and flashed her eyes at him. "So, what do you make of Mason, now that you've met him?"

He pondered that question. His feelings about Mason were complex and ambivalent. On the one hand, he could be fun, remarkably insightful, and other than a little "friendly" drinking competition, Mason had been nothing but cool with him. On the flip side, he hated every bone in Mason's body for his involvement with Lotte, even though it was completely unfair to do so—*though all's fair in love and war*—and he could definitely be obnoxious. He clearly enjoyed pushing people's buttons, Lotte's in particular. The issue of Mason's highly questionable character, however, loomed largest in his mind.

"Tough to say," he finally replied. "I was surprised you told him everything about the Afrit, especially the stuff involving Dr. Esfahani. I'm not sure I totally trust him. Are you certain that was a good idea?"

"I understand what you're saying. It's a risk, but to be clear, we have as much on him as he has on us. If we go down, he'll go down. UNESCO would have a lot to say about what he did with those artifacts, but I don't think it'll come to that. I mostly told him because, as we learned, the details are important. He has to understand how these creatures work, and what the price may be for playing their game. It may be him, or you, that has to bargain with this other entity. Who knows if it likes women? He needs to understand everything, as you do."

That gave him a chill. "Wow, okay. Hearing it that way, I guess you're right. I knew we kept you around for some reason."

She gave a hearty laugh and stuck her tongue out at him. "Well, someone has to use their brain around here, don't they?"

He laughed in return. "Anyway, to answer your question, he's not what I expected. I have a hard time seeing you two together. You even said that yourself."

"Yeah, I'm not sure what to say to that. At first, he seemed to be one thing, but the more I got to know him, he turned out to be the same as everyone else, perhaps worse. It was odd being at university. So many people always seemed to be 'on the make.' I quickly realized I had a power. I could have any boy I wanted. They'll do almost anything for an attractive girl, but they don't want the whole package. They just want the pretty wrapping paper. It was shocking, really. I suppose I was insulated from that in high school, being with you."

Glad to have been of service, I guess.

"In any case, Mason seemed far more focused, at least at first. It helped that we shared similar interests. We talked a lot. He never put any pressure on me, and as time went on, I realized he was everywhere in my life. So, when it happened, it was very natural. Quite like you and me."

Oh no, nothing like you and me. Mason and I are not alike at all. Perish the fucking thought!

"Once that line was crossed, though, all bets were off. It became all about... well... the physical stuff. Just like it seemed to be with every other boy."

La la la la la la la la la!

"Then the whole thing with Emilia happened. That was obviously the last straw. It was a lesson, I suppose. Looking back, not the only lesson I learned those first two years of school."

"And that was it? No other romantic relationships to surprise me with at the last minute?" Mason had hinted at this last night, but he wanted to hear it straight from her.

She made a sour face in his direction. "No, you little shit. I suppose I went on a date or two, but just dinner or a concert. Nothing serious. I was busy graduating at the top of my class, traveling to dig sites, going to every lecture I could attend. I held a part-time job at the Ashmolean. I had too many things to do for the meat-market parties. I was too busy for the frivolous hook-ups and the needless drama."

You were too busy to talk with your supposed friend when he needed you the most. Whatever.

She took a breath and calmed herself. The scalpels had flashed, but not at him. "In any case, no. No other relationships like that. No more surprises, you'll be glad to know."

Actually, he *was* glad to know that. *Very* glad. It felt like more than enough just trying to get his head around Mason.

I'll be chewing on that for the next. oh... decade or so, at least.

"So what about you?" she asked.

"What about me, what?"

"Well," she said, coyly. "You now know all my secrets. What about yours?"

"Oh, you mean girlfriends," he reluctantly said. "Well, honestly, there's not much to tell."

Honestly, there wasn't much to tell.

You really can't count.... God, what was her name, Nicole? Yeah, Nicole, he finally decided, though he still harbored some doubt. He woke up with her in his dorm room one morning during that first semester, after a particularly outrageous party. They were both naked, but he didn't remember if anything had happened. She mooned around for a while after that, but he hadn't been interested. Lotte didn't need to know about Nicole, and she already knew about Erica, so that just left....

"Jennifer," he quietly said. "There was Jennifer. I'm not sure she was my *girlfriend*, but we were, well, how did you put it? Involved. I met her at a fairly low-key party at my dorm the semester I started back. We were both going for the seltzer water at the same time. I think we were the only ones drinking seltzer water. She was nice, a theater major, but her love was really dance. She invited me to a dance recital where she'd be performing. She was amazed I went. What the hell else did I have to do?"

"Tell me about Jennifer," Lotte calmly said.

"We got to be friends. She knew I was into fitness stuff, and she showed me the dance and yoga routines you saw me doing. She sort of let me into her world, the theater, dance, artsy types. I like being around them, even though I don't have an artistic bone in my body. They're fun, and they sort of take you as you are, because they're all self-proclaimed 'freaks and geeks.' She liked hanging out with me because, loveable as they are, there's constant drama. It sort of wore her out, and she liked getting away from all that from time to time."

She laughed. "I know the types. They wear me out too, but I like them."

"Yeah, so it worked. Mostly, we just hung out. We did stuff off campus because I had the car. Once, we went to Boston the see the ballet."

They went to see a Saturday matinee performance of *Onegin*, one of her favorites. The scene where Tatiana danced over a sleeping Onegin, floating *en pointe* from one side of the stage to the other, with only her feet moving as she cradled her chin under her folded arms, almost brought him to tears. The beauty and the expression of emotion astounded him, but maddeningly, it only served to bring Lotte into his thoughts.

He took Jennifer's hand in the seat beside him.

She smiled, and squeezed his hand in return.

Afterward, they went to the North End for dinner. He couldn't bear another trip to the restaurant they'd been to before—too many memories—so they picked another, which turned out to be equally fantastic. They found a different pastry shop as well for dessert, and he ordered the *Tiramisu*. It was both as good, and not as good, as he'd remembered. After dessert, they slowly sauntered toward Haymarket to catch the T, back to the same garage by the Wang Center where Mr. Schwarz had parked.

"I'm tired," she said. "Are the hotels around here super-expensive?" They were, as he soon discovered, but he never missed the money. That had been the first time.

"So, what happened?" Lotte asked. "You seem to really care for this girl. I'm surprised you're not with her."

"Nothing happened," he replied. "At least, nothing we both didn't know would happen from the beginning. Like I say, she wasn't really my *girlfriend*. We were just friends, with... well... more, from time to time. She didn't come back for her senior year. She got a job in a touring company. It was a great opportunity, and I was thrilled for her. We were never meant for the long haul, and we both knew it. We're still friends. We email or text from time to time. With Jennifer gone, I took extra credits in my last year and wound up finishing on time. It all worked out. She gave me Langsam before she left."

"Oh, she gave you your turtle. How sweet! Was it like the Tortoise and the Hare? She thought you were slow and steady, consistent and reliable?"

He replied with annoyance, though not directed at Lotte. "It was more like one of her friends had a turtle they were about to release into the wild to fend for itself because they were done with it. So irresponsible! Awful for the turtle, and the native environment. Whatever. When Jennifer gave her to me, though, she said it was because she thought I was hiding in my shell, and maybe the turtle could remind me to poke my head out every now and then."

"Oh," she replied.

They were silent for a time after that. A long time.

Eric shook from hunger, and from the lingering effects of having drunk far too much the night before. At about 12:30, they pulled into the parking lot of his apartment building. He inventoried the things he needed to do: *Turtle, Mom, Dad, Margot, Erica, van, Afrit, drive back to Bailey. Something's missing. Oh, yeah. Eat!*

Lotte had to pee—like, wicked bad—so he let her out and went to get some subs to go.

They ate rapidly at his little kitchen table. She made more of her awesome coffee, and he drank two cups. He knew he'd need it. Together, they loaded Langsam's terrarium into the Mazda. He thanked her and made for the car door to leave.

She stopped him and gave him a gigantic hug.

Weird. Whatever.

He made the familiar drive to Rolling Meadows. The house looked the same, but it was no longer his house, his home. In some sense, he had no home, though he didn't feel homeless. He didn't have to ring the bell, but he did anyway, and then walked in.

"Hey, it's Eric!" he called. "Anybody here?"

"Out here, honey!" his mom called from the back. It sounded like she was on the porch.

He walked through the house toward the rear. He glanced at the alarm panel by the sliding doors as he exited, remembering the most dangerous nights of his life.

So far.

"Hey!"

His mom sat at the patio table under a large umbrella, reading a book. "Hi, honey! Are you back already?"

"Nope, I'm just a mirage, sent to torment you. The actual Eric will be back in five hours, then the real fun will begin."

She laughed. "Always mister smarty pants. How's Lotte?"

"Lotte's fine, Mom. Amazingly, I, your actual son, am also fine. Thanks so much for asking."

"Oh, honey, you know what I mean! How did all this business with her go? Is everything all right?"

"Well, it's good news, bad news," he said, lying through his teeth. He knew quite well that it was all bad news. "We have to go back, like today. I have no idea for how long. I was hoping you'd watch Langsam for me. Actually, I brought her here. I even stopped and got some worms. Maybe you can get Dad to feed her those. I thought you might like to take her out for walks, if you have time—that is... of course... please? Also, maybe you could help me get her terrarium out of the car?"

She stared at him. "Is that the good news, or the bad news?"

"Umm, that's all the news. To me, it's both good and bad. Take your pick. Is Dad here?"

"No, honey, he's golfing. They may be done by now, but he's still at the club."

"Crap, I'll have to call him later. Listen, I have a zillion things to do before we leave. It would mean everything to me if you could watch Langsam. This is important, Mom. Seriously."

His mother lowered her sunglasses and looked him up and down. "You look pale, honey. Did you not sleep last night?"

Well, sleep was among *the things I did last night.*

"Of course, I'll watch Langsam," she finally said. "You go and do what you need to do, but, honey?"

"What, Mom?"

"I'm not feeding that turtle those worms."

His conversation with Margot went more easily.

"You back already?" she asked when he called. "This is either really good, or really bad."

"It's really neither," he replied. "I need to shoot back out. This has turned out to be more complicated than we anticipated. I'm gonna need the week off, maybe more. I'll be calling my dad later to ask if he can go to the purchasing meetings with you. Can you handle it?"

"I don't know. We'll find out. I'll sink, or I'll swim, but I'll do my best because I want this for you. Do what you need to do. We'll figure it out. If you fuck it up, though, I'll kick your ass. Just sayin'."

He laughed. "That sounds like a bargain to me."

He hung up and decided to cheat on his priority list. He swiped to Ricky Vitis's number. "Ricky, you guys open today?" Ricky worked for his father, Stan Vitis, who co-owned Vitis Brothers, a company that frequently rented trucks and vans to Schneider when they needed an extra vehicle, or if one had a breakdown. He and Ricky had been pretty good friends when they were little kids, and they maintained some relationship through middle and high school, though by then they largely ran in different circles.

"No, man," Ricky replied. "What do you need, though? I'm just chillin' by the fuckin' pool."

"I need a cargo van, today, if possible. I'll pay, full price. I may need it for like a week, or more. You got anything?"

"Yeah, man," he said. "It's a piece of shit, but it runs, and I'll cut you a great deal too. Meet me at the store in an hour."

"Done! Thanks, Ricky, I owe you one!"

That business complete, Eric faced one of the two most challenging tasks: Erica. Her phone rang a long time before she answered.

"Eric!" she said, breathlessly. "I wasn't expecting you back so soon. How are you?"

"Umm, fine, I guess. Listen, where are you?"

"I'm out on my bike."

"Where, exactly?"

"Jeez, right now? I'm on, just a second, I can't see the street sign. Arnold Lane."

He tried to picture where that was. "That's on the hill not far from the high school, right?"

"Yeah, I can almost see the high school from here. Why?"

"Hey, you know that cemetery on Pleasant Street? Could you meet me there in like, ten minutes?"

"Hold on," she said. "Google says I can be there in eleven minutes and forty-two seconds."

"Great, see you there shortly."

He banged a U-turn and made for the cemetery.

He beat her there, and drove along the main road and parked his car near the second small cross street. Soon, he saw her riding her bike in the rear-view mirror. He got out of the car and waved.

"Hey," she said as she pulled up. Her blue bike, blue outfit, and blue matching helmet almost made her look like a police officer. "This is a pleasant surprise."

Enjoy it while it lasts, he thought with dread. "Let's go down this way. There's a nice spot over here."

She walked her bike as they strolled along the crossing road to the edge of the cemetery. Beyond a thin strip of grave markers, a row of bushes nestled in front of a tall tree with a thick trunk. He helped her navigate her bike through the underbrush, and soon they stood in the familiar little clearing.

"Wow, this *is* a nice spot." She grabbed her water bottle and sauntered to the base of the tree, and happily sat down.

Déjà vu all over again. "Yeah, no sign of zombies anywhere. Just a few ghosts."

"Huh? Eric, you are so weird sometimes. So, what's going on? Everything work out with that girl and her friend?"

"Well, kind of. Look, Erica, you're not gonna like this, but you want me to be honest with you, so I'm gonna be honest. This thing with Lotte has turned out to be a little more complicated than I thought. Her friend needs more help, and we're going back, probably later today. I don't know how long we'll be gone, maybe a week, or possibly more. It's not something I can get out of at this point. It's just something I need to do. I'm hoping you'll understand."

She took a long swig from her water bottle. "Are you in trouble, Eric? You look really pale. Is something wrong?"

Trouble. Hmmmm. "Not really," he lied. "We just had a late night and I have a ton of stuff to do. I'm fine."

"Late night, huh?" she said with skepticism. "A late night with *Lotte*?"

Ugh! I deserve that, but still... ugh! "No, it's not like that. Lotte had gone to bed. I was doing, well, other stuff, related to this friend of hers. He needs a lot of help."

Yeah, help finishing a fucking bottle of rum.

"How am I supposed to know what it's *like*, Eric? You never take *me* away for a week. I mean, you never seem to take any time off at all! Now *she* shows up and you're suddenly gone indefinitely! What am I *supposed* to think about this? How am I *supposed* to feel?"

He recognized these feelings. When Lotte went away, and when she didn't have time for him that first semester, this had been precisely how he'd felt. He hadn't known what to think or feel either, but he never really got her side of the story. He'd never asked. Maybe deep down, he hadn't really wanted to hear the answer, or perhaps there really wasn't an answer at all. It was merely "one of those things," the tidal wave of life just sweeping over you.

"I understand how you feel, Erica. You'll have to trust me that the reason I'll be gone has less to do with Lotte than helping her friend. That's the truth. How are you supposed to feel? Hurt, confused, angry, abandoned, frustrated, you name it. All of those are legit. I've been there, but I guess sometimes that's just unavoidable. I'm sorry to be the one bringing that into someone else's life like someone once brought it into mine. In certain situations, though, you just have to do what you have to do, and hope that others will understand."

He knelt beside her and took her hand.

She looked at him with teary eyes.

"I'll make you a promise, though," he said. "When this is over, I'll give you clarity. You'll know where we stand. This is the one and only time you'll need to do this for me. So, I'm asking for your patience, which is all I can really ask for. If that's too much, I completely understand. Believe me, I do."

Ricky stood outside the front door of Vitis Brothers smoking a cigarette when Eric pulled up.

"Hey, Ricky!" he said through the open window. "Thanks so much. Listen, I'm gonna need to leave my car here. Is there somewhere I can park it?"

"Yeah, man, just put it anywhere by that fence over there. Nobody will fuck with it. Jesus, you look like shit!"

Ignoring the comment, he parked and locked the car, then he and Ricky walked to the back lot where the trucks and vans were parked. They approached a rather beat-up white cargo van. It had only two seats. The back area was all for storage, with various ropes and cords tied to clamps to secure cargo. It reeked of stale cigarettes. Despite being a piece of shit, it would be perfect for their needs, and Eric knew he'd gotten lucky to find something like this on a Sunday.

"It's awesome, Ricky. I'll take it."

They went inside and filled out the paperwork. He paid for the extra insurance, unsure of what the hell this thing might face on those mountain dirt roads.

On the drive back to his apartment, he stopped at the drugstore to get some little hanging pine-scented air fresheners for the van. He feared that Lotte wouldn't tolerate the smell. She hated smoking, which felt like a bit of cognitive dissonance given that so many of her weirdo band shirts featured people with cigarettes.

It was about 3:45 when he returned.

Lotte lay on the futon, taking a nap. "Hey!" She stretched her arms. "Any luck?"

"Yeah, everything's basically done. Got the van outside. We just need to pick up the... well... the stuff. I'll call my dad from the road. You ready to go?"

She got up and walked over to him, seemingly oblivious to the fact she was only wearing a t-shirt and her underwear. "Eric, you don't look well. Are you all right?"

Sure, I'm fine, if you ignore my stomach, which is still doing somersaults, my slightly blurred vision, and that I'm so tired I could fall asleep standing up. "I'm tired, but I'll be okay. Don't we need to get back up there?"

She put her hand on his forehead. "We do, but you're in no condition to drive. You look like a ghost."

Takes one to know one.

"Come on, you need a nap." With that, she dragged him to the bedroom. "Give me your phone. What's the password? I need to make a call."

"From *my* phone?"

"Yes, I don't have the number. Take a nap. I'll wake you in a couple of hours, and we'll see how you feel."

He gave her his phone and the password, and she closed the door.

He took off has pants, collapsed on the futon, and fell asleep faster than you could say, "Afrit."

A gentle chime woke him from a deep slumber. He'd been dreaming of the house in New Hampshire, and of being on the road. For a moment, he didn't know where he was. Then he noticed Lotte's hand on his shoulder, and her body behind him on the futon.

She moved to turn off her phone alarm. "How do you feel?" she asked.

"I'll have to get up and see, but I can't imagine that was *bad* for me."

"Good. I made more coffee. You need to pack, and then we're all set to pick up the artifacts." She got up and walked out the door, still wearing only her t-shirt and underwear.

He dragged himself from the futon and somewhat indiscriminately began throwing a bunch of things into his duffel bag. Aside from what he wore to work, he didn't have a lot of clothes. She brought in the coffee, and he drank while he finished getting his things together. Then he took a quick trip to the bathroom to brush his teeth and pee.

A fully clothed — *Damn!* — Lotte awaited him when he emerged. Before he closed the door to leave, he nabbed his old Bruins hoodie from the closet, in case it got cold at night. Then they grabbed their things and trundled down the stairs.

"Hey, we'll be riding in style!" she said sarcastically when she saw the van. "I didn't know the Goodwill store rented trucks."

"Very funny. This is the best I could do on short notice, and on a Sunday. It'll get us there, and hopefully back." He opened the side door so she could stow her bags.

"*Alter!* Eric, it stinks! It smells like an old ashtray had a fight with a Christmas tree, and they both lost and died in here! I'm not spending four hours in this awful thing!"

"Lotte, what do you want me to do? This is all there is. The big rental companies don't open in little towns like this on Sunday. I'm not even sure they'd be open in Worcester. Plus, there's no guarantee they'd have a van like this. This is it! Maybe we can go to the store and find some better air fresheners."

"Oh, all right, if we *must!*" she said with disgust. "I wish I could sacrifice whoever invented smoking to the Afrit. I know, that's awful. I don't mean it, but it really is just so horrid."

"Yeah, I don't like it either, but let's just get going. Speaking of which, where are we going?"

"Yes, I called, and we're all set. Drive to your grandmother's building."

"Lotte, we don't have time to visit Grandma right now. We've got to get those artifacts and go."

In reply, she simply gave him an odd stare.

Eventually, he got the idea. "You've got to be kidding me."

When they arrived, she left him in the lobby while she went up to his grandmother's apartment. She returned with a ring bearing two keys, one of which opened a door near the elevators. Behind were some stairs leading down, along with a freight elevator. They took the stairs, and she led him through a basement hallway with fenced-in storage areas. At the unit marked with the number of Grandma's apartment, she opened the lock with the other key.

He could see Grandma's Christmas decorations and fake tree, along with some other boxes. A large white tarp covered a pile of items that dominated the right side of the unit. She pulled back the tarp, and there they were... sort of.

He saw four large, black, flight cases with locks and multiple handles. Three of them rested on substantial six-inch casters as they brooded on the concrete floor. The largest case, which obviously housed the mirror — or rather, un-mirror — had a small, detachable hydraulic lift. This would make it easier to set upright, or lift into the van.

"We'll take the frame first," she directed. "Thankfully, it fits in the elevator."

"Where did you get these cases? They must have cost a fortune!"

"They did, but the sale of the furniture more than covered the cost. My father didn't care. He just wanted the things gone and left it to me. I had them custom built. Everything's here, one case for the frame, the smaller one there for the marble board, and the boxes for the bowls and the papers are divided between the last two with wheels."

Wheels or no, getting the cases out through the narrow aisles in the basement still presented challenges, particularly the case with the frame. After close to an hour, they had all the gear loaded and tied down. The wheels on the cases had locks, so they'd be less likely to roll in the back.

Lotte returned Grandma's keys, and they set off.

Well, off to the grocery store to get some more substantial air fresheners. We also need to pick up candles. Many boxes of candles. You can't have too many candles.

CHAPTER 9

Central Etruria, 593 BC

Fire spread into the trees behind the workshop as Rika stumbled after Larce and the half-dozen men who accompanied him up the rise toward the temple. The large, south-facing doors all stood closed. Were anyone inside the structure, they must have used the single entrance into the central section of the building on the opposite side, near the residence.

As they approached, she heard shouts from behind the temple, and more ominously, observed smoke as it wafted out from the doorways and between tiles in the roof. Her fears had become reality: the holy building represented the true target of the attack. The workshop fire had merely been a distraction to lure away the guards, along with those who might rush to help stave off this more sinister blaze.

They rounded the corner as men ran out of the open doorway, obviously alerted to the party's approach by some lookout. Several guards drew what weapons they had at hand and gave chase, but three remained with their lord as he rushed inside the burning temple.

Rika followed them into the mayhem.

The inner wall of the eastern section already blazed, and the timbers that supported the roof had begun to burn as well. The brilliantly painted statues that guarded the doors of the sanctuary, presumably Antenor and other early ancestors of the Zalthu, lay smashed on the ground. The head of one figure, with its wide-brimmed hat, gazed pleadingly at her, as if beseeching her to somehow halt or reverse the inexorable process of destruction. The broken object lay in a pool of blood that dilated sluggishly outward across the cool stone floor, fed by a ragged gash in Hathli's neck, whose body slumped nearby.

Angry words of challenge and defiance woke Rika from her stupefied paralysis. Larce and the guards stood at the inner door to the western chamber, the one she'd observed that fateful night, now months past. With effort she pushed past them to see inside.

Cutu's body lay sprawled across the altar stone. Blood streamed from a wound in his neck, similar to that his wife bore.

Thana Zalthu stood nearby, secured by three men, one of whom held a knife to her throat.

In truth, Rika quickly realized, there were two men and one boy. To her alarm, the youngster was Arte.

His face appeared to drop when he saw her, and he closed his eyes and slowly shook his head.

"Let her go this instant!" Larce commanded. "You know not what you're dealing with here!"

"We know enough!" the man with the knife retorted. "You're a fool to think all your guards are so tight-lipped. Many have wives or mistresses in the villages. We know what happens here, and who's responsible!"

At this, Rika noticed some uncomfortable looks on the faces of the men around her, but the man with the knife quickly went on. "Today, though, it ends! Your precious temple and its tenders will be no more, and these feasts of blood shall cease!"

"You don't understand what's at stake! Yes, sacrifices must be made—terrible sacrifices—but the gods must be appeased, lest they withdraw their beneficence."

"Easy for you to say. It isn't *your* noble blood being spilled! You take from among the very folk who've served you loyally. Why not harvest the souls of our enemies, as it's always been, or get other wealthy and powerful landowners to share in the burden? You don't even send these... *things*... whatever they are, out to do their own dirty work. It's pathetic!"

"It's a complicated and delicate matter," Thana interjected as she strained to speak over the restraints of her captors. "If you think the arrival of guards in the night is frightening, consider seeing something come alive from your very nightmares. It would cause panic, useful against one's enemies, but counterproductive amongst those who till your fields, hunt your game, or mine your ores. There are webs of alliances, fragile treaties of peace, and jealousies at the wealth and power our family have accumulated, with little understanding of the accompanying responsibility. Above all, we need secrecy, lest true knowledge of what power we possess spread wider into the world. For now, this is the way of things, but it shall not always be so. A *burden*, you call it. This is true, but it is *our* burden, and those who work for us live lives both longer and more prosperous than most. Your lack of perspective in this is more dangerous than you realize."

"We'll see," the man huffed. "Perhaps a family of charlatans hide behind your fancy words! Gods have come, gods have gone, and new gods have replaced them. Somehow, life proceeds onward. Let's find out what that life might be like when the temple of Zalthu is destroyed, and all its priests are eliminated."

Thana gave a sly laugh. "Not all. One is yet beyond your reach."

Rika felt the woman's icy gaze upon her.

"You know what you must do, child. Someone else must finish the instruction in your letters, but the illustrations on the receptacles will be easy for you to follow with the essential information I've imparted. Use this knowledge wisely, and make me proud of the confidence I've placed in your spirit."

The man howled in anger and frustration, and despite desperate proclamations of clemency from Larce that even Rika knew to be fictitious, his bloodstained knife deliberately creased Thana's neck, and drenched crimson her beautiful white robe.

Rika shrieked in bewildered misery and began to run forward, but Larce caught her arm and held her fast.

"It's too dangerous, young one." The gentleness in his voice belied the firmness of his grip. "If Thana's last words were true, then you are our only hope."

The guards rushed past them into the room. Despite being armed with only light weapons, they quickly overpowered the man with the knife, and the other who wielded only a wooden club. Their blood mingled with Thana's and Cutu's by the ancient altar stone.

Arte cowered on his knees, still tightly clutching Thana's lifeless arm. A guard roughly grabbed him by the collar and pulled the trembling boy to his feet.

"Run him through!" Larce screamed. "The bodies of these and the other renegades will be displayed as a warning!"

"No!" Rika shouted, uncaring that she contradicted a noble. "Stop! Don't spill his blood!"

The guard hesitated, but Arte spat a defiant reply. "No! Better you end my life than I be spared by the mercy of a traitor! How could you, Rika? You lied to me, and you betrayed our people. I wish not your charity. You dirty me with your sentiment. I want no part of it!"

She fiercely pulled herself free of Larce's grip and ran to Arte, but when she reached his side, she looked past him — toward the inner part of the north wall of the room, which she'd never seen.

There, a great, solid stone, perhaps five cubits high by three cubits wide, loomed in the center. Ruddy and rusted patches smudged the great rock's dark surface, and in its face, a recessed rectangular area the size of a doorway had been carved. The smoothened surface within this space bore a myriad of tiny indentations.

To this object's left, along the western wall, a ceramic box about two cubits wide stood on a sturdy rock base. She knew that inside this container lay the strange and ancient stones which represented the true power of the Zalthus. Its surface contained the important images Thana had referenced, but which Rika had never before seen. She needed to get the coffer to safety.

She turned back to Larce. "There's no time for this! We have to get this box and the one in the eastern chamber out of here before the fire brings down the building. Quickly. It may already be too late!"

Likely prompted by Thana's final words, Larce commanded one of his men to run for help. The guard dashed from the room.

Rika rejoined Larce near the inner door. The eastern wall and the ceiling in the central chamber already burned. It wasn't clear they would have time to retrieve the precious items in the other room before the structure began to collapse.

At that moment, more people arrived in the temple's central chamber, led by the woman who had been with Larce earlier. "It's hopeless, Cousin! The workshop and the surrounding foliage burn uncontrollably. We saw the flames here and feared for your safety. Your messenger came upon us outside."

"You men!" Larce commanded. "Fetch axes and cut through the wall of the eastern chamber from the outside. You must get inside and retrieve the box before the fire spreads! The rest of you, come to this chamber and help us get this box to safety. We must retreat from this area quickly. I fear the entire plateau will burn this day."

Rika felt hopeful that the irreplaceable items would soon be safe. She rushed to where Cutu's bloody body lay draped across the altar stone. On his finger, he wore a spiraled silver ring with small black globes at each end. She worked to remove it, as well as another larger ring of similar construction that he wore on a leather thong around the gory ruin of his neck.

"What of this one?" the guard who held Arte gruffly inquired.

Once she had completed her task, she rose and approached Arte. "I have to retrieve the rings from Hathli before it's too late. Just bring him with us. I have need of him."

"I told you, Rika!" the boy protested. "I won't countenance your sympathy! What *need* will you have of one who declares himself your sworn enemy?"

"Oh, Arte, I need to thank you. Thank you for acting now before you and I went any farther, and for sparing me such heartache and sorrow.

Oh, and Arte, soon... soon, we'll all give thanks to you. We'll all sing praises to your name when the Gatekeeper comes and escorts your soul through the portal, and into the land of the dead."

Somewhere near Hopkinton, Massachusetts, Sunday, July 28, 2013

"So, how long have you been conspiring with Grandma?" Eric asked once they hit I-495 headed north. He felt somewhat refreshed after his nap.

Lotte leaned heavily against the passenger door of the van, desperately trying to breathe fresh air through the open window. She looked miserable. "I wouldn't say *conspiring*. I stayed in touch with her, as I told you. I had to come back to Southby about a year-and-a-half ago, when my father was selling the house and the furniture. I visited your grandmother then. I mentioned I had some things to store. She gave me the keys and told me to look at the space. It was perfect. That's really it."

"She never mentioned it to me."

"I asked her not to, just as I asked her not to tell you about the postcards I sent to her. I thought that would be best, and what you wanted. The same with my conversation with your father."

"Shit! That reminds me. I forgot to call Dad. Can you find his contact on my phone and ring him? I have to talk with him now."

She opened his phone and started the call.

"Hey kiddo!" he answered. "I was wondering if you'd forgotten me. Your mom said you were headed back out of town."

"Yeah, Dad, sorry. Meant to call earlier, just so many things happening. We have to help this friend of Lotte's. We got a cargo van from Vitis Brothers. We have to move a bunch of... well... stuff."

She laughed beside him.

"Is that Lotte I hear?" his father asked. "Tell her I say, 'hi'"

"Dad says, 'hi.'" Returning to his father, he said, "She says, 'hi' back. Listen, this may take a while. I'm probably gonna need to take this week off. If it goes longer, I'll let you know. I hate this being so last minute. You know that's not me, but it really means a lot to Lotte's friend—and Lotte."

His dad was silent for a moment. "Well, in theory Margot can handle most everything. This is a good chance to see how she does without you there. There's purchasing meetings this week. I'll lead them, and she can start to get the idea of how they go. So, it's fine, but, Eric, keep your head screwed on. Things seem to be happening really fast. Don't rush into anything. Think it all through."

"I hear you, Dad. I totally hear you. I'll call as soon as I have more details. I really appreciate it."

Whew!

The whistling wind from the open windows stifled any conversation as the bedraggled pair sped up I-93. They stopped again near Concord for a quick break and a bite to eat. Lotte had continued to suffer in the van, so Eric investigated the ash tray while she used the restroom one last time. It was jammed shut, but once he forced it open, it turned out to be full of ancient cigarette butts. He removed the tray, dumped the butts in the trash, and took the foul thing to the bathroom to wash it out, gagging the entire time. He then sprayed it down with air freshener.

Once they'd driven a few miles up the road, she said, "That awful smell... it's better now. What did you do?"

"I cleaned out the fucking ash tray while you were in the bathroom. God, was that gross. I'm glad it helped. I could see it was really bugging you."

She smiled and squeezed his shoulder. "Thank you. You can't imagine how much that means to me."

The lights were still on in Mason's house when they finally arrived around 10:30. It had started to rain, and the dirt roads were already muddy. A light near the stairs on the slope leading to the house went on as they unloaded their bags. Mason must have heard them.

"Hola!" he called as they got close to the porch. "Welcome back, my friends, to the show that never ends. We're so glad you could attend. Step your pretty ass inside!"

"Oh, Mason," Lotte said with weariness. "How sweet of you to notice. I'm flattered, really. Don't you have some cartoons to go watch, or are you not allowed because it's past your bedtime?"

He found that hilariously funny. "So where is this fuckin' thing?" he asked when he'd finally stopped laughing.

"Everything's in the van," she replied. "We'll need to bring it in here and set it up in the living room. You boys get the cases. I'll start moving the furniture."

"Wait a minute," Eric said. "We're gonna set it all up now?"

"Oh, yes. We have to conduct the summoning right away. We've waited too long as it is. More people could have been... well... taken."

He sensed she was softening the blow for Mason's benefit.

"Well, partner," Mason said to Eric. "Let's do this thing!"

The light rain made the dirt driveway and the stone steps slippery, and the cases' wheels didn't help much on the stairway. Nevertheless, it didn't take the pair very long to get the items into the house.

Lotte directed that the un-mirror be set up with its back toward the stairs to the second floor. The ingeniously designed case contained a set of collapsible, custom-made supports that connected to the sides of the giant rectangular box. These held the case upright once the lift brought it into position. Then, one simply removed the front and back, and the un-mirror, secured in the central part of the case, stood upright. The thick pane of ancient glass and the *Alkuartiz Alnaar* sparkled in the light from the fireplace to the right.

"Mason," Lotte said. "I want you to cut the candles in these boxes into thirds. Here's a very sharp knife. It'll do nicely." She lifted a knife from one of the two matching cases.

Eric almost fainted. "That's... that's... that's Dr. Esfahani's knife! What are you doing with that? You told me you put it in her purse and disposed of it!"

"I did?" she replied. "Oh, yes, I suppose I did. I'm sorry, Eric. I kept it, thinking it might come in handy. It's perfect for cutting the candles."

"Yeah, and my throat! That was a dangerous thing to hold onto, Lotte."

"In a way, perhaps," she causally replied, "but if the police found the knife, they'd have already had enough evidence to search our house. Eventually, they'd have found everything else anyway. Keeping this didn't add to the risk we'd already assumed."

"You keep anything else of hers?" he asked with annoyance. "Her *hijab*, maybe?"

"I almost did keep her *hijab*. It somehow felt wrong to dispose of it. But, no, I didn't keep that. I did keep these, though." From the same case, she pulled out a small box and opened it. Inside, the gold ring and the bent filigreed bracelet danced in the light from the fire. "These, we'll surely need."

Eric went silent. He recognized the logic in what she'd done, but he still felt it had been a terrible risk, and he wondered why she hadn't told him. That hurt most. They'd never really seen eye to eye on keeping the artifacts, but he'd never lied to her. True, she'd probably done that to avoid an unnecessary and unproductive confrontation, and possibly to spare him additional worry. Still, it made him wonder. If she'd do something like that to get what she wanted, was she truly the right person for him?

He tried to banish these troubling thoughts from his mind, as together they set the semicircular black marble stone on the floor. She placed the shallow bowls in their slots and under the outcroppings at the base of the frame, and then he helped Mason place the candles, six per bowl as she instructed.

Everything seemed to be in place.

"Now listen to me," she directed. "I have an idea. It's delicate, but I think we can do it."

"I'll do it any time with you, baby!" Mason said with a self-satisfied grin.

"Mason," she said, trying to contain her anger, "not now. You need to listen. If we make a mistake, we could be in deep trouble." Her tone seemed to chasten him. "So, there are six candles in each bowl, but I only want you to light five. Save the last for an emergency. Using five candles will heat the frame rapidly, but when I signal, I want you to extinguish all but one candle in each bowl. I want to cool things down, but not shut it off entirely. So, you have to make absolutely certain that last candle remains lit. Got it?"

They nodded.

"Eric, I want you by me. You're going to have to watch all the candles on the marble board. Focus *only* on this, nothing else. I don't care *what* happens, look only at those candles, and keep your concentration, unless I yell, 'run!' Can you do it?"

"I think so," he replied. "Yeah, I'm on it, no problem."

"All right," she said, and then turned to Mason. "You'll need to watch the two bowls near the frame. It'll be hard, because they're on opposite sides, and I don't want you reaching under. I have no idea how the Afrit would respond to that, especially to a male being so close, so you'll have to go around, behind me, and you'll have to move quickly. Again, focus on *nothing* else. Nothing! Do you hear me, Mason? I don't care what you see, I don't care what you hear, don't let those candles go out!"

Sensing her seriousness, he just nodded.

"Okay, here are some lighters I bought when we stopped in Concord. Take two each. Make sure they work. Get some wet paper towels from the kitchen if you don't think you can put the candles out with your fingers. When you're ready, Mason, turn off the lights."

They scurried to the kitchen to fetch wet paper towels, and then all decided to use the bathroom one last time—just in case.

Mason then turned out the lights, and by the glow of the fire, they lit the candles.

Eric sat on the floor by Lotte at the apex of the curve on the black marble board. He noticed the rings by her feet.

Mason stood behind, ready to move to either side as needed.

She closed her eyes and began to nod and sway in rhythm to her whispered chants.

Soon, the flames from the candles heated the quartz outcroppings and the base of the frame. They started to glow, dim at first, but ever brighter as they channeled heat upward into the rest of the large frame. The *Alkuartiz Alnaar*—the so called "Fire Quartz"—at the bottoms of the bowls also took on a similar radiance.

Lotte occasionally opened her eyes to examine the glass in the frame. Her voice grew louder as the heat emanating from the ancient and mysterious artifacts lent its warmth to the room. "Hear my call. Come to me. Come and we'll speak. Come to me and we'll bargain."

With alarming swiftness, a shimmering black mist appeared in the glass. It billowed and wound its way across the shining surface until the entire un-mirror had darkened. Slowly, a tendril of ash probed outward, twirling slightly as it groped toward the large bowl at the center of the black marble board.

"Get ready," she said, as if in a trance.

The shimmering appendage reached the flame about three feet off the ground, then curled upward and started to rotate.

"Now!" she commanded.

Eric immediately began extinguishing candles, carefully leaving one burning per bowl. Mason ran first to the right to do the same, then around to the left. Neither used the moist towels. The adrenaline masked whatever slight pain they may have felt.

The tendril of ash continued to spin, but more slowly, and the volume of sparkling black particles that flowed from the pane of glass noticeably decreased.

"Speak with me," Lotte intoned. "Before you're fully formed, before we've begun to bargain, I need you to speak with me. The line has been broken for countless generations. Our memories are lost. You know me. You've dealt with me. You must teach me! Answer my questions so I can bargain in good faith. Make me understand so we can forge a proper deal."

The misty appendage seemed to quiver slightly, and its rotation almost imperceptibly quickened.

'*Ask!*' They all heard the words in their minds, vague and distant, but unmistakable.

"Holy fuck," Mason said from behind them.

Eric glanced around and saw that, astonishingly, Mason hadn't taken his eyes from the candles that commanded his attention.

'*Ask!*' the baleful and disembodied voice repeated. '*For you, you who freed us, we will answer as we can.*'

"I have spoils for you," she replied with remarkable confidence and calm. "Powerful spoils. One we need eliminated from our world, but I've never seen this one, and I know not where it is. How do you track it... find it? What do we have to do so you know the exact person or entity we wish taken?"

The candle in the large bowl beneath the artery of black ash began to sputter. Eric lit his lighter and cautiously positioned himself, ready to light another should that one go out. The misty appendage above his head again seemed to quiver.

'*One is brought before us, one who has seen. We look into their mind, capture this image, and then we can sense the being you seek.*'

She silently absorbed this information. "I understand. We're not ready to bargain. We can't bring anyone forward who's seen the one we seek. When we can, we'll summon you, and we'll bargain. This I swear. Will you now return to your home and wait for us to be ready?"

Again, the ash quivered, and at just that moment, the candle Eric had been monitoring in the central bowl faltered and went out. He held his lighter to the wick of another, praying it would light in time. For a brief moment, there seemed to be no flame in the bowl at all, but then the new candle lit.

Holy crap! Maybe the lighter kept enough heat going for the ash to keep its form. Stupid cheap supermarket candles! I'm going online to order a bunch of really good ones. This is ridiculous.

The voice of the Afrit brought him back to the moment. '*We agree. This once we will comply, as you have bargained in good faith in the past. Summon us when you are ready. We will be waiting.*'

With that, the tendril of ash receded gradually back into the mirror, and the mist in the glass dissolved.

They all remained motionless for a time. The fire crackled to their side, and the candles in the bowls began to burn low.

"Can I stop looking at these fucking candles now?" Mason finally asked. His voice sounded like thunder in the stillness of the room.

"Yes, Mason," Lotte replied, weariness in her voice. "It's gone. You did well. You both did very well. Eric, you may have saved our lives lighting that candle. I had the rings, but I had no back-up bargain. There's only so much planning you can do."

"How did you think of that?" Eric asked. "How did you know the Afrit would talk with you that way?"

"Several things. What happened when I first tried to summon the creature taught me something, but I didn't know it at the time. On that attempt, I used very few candles and very low heat. It took a long time for the Afrit to come, and longer for it to form, but once the ash was actually in the room, it spoke with me throughout almost the entire process. Then, when my father interrupted, I put out the candle in the central bowl. The ash that had partially formed the head and shoulders of the creature became trapped in our world, though it didn't have the energy to retain its shape. It needed more flame, and that's what eventually became the impish Afrit that we destroyed."

Eric rubbed his thigh where he still bore the scars of that encounter.

"The rest of the ash that hadn't formed, though, went back into the mirror. It might be vulnerable until it forms here, so it immediately retreats if it hasn't undergone enough of the process before the flame goes out. I began to think that maybe, if we could keep the frame at a low enough temperature, we'd have time to talk with the Afrit, and that it would go back to its own realm because it didn't want to lose part of itself in our world. It was a gamble."

"Okay, but how did you know it would answer your questions, and how did you know what question to ask?"

She gave a little laugh. "Well, I didn't really. I hoped it would talk. If it didn't, I'd threaten to extinguish the flame. I don't think the Afrit would have liked that, but it was my fallback position. As far as the question... well... I had to ask myself: how did this relationship evolve? How did the *Sadat Alnaar* get to a stage where they knew how to work with this creature? At some point in the past, it either told them what it wanted, or someone else did, or they asked. I decided to ask. It seemed reasonable, and the Afrit can be remarkably reasonable, within certain parameters."

"So, what exactly have we learned?" Mason asked. "What is this about 'one who has seen,' or whatever, being brought to this thing. What's that all about?"

"Spies!" she said with excitement. "The *Sadat Alnaar* used spies to get a look at the people they wanted eliminated — generals, politicians, soldiers in key strategic or communications positions, what have you. At first, it had probably been blood feuds in a very local area, very easy to identify the targets. Later, though, when the scale got bigger, they had to send out spies. They returned with the image in their heads of those who needed to be taken as spoils by the Afrit. That served the *Sadat Alnaar's* purposes, or the purposes of those who paid them."

"Wait a minute," Eric interjected. "You want the Afrit to take whatever it is that's out there as *spoils*? I thought you said you wanted to lure the thing back to its own portal, try to *bargain* with it... send it home. What happened to that?"

She nervously rubbed her lips with her hand, smudging what was left of her black lipstick. "I abandoned that idea, though it's still Plan B. Something about all this just... well... worries me. This creature doesn't appear to be like the Afrit. This creature is killing — "

Mason let out an angry wail.

"Sorry, we don't know that. This creature is *taking* people, but not returning to its portal. That could be due to Emilia not having the rings, and not striking a bargain with it right away. I'm not certain, but whatever this thing is might feel perfectly free to do whatever it likes here, exactly what we've always feared might happen if the Afrit got loose. I'm just not confident we can bargain with it. I think we need to be done with this thing, and the three of us lack the power to make that happen. So, we're going to get the Afrit to do it for us, and hope it's bloody well strong enough get the job done."

"So," Eric said with growing unease, "that means we need to find someone who has seen this... this... whatever it is, and we need them to transmit that image to the Afrit. Who the hell are we gonna get to do that?"

She smiled. "That's our job, Eric, but unlike our predecessors who were sent out to identify human targets, we're spies of a different type. Get ready, boys. We're going monster hunting."

CHAPTER 10

Central Etruria, 584 BC

A commotion began when he arrived, though it could hardly have been from surprise. They'd known of his approach for days. News traveled quickly through the network of spies and informants that encircled the monumental structure, which now stood atop the majestic plateau. A trader, they recounted, came from somewhere in the east, though the exact whereabouts were uncertain.

His business in the house of Zalthu likewise remained unclear. Few merchants bothered to peddle their wares in such remote inland locations. They typically left that to middlemen who bought goods in ports like Fufluna or Pyrgi, and who had the means to transport items safely and inexpensively across the great cities of the League.

Instead, this one arrived on horseback with one hired bodyguard, who also served as his guide. They had two donkeys in tow, laden with packs that carried what minimal and mysterious bounty this peculiar trader felt justified such a journey. Perhaps the novelty of this curious sight had safeguarded the small party from bandits, or perhaps, whatever strange god that held this odd man's allegiance found him fit to protect.

In any case, the arrival caused excitement in the relatively regimented lives of the folk who lived in and around the new complex. Visitors were once again uncommon to this region. It had been nine summers since the terrible fire that had destroyed everything. The colossal building they'd erected to replace those lost, however, had initially attracted much attention.

After the blaze, the Zalthus had called in every debt and favor to construct the massive structure, a great square whose wings measured 120 cubits per side, and surrounded a colonnaded courtyard. The apex of the tiled rooves sported opulent and brightly painted statuary, including representations of the Zalthu's esteemed ancestors, copies of those destroyed during the rebellion, and as always depicted with square beards and adorned in their signature wide-brimmed hats.

Rika assumed Antenor had brought this unique fashion with him from his native lands in the east, but no one really knew anymore.

These statues were punctuated by graceful and detailed figures of felines, horses, hippocampi, griffons, and sphinxes. Outside, the imposingly gnarled faces of gorgons ran along the roofline to ward off the "evil eye." A grand and sturdy tower guarded the great structure's northeastern corner, a late but welcome addition to the plans, as it provided a panoramic view down the hill to the north and east. Dense vegetation protected the western edge of the plateau.

The palatial building had done much to restore the Zalthu's prestige among the nobility, and many had come to see it. No doubt the increased defenses and augmented cadre of elite warriors, sworn to secrecy and unquestioning service, had also eased concerns about the safety of the holy relics, and the family's ability to deliver aid in times of need. Despite ever increasing mercantile undertaking, the temple remained at the heart of the Zalthu family's power, of which Rika was now an integral part.

Indeed, she now resided on the third floor of the guard tower, and from one of her windows, she now briefly glanced down over the statuary on the roof of the northern wing, and into the courtyard below. She observed the merchant and his companion, as well as those who excitedly clustered around them as they walked through the eastern gate, but the sight failed to maintain her interest. This visit didn't involve her, and since Larce, ravaged by illness, had willingly given himself to the Gatekeeper several years ago, it seemed unlikely she'd even be invited to attend the ceremonial dinner.

Surely, this man had come to solicit Marce's daughter, Arathia, or those who spoke for her in matters of trade, as she was just a girl of eight. Why the visitor hadn't simply presented his wares to her father in Tarchuna was a mystery to Rika.

No matter.

She turned back to her work, marking the soft beeswax on the flat surface inside the carved ivory frame with questions, just as Thana had done for her when she was a youngster. These were not the same writing tablets the old woman had given her. Those had been lost and broken in the confusion of the fire, along with her cherished loom weight that bore her name.

She prepared this lesson for Rasce, the nine-year-old son of her oldest brother, Kavie. For now, these were merely exercises in reading and writing, as they had been for several years, but she could see the boy's potential, as well as his devotion to his kindly but reclusive aunt. She knew that in time, she would need assistance in her obligations, and felt certain the bonds of family would eventually prove invaluable.

She whispered a quiet prayer of thanks to Uni for preserving her kin through the horrors of the fire, and the days of violence and recrimination that followed. No aspersions could be cast in the direction of any Matuna. All had been witnessed as they fiercely but vainly fought the consuming blaze, save Sethra, who lived in a farming village to the east with her husband. Rika's parents and brothers were fortunate to now occupy some of the fine stone houses in the village. The previous occupants were not so lucky, their bodies having been left to the vultures to pick clean after the dreadful purge.

Nepotism, however, had not brought Rasce to her attention. She always sought children with potential, with that spark of curiosity and fearlessness that Thana had once seen in her. Only the great god Tinia himself knew how she had tried with Marce's daughter, Arathia. Sadly, the child had been spoiled by a life of idle opulence, and had no time for the High Priestess's "tiresome games." That the girl now seemed poised to inherit the Zalthu's fortune, as well as their responsibilities, did not bode well for the future. Still, Rika stifled her sometimes overactive tongue and instead counted the blessings the gods had seen fit to gift her and her family.

A knock at the door surprised her.

"Enter," she directed, in the voice of command she'd come to master since all had so abruptly changed for her.

"I beg pardon for interrupting you, Priestess," the rather worried guard said through the crack in the door that marked the limit of his courage. "The man who's arrived just now, he wishes to speak with you."

"With me? What business could he possibly have with me? How does he even know of me?"

"He... well... he didn't ask for you by name. He told us his business is with the High Priest of the Temple of Zalthu. We explained that you were the High Priestess. He just smiled and asked for an audience."

Her mind slowly turned. She couldn't fathom what this might be about, but couldn't deny being intrigued. "Where is he now?"

"In the great hall. The mistress and Arathia are there with all the advisors."

Ugh, too many prying eyes. This matter could be delicate. It demands privacy.

"Search the man and make sure he isn't armed, then have three guards escort him to the roof of the tower. I'll be waiting for him there."

Bailey, New Hampshire, Monday, July 29, 2013

A rustling in the kitchen finally woke Eric. Even the birds hadn't stirred him from much-needed sleep. His phone said nearly 8:00 a.m., but lingering clouds still darkened the sky.

The somewhat dated plaid couch where he slept had been pushed away from the fireplace to make room for the artifacts and their various cases. The coffee table had been crushed close to the sofa, with only just enough room to squeeze in. Beyond that sat a jumble of chairs, end tables, and a folded rug where they'd been unceremoniously dumped.

Lotte had let him stow his duffel bag in the guest room upstairs where she slept, so he padded to the kitchen in the sweats and the t-shirt he'd worn while sleeping.

"*Guten Morgen*," he said, seeing her searching through cabinets, many of whose doors now stood open.

She flashed him a frustrated look. "Well, there's nothing particularly *Guten* about it. There's no tea, and there's nothing to eat here but canned soup! What does Mason live on? Does he trap squirrels and cook them on the barbecue? I wouldn't put it past him. Anyway, there's coffee. I started that for you. I don't particularly like it, but I may have no choice this morning. I'll get a caffeine headache otherwise."

He didn't know why, but he smiled. She periodically threw him some major curveballs, but for the most part he found everything she did completely enchanting, and this had never hinged simply on her looks. Rather, for him it had always largely been something in her manner, something in her completely unselfconscious style that exuded confidence and complete comfort in her own skin, contradictions and all. She could be utterly self-centered about many things, then thoughtful enough to start coffee she wasn't even going to drink.

Well, not normally anyway.

He took a deep breath. It smelled really good. Like gummy bears, coffee had become an aroma of Lotte, an exotic scent that would henceforth evoke thoughts of being with her. Unbidden, he relived those glorious afternoons lying on the couch studying with her under the great glass wall at 246 Holton Hill Road, and the look of excitement on her face when she won yet another game of *Trivial Pursuit*. These were the mundane little moments he missed so much, when she bent time and space by doing exactly as she wished, and had allowed him to hitch a ride and happily travel along in the wake of her stardust.

"Let me take the van and go to the grocery," he offered. "We should make a list of what we need."

"Nah, I'll do it," Mason said as he dragged into the kitchen, yawning. "I gotta get some gas anyway if we're gonna drive around looking for this fuckin' thing. Make your list and I'll head out after I have one cup of that coffee."

"Oh, Mason, that's great," she said. "While you're out, would you mind letting me on your computer? I want to look at Emilia's photographs."

He grabbed a sheet of paper and pencil from the pad that magnetically clung to the refrigerator and scribbled something down. "Here's the password. Go to town. There's tons of porn on there too if you're so inclined."

She gave an exasperated sigh and rolled her eyes.

Eric went outside to exercise while Mason went to get the groceries in his RAV4.

Lotte stayed inside to look at the photos, the ones she wanted to see anyway.

When Mason returned, Eric went down the stone steps to help him with the bags.

"They found one of the hikers," Mason said with a serious expression. "Trudie at the market told me. She dates Vern Deckard, the local deputy, and he was at the scene... said the guy had his head pounded in, like practically driven into his fucking body!"

"Could it have been an animal of some sort? What could do that?"

"No fuckin' animal I know of. I think we know what did it, but who the hell knows how."

"What about the other hiker? Any sense of where it might have taken him?"

"Her, actually. It's the woman who's still missing. So, that's the other thing Trudie said. Vern told her there were no tracks anywhere. There were some strange marks in the ground, almost like some big fuckin' bird had been there, but nothing leading away from the scene at all. It's like she just freaking vanished into thin air."

Eric shuddered, remembering the Afrit's great bat-like wings. He imagined the creature plucking its victim from the ground and flying away. "We better go tell Lotte. This doesn't sound good."

Once informed, she appeared as displeased as they were, but expressed greater interest in where the hiker had been found.

"Trudie didn't say, exactly," Mason tried to answer, "but it can only be one of two places. The south and east face of New Speck Mountain are too steep for hiking — too many rock cliffs, like the one on that little plateau up the path where we set up the portal. There are hiking trails on the north and west face, so it has to be one of those two areas. If Vern was involved, I'm guessing they found the guy on the west face. There's another little town on the other side of the mountain from here, and their deputy would probably have been on the scene if they found the body to the north."

"Well," she said, "this tells us something. How do you get to those hiking trails to the west?"

"Unfortunately, there's lots of ways. There are trails all over the damn place, and lots of entrances to get to them. If you follow New Speck Lane to the end, there are some dirt roads that cut up the mountain and take you to the trails from the south. Larry Henderson, the other guy who's missing, lives out that way."

"This tells us something as well. Where else?"

"Well, if you go back through town, there's a road that cuts north. Follow that to a side road and you get to the old quarry. There's an entrance to the trails near there, but very few people use it. The quarry is kind of a shithole. There's an old, abandoned building there, and people party and shoot guns in the pit where they used to mine the gravel. Past that, there's another entrance even farther north. The west face is a huge area. Finding this thing is gonna be like finding a particular electron in a fucking particle storm."

She sighed. "Well, there's nothing for it. We have to try. Where should we start?"

They all exchanged confused looks. "You said Larry Henderson's place is nearby," Eric finally said. "That's closest, so why don't we start there?"

Having no better alternatives, all agreed.

After breakfast, they loaded into the old blue RAV4. Lotte rode shotgun, and Eric sat in the back. Mason navigated the dirt roads down the hill back to New Speck Lane, where he took a right and headed due west. After a short while, they could see Baily farther down the mountainside to the left, and the blue of the lake beyond. The nearly eleven o'clock sun made the water sparkle. The clouds had cleared, and a beautiful late July morning unfolded before their eyes.

New Speck Lane continued another mile or so past town to the west. Houses became sparser as they went on. The end of the road appeared to be ahead when they saw some vehicles parked on the shoulder, one clearly a police car.

"I think that's Vern's car," Mason said as they got closer. "Let me stop here and go see what's up. Larry's place is down the hill there to the left. It looks like those cars are parked by the dirt road that leads to the trails." Lotte and Eric started to get out, but he stopped them. "Let me talk with him alone. I know Vern. He might get a little spooked if he sees strangers, won't be as willing to talk. He might think you're reporters."

"Do we look like reporters?" Lotte asked.

"How the fuck do I know what reporters look like? I just want to get as much as I can from Vern. So hang here, okay?"

She surrendered, and they watched as he walked toward the vehicles.

"What do you make of that hiker's head being pounded in?" Eric asked as they waited. "That doesn't seem like something the Afrit would do, at least in terms of abandoning the body."

"I agree. I think the creature simply killed that poor man. The woman, I'm guessing, it took. It can probably only carry one person. What it's done with her is anyone's guess."

Mason reappeared, jogged back to the car, and hopped in. "So much for that. The whole freaking area is cordoned off. State cops are up there looking for clues."

"They'd better not find any," Lotte said. "They may get more than they bargained for."

"Seriously. Vern said they'd be done today. Apparently, they're not finding shit, but we can't go up there until probably tomorrow. So, where to now, ice princess?"

She scowled, but didn't take the bait. "I'm curious about this quarry. I know it sounds a bit shady, but I think it's worth investigating."

Mason hesitated. "Well, okay. If there's nobody there, we can have a quick look around, but the dudes who hang out in that place are some mean motherfuckers. Trust me, we don't want trouble with them."

"Fair enough," she agreed.

Mason banged a U-turn and headed back down New Speck Lane.

The ancient pavement on the side road leading to the quarry was cracked and riddled with potholes. The road wound through tall trees and thick underbrush, so it wasn't clear what lay ahead until the dusty RAV4 emerged into a large clearing.

To the left sat an enormous, corrugated metal structure with a massive conveyor belt, which faced the mountain. The building had once been gray, but now rust predominated. Broken windows, sagging roofs, and prolific graffiti completed the study in dereliction.

Perfect setting for a horror film. Wait a minute, this is *a horror film!*

Up an incline in front of them, the gravel pit looked like a giant valley carved out of the rock of the mountainside.

Mason idled the car and scanned the area. "It doesn't look like anyone's here," he said, suspicion in his voice. "I'm gonna do a quick turn by the gravel pit, see if anyone's over there. If not, we can look around. I assume you want to go in there?" He pointed at the menacing building to the left.

"Well," Lotte replied. "*Want* isn't really the word I'd choose, but if I were a monster, this might look quite appealing."

Mason drove to the entrance of the pit, and they saw more graffiti, trash, and some bales of hay seemingly set up for target shooting. Not a soul could be seen. Satisfied, he drove the car toward the side of the building that faced the road. He swung around the corner and parked behind a pile of old boxes and rusting oil drums, where the car would be out of sight.

"If anybody comes in," he explained, "we can try to sneak out without them seeing us. We'll have to haul ass, though. Dudes up here will chase you just for sport."

They exited the car and walked back toward the front of the building.

The part of the structure next to which they'd parked appeared to have been a garage. They glanced through some broken windows and large, ill-fitting sliding doors. Old tires and shelves with tools and oil cans gave testimony to the days when gravel trucks had been stabled and maintained here. The large area appeared empty and didn't seem worthy of further investigation.

The massive machinery of whatever mechanism chewed the rocks of the quarry into pebbles, along with the conveyor belt that fed its voracious maw, dominated the opposite side of the building. Precarious metal staircases clung to the sides of these structures, but clearly there was very little to see inside. That left the building's center, which appeared to have been the administrative heart of the complex. It rose several stories above the other portions of the facility, like the bridge of a great battleship hovering above the fore and aft decks. A large opening granted entrance to the darkened interior. Once, this had been the main entrance. Now, broken and rusted hinges were all that remained of the missing metal door.

The trio stood at the threshold and gazed into the gloom.

"Sure you want to go in here?" Mason asked.

"I'm absolutely certain I don't," Lotte replied, "but it's why we're here. Come on."

With simultaneous sighs of resignation, they strode forward and went inside.

Their eyes adjusted rapidly to the darkness, assisted by dim light coming in from the many broken windows. A concrete stairwell ascended up the right wall. To the left, large doors probably led to the garage area they'd examined from outside. They walked along a hallway, past the stairs, toward the rear of the building, and emerged into a large room of indiscriminate function. The walls served as a gallery for decades worth of colorful scribbles. Beer cans, cigarette butts, and broken glass littered the floor.

This area appeared empty, so the three backtracked to the stairwell and cautiously went up. The second and third floors had clearly once been offices. Some still had the remnants of desks and file cabinets, which sat forlornly among the used condoms and broken crack pipes that added to the charm of the beer cans and other trash.

Lotte covered her nose. "Disgusting! How desperate would you have to be to accept partying in a rubbish heap like this?"

"Desperate pretty much explains it," Mason answered. "Cops around here don't put up with much. The livelihood of these towns depends on stuck-up vacationers, who don't want to look at a bunch of lowlifes. Vern may not seem like much, but he can call in a fuckin' airstrike of regional police, so kids, junkies, bikers, you name it, come here. Yeah, it's a shithole, but it's *their* shithole, and for the most part, nobody bothers them."

The fourth floor seemed to have once been several large conference rooms, but most of the inner walls had been torn down. Old clothes, blankets, moldy sleeping bags, and abandoned duffel bags lay strewn about the room. It looked as though people may have been living here at one time, but not recently.

Only the fifth floor remained to be searched. They carefully ascended the stairs and emerged into what had probably once been a reception area. To the left were some smaller offices, and to the right, toward the back of the building, was likely where the company's owner or CEO had once held court.

"Executive suite," Mason said sarcastically. "Let's start with the big one."

This office still retained its large, metal door. Eric gave a push and it reluctantly swung open with a rusty creak. To the right, large windows looked out over the conveyor belt toward the gravel pit and to the mountain beyond. It would have been a beautiful view, but something had smashed a large section of the glass. The metal frames that once held the square window panes bent violently inward, and shards of broken glass covered the floor.

An old folding table with some rickety chairs sat in the center of the room. On the table were all manner of drug paraphernalia, and what looked to be a sizeable amount of heroin in little brown bags.

"Shit!" Mason said. "This is worth some money. I can't believe they'd leave it all abandoned like this."

To the left, many cardboard boxes and wooden crates had been stacked, seemingly to build a divider that separated the area behind from the rest of the room. They could see the far window over the top of the makeshift wall. Mason went to the table, while Eric followed Lotte as she crept toward the gap between the boxes and the back wall that led to the segregated space.

Cautiously, she peered around the corner.

Without warning, she violently reared back, colliding with Eric as she frantically fled from the opening. She clasped her hand tightly to her mouth, but even this couldn't stifle a terrible moan of horror and revulsion. He tried to steady her, but she wrenched free of his grasp, then stumbled to the center of the room and collapsed to her knees, gasping and sobbing. He ran to her and grasped her shoulders as she shook and gagged.

"What the fuck!" Mason cried as he left the table and bolted for the gap in the wall of boxes. He rounded the corner and froze. His hand now also slowly rose to cover his mouth as his wide eyes locked on what saw. He leaned his back heavily against the wall. "Oh, my fucking God."

"What is it?" Eric asked with alarm. He still held Lotte, who began to cry. "What do you see?"

"I don't think I can describe it, man. Get her calmed down, and you're gonna have to look for yourself."

He spent a few minutes crouched on the ground with her. When it appeared her tears were mostly spent, he reached for one of the chairs. "Listen, try to sit here. This floor is disgusting. You'll get leprosy or something." She let him lift and guide her into the flimsy chair, which he hoped wouldn't pick this moment to finally collapse. He wiped her eyes and stroked her hair until her shaking diminished.

"Thank you, Eric. It was just such a shock. Go have a look. Give me a moment, and I'll be over in a second. I need to gather my wits and focus. There may be clues here."

"All right. I'm right here if you need me, though. Just call."

She gave a nod, and he rose and walked with determination toward Mason, who had collapsed into a seated position against the wall. Eric knew that he could never un-see what he was about to see, so, with a deep breath, he peered past Mason into the enclosed space.

A body lay on the floor. The shoulder blades, or what remained of them, were flush to the wall, and slightly elevated the torso. A massive spray of blood and fleshy matter covered the surface behind the corpse and the floor in front, as if a million raspberries had exploded. Blood still dripped and oozed from a flattened, pulpy mass atop the ruined neck and shoulders. He realized this had been the head, pulverized by a force that had driven the skull down the spine, and then deep into the sorrowful victim's chest.

He'd seen images like this a thousand times in the horror movies he'd watched as a kid. Somehow, the distance had shielded him from the true horror of a grisly and violent end. The screen couldn't project the musky smell of blood and death. The sound couldn't capture the ambient noise of utter and ultimate silence. The unreal images did, however, mitigate his shock at seeing something so graphic, so unambiguously grotesque and horrifying. This completed the circle, and somehow, he felt braver for not having flinched, for not having turned his head in revulsion at the reality behind what the movies use to frighten—and to entertain.

Lotte brushed against him. She grasped his arm as she stepped into the enclosure. He felt her tighten as the corpse came into view, felt her hands squeeze his bicep to the point he had to flex to resist the pain.

Then she relaxed her grip and, with a deep breath, began to look around. "It burst in through the window back there," she said, voice still trembling. "This is recent, otherwise there wouldn't be fresh glass on the floor like that. Also, this blood is still dripping. No decomposition either. This may have happened last night, or even earlier this morning. It may have seen light through the window. There's a candle on the table that recently burned down."

She rifled through the space. There were a couple of sleeping bags with blankets, duffel bags with clothes, boxes of cereal and dry goods, along with McDonalds and Wendy's bags.

"Two," she said with clinical dispassion, her calm largely restored. "There were two, at least—two sleeping bags, two sizes of clothes. One liked McDonald's, the other Wendy's. Just as before with the hikers, one was taken, and one killed."

She looked out the window at this end of the room. "Eventually, they threw their trash down there. Someone was bringing them the food because there's no car here. That person, or people, will be back. We need to go."

As if on cue, they heard the sound of revving engines coming from the road.

"Shit!" Mason cursed. "Hold on. These fuckers are selling heroin. There's gotta be a gun around here somewhere. Eric, toss that area there. I'll look here! *Do it!*"

Eric searched one of the sleeping bags, but found nothing. Mason also came up empty. They looked at each other, and then to the ruined corpse against the wall.

"Wanna flip for it?" Mason asked with a sardonic smile.

Eric just shook his head and bent with grim determination to search the blood-drenched body, the gore of the pulped skull a mere eighteen inches from his face. Sure enough, under a t-shirt that was more liquid than solid, he found a gun tucked in the dead man's belt. He carefully extracted it and handed it to Mason. He'd never fired a gun, and didn't plan on making this moment his first lesson.

"Fuck, man," Mason said. "That took guts. Eric fuckin' Schnitzel-Schneider the Great. Lotte didn't lie about you, man. You're the real fuckin' deal."

Despite the urgency of the situation, Eric took a brief moment to enjoy that oddly phrased compliment. It wasn't so much that Mason had acknowledged him, though that carried the unique thrill of vindication in the implicit challenge of their relationship. Rather, he realized that Lotte had spoken well of him. Perhaps, at some level, she too thought he was the real fuckin' deal, and that maybe he'd had some fraction of the impact on her life that she'd had, and continued to have, on his.

In that nanosecond, it seemed anything was possible, but they had to run.

They fled through the creaking and partially jammed metal door, which hindered them briefly, to one of the smaller offices toward the front of the building. There, they peeked out of a cracked pane of glass to the clear area below.

Three motorcycles. Five riders. Three male. Two female. Three walking toward the gravel pit. Two headed our way. Shit!

"What are we gonna do?" Eric loudly whispered.

"We have to see where they go," Mason replied. "It's a guy and a girl. They might be coming in here to make out, or to get high, or score drugs for the dudes up here. If they go in one of the rooms downstairs, maybe we can slip out. If they come up here, we'll hear them on the stairs. We'll just stay here. They'll probably go into the big room, and we can get out then. Either way, we just have to chill and wait."

That made sense. They waited, but they didn't exactly chill. Five minutes passed. Nothing happened. In theory, if they'd come up the stairs, they be on the fifth floor by now, but nobody had heard anything.

Mason crept to the top of the stairwell, looked down, and then motioned for them to join him. "They probably went in one of those rooms on the first three floors. Let's go down. At least the fourth floor should be safe." They started down and had almost reached the floor below when Mason stopped. "Wait a minute! The heroin! That's worth a fuckin' fortune. Just hang here for a second. I'm gonna grab it."

Lotte seized his arm. "Mason, there's not time. It's not worth it. Let's just go."

"I'll be right back." He pulled away and slipped up the stairs.

The pair sat on the steps, listening and peering around the corner for any sign of the bikers. Suddenly, they heard the loud grinding of rusty metal from above, and a resonant thud when it seemed as if something had given way. The sound echoed in the concrete stairwell, dispelling the cathedral-like quiet.

The two sat perfectly still. Not even the sound of their own breath reached their ears, though perhaps the throbbing of their hearts drowned it out. After a time, Mason reappeared and slipped down the stairs, a small bag over his shoulder.

"Fucking door," he whispered. "Must have gotten stuck when we went out. Did you hear anything downstairs?"

"No, Mason," Lotte hissed back with anger, "but that was incredibly stupid! If you do something like that again, Eric and I are going home. Good luck with your fucking monster! This, of course, assumes we can still get out of this damn *building*!"

"Yeah, yeah, fuck, Lotte. That was dumb. I got greedy. My bad. Let's just get the hell out of here. I'll make it up to you, promise."

She just rolled her eyes.

They stayed put for another five minutes, then, having heard nothing, decided it should be safe enough to move again. On the fourth floor, Eric picked up a sturdy piece of wood from one of the broken walls. Mason grabbed a palm-sized wedge of concrete that had chipped away from a large support beam, and held it in his left hand opposite the gun.

The trio proceeded to the third floor.

Delicately, they skulked into the hall that looped around to the stairs going down on the opposite side, like an escalator in a department store. Mason led the way, and Eric took the rear. When they reached the stairs, Mason looked down and flashed a thumbs up. They inched forward, aware that the couple must now be close.

The second floor seemed as if it would be a repeat of the third. Mason edged silently toward the final staircase. As he neared the turn, however, a woman suddenly stepped out in front of him, a casual and mocking look on her face. A dangerous looking hunting knife danced in her hand.

"Well, well, well... what do have we here?"

Mason raised his gun. "We have people who just want to get the fuck out of here. Step aside or get a taste of this."

"I wouldn't if I were you," a man's voice came from the doorway to the room nearest them, "or this little lady is gonna get a bullet right in her head." He emerged from the darkness, pointing a handgun straight at Lotte. "Drop the gun, asshole. And you, drop that board. Do it, *now*! Then turn around and put your hands against the wall."

Mason reluctantly dropped the gun, and Eric dropped the plank he carried.

They began to turn toward the wall, but Mason swung out with the piece of concrete in his left hand. He connected squarely with the man's temple and he stumbled backward.

Eric grabbed Lotte and flung her behind him just as the woman with the knife attempted to strike. She quickly reoriented on him, waving her weapon in front of her.

She slashed once, but he dodged back. Then, as she prepared another thrust, the piece of concrete slammed into her chest. He realized Mason had thrown it right over his shoulder. The woman collapsed in a heap, writhing in shock and pain on the dirty concrete floor.

He turned to thank Mason, but the man with the gun instantly drew his attention. The biker had seemingly regained his senses, but before he could bring his weapon to bear, Eric pushed Mason aside and dove on him. He drove the man hard into the ground, and the man grunted as his back slammed into the concrete floor. Before he could recover, Eric grabbed the biker's wrist and secured his gun to the floor. Then he reached back with his right hand and punched with all his might.

He'd never hit anyone before. It hurt like fucking hell. He figured he'd broken every bone in his hand and that he'd probably never write "Lotte" in small letters on another envelope again. Sensing the guy still maintained consciousness, he elbowed him. That seemed to do it.

Mason knelt beside him and grabbed the guy's gun. He already held the one he'd dropped, and Lotte now wielded the woman's knife. All three bolted for the stairs, past the biker woman who still struggled for breath where she floundered. When they got outside, they heard the distant sound of gunfire.

"They're shooting in the quarry," Mason said. "Lotte, take my keys. Run to the car and start it up. We'll be there in a minute. Come on, Eric!"

He followed as Mason ran toward the parked motorcycles. "Help me push them over!" Soon, the three heavy bikes lay awkwardly on the ground. Mason looked toward the gravel pit, then back at the building. All seemed clear. "Okay, let's get the fuck out of here!"

Together, they ran to the RAV4. Lotte had the engine running and sat in the passenger's seat. Mason and Eric jumped in, and they drove madly for the road. Eric looked out the back window. He didn't see anyone come for the bikes from the quarry, or emerge from the building.

If we can get back to the house, we may have gotten away clear.

"You damn fool!" Lotte angrily spat at Mason. "You could have gotten us killed! For what? For what, Mason? What will you do with this 'fortune' in drugs? You're so brilliant. You can be so bright when you put your mind to something. What a waste!"

"I got us out, didn't I?" he retorted, not as angry as he ought to have been. "You're right, Lotte, it was a dumbass move, but I got us out."

"*You* got us out? Funny, from where I saw it, Eric saved *your* pathetic life! Actually, credit both of you. In that moment, each of you were truly a wonder, but, come on, Mason! Get it together! Start using that brain of yours, or we'll be as horribly dead as that grotesque lump of oozing flesh we saw back there! Is that what you want? No? Then damn well act like it!"

They drove the rest of the way to the house in tense silence.

CHAPTER 11

Central Etruria, 584 BC

The guard gave a slight nod and pulled the door shut, and Rika heard him scurry away to fulfill his orders. Arathia and her mother would be furious, but likely wouldn't dare challenge her authority. The merchant had asked to speak with the High Priestess. This implied the gateways, and the beings they summoned, might be involved. In this purview, her word typically prevailed, though she always tried to exercise caution. She had no desire to upset any faction, and good relations with all only furthered her influence.

She'd used this influence to help the Zalthus navigate away from their increasingly shortsighted and destructive patterns. The most delicate issue had been the one that led to the revolt that destroyed the previous compound. The beings the family tended required periodic *appeasement*... easy to accomplish in the days when various factions of the Rasenna fought amongst themselves, or later against enemies who encroached upon their immediate borders.

This era, however, had long since passed. The relative unity of their lands, as well as treaties with those who subjugated the Latini, meant that the threats were much farther away. As she'd quickly learned, the creatures she tended had a somewhat limited range. Long journeys taxed their finite energy, and the Zalthus were fearful of traveling too far with the materials that summoned them forth, lest they be lost or stolen. This parochial and insular attitude put untenable pressure on their local population, which had finally flared into open rebellion.

Rika had immediately taken a bolder approach. She proposed they travel with the portals to distant areas where their people's lands drowned in a seemingly unstoppable flood of Hellenes. The godlike entities could support the far southern colonies, aid in the protection of vital shipping in what were once safe waters off the western coast, and even help safeguard the eastern borders against the ever-troublesome Umbri.

The member cities of the newly founded League of Twelve had squabbled furiously about whether to take a more bellicose approach in some of these areas, or if diplomacy and compromise would better ensure long term prosperity. Trade with Hellenic states like Corinth and Athens brought crucial riches to the land of the Rasenna. Their colonies on the peninsula, however, were aggressive and opportunistic, and posed a substantial threat.

In the end, the League of Twelve narrowly agreed to her proposition, bolstered by the support the mighty beings would bring to their military operations. The creatures could again feed on the blood of others, as always it had been. Her challenge then became the oversight of safe and secret passage of the gateways to these distant areas, the establishment of the necessary infrastructure to operate the portals, and to ensure that all concerns, both mortal and immortal, were satisfied. So far, she herself had spearheaded these endeavors, but clearly more acolytes would be required to oversee dangerous journeys in the future.

Though they feared her mysterious power, many of the elite warriors of the compound recognized and appreciated the changes she introduced. They also admired her independent and active ways, and often congratulated her for the vigorous rides she enjoyed on the Zalthu's prized steeds, one of many privileges that offset the heavy burden she bore. Likewise, the men enjoyed to watch as she easily traversed the ladders and crawl-spaces of the watch tower to enjoy the breathtaking view, sunshine, and breezy air on the top floor, an activity that eventually won her safe and desirable quarters in the tower itself.

Now, she nimbly scaled the ladder to the roof and squeezed through the trapdoor as she had so many times before. She stood and drank in the beauty around her as she centered herself in anticipation of what might be afoot.

All too quickly, a guard pulled himself out of the opening in the roof, followed closely by another. Behind them came the man she'd seen arrive earlier, followed by one final warrior. The newcomer had bronze skin with obsidian hair and a light beard. His sharp, amber eyes darted and danced as they deftly surveyed her from head to toe. Now that she could see him up close, he appeared younger than she'd surmised, probably not far in age from her twenty-one summers.

To her surprise, the man abruptly prostrated himself before her, and spoke loudly into the sunbaked stucco of the tower's roof. "Praise Melquart and Astarte, I've found you! I submit myself as your humble servant, and ask only for shelter that I may honor my family's directives."

She found herself at a loss, confused as much by his words as his highly unusual deference. The High Priestess commanded authority, but the Rasenna prostrated themselves only to a deity.

"Rise," she gently urged, once she had found her voice. "You need to explain more clearly why you're here, and that would be far easier if you weren't speaking to my feet. Stand up and tell me your name."

The man hesitantly complied as the guards crowded close around him, unwilling to risk any threat to their all-important charge. "I am Abirami. I come from a merchant family of the city of Tyre, in the lands of Canaan. Our network extends beyond the Pillars of Heracles, and we have long traded with your people. I have visited these lands before, though never so far inland. This is how I come to know your language, and in part why I was chosen for this task."

"And exactly what *task* would this be, Abirami, and how does it involve me?"

He seemed to stumble for a reply.

His journey has taken him over halfway across the Great Sea, and he doesn't know why he's here?

Caught between annoyance and amusement, she betrayed no emotion to her unusual visitor.

"It will sound strange," he finally offered. "My city is besieged for three years now by Nebuchadnezzar of Babylon. Tyre is on an island, and the Great King has no ships, but he tries to build an embankment from which his innumerable forces can overwhelm us. It is a great danger. The leaders are trying to negotiate a peace, but there are no guarantees this will work. I have been ordered to come to this place by my family, and those they serve. If the need arises, I will receive word of the action they wish me to take. Until then, in truth, I know as little of why I'm here as you."

She harbored doubts about this, but without clear evidence to the contrary, or a better understanding of the circumstances, she hesitated to take a provocative action. "So, all you wish is shelter until the siege is resolved or you are contacted. Interesting. I'm still not clear why you came to our door, or to me in particular. Are you sure you have nothing to add to what you've told me?"

He briefly touched his chest, then bowed his head. "I... I can add only that I have brought goods from afar as recompence for your hospitality. I wish not to be a burden. You'll hardly know I'm here, I swear to you. The entire matter should be settled soon, and I'll likely be gone from your life as if I'd never been here at all."

She laughed. "Of all the things you've told me, Abirami, this last I find the most unlikely. I bid you welcome to the house of Zalthu. Guards, escort our guest to a room in the eastern hall. Make sure he has complete privacy, and utmost *security* in addition to our normal comforts. Tomorrow, you must join me for a ride, and you can tell me all about your city, in the faraway lands of Canaan."

Bailey, New Hampshire, Monday, July 29, 2013

When they got back, Lotte stormed up the stairs, slammed the door, and sequestered herself in the guest room.

"I think I better make myself scarce for a while," Mason said. "I'll be back in an hour or so." He returned to his dirty RAV4 and left.

At about 2:30, Eric ventured upstairs and knocked on her door. "Lotte, you want some tea? How about a snack? You okay?" He heard movement, and soon she appeared.

"Come on in," she said, seemingly calm.

He entered, and saw a book lying face down on the rather flimsy looking double bed.

She noticed him looking at it. "I started that at your apartment and wanted to keep reading it. Reading relaxes me, and after what we saw, and then idiotic *Mason*, I just needed some time alone. I hope you don't mind I brought it."

"Not at all. What book did you pick?"

She smiled. "Stacy Schiff's book on Cleopatra. It's quite wonderful. I've never read it. You have such an odd array of books — all sorts of subjects, all periods of history. There were many I'd have liked to have read."

"Hey, you know where they are. Knock yourself out. Yeah, I guess that's right about my books. A wise man once told me to 'cast a wide net.' I thought that was good advice, especially for me. I don't have this... like... single burning passion, this one area of interest, like you and Mason do."

She scoffed. "Mason's single area of interest is *Mason*! He chose archaeology because he thinks he can be a big flashy fish in a small pond. Make some 'important discovery' and then do television documentaries. It's maddening! Where is he, anyway?"

"He went out. He'll be back soon." He pointed toward the road.

"*Alter!* What happened to your hand?"

"Yeah, that's from when I punched that biker guy. It's bruising up pretty good, and it's all red right now because I've been icing it. Physically, it's okay, nothing's broken, even though it felt like it when I hit him. Talk about casting a wide net. That's the first time I ever punched anybody. It was more the shock than anything. I don't think I'll be making a habit of doing that. What about you? Are you feeling better? We'll need to talk about what we're gonna do when Mason gets back."

She squeezed his arm and then sighed. "I'm fine. Mason just tries my patience. He's already put us in enough danger, then does something foolish like that. It would serve him right if we just left, but you and I both know this is only the beginning. This creature is voracious. It'll keep on killing. We have to find it... *see* it so we can give that image to the Afrit. This thing has to be stopped." They heard the front door open. "Well, speak of the devil. Let's go down and torture him a bit, shall we?"

She flashed a conspiratorial smile and led him back downstairs.

"I brought doughnuts," Mason said as they entered the kitchen. "It's a peace offering. Tea and coffee there too. Doughnuts are fresh. There's an ice cream parlor down by the lake that makes them."

Lotte rudely grabbed the bag from his hands and took it into the kitchen. She shot Eric a sly look, sat at the table, and started divvying the contents between them.

After a bit, Mason hesitantly joined them. He sat for some time before she finally slid the box of doughnuts his way.

"Tomorrow," she said, licking white powder and stray raspberry filling from her fingers, "we have to start searching the west face. Hopefully, the police will be done."

"What makes you think it's there?" Eric asked. "It could be in another part of that abandoned building, or near the peak of the mountain. It may just be a coincidence all the victims are in this area, or there may be more bodies we don't know about."

"All that's possible, but we can only act on the evidence we have. Larry Henderson's house is just to the south of the entrance to the hiking trails. That's where the police were yesterday, so it's reasonable to assume they found the hiker somewhere in that area as well. If you go down the hill due west from there, you run into the quarry. The logical central point is somewhere on that west face, a bit closer to us than farther north. Predators have a territory. Using the spots where we know victims were found, we can home in on the center of its domain."

"Assuming you're right," Mason interjected, "and you probably are, that's still a massive area to search. The police have been there, probably with dogs, and Vern reiterated this morning when I talked to him that they haven't found anything, not even a hint of a clue. Maybe that's changed, but I doubt it. So, what are we gonna do that the freaking cops can't?"

"That's what we have to figure out. The police are looking for a man. They're looking for tracks and prints, trails of scent their dogs can pick up. They're not finding anything because there's nothing like that to find. We don't know much about this creature, but at least we know it's not something of this world. That gives us an advantage. So, what do we actually know about this thing that can help us?"

"It probably flies," Eric suggested. "I didn't see any way up to that window on the fifth floor that it seemed to have burst through, so it likely flew in."

"Yeah," Mason said enthusiastically. "Maybe we can find a spot higher up that we can keep a lookout. They sell binoculars in the general store. If we see it when it flies out, we can get a look at it from a distance, then we can pass that image to the Afrit."

Lotte pondered this. "It's not a bad plan," she finally said. "The problem is the creature may hunt by night, or fly so close to the trees we won't see it. We could be up there for days looking for something we'll never lay eyes on. Let's try to think of something we can do to locate it more quickly on the ground. What else do we know?"

"It's got massive hands," Eric said. "To pulp someone's head like that, it must be big, and strong."

"But it's not," she countered. "Strong, perhaps, but it's not big. The ring, which I assume is used to seal the pact with this beast, is substantially smaller than the one we used with the Afrit. This is why I have confidence that the Afrit can overpower it. I don't know how it's crushing its victims' heads. Maybe it has some power like the Afrit has with fire."

"Magnetism," Mason said. "The portal is highly magnetic, so maybe its power is magnetism."

Her eyes went wide with excitement. "No! Magnetism wouldn't explain how the creature is killing, but Mason, you may have hit on how we can find it. The portal that calls the being is magnetic, just like the one that calls the Afrit is hot and uses flame. The monster is probably attracted to magnetic fields, and more than likely has magnetic properties of its own. It's possible we could find out where it is, if we can somehow track that magnetism."

"What if we used a compass?" Eric asked. "If we move near enough to a magnetic anomaly, it may divert the needle from north. That seems like a simple solution."

"Yeah," Mason skeptically replied, "but simple solutions aren't always good solutions. The magnetic field we'd be looking for might not be strong enough to move a compass needle, and even if it is, we'd only have a really rough sense of directionality. That's not good enough in such a huge area. I think we need something a lot more sensitive, like a magnetometer. I've used them on dig sites."

"So have I," Lotte said. "Werner equipment has them built into all their scanners. The problem is, where can we get one around here?"

"Well, shit, if we could get on the fuckin' internet, we could answer that question. That's what sucks about being up here. Hell, there might even be a magnetometer app for our phones we could download."

She shook her head. "Not a bad idea, but I don't think an app will be precise enough either, and we'd still need to get somewhere with a cell signal."

"We could drive back to Berlin," Eric suggested, "download the app, then look up what else might be available."

Mason nodded. "Yeah, we'll have to... wait a minute! I know who might be able to help us out—Ethan McCarthy. He lives east of here and runs fishing tours for the summer residents, but he's into all kinds of electronic shit. He's a crazy-ass conspiracy theory survivalist freak: government surveillance, contrails, alien abductions, vaccine mind-control, deep-state Illuminati, what-the-fuck-ever! All that stuff freaks him out. That's why he lives in the damn middle of nowhere. He might have what we need, though, and it's easier than schlepping down to Berlin."

"All right," Lotte agreed. "How far away is he?"

"Just a couple of miles up the road. Let's go."

The makeshift wooden sign by the side of the road announced, "Fishing Tours Daily." A gravelly driveway led through the trees to a rundown white house with peeling red shutters. Several small boats on trailers or racks lay strewn about the weedy yard. A beat-up old red GMC pickup truck sat in front of the house.

"Good, looks like he's here," Mason said as he parked the car. "He usually does his fishing stuff in the morning. Come on."

"You sure he'll be happy to see us?" Eric asked. "This place looks kind of creepy."

"Ahh, Ethan's fine. He's all bark and no bite. Truth is, he'll be more afraid of you than you are of him. All this conspiracy theory survivalist crap is just deep-seated insecurity. Play along with his bullshit and you'll be fine."

They approached the front door and Mason knocked, and a dog barked in the back yard. No one came to the door, so he knocked again.

"I'm coming, I'm coming," a voice came from inside. The door cracked, and a man with a grayish beard poked his head out.

"Hey Ethan!" Mason cheerfully greeted him.

"Mason!" he replied with sudden recognition. "You little motherfucker! I haven't seen you in years. What kind of shit are you in that brings you to my door, and who are *these* people?"

"These are my friends, Ethan. They're cool. Listen, I just have a quick question for you. Do you have a device that measures magnetism?"

He recoiled slightly. "What in the hell do you want to do that for? You think somebody is screwing with magnetic fields, trying to fuck things up like the goddamn contrails did with the climate? Boy, did *that* experiment ever backfire! Man, these motherfuckers won't quit until they've f'd up the entire planet!"

Mason tried to suppress his laughter. "No, no, nothing like that. We just think something is screwing with our radio signal on the hill and wondered if we could get some device to see if it might be a magnetic field of some kind."

"Well, that would be RF interference if it's fuckin' with your radio, but it don't matter, 'cause the same device will usually measure both. What you need is a gauss meter."

"Do you have one?"

"Sure do. I've got an EMF meter that measures electric field, radio frequency, and magnetic field. They say it's one of the best on the market, but it only works around AC power."

"Meaning the source of field has to be some sort of electrical current," Lotte said.

"Bingo." Ethan nodded. "If the magnetic field is due to a DC power source, or is what they call a 'static' field, like a concentration of iron ore in the ground, or some other non-electronic thing that's causing the problem, then you need a different kind of unit."

"I doubt that an AC power source is what we're looking for. Do you have one of these other kinds of meters?"

"Nah, I don't got one, but I think I know somebody who might. Come on in, and let me make a quick call."

"You have a phone?" Lotte asked.

"Yeah, I live on a main road. We get phone service, not like up on the hill. Why, you need the phone, little lady? Women are forever talkin' on that damn phone. You wanna stay with me?"

She cringed slightly. "No, but thanks for the offer. I was just curious."

He laughed. "Too bad. You're a hot little ticket. Hold on... let me see if I can find that number."

He directed them into a room off the front hall that had probably once been a living room. Now, all manner of boxes, old radios, TVs, and electronic gear crammed almost every conceivable space. Lotte sat on a box while Eric and Mason milled about.

"The graveyard of yesterday's technology," Mason said with amusement. "All the crap we thought we couldn't live without, now replaced by other crap we don't think we can live without. Unbelievable. This is the shit archaeologists dig up. We think it's all 'high status grave goods,' but more likely it was just, 'What the fuck do we need with this old comb? Toss it in Aunt Octavia's funerary urn. Who gives a good goddamn?'"

They idly waited for a time until Ethan shuffled back into the room. "Okay, here's the deal. There's a place called SmartWaves Radio. It's on Diana Street in Berlin, right near the hardware store. They sell all kinds of specialized electrical equipment because of all the people who hunt for ore in the hills around here. They have exactly what you're looking for. It's called an Earth Magnetometer. It's pricey, though, about eight-hundred dollars. Too rich for my blood, but it should be able to help you track down the source of the magnetism."

"*Alter!* That is expensive, but I don't think we have much of a choice."

Mason nodded in agreement. "Looks like we'll be going to Berlin after all."

Ethan shrugged. "Hey, it's your money. It'll probably take you about forty-five minutes to get there. They close at five, so you better hurry if you want it today."

"Ethan," Mason said, "can't thank you enough, man! This is awesome. Come up to the house for a beer some time. I owe you one."

His eyes went wide. "I ain't going up there if you have fucking magnetic field shit going on! They could be doing mind control experiments in some underground bunker you have no idea is there. Or maybe that's why all these people are going missing? Maybe aliens are using magnetic ray guns and killing them. They could have parked their magnetic spaceship right near your damn house and that's what's fuckin' up your radio signal. Shit, maybe it's the fuckin' Chinese, preparing the invasion. That's comin', don't doubt it. No thanks, man. Just drop a six pack on my porch some time. That'll do fine."

When he'd exhausted himself with his rant, they politely thanked him, went back to the RAV4, and quickly departed.

"Can you fuckin' believe that?" Mason guffawed. "Backfired contrail experiments, spaceships, magnetic ray guns! What a load of horseshit. Who believes this crap?"

They all laughed, but then Lotte said, "Wait a minute. What if he'd said some sort of magnetic force had summoned a being from another plane who was running around smashing people's heads in? How do you think *we* would have responded to that?"

They drove for a time in befuddled silence, until Mason spoke. "Yeah, we probably wouldn't have believed him, but we'd have given him an 'A' for creativity. I know I'd be pretty impressed if somebody made up a wacked-out situation like this."

They made it to SmartWaves by about 4:30, and purchased the Earth Magnetometer, along with a few extra batteries. Lotte was excited to try it out, so they unpackaged the device and set it up in in the backseat of Mason's RAV4. The unit consisted of a handheld box about eight inches tall and four inches wide, and a roughly yard-long stick with a white plastic tip, assembled from three interlocking pieces, which connected to the meter with a short cable.

Mason and Eric waited patiently while Lotte digested the three-page instruction sheet. "Well, it seems simple enough," she finally related. "Like any magnetometer, you just point the tip of the stick in various directions and look for the highest magnetic field rating. The devil is in the details, though, and there are a couple of options. There's a 'fast scan' technique, where you just walk along and monitor the field strength, but it's really dependent on the angle of the stick."

"What's the other option," Mason asked, "some kind of stationary reading?"

"Exactly. We'd stop at various points, get readings, and compare those to previous peak values. That's more time consuming, but more accurate. We may have to use a combination of both methods."

"Yeah, I think you're right. Let's give it a whirl. There's a big-ass water tower across the street. I bet you'll get all kinds of readings from that, and we can test how it works from different directions."

"Fantastic. We'll have to leave our cell phones in the car, as well as anything else you think might generate a magnetic field."

Feeling they were in a relatively safe area, they tucked their cell phones and Mason's and Eric's car keys, the only metal of any consequence they had on them, under the seat of the RAV4. The trio then walked down Diana Street and crossed Route 16. A huge water tower, painted bright blue, loomed just to the right, fed by a massive horizontal pipe that snaked off to the north, presumably toward the Androscoggin River, which they'd crossed to get into town.

Lotte started to take readings once they'd crossed the street. She moved from the sidewalk to a grassy embankment, walked past the water tower, then toward another street in front of an industrial building, where she stopped.

"Well," she said, "I'm definitely getting some wide variation around here. The meter reads in microteslas, abbreviated 'uT,' in a range of zero to two hundred. It registered in the mid-forties at the street, and up to a peak of about fifty-three near the water tower. The building dead ahead is already around sixty, and I'm sure that would get a lot stronger if we crossed the street. I think that's a hydroelectric plant. There's also another magnetic source off to the right. I'll bet it's that white junction box near those bushes."

She slowly tracked south, stopping periodically to take scans, before she again crossed Route 16 to a little triangular park between that road and Pleasant Street to the west. At a gazebo near the tennis courts at the northern end of the park, she halted and gathered a series of readings in several directions. "Okay, this is good. The magnetic field is still reading higher to the east, toward the hydroelectric plant. In this case, we know the likely source, but on the trails, we'll have to investigate any meaningful variance beyond the norm until we find what's causing the fluctuation. It'll take some time, that's for sure. Speaking of time, what time is it? I'm getting hungry."

"It's five-thirty," Mason replied. "I'm starving too. We haven't really eaten since breakfast, other than a doughnut. How about I take you guys to dinner? Beats driving all the way back and then having to make something."

There were no disagreements. They drove around a bit and found a nice little pub on the north side of town. Once settled, Mason ordered a round of beers, which after a long, hot day, even Lotte didn't turn down. Mason pounded his, but Eric drank slowly. He didn't want a repeat of the other night, though he really never got seriously drunk from beer.

Nonetheless, at an opportune moment, he excused himself and found their waitress. "Hey, do you guys have O'Douls or some kind of non-alcoholic beer?"

"We have Clausthaler," she replied. "Is that okay?"

"Perfect! Listen, could you do me a favor? I think my buddy is going to be ordering rounds. Whatever he orders, would you just put a Clausthaler in my glass? I'd really appreciate it."

"Absolutely, honey!" she said with a sympathetic look.

The food tasted great, and they had a nice time relaxing after an incredibly bizarre and sometimes terrifying day. Mason told them about the trails on the west face of New Speck Mountain, which ran a large loop on the perimeter with crossing paths that cut down or across the slope. They started to formulate a plan to follow the loop south, then cut up at the first path to isolate the southwestern corner, which Lotte believed to be the most likely area the creature may have established itself. They'd investigate other areas as needed.

As anticipated, Mason continued to order rounds. Lotte put her foot down after two, but Eric accepted a few more, knowing he'd be safe. She flashed him a worried glance, but when Mason wasn't looking, he waved his finger over his drink and shook his head and mouthed, "No alcohol."

She smiled and winked.

After dinner, Mason graduated to tequila shots. Eric took the simple route of proclaiming himself designated driver, to which Mason couldn't really argue. It did, however, seem to give him an excuse to drink more. Finally, Lotte went and paid the bill, and they coaxed their inebriated companion out of the restaurant.

"But I was gonna pay!" he said, slurring his words.

"You did pay, Mason," she responded, almost like a mother to a child. "Don't you remember signing the credit card slip? You must be more drunk than you realize. Why don't you lie in the back and we'll be home soon."

They piled him in the car, and Eric started the drive back to Bailey.

Mason drunkenly mumbled from the backseat, "Whole *Lotte* shakin' goin' on back here. I ain't fakin', whole *Lotte* shakin'! I was in a whole *Lotte* trouble. Whole *Lotte* trouble, so I had a whole *Lotte* alcohol. Now I feel a whole *Lotte* better. Wait a minute, that ain't goodly English. I should say I feel a *little Lotte* better. Nah, that sucks too. I'm just gonna take a fuckin' nap."

Eric couldn't help but laugh a bit, and even Lotte smiled.

"How's your hand?" she asked, brushing his arm with her fingers.

"It's throbbing. I can't really make a fist. I'll ice it some more and take some ibuprofen when we get back. It'll be fine."

"You may have saved my life again today, Eric Schneider. Doesn't that put me in your debt, or some-such?"

He laughed. "You don't owe me anything. I mean, practically three years of tutoring *me* in German? I probably still owe *you*."

She giggled. "That's not true. You weren't *that* bad. In truth, you were my best student."

"I was your *only* student!"

"Well, that's partially true. The others didn't stick with it. Whatever. I'm sure they did fine, but you kept working at it. You weren't at the top of the class, but you more than got through. Mr. Meier was extremely proud of you. I was proud of you."

"Yeah, well, credit the tutoring more than the student. It was mostly you. You made everything make sense for me. You gave it a purpose, a meaning. You made it fun, and exciting. In the end, it was you. You led, and all I had to do was follow."

She stared quietly out the windshield at the rapidly darkening sky. Black clouds billowed in from the west. More rain would fall tonight, possibly thunderstorms. The wind had already picked up, and Eric could feel its tug at the wheel of the RAV4.

"That was our pattern, wasn't it?" she whispered.

Mason stirred in the back seat, and again muttered to himself. "Whole *Lotte* shakin'. Whole *Lotte* trouble. Whole *Lotte* love."

Together, they escorted Mason up the stairs to his room.

"I love you guys!" he said in a sappy, drunken voice. "Especially you, Mister Eric Schnitzel-Schneider the Great. Don't fuckin' play coy. I see the way you look at me, man. We were meant for each other! True love. Fuck all these weirdo girls and their dumbass music."

"Mason," Lotte interjected, as she strained to push her stumbling comrade up the stairs. "I'm so happy you've finally found love. Now, can't you try to lift your leg a little higher and climb the stairs so we can all go to bed?"

He whooped with woozy excitement. "All go to bed? Lotte, baby, if you mean you want a threesome, I'm all fuckin' in! *Woo hoo!*"

"No, Mason, that's not at all what I mean. Get your mind out of the gutter, or raise it up enough so at least it reaches the damn gutter."

He stopped cold on the stairs, head wobbling. "So, you only want to go to bed with me, right? Okay, I surmended, I mean I surmender, I mean... damn... I take back everything I said. Girls are the best. Sorry, Eric, it just wasn't meant to be. It's not you, it's me."

They finally dumped him onto his mattress, closed his door, and exchanged a look of mutual relief. She gave him a little hug goodnight and went to the bathroom. He took the opportunity to grab his sweats and a t-shirt from the guest room, used the bathroom off the kitchen, and settled in on the couch.

No fire would warm him tonight, but it wasn't cold, and he had a fine, thick blanket. Outside, the wind howled as the trees loudly rustled, and periodic bursts of rain lashed at the window behind him.

None of this kept him from sleep, but the thunder and lightning did.

A violent storm struck just after midnight. It seemed to be passing right over them. Bright white flashes brightened the sky, almost instantly followed by deafening thunderclaps. Tree branches scraped and clawed at the roof of the house in the gale-force winds.

Well, so much for a good night's sleep.

He was about to get up, when the light in the stairway went on. Lotte padded downstairs, wearing nothing but her black Lemmy t-shirt and her underwear. The storm raged as he quietly watched her slip into the kitchen and click on the light.

After a time, she emerged with a mug in her hand, presumably tea from the box of herbal blends she'd instructed Mason to purchase from the little market. She turned off the light in the kitchen, but then bypassed the stairs and walked toward where he lay on the couch.

"Eric," she whispered, "are you awake?" A massive thunderclap sounded, and she jumped slightly. She spilled some tea, and stood on tiptoe to avoid stepping in the puddle.

"I am now," he answered.

"Oh, I'm sorry to wake you. I'll go."

He laughed. "No, no, Lotte, I was totally kidding. You think I can sleep through this? I'd need more beer and tequila than Mason had. Plus, I heard you in the kitchen. Plus, there's a girl standing in front of me wearing nothing but a t-shirt and her underwear. You think I'm gonna miss that show?"

She giggled. "Oh, silly. It's nothing you haven't seen before. Can I sit with you?"

"Sure."

She put her tea on the coffee table, went to click off the light in the stairs, and carefully navigated her way back. He watched her movements as if she walked in a strobe light, illuminated intermittently by the flashes of lightning.

"Verdammt!" she said as she slipped under the blanket and sat cross legged near his feet. "I stepped in the tea I spilled."

He felt her dry her foot on the blanket's corner.

They sat and listened to the rain, and the wind, and the mighty claps of thunder that shook the little cabin. He saw her in milliseconds of time, like a series of black and white photographs. He could have titled them: Lotte Reaching for Mug; Lotte Drinking Tea; Lotte Placing Mug Back on Table; Lotte Gazing at Me in the Darkness.

"Can I ask you a question?" Eric said.

"Of course," she replied in between explosions of thunder.

"Where do you think these things come from? We call the artifacts we found 'portals.' Where are the creatures that come through them 'portaling' in from?"

"Well, we don't know. It's like Cleopatra — we know so little about her, we have to extrapolate from the lives of other people from that time, use what little evidence we have to formulate the best picture possible. This is why I love archaeology. It makes you have to work things through. Even if more evidence later changes your view, it's always an interesting and productive challenge to speculate intelligently."

"Do you have any working theories?"

"Sort of. It's not really my area of specialty."

"You mean there's some area left that you're *not* specializing in? What is it, quantum astrological architectural gardening?"

She gave a hiccup of laughter. "Little shit. It does feel that way sometimes, though. No, it's far more mundane. It's just physics, but very theoretical. I can't do all the math, but it involves multiverses... other universes overlapping with ours, or from which our universe sprouted like a gigantic balloon. It makes you realize there may be spaces where the laws are entirely different, either other universes, or the places in between them."

"How do these universes connect?" he asked, intrigued.

"That's where the portal material comes in. I don't think either the *Alkuartiz Alnaar* or this magnetic gateway are made of material from our universe, at least at some level. The substances may have been locked in our planet when the solar system formed, or possibly they landed here on an asteroid. Either way, they always appear in small, precious quantities. I'm beginning to think this material is a remnant of some other universe, or universes, or the space in between universes that *formed* our universe. Through these materials, we can reconnect with that other space, or spaces."

"And when the beings from these other spaces come here, they take on the properties of this universe — like a symbiosis. They learn from us, so they can interact with us and get what they want."

"Precisely. You understand. That's basically as far as I've worked it through, although... there is one other thing."

"What?"

"It's the whole setup — the portal, the items on the ground, the rings. How can it possibly be that both summoning mechanisms look so much alike, and that they function all but identically, save the *element*, as it were, that drives them?"

"I have no clue," he said, having, in fact, no clue.

"Well, here's my theory. They both learned how to do it from the same source. Someone else figured it out, and that knowledge was transmitted into Etruria, and wherever the *Sadat Alnaar* originated — Persia, most likely, though perhaps elsewhere."

"What does that mean, exactly?"

She drained the last of her tea. "Well, it means there's almost surely more of these portals. Obviously, I already expected that, but now I'm all but certain. Moreover, though, it raises questions. How far back does this go, and what's the source of this knowledge? Could these have been *linked* in some way at one time? Is there something *more* going on that perhaps we haven't yet seen?"

The storm had receded, though thunder sounded persistently in the distance, rain continued to steadily fall, and the trees still rustled loudly in the wind. He felt her arm across his bent knees, her body pressed against his shins. He mentally framed and hung the black and white photograph entitled: Lotte Gazing at Me in the Darkness.

It would be on exhibit indefinitely.

CHAPTER 12

"Why don't you two get a fuckin' room?"

Mason's quip jolted Eric from sleep. He found himself entangled in Lotte's legs, one of her feet on his shoulder, resting against the side of his head. He felt her stir at the opposite end of the couch under the blanket they apparently shared.

She yawned. "What time is it?"

"Fuck if I know," Mason replied in a grumpy tone as he rounded the corner toward the kitchen. "I need coffee."

Eric grabbed his phone from the coffee table: *8:20*. They'd slept fairly late as clouds still darkened the sky, and a light but steady rain provided a soothing backdrop for sleep. He looked at Lotte, who shuffled on her elbows in an attempt to extricate herself from the knot they had somehow created.

She smiled. *"Moin!"*

"*Moin* yourself. Guess we fell asleep, huh?"

"Looks like we did. Best I've slept in days, once the storm cleared."

Me too, though I also slept pretty well that first night you arrived.

"While he's in the kitchen," she whispered. "I'm going to sneak up and put on some clothes. Then you can get your things."

He watched as she slipped off the couch and pranced up the stairs. He took a moment to absorb that enticing image, and then strode into the kitchen.

Mason stared at the coffee maker. "I need coffee before I can make fuckin' coffee." His voice was raw.

"Just sit down. I'll do it. I'm amazed you're even up. We figured you'd be out until noon."

Mason collapsed into one of the chairs at the kitchen table. "Nah, I'm cool. Get me some eggs and bacon and I'll be good to go. Speaking of good to go, what's up with you and Lotte?"

"What do you mean?"

He laughed. "I mean what's up with you two sleeping together all of a sudden?"

"Oh, the storm woke us both up."

"There was a storm?"

Eric snorted trying to contain his amusement. "Yeah, man, big storm, lots of noise. You must have slept through it, which is probably why you're among the living right now. Anyway, Lotte and I, we were talking, and I guess we just fell asleep."

After a pause, Mason said, "She likes you."

"Yeah, we've been friends a long time, or at least we *were* friends a long time ago."

He shook his head. "No, that's not what I mean. I mean she *likes you*, likes you. She would never do something like that, sleep in some guy's bed, even if it wasn't, like, a sex thing, unless she liked them."

"She's always been a kind of 'touchy' person. She usually seemed pretty casual about stuff like that to me."

"Well, that wasn't *my* experience, even when we were together. I've never seen Lotte act like this around anyone but you. Of course, that's not a scientific examination of every relationship she's had, but Lotte doesn't fuck around, man. She doesn't do shit unless she has a reason. I don't know if she's what you want, but I think she'd be into it if you were."

"I'd be into what?" Lotte asked as she entered the kitchen.

Eric stumbled for words, but Mason saved him. "Into eggs and bacon, if Eric were willing to make them. What do you say, Eric Schnitzel-Schneider the Great?"

He grinned and gave Mason a wink. "I say, how do you all like your eggs?"

It was nearly 10:30 by the time they were ready to leave, after they'd all eaten a leisurely breakfast and taken showers. The rain had stopped, but the sky remained overcast. They opened the door and scurried down the stone stairs to the cars. Debris from the storm littered the area, and some large branches had fallen from several trees.

"Mother fucker!" Mason shouted as he rounded his now leaf- and twig-covered RAV4. "I cannot fucking believe this!"

Lotte and Eric ran to where he stood by the hood of the car. A large tree branch had embedded itself in the windshield, which had buckled and shattered into a web of fractures.

"Oh, Mason," Lotte sympathetically said. "This is terrible. What will you do?"

"I don't know," he replied, prodding at the branch. "Maybe it isn't as bad as it looks. Can you guys help me get this damn thing out of there?"

Working together, they pulled the branch from the windshield, which left a nasty scrape as they dragged it across the car's hood then dumped it on the ground. In the process, the windshield further cracked and disintegrated. Shards of glass poured into the vehicle and covered the seats.

Mason shook his head. "Yeah, I'm not gonna be able to drive it like this. Eric, maybe you can run me down to Red's Auto Body later in your van. It's on the road back to Berlin. I'll see if he can get somebody up here to fix it, or if he can tow it, or something. Shit!"

"Yeah, sure," Eric replied. "Whatever you need."

"Great. Listen, Red usually spends his nights drinking at Murph's Tavern, so he's useless until after lunch. Let's go down there later. It's not like the car is going anywhere. We're all set to go. We'll just have to take the van." They started moving toward the other vehicle, when he suddenly cried, "Wait a minute!"

He ran around to the passenger door of the RAV4, opened it, pushed aside some debris and broken glass, and went for the glove compartment. "Should we bring these?" he asked, holding up the two handguns they'd taken from the bikers the previous day.

"*Scheiße!* I'd forgotten all about them! They were in the car all day yesterday in Berlin? Where are the drugs, Mason?"

"Yeah," he ruefully replied. "They're in the back of the car. I forgot about them too. Guess I should stash them somewhere, huh?"

"So, let me get this right," she said, trying to contain her anger. "We drove around all afternoon yesterday with a bag full of heroin and two guns in the car. Correct?"

"Yeah, and this knife." He produced the weapon from the glove compartment and dropped it on the roof of the RAV4. "It was a crazy day, Lotte. I just fuckin' forgot about them. My bad, okay? In fairness, so did you guys."

She just stared at him. Finally, she broke her gaze and with sufferance said, "By all means, Mason, go hide your drugs. I don't think guns, or the knife, will be useful on this creature, and if the police are still in the area, we run a terrible risk. So hide them as well. Do it quickly, and let's get going."

"Yeah," he said as he skulked away. "I'm gonna stash these in the shed. I'll be right back."

They took off a couple minutes later, and drove in silence along New Speck Lane toward the entrance to the trails. Mason sat on a small fold of metal behind Lotte's seat, to which he clung for extra stabilization. Leaves and twigs blown by the storm covered the road, and at one point they stopped to pull a particularly large branch off the weathered pavement.

They saw no police cars at the entrance to the dirt road that hooked northwest and twisted upward toward the trails. The van bounced and lurched on the muddy and pothole-ridden dirt track as they ascended. Trees formed a canopy above them and obscured the still cloudy but brightening sky.

Eventually, the road widened slightly and emerged into a small circular clearing. A dilapidated wooden sign showed a map of the trails. Two trees with weathered orange markers nailed to them indicated the entrance. Yellow police tape, tied between the trunks, draped across the path.

"Looks like they still don't want us up here," Eric commented. "What do we do?"

"I have an idea," Mason said. He slid open the side door of the van, walked to one of the trees, and carefully untied the police tape. When it came free, he motioned for Eric to drive forward, who pulled up in the van and rolled down the window.

"What do you want me to do?"

"Just go up a little. Let's get the van out of sight. That way, if someone comes, they won't see it parked here and know people are on the trails. There's plenty of tire tracks. They obviously drove up this way yesterday, so one more set won't be too suspicious. I don't think they're searching anymore. I just think they've closed the area down, which suits us fine. I'll tie this tape back when you're through, and catch up with you."

"All right. This trail is really narrow, though. I'll go as far as I can. I'm never gonna be able to turn this thing around. I'll probably have to back out."

"You can do it, man," Mason replied encouragingly.

Eric navigated the van through the trees and up the narrow path. He soon came to a T-junction where the trail led left, downhill toward the west, and right toward the east, up the mountain and back in the direction of the house. Somehow, he managed to make a left, and then backed up and parked.

"Whew, that was lucky. I should be able to squeeze out from here."

Mason jogged up, panting. "Great, this should work fine, unless the police come back up here. Then we're fucked, but we'll fall off that bridge when we come to it. This is the orange perimeter trail. If we go south from here, it'll wind down near the quarry. We'd then take the blue trail back up the hill, and right at the green trail to get back here, a little farther behind the van. Lotte, this'll isolate the area where you think the thing is most likely hiding. Ready?"

She nodded, hopped out of the van, assembled the metal probe, and attached it to the Earth Magnetometer. They again left their cell phones, keys, and anything else they thought might be magnetic in the vehicle. Sunlight had begun to poke through the clouds, and the muddy trail had already started to dry out as they trekked down the tree-covered path.

Lotte used the fast scan approach to try and determine a baseline reading. "I've gotten a peak of thirty-eight uT, but that vanished pretty quickly — probably some magnetic ore in the ground. Otherwise, it seems to hover around thirty-six or so. We'll stop and get more detailed readings if I detect a variance larger than that."

Eric said, "What if the path is too far away to detect the magnetic field?"

"Then we'll have to cut through all this underbrush, and it'll be far harder. I'm really hoping to find something along the trail. Come on, let's finish the loop and see if we get lucky."

This didn't especially buoy his confidence. Nonetheless, he dutifully trooped behind her as she navigated deliberately down the hillside. Several times, she stopped and probed into areas to the left or right, but quickly abandoned the hunt when the readings didn't persist. After a time, the trail began to flatten out and curve right, to the north. At a clearing, they looked farther down the hill and saw the rusty corrugated roof of the building at the quarry.

"I'm getting a slightly higher reading in that direction," she related. "It's not much, but if it persists, or gets stronger, that'll be the most consistent variation I've gotten so far."

"I think we know that's the building," Mason replied. "We may have to get farther away from the quarry to pick up a weaker signal."

They continued until they reached the marker for the blue trail, which led up the hill to the right. To the left, they could now see the entire building and the quarry. There was no sign of the bikers, or anyone else.

"Anything?" Eric asked.

"Nothing to the east, up the hill. I'm actually getting a slightly lower baseline reading in that direction because I'm facing directly away from the quarry building, so that field is subtracting from the total. There's no other substantial magnetism in this area that I can detect. I think we need to carry on."

"This trail is smaller," Mason said, "and has a steep uphill incline, so this will be tougher going. You'll need to focus on walking, and not dropping the magnetometer. We'll stop every fifty yards or so to take a reading. *You can stop every forty-five meters.*"

She snorted a little laugh as she tucked away the device. "Very funny. I suppose even a broken clock is right twice a day."

The trio valiantly pushed ahead, but as Mason had indicated, it proved to be quite rough going. The blue trail was steeper, had far more mud, and many places where the rocks were still slick from pooled or draining rainwater. Both Lotte and Eric slipped and got mud on their pants. It started to get hot and muggy as well.

"Did we bring water?" she asked.

"Nope," Mason replied. "Didn't even think about it. Some fuckin' outdoorsmen we are, huh? Let's finish out this loop and head back for some lunch. We can get better prepared and come back in the afternoon."

The periodic stops to gather data provided a brief respite to catch their breath. The meter had returned to its baseline reading, losing even the effect of the building at the quarry as it grew more distant behind them. Panting from effort, they came to the intersection with the green trail. Going left would take them north along the face of the mountain, but they went right, headed back to the orange perimeter trail and the awaiting van. The footing became easier here because it was substantially drier and either level or slightly downhill.

Lotte again used the fast scan, and after a short distance, she stopped and took a series of readings from downhill to the west, to uphill and to the east. She then walked about ten yards and repeated the process, then walked another ten yards and did the same thing again.

"Hmmm, strange," she said. "I think I've got something. It's not in the area I thought. It's uphill to our left—a small variance, but it seems to be directional. It's getting a touch stronger as we move south." She strode on, and stopped to take readings at ten-yard intervals, pointing the meter at an increasing angle until she held it perpendicular to the trail, pointing almost due east. "It seems to be straight up this way. It's stronger here. I'm getting a peak reading of forty-three uT. That's higher than the norm, and it's the largest consistent fluctuation I've detected, other than the building."

"Trees are too thick in this area to see much," Mason said. "I'm guessing we're about a quarter of the way back to the perimeter trail, maybe more. Listen, I have an idea. Why don't we stop down at the general store and pick up a pair of those binoculars. We can come back after lunch, go up the orange trail, loop around, and scan this area with the binoculars from above, see if anything sticks out. We just have no idea how far away this anomaly is, and cutting through this fuckin' underbrush uphill is gonna suck. Better to approach it from the top, or the side, if we can pinpoint what we're looking for."

All agreed, and they quickly hiked back to the van. Eric successfully navigated the tight turn, and Mason again untied then retied the police tape. They banged down the hill on the dirt road and soon emerged onto New Speck Lane.

Lunch and clean-up were the top priorities. Lotte and Eric changed their pants, then washed their dirty pairs in the kitchen sink and left them to dry on the old wooden bench outside. After eating, they drove the van past town to Red's so Mason could find out about his car.

He went inside while they waited, and soon emerged from the body shop and jumped in the back. "Red's gonna have to tow it. The insurance people will fix it, but they need to inspect the damage and they aren't gonna drag up the hill. I'm just gonna leave the keys for him. He'll get it while we're on the trails."

They stopped at the general store and bought binoculars, then backtracked toward the trails, where they arrived around 2:30 p.m. It had turned into a sunny day, and plenty of daylight remained. Mason and Eric repeated the procedure with the police tape, and soon they had the van parked out of sight once more.

"Hey, Eric?" Mason asked. "Do you think you could back the van up the trail and get us closer? Might be easier than schlepping all the way on foot."

"I can give it a shot. It's wide enough here, and it seems to have dried out since this morning. If it stays this way, it's no problem, assuming it doesn't get too steep."

Mason opened one of the back doors so he could help navigate. It was slow going, but it beat walking. The orange trail wasn't as steep as the blue trail, being a bit farther from the mountain itself. Once they passed the green trail, however, the incline increased.

After proceeding a bit farther, Eric felt he had to stop. "This is about as far as I think I can go."

"This is excellent," Lotte said as she jumped out of the van. She traipsed up the path to get clear of the vehicle's magnetic field and took a reading with the magnetometer. "The field rating is weaker here, just a bit above thirty-six uT to the northeast. We're farther away, but we still seem to be in range of the source. If we walk up the orange trail to a point where the strongest field rating is perpendicular, it should be straight in that way."

"Tell you what," Mason interjected, "let's walk a bit farther up and then cut in, see if we can find a spot we can look down with the binoculars. I'd rather not just walk into this blind if we can avoid it."

That seemed a good plan, so they again hit the orange trail. This time, Mason and Eric carried packs with bottles of water, and even some trail mix he'd had in a cupboard.

Who knows how old that stuff is, though.

After a series of scans, Lotte identified a point perpendicular to the path. "It's dead ahead that way. Peak is now up to just under forty uT. We're still a little farther away. Based on where we were on the green trail when we were perpendicular, I'd say it's about a kilometer, perhaps a bit more."

"Umm," Eric sheepishly asked. "How far is that in Celsius?"

She giggled. "It's about two-thirds of a mile, *Dummkopf.*"

They walked on, and the trail steepened even more. To the left, the slope became greater, and bare rock began to appear.

"Let's cut in here," Mason suggested. "It's getting steeper. Maybe we can find a hill with a clearing that looks down."

Again, the going got very tough as they left the path and ascended the sharp slope. Things had dried out and weren't as slippery here, but finding purchase still proved difficult. Eventually, the trees thinned and bare rock became predominant. A ridge soon appeared, and with great effort they hauled themselves to the top.

Man, this sucks! People actually climb mountains like this for fun? Hopefully, I won't have to make this trip again, but I have a bad feeling that I will.

The trio caught their breath on a rocky outcropping and looked down on the area below. Lotte scanned with her magnetometer.

"There!" she said, pointing at two mounds that poked above the treetops. "The reading is coming from those hills. Peak is up to forty-eight uT, definitely much stronger."

Mason got out the binoculars. "I don't see anything. There's a stream down there. It winds between the area where you're getting the reading and that other hill there." He pointed to his left, and they saw a rise closer to the trail. "That's nearer to the double hillock we want to investigate. If we follow the stream bed, maybe we can go up there and get a better look. The way down on this side looks a hell of a lot easier than what we just came up."

This turned out to be accurate. An almost gentle, grassy slope led to the bottom of the little valley. They found the stream and followed it as it curved southwestward, until it was diverted by the rise of the hill that was their destination. Like the one they'd just descended, the slope here proved far less treacherous than the steep incline they'd first tackled.

Occasional trees dotted the hillside as they ascended. Finally, they emerged onto another rocky ledge that looked back down into the valley, and out onto the double hillock across the stream some three hundred yards away.

"We're up over fifty uT now," Lotte said. "The magnetism is increasing greatly as we approach. There's definitely something magnetic in that double-hill area."

Again, Mason got out the binoculars. "I still don't see anything. There's a higher point up this way." He pointed farther up the ridge where they currently crouched. "Stay here for a minute. Let me see if I can go and get a better look."

They drank some water and watched while he scooted along the ridge. As he neared the outcropping he was headed toward, he disappeared down a small incline. After a few moments, he still hadn't emerged.

"What's he doing?" Lotte asked.

"Probably taking a piss. I could use one too."

Just then, they heard him let out a terrible wail. "Nooooooo! Nooooooo!"

"Come on!" Lotte commanded.

They both scurried toward where he'd disappeared. When they crested the little hill, they saw him on his knees, sobbing and howling with grief. They ran to him, but when they got close, both stopped in unison and stared with horror.

Just beyond where he knelt, crying and pounding his fists into the dirt, lay a desiccated body. It looked like an Egyptian mummy. Flesh clung to the bone, flattened and wrinkled, drained of all liquid, and gray, like ash from a fire. Black holes marked where the eyes seemed to have shriveled. The arms and hands were skeletal, fingernails swollen and sticking out like the backs of cockroaches on the tips of each stiff and contorted finger. Only the golden blonde hair and the tattered clothes gave any clue this had once been a living being.

"Emilia," Lotte whispered in shock and dread.

Eric looked around. Another corpse lay nearby, just as grotesquely disfigured, having worn shorts and hiking boots. "The female hiker. It's either killing them here, or this is where it's dumping the bodies. It could be close."

He noticed the binoculars abandoned on the ground where Mason had dropped them. He grabbed them and raced to the outcropping, which had been Mason's original objective. On the way, he noticed another body, seemingly tossed haphazardly into the bushes from the higher ground above. By the look of the clothes, this appeared to be a man.

Maybe Larry Henderson or the other drug dealer.

He didn't have time to investigate. He reached the top, brought the binoculars to his eyes, and frantically scanned the double hillock. Back and forth he searched. Back and forth, back and forth, and then....

He saw something. It was just a flash, something in a tree, gone before he could see what it had been, but the branches still rocked from a sudden movement.

"Guys!" he shouted. "We gotta get out of here, right now!" He ran back to where Lotte crouched by Mason, trying to calm him. "Lotte, I saw something. I think it's out there. We've gotta get the hell out of here!"

"Mason!" she spoke sternly into his ear. "We have to run! There's nothing we can do for Emilia. If you want to live, we have to go! Now!"

He looked at her, tears running down his cheeks.

She got up and extended her hand. He took it, and she helped him to his feet. "We have to get back to the van. What's the quickest way? Mason! Concentrate! What's the quickest way?"

Slowly, his eyes gained focus. He looked around and seemed to regain the bearings he'd so completely lost. "Back the way we came," he finally said. "Then into the trees to the right. The trail isn't far. If we're quick, and quiet, it may not be able to find us."

They ran.

They bounded back down the grassy hill, but rather than follow the slope to the bottom by the stream, they made for cover back toward the trail. Mason led the way, and Eric took up the rear. They moved swiftly, but with caution, and as quietly as possible. Eric frequently looked behind, and above. He saw nothing, but right as they spilled out onto the trail, he heard something like the pumping of gigantic wings sweep above them.

"It's close!" he loudly whispered. "We have to run. The van isn't far."

The downward grade both helped and hindered them. They didn't have to fight against an uphill slope, but they couldn't run full speed for fear of losing their balance. Instead, they shuffled sideways as quickly as possible.

At one point, Lotte slipped and fell. She slid forward and then skidded to a stop, desperately clutching the magnetometer to her chest.

Eric came up behind her and lifted her by the shoulders. A dark shape passed above them above as he helped her up, barely visible through the canopy of trees.

By the time he and Lotte arrived, Mason had already climbed in the back of the van.

Eric jumped in, grabbed the keys from where he'd left them under the seat, and started the engine. "Lotte, fasten your seatbelt! Mason, hold on! This is gonna be bumpy." He threw the creaky van into drive and drove as fast as he could down the narrow trail.

With surprising speed, they reached the turn leading back to the dirt road. He slowed the van to navigate the tight space, and had almost completed the maneuver, when they heard a loud rustling in the trees above, then a loud thump on the roof.

They stared, first at each other, and then toward the ceiling of the vehicle. Mason gestured upward with his finger and then pointed at the trail ahead. Eric nodded and gunned the engine. The right fender of the van scraped loudly along a tree trunk.

Good thing I took that extra auto insurance! Good thing I took out that life insurance too, 'cuz I'm pretty sure we're gonna die!

They bounced and heaved down the trail. At one point, they heard a loud scraping on the roof, as if something had pushed off. The van rocked slightly, and the handling improved a bit.

"It's gone!" he yelled. "I don't think there's anything on the roof of this van for the thing to cling onto when we're up to speed. We have to keep moving."

The yellow police tape between the trees loomed ahead. He sped through like the lead runner breaking the tape at the Boston Marathon. They skidded out into the circular clearing and were headed for the dirt road when, without warning, something slammed into the solid side door of the van behind Mason. A conical indentation about six inches wide and flat at the top appeared.

"Holy shit!" Mason screamed. "What the fuck was that?"

Nobody had an answer.

Eric focused exclusively on the road, hoping his speed and the cover of trees would lose the creature. The shock absorbers of the tortured van loudly slammed as they repeatedly bottomed out in the myriad potholes. Muddy water splashed on the windshield, and he had to divert his attention to activate the wipers and washer fluid, which only served to leave dirty streaks and smears across the glass.

They rounded a tight turn and the cracked asphalt of New Speck Lane came into sight. "Hold on!" he cried as he banged a hard left onto the road. The van rocked and teetered, but miraculously resisted tipping over. He jammed his foot onto the accelerator and began to gain speed, but then they all heard the familiar sound of something landing heavily on the roof.

Shit! What do I do now?

Almost on impulse, he slammed the brakes. The van skidded to an abrupt halt and Mason plunged into the space between two seats. Through the dirty, streaked windshield, Eric watched as something tumbled from above. It smacked into the pavement in front of them, and skidded to a halt on hands and knees.

It had great wings, grayish-blue and tipped in black—not elegant like an eagle's, but bent, like those of a vulture. A large, hooked beak extended from its face, and evoked a vulture's visage. From the lower jaw of this beak, the tusks of a boar protruded upward, while coarse fur that recalled the black beard of a man dangled below. The creature's head bore thick, fibrous strands that looked like snakes. Its pointed ears and heavy brow twitched as the beast tried to right itself.

Its torso and arms were recognizably human, but a sickly, pale blue in color. Each finger sported a thick, claw-like nail. The beast's biceps were ringed with more of the fibrous snake-like strands, mirroring those on the crest, while the monster's legs ended in enormous, gleaming, three-toed claws. Its motions were abrupt—sharp—like those of a bird. One moment, the creature looked in one direction, then instantly in another.

Most curiously, the monster appeared to have dropped something that sat by its side on the cracked pavement of New Speck Lane—a jet-black stone about a foot in length and in the shape of an elongated "T."

Before Eric could react, the creature sprang to its feet. In a split second it looked to the trees, then to the van, then to the road, then finally settled its icy stare on the black stone lying on the ground. It extended its palm and the item quivered, then flew directly into the being's muscular grasp. The beast clutched the object to its chest, and it began to surge and glow. Before their eyes, the T-shaped stone grew, extending in both directions and gaining girth and mass, until the monster held in its hand a massive and imposing five-foot-long hammer, reminiscent of a gigantic croquet mallet, but infinitely more menacing.

Mason poked his head above the dashboard. "Fuck. Lotte, are you fuckin' seeing what I'm seeing?"

"Yes, Mason, I see it. I know what it is. Eric, back up! It's going to attack!"

He looked at the creature.

With a flick of its neck, it had focused its wild-eyed gaze on the idling white van. Slowly, it raised the massive hammer that it cradled in its arms and strode boldly forward.

"There's no place to go behind us. The only way out is *through!*" He slammed his foot on the gas, and the white van accelerated toward the otherworldly monster.

Like the battle of Waterloo, it was the nearest run thing you ever saw. One millisecond more and the beast would have struck the windshield and shattered it, and Eric, and Lotte, and likely Mason as well, though Mason had somehow managed to retreat to the back behind the dirty pleather seats. Like Wellington at Waterloo, however, the aged, dirty, stinking white van slammed into the creature first. They all felt the violent collision as the van bucked and staggered, and heard the rocking *badabump, badabump* of two sets of tires running the ghastly thing over.

For fear of losing control, Eric had to release his foot from the accelerator and apply the brakes. The van stood motionless. He looked in the side mirror at the overrun monstrosity. It lay in a dazed state and had again dropped its weapon. The object lay by its side, a scale model of the horror it would become when wielded.

For a brief second, he contemplated getting out and grabbing it, but with a lightning-fast twitch, the creature righted itself and again extended its palm to the black stone. The T-shaped object responded as if born to this function, and sailed into the beast's outstretched hand, where it again immediately grew to fear-inducing proportions.

Eric hit the gas. The back tires of the tired van screeched in protest as smoke rose from the burning rubber. In the mirror, he saw the beast take three steps, then launch into the air.

But there was nothing he could do.

With a resounding thud, the creature again landed on the roof. With a dull crash, the head of the monster's terrible hammer smashed through the roof near the rear. Hoping for a repeat performance, Eric slammed on the brakes, but the hammer sliced through the top of the van as easily as Mason had cut his eggs at breakfast—a nice, clean line from back to front.

Then, before he could reapply the gas, the opening in the roof burst apart as the monster thrust its torso through. Lotte reached for her door in an attempt to escape, but Eric threw the van into park and went between the seats to grasp for Mason, who floundered on the floor of the cargo space. He grabbed his hand and tried to pull him forward, even as the creature clutched at his endangered companion with the arm that didn't secure its abominable weapon.

But there was nothing he could do.

Mason didn't scream. He held tight to Eric's grip and tried to kick out behind him, but the beast easily fended off this assault, grabbed his ankle, and began to lift him upward. Mason held Eric's gaze as he pulled with all his might and tried to free himself, but all too quickly, the only thing that kept him in the van was Eric's hand—the hand he'd injured punching an angry biker the day before, and which now couldn't quite grip tightly enough to keep his comrade from slipping away.

Mason looked straight into his eyes and smiled. "Eric the fuckin' Great."

He forced the words from lungs that strained from being literally pulled apart. Then, Eric felt the loosening, the giving up, the surrender, like Napoleon's Immortal Guard finally giving way under the relentless and undeniable onslaught of defeat.

He watched in silent terror as Mason disappeared, sucked through the hole in the roof of the van. The arm to which he so recently clung caught on a jagged piece of metal. Momentum severed the limb from the body at the shoulder in a shower of crimson, and it landed with a cold thud on the dirty metal floor of the cargo space. Blood and cartilage dripped from the gaping, ragged tear.

Instinctively, Eric grasped for it, clutched for the hand still outstretched, palm down and fingers limp, like Adam's on the roof of the Sistine Chapel. He took Mason's hand in both of his and held it, clung to it, cradled it. He willed and begged for it to return to life.

But there was nothing he could do.

There was nothing he could do.

There was nothing he could do....

CHAPTER 13

Central Etruria, 573 BC

Rika knew it to be completely improper, but nonetheless she pressed her eye to the wall and looked through the small slit into the room beyond. It reminded her of peeking through the cracked daub and broken wattles into old temple all those years ago, driven by her insatiable curiosity and her childlike ignorance of the dangers involved. The day, however, had finally come, and once again, she had to know. She had to see it with her own eyes. That it had taken almost ten summers for Abirami to receive word from his family had greatly surprised all concerned.

Not all surprises, however, were unwelcome. The time had been a gift to both of them, during which ever closer ties, and the routines of a life together in so many things, had obscured the concept that at some unforeseen future moment, it could all come to an end.

Could that moment be now?

If so, she decided to face it head on. Thus, she superstitiously observed the two men through the spyhole, constructed for exactly this purpose, as they sat in the meeting chamber on the southwest corner of the complex. This secret had served the Zalthus well in their various dealings, but today it would benefit a Matuna.

The newcomer looked much like Abirami—a relative perhaps, but if so, not a close one, as their dealings were stiff and formal. They faced each other from couches on opposite sides of a central carpet. Small lamps augmented the dim illumination from narrow windows into the colonnaded courtyard. Abirami sat with his back to her, but she knew the graveness of his expression, as all life had vacated his eyes when she'd told him of the man's imminent arrival from the coast, and he'd been downcast and sullen for days while they'd both nervously waited.

Now the men spoke, but they used the strange eastern tongue which she'd never mastered beyond a few perfunctory words. Short and polite at first, the conversation rapidly become curt and testy. They disagreed on some matter she couldn't comprehend. Their visitor clearly wanted something, perhaps for Abirami to accompany him back to their lands. For her, this would be the most devastating outcome, but she maintained hope, as it also seemed so unwelcome to the man who over time had become her friend, her lover, and the father of her two children. The pressures of family clearly assailed him from two sides, and for now, it remained uncertain which would prevail.

The newcomer abruptly rose, his tone angry and chastening as he berated Abirami. She imagined his words based on his tone. *'Are you mad? Have you lost your mind... your sense of duty?'* In disgust, he finally sat back down, and for a time, both men were still. Then, in a resigned tone, a final question, succinct and ultimate, as the man deliberately extended his palm outward.

Abirami rose, reached over his shoulders, and pulled off a necklace tied with a leather thong. She'd seen the strap many times, but always the trinket it suspended had been concealed from her. He never wore it to their bed. She'd assumed it to be the symbol of his patron god, Melquart, or that of the mistress of his city, Astarte... an item of deep personal and private reverence upon which she'd never dared transgress. With his back to her, she still couldn't clearly make out the roughly palm-size object her love handed over, but his stance showed strength and resolve.

With that, the conversation appeared to be at an end. The visitor pocketed the item, the two men briefly hugged, and then the man left. Abirami left shortly thereafter, and Rika realized with a start that she needed to get back to her quarters lest she raise suspicion. She let go of the cloth that covered the tiny hole, got up from the stool on which she sat, exited into the hallway from the small ancillary area of the workroom in the western wing, and then dashed out of the doorway.

The wall under the loggia, which ran along the building's southern wing, sported a series of frieze plaques that depicted a horse race. They were part of a cycle that portrayed the arrival of a noble bride, and the games and banqueting in celebration of the impending union. The final sequence that ran along the eastern wing showed the regal groom and bride together, a powerful reminder to all who visited the complex during festivals and ceremonies of the influential connections the Zalthus enjoyed with the wider world.

Rika simply enjoyed the beautiful shapes of the majestic equine creatures she passed, given even greater brilliance by the lush red and white paints that faded little under the shade of the colonnade. Despite her urgency, she couldn't help but smile at them as she rushed by.

"Done with your spying for today?"

Rika jumped at the unwelcome and completely unexpected question. "Arathia! You startled me. What are you doing here?"

"What am I doing? This is *my* house, Priestess. I have no need to explain my presence to you, or anyone."

She cringed. The girl had always been to her like bitter sediment in wine, and she'd grown only worse with age and entitlement. This time, however, she spoke true, and Rika knew she'd been caught. She guided her nemesis through a door, between the images of her beloved steeds, where Abirami couldn't see them as he crossed the courtyard.

"You're correct, of course. My apologies, noble one, I didn't mean it in that way. I wonder only what might interest you in a matter such as this."

"I could ask the same of you, but I think I know why *you're* here. Perhaps, if I finally gain an answer as to why we've been burdened by this man's presence for the past decade, and what this 'matter' you speak of has to do with the business of my family, then you'd understand why I stand before you."

"Abirami has never been a burden," she countered, with as much diplomacy as she could muster. "He paid his way many times over with the fine gifts he brought, and the trade connections he offers would be of incredible benefit to the house of Zalthu, if only your father did not spurn them."

"We seek new partnerships. The winds of change blow over the Great Sea, and our sails must be unfurled to ride the course they chart."

"Your father's associations in Tarchuna, and with the Hellenic colonies, walk a fine line, Arathia. Now is not the time to weaken bonds with our historic and honorable allies from the east and Carthage."

"So says the Priestess whose children are the product of one such *honorable* ally. Recently, little else of good seems to have come from our dealings with these Canaanites. They appear to be as powerless as we are to stop the onslaught of the Hellenes. Perhaps the web of fate is revealed to us, if only we have the courage to keep open our eyes, no?"

"Many think not. If we can but maintain unity and coordinate our efforts, perhaps the winds may blow differently. So the majority of the League has proclaimed, and so I have acted in accordance with their wishes, while representing the good name of your house."

"Hurrah! We're all so proud that you didn't flinch even once while you spied on your lover!"

"That's a private matter, Arathia. In truth, I well might answer your questions about Abirami's presence here, and what today's visit was about, if I were able. Sadly, I remain in the dark, but still, I got what I came for. I'll trust in your discretion. Little good would come of him knowing I'd been here. Please excuse me."

There wasn't really much Arathia could do to stop her. The practice of subterfuge was accepted at some level, and other than the personal affront Abirami might feel, Rika had done nothing that any Zalthu seeking information might not attempt. It would have been easier if she hadn't been noticed, but as she drew close to her chambers, she forced the minor irritation from her mind.

Abirami had already arrived. He stared out the same window in the tower from which she'd first seen him, gazing into the grand colonnaded courtyard below as he waited.

"Where were you?" he asked in a distracted tone.

"Checking on the children," she lied. "Today they're helping feed the baby goats. So precious. It's a part of life I thought forever closed to me. Now, I wouldn't trade them for all the world. What happened in your meeting?"

He turned as he answered. "The siege is ended. My city has a new king who has agreed to serve as vassal to Babylon, but we retain much of our independence in trade. The threat being over, I received instructions to return."

"And shall you?"

He smiled. "So lovely, and so wise, but so unable to answer such a simple question. True, it's not easy. I'll likely never see my lands again, but my life is here now, with you, with our children. How can you not know I would never abandon you?"

She fought back tears. "I know not why you came here, what burden they placed on your shoulders, or what impact that might have on your ability to turn them away."

"And I know not where you go on those mysterious journeys that venture forth in the dead of night. I've never seen inside the innermost sanctum of the temple you tend, which dominates the first two floors of this very tower, or been party to the strange rituals that are said to be at the heart of your people's power. I'm shooed away before they begin and forced to sleep with the baby goats."

"You lie, you rascal! A fine apartment in the eastern wing always awaits you."

He laughed. "I exaggerate, only to show how much we conceal from each other. Still, here we are, and despite these things unknown, we could never deny what we felt for one another, could we?"

"No," she agreed. She realized they both harbored secrets that may never be fully revealed. "We could not, and cannot. What do we do now?"

"Well, I told my cousin, Ahumm, that I could help the family with business from here. I may venture to Fufluna more frequently, especially if I can convince Marce to get involved."

"Unlikely," she scoffed. "He seems enchanted by his association with nobles from Tarchuna, who are as unwilling to upset their Hellenic partners by trading with Tyre or Carthage, as they are eager to break the monopoly in ores the Paithna family controls from Cisra. It could be a dangerous game you play. Be wary."

"Just as I surmised. No matter. There are many deals to be made in a busy port, and I'll ensure Marce and the family get a healthy cut so friction here is minimized. Unless, of course, I can convince you to run away with me?"

She laughed over her tears. "If only it were possible. As a youngster, I gave my allegiance to all of this. At the time, I didn't fully understand what that might come to mean, but I felt certain in the knowledge that my life would be uncommon. This it surely has been. I must uphold my end of the bargain."

He took her in is arms. "It doesn't matter. Perhaps one day I will visit my lands when things there have settled, both politically and personally. I have more than I could have ever wanted right here with you."

She spoke few words in Abirami's tongue, but she knew how to say, "love."

She said it now.

Bailey, New Hampshire, Tuesday, July 30, 2013

"There was nothing I could do. There was nothing I could do...."

"Eric."

"Nothing I could do. Nothing I could do...."

"Eric, it's all right. Come on, let's get up."

"Nothing. Nothing...."

"Come on. That's it."

Lotte braced him as he let go of Mason's lifeless hand. He slowly rose on trembling legs.

"Nothing. Nothing...." He chanted in breathless little whispers as tears streamed down his cheeks.

"Oh, Eric, you did everything you could. You risked your life to save him. Come on, sit here."

He felt the seat of the van under him. His left arm touched the steering wheel. Lotte's face hovered in front of him like a full moon on the darkest of nights, a tender smile on her lips, but with eyes bloody red from tears of her own. She touched his cheek and held his hand, the hand that felt Mason slip away, and which now throbbed with the pain of exertion... and failure.

"Eric," she said in a gentle voice. "Can you get us back to the house? We need to go. That thing might come back. Can you get us just that far?"

He looked up and around. Slowly, his surroundings came back into focus, replacing the persistent image of Mason's stony gaze as he disappeared through the torn and jagged roof. He looked toward the back of the van, still spattered with blood from the severed arm that lay on the floor of the cargo space. Blood stained the knees of his pants, where he'd knelt as he tried in vain to resurrect the dead.

"Where are the keys?" he managed to ask, remembering vaguely that keys were needed to start vans, whatever vans were.

"They're in the ignition," she replied with obvious relief, "but, my love, the car's running. All you have to do is drive. Can you do that? Can you get us home?"

He listened. Sure enough, he heard the sound of an engine.

Drive. Put it in drive. And steer... with the wheel. Straight. It's right up the road.

He swung his legs around and, by sheer muscle memory, found the gas and the brake. He put the van in drive, and they began to move.

She kept her arm on his shoulder and whispered in his ear. "You're doing great. Just take it slowly. That's it, *langsam*."

They reached the house. The old, dirty, blue RAV4 with the fractured windshield had vanished. It had been towed away, like Mason had been, but Mason wouldn't be coming back. Surely, by now, his body had been shattered beyond any hope of repair.

Lotte guided him up the stone steps, through the front door, and toward the couch. He put his knees on the seat and fell to his side, his back to the room. He felt her untie and remove his shoes, and then slip the blanket over his shoulders.

He stared at the deep red, blue, and cream plaid pattern on the back of the sofa. He lost himself in the details of the stitching... the areas where one color bled into another... where the lines were indistinct and fuzzy... neither blue nor red, good nor bad, right nor wrong. No living, no dead, it just... *was*. For now, that was all there could be.

Eric opened his eyes and saw little but darkness. The room glowed slightly from the fireplace, and dim light emanated from the kitchen. He smelled something cooking, which made him hungry, even though he didn't feel like eating. He did have to pee, though.

He got up still wearing his pants, dried and caked with mud, dirt, and blood. He hoped he hadn't stained the plaid couch. A glass of water sat on the coffee table, and he vaguely remembered Lotte telling him to drink. She'd held his hand to steady his trembling, then run her fingers through his hair when he'd collapsed back on the sofa and returned his gaze to the infinite nothing that beckoned him.

He shuffled to the kitchen and saw her stirring a steaming pot, illuminated only by the little light above the stove. She didn't see him, so he watched her for a while. It calmed him to observe her performing such a normal activity — the slow stirring, the steam rising. It made it seem like at least something — *anything* — was still as it should be.

She turned to reach for a bowl in the cupboard and saw him. "Oh!" she said with a little start. "You scared me. I didn't hear you get up. Are you feeling better? I'm making some soup. You must be hungry. Do you want some?"

Unable to process all these questions and concepts, he started to sluggishly drag himself toward the bathroom.

She stopped him, put her arms around him, and squeezed tightly, cracking his spine.

"I know you're hurting," she said into his shoulder. "I know how awful that must have been, but Eric, I must tell you, I've never seen anyone so brave — so selfless. I know it's hard, so very hard, to move forward after something like this, but this is why I knew I needed you by my side, and I still do. I still need you. Can we have some soup together and talk? This isn't over, and I know I can't finish it without you."

He lost himself in her embrace. For a brief moment, the weight lifted from his mind and he saw clearly. She wouldn't give up. Even if he left now, she'd never stop hunting, and if she died trying, he could never live with himself for having abandoned her. Terrifying and dangerous as it might be, he realized this was his fight too. She needed him. She would lead, and he would follow. In some sense, it simplified matters.

"Can I pee first?" he asked.

She tightened her grip, and forced the last of his breath from his lungs.

He went upstairs to use the bathroom and change, then returned to the kitchen and settled in at the table. "What time is it, anyway?"

"Close to ten. You were out for six hours. I didn't dare wake you. I think you were in shock, you poor thing."

"Yeah, that's what it felt like. I tried, Lotte. I really tried. I just — "

She put her hand on his arm. "I know you did. You did all you could do."

He tried to refocus. "What happened with... with, the... you know... in the van."

She took a deep breath and closed her eyes. "I cleaned the car." She nodded toward a red plastic bucket that sat drying near the kitchen sink. "We'll have to bury... well... Mason, tomorrow. I'll need your help. Do you think you'll feel well enough to do that with me?"

He nodded. "Yeah, I'll be okay. I think I just needed to clear my mind for a while, forget about it. Some things are coming back to me, though. Did I hear you and Mason say you knew what this thing was?"

"You did. We both recognized it almost instantly, though how myth and reality intermingle always poses a slight challenge. The hammer was the giveaway, then the other pieces fell into place."

"So, what is it?"

"It's Charun, Eric."

"What's a Charun?"

"Not what. *Who.* In Etruscan mythology, Charun is one of the psychopompoi... a spirit or deity responsible for accompanying newly deceased souls from Earth. His name was adapted from the Greek 'Charon,' the famous ferryman who transports souls across the River Styx and into Hades, the underworld."

The classic rock song *Come Sail Away* suddenly took on an entirely new meaning in his mind.

"The Etruscan Charun, though, is likely much older, and is fundamentally different from his Greek counterpart. He's depicted with a hammer, his religious symbol, and is often shown with pointed ears, snakes around his arms, and a blueish coloration symbolizing the decay of death. In some images, he has enormous wings and snake-like hair, a vulture's hooked nose, large tusks like a boar, a black beard, heavy brow ridges, and fiery eyes. Sound familiar?"

"Shit, very familiar. I guess that makes sense, given that Mason and Emilia found this thing in Tuscany."

"Precisely. Think about it: the Etruscans spoke a non-Indo-European language. Their ancestors held out in Etruria when all others fell, and eventually they emerged with a thriving culture that rivaled the Greeks and Carthaginians for several hundred years. For a time, they even dominated the *Latini*, who eventually became the Romans. They may have even founded Rome itself. They had powerful colonies around Campagna and Corsica, and were well on their way to competing with Carthage and Greece for domination of Sicily."

"So, what happened?"

"It's not clear. Sometime in the last decades of the sixth century BC, the tide started to turn. They were chased from Rome in 509 BC, and in

474 BC, they lost at the battle of Cumae, effectively ending their period of dominance. The Romans eventually absorbed their culture, though they borrowed a tremendous amount from the Etruscans as well, particularly in religion and divination."

"It's almost like the expansion of Islam—rapid rise and dominance for a period, then a sudden collapse, or at least the ceasing of expansion."

"Exactly like that. What if the Etruscan's power was predicated on bargains with Charun to eliminate key enemies, similar to those agreements the *Sadat Alnaar* worked out with the Afrit? What if Mason and Emilia stumbled on the temple or sanctuary where they conducted the summoning? It appeared to have been buried during an ancient earthquake. Maybe that occurred around 510 BC, or thereabouts, and that precipitated their decline. Maybe all the priests were killed. Maybe the location was kept secret, and no one could find it to be able to dig out the stones. Charun became lost to them. This may be why you see his image, or images of demons, like the one in the Tomb of the Infernal Chariot, or the Blue Demon in Tarquinia, begin to appear in later Etruscan art. They may have been praying for him to return to save them."

"So, how does all this help us get rid of the damn thing, and what's up with the magnetic portal? You didn't say anything about that in legends about Charun."

"You're right. The magnetism is still a mystery. There's nothing about that in the mythology. As far as getting rid of him, I'm not sure knowing who, or what, he is helps that much either. But we do have one key piece of the puzzle."

"What?"

"We've seen him! We now know what he looks like, and we can impart that information to the Afrit. Now the Afrit can help us be rid of him. So, are you ready?"

"Ready for what?"

"Ready to summon the Afrit, Eric."

Damn! I knew she was gonna say that!

"No time like the present, right?"

Again, the black mist clouded the ancient glass of the frame, obscuring the reflections of candle and firelight that lit the room. The bowls blazed with five candles each, and Lotte bobbed and whispered as she sat cross-legged at the apex of the black marble board. The gold ring and the bent filigreed bracelet rested on the floor in front of her.

Eric waited nervously behind her. He didn't like or trust this being, and apparently the feeling was mutual. He wondered if it were due to some ancient offense that a man, now lost to history, had committed, or if the Afrit simply preferred some intangible aspect of the female psyche.

Doesn't make any difference to me. I'm keeping my distance. Let her bargain with the damned thing. They seem to understand each other.

The familiar tendril of ash soon reached for the flame that rose from the marble board. The creature's head and stout shoulders assembled above the large bowl in the center, then its body and wings took shape behind. Once more, the beast towered above them, seven feet of solid, shining black ash that glistened in the light of the fire. Its pupil-less eyes surveyed the room, as the monster's goat-horned head drifted from left to right. Its bony, bat-like wings twitched as if in anticipation of flight.

Lotte stood, and the Afrit crossed its arms and gazed down at her. "I want to bargain!" she said with a commanding tone. "Search my mind. In it, you'll find the image of the one I wish taken. His energy will be yours, the spoils to enjoy when your task is complete. Then, you'll be free to go. We'll tend the portal and the flame that will send you back. This I swear, and you know my word to be true. What say you?"

The hulking beast swayed from side to side and lashed its barbed tail. Eric could feel it probing, even in his mind, for the image of Charun. He concentrated on what he'd seen when the bird-like creature had stood before him on the cracked pavement of New Speck Lane, when it had run at the van with its terrible hammer, and when it had reached for Mason on the dirty floor of the cargo space.

'We see!' the Afrit finally said. Its gravelly and unintelligible words echoed in the quiet of the house, but their minds understood perfectly. *'We can sense him even now. Close. Very close. In this one, we see a challenge. Not like you small beings who quiver in fear and are easily subdued. This one will fight.'*

"Can you overcome him?" she asked. "Can you do as we ask?"

Again, the beast swayed. Its wings unfolded slightly and fluttered. *'We will need flame. You must tend a large flame nearby for us. This is part of our bargain.'*

Nearby? Eric thought with alarm. *How close is nearby? Like, is Jamaica close enough?*

Lotte spoke before he could voice an objection. "We agree. You'll have flame. We'll see to it."

At this, the Afrit ceased its swaying and its wings became still. Then, it lifted its massive head and gazed at the ceiling, though Eric sensed it looked beyond the rustic beams and boards above them.

'*Too far,*' it said, its voice wary in their minds. '*He must be closer, must be nearer the flame. He is too strong for us to bring here. The doorway must be brought there.*'

Lotte hesitated as she clearly struggled with the same concerns that flooded into Eric's mind. *How the hell will we bring the portal to Charun's location? Where will we set it up? How can we transport the massive un-mirror across that rugged terrain? This is gonna put us in a lot more danger, too!*

She turned her head and gazed at Eric with a questioning look.

He shrugged. "I don't know, Lotte. What choice do we have? I guess where there's a will, there's a way. It's your call."

She returned her attention to the Afrit, who remained perfectly still. "We agree, but this will take some time, and we have to do it in daylight when we can see. It'll also be dangerous for us to do all this so close to the one we seek. He may hear us and come out of his hiding place. He's already taken our friend. You'll have to watch over us. We'll light a flame when we find a suitable spot to set up your gateway and the fire you requested. Will you come to us when you see this signal?"

The ashen monster gave an almost imperceptible bow.

"Excellent. In the meantime, stay out of sight. Don't engage with anyone else, and harm no one! Do we have a bargain?"

Slowly, the Afrit extended its muscular arm and unfolded its talons. '*Let the rings bind our pact!*'

She reached down and picked up the jewelry, put the ring on her finger, and then carefully slipped the bent filigreed bracelet over the creature's claw. The beast's skin rippled slightly and expanded to secure the fit.

She backed up and motioned for the creature to follow. Its massive cloven hooves strode across the oak floor of the living room. Its footfalls were tentative, almost gentle. The beast glared at Eric as it passed by, flicked its barbed tail, and chuffed in disdain.

Yeah, back at ya! Charmed to see you again, too.

Lotte opened the front door and exited. The monster bent down as it followed, then straightened its wings to twist through the un-accommodating opening.

Eric didn't bother going outside to watch the thing slip silently into the night sky. He'd seen it all before, and he cursed having to bear witness to the monstrosity's presence in his world again.

Despite having slept a bit earlier, Eric still felt exhausted. It was past 1:00 a.m., but they both wanted to get things prepared for morning. They'd already packed up the un-mirror and stowed the black marble board in its custom-made case. Now, they cleaned the bowls lined with *Alkuartiz Alnaar* in the kitchen sink, and placed them carefully in their boxes.

When they'd finished tidying up the kitchen and living room, Lotte dragged herself upstairs.

When he heard her close the bathroom door, he scurried up to the guest room to grab some clothes to sleep in. With Mason gone, he somewhat sadly realized that he no longer needed to keep his duffel in her room. He'd begun to gather up his things to take downstairs when he heard Lotte behind him.

She stood in the doorway, half in and half out of the room, her elbow propped on the frame as she eyed him expectantly. "Eric," she said, her voice full of curious anticipation.

He stared at her. He felt he knew what might be next, but what would he do if his instinct were right? If she asked him to stay, would he? What would happen? What would that mean?

For him, it would cross the boundary line to which he so tenuously clung. The last remaining distance he'd managed to achieve over years of struggle would collapse. He would again want her, need her, long for her with no buffer, no filter. The decision of what to do would be out of his hands.

His father's words came to him, *'Take it slow. Think it through.'*

Right now, things were moving at warp speed. Dilithium crystals strained to power the Enterprise to ever more perilous speeds. He knew what it would mean to *him*, but what would it mean to *her*? Lotte, so casual, so uninhibited, so willing to share tenderness when it suited her, but then... gone. Lotte, half in and half out of his life, like she stood now, half in and half out of the room.

First, he had to know what it meant. She had to tell him, make it clear. Either that, or else he had to ask her, and now simply wasn't the time given what they needed to accomplish together. If she said, "no," he wouldn't be able to focus, and that would put them in danger.

He rose and tried to act casually. "What's up?"

Only her eyelids moved. They blinked in a precise rhythm as she held his gaze. Finally, she turned her heard toward the flimsy bed. "Nothing. I'll see you in the morning."

He abandoned his duffel bag and left the room. He'd sleep in the clothes he already wore.

CHAPTER 14

The door to the shed stood before them. Once, it had been painted red. Now, bare wood showed through the few remaining flakes of peeling scarlet pigment.

They opened the door. Sunlight danced across shelves laden with years of accumulated relics: watering cans, saws, hammers, an old lawn mower, horseshoes and iron spikes, an old badminton net with rackets, and boxes and cans filled with all things put aside for another day that would likely never come.

A Hefty garbage bag, tied tightly with twine, sat on a workbench that overflowed with packages of nails and scraps of wood. Lotte picked it up, and Eric took the shovel. He dared not think of what was inside that bag, though he knew, of course.

They walked up the path to the little plateau that overlooked the house, and the town, and the lake beyond. The morning sun lit their way. When the trail evened out, they saw the obsidian magnetic portal gleaming on the face of the rock. The tent had blown away, most likely in the violent storm of the night before last. It sat akimbo in the trees to the right. The flimsy folding table and chairs had similarly blown over, and away.

They walked to the left, where the grassy part of the plateau gave way to scrubby bushes before surrendering to the trees. The earth smelled rich here. Dirt from the mountain and decaying plant matter had made this area lush. Once they cleared a spot, the digging went easily, as if the ground welcomed a gift about to be bestowed.

She packed the pieces of the portal into boxes while he dug. The stones on the ceramic stands had fallen over, but thankfully nothing had broken.

When both had completed their tasks, she lifted the rolled-up garbage bag and deposited it with care into the hole. She took his hand as they stood and quietly gazed down. Mere days ago, the reality of Mason had brought him to tears. Now tears flowed down his cheeks for Mason's passing. It didn't make sense. It didn't compute.

But there was nothing he could do.

She watched as he filled the hole, and then they raked debris over the freshly shoveled dirt to further disguise the area already obscured by thick underbrush. Once done, they each picked up a box full of the magnetic stones. They'd have to make several trips to get all of them plus the propane, the generator, and tools that had been left to soak in the rain.

They would leave the tent, table, and chairs to fend for themselves.

Eric found a mallet-like hammer in the shed, possibly the one Mason and Emilia had used to chisel rock before they purchased the air hammer. With it, he pounded the jagged metal of the roof of the van back into place, or at least close enough. The sharp, twisted edges no longer threatened to slice the tops of their heads as they loaded equipment into the cargo area.

They found it vastly more difficult to transport the un-mirror and the larger boxes out of the house without Mason's help, but together they managed. When finished, they drove back to New Speck Lane, then toward the trails. Muddy streaks on the windshield still hindered visibility. Eric wished he'd cleaned it off before they left, as the van's dilapidated wipers and low-pressure wiper fluid served only to smear the mess around.

They soon arrived at the circular clearing. The police tape remained draped from the trees as they had left it yesterday, broken in the middle.

He stated the obvious. "This will be a problem, if it isn't already. I hope the police haven't been up here and seen this. That'll make them super-suspicious. What are we gonna do?"

She got out of the van and inspected the tape where it was tied to the trees. "Come help me. There's extra here. Let's loosen the knots and produce some slack, then we'll tie it in the middle."

"It won't look right. It'll be obvious that it's tied."

"Possibly, but if they just quickly drive by, maybe it'll pass. In any case, do you have a better idea?"

He didn't, so he loosened one end while she worked on the other to create the slack they needed. He hopped back in the van and drove through the trees, and she proceeded to tie the tape at the break. She tried to curl over the loose ends so they covered the tight knot. As anticipated, it wasn't perfect, but it would have to suffice.

She got back in, and again they drove down the path, then reversed direction at the T-junction and backed the van along the orange trail to get as close as possible to the hill where the creature seemed to be hiding.

"So, do you have a plan?" he asked as he shut off the ignition. "Any idea where you want to set up all this stuff?"

"I'm not certain, but I think that first hill we were on gives us the best hope. I feel safer a bit farther from that double hillock where we detected Charun, and I really don't want to go up that other hill and see... well... you know...."

He did know. He didn't want to see Mason as a desiccated mummy-like monstrosity either.

"Anyway, if we can just get the frame over near the stream bed, or perhaps not even that far, the slope becomes much easier. We can roll the case with the frame up on its wheels. The rest we can carry. So, I think we should try to cut in and look for an easier way before we hit that steep area with all those rocks, where we climbed up the first time. Let's bring the lighter fluid and starter paper we took from the house. We'll gather some firewood, and then summon the Afrit. It can watch over us while we get the rest of the stuff set up."

He harbored certain doubts about that, but in the end figured he'd have a better shot with the Afrit than Charun. They grabbed what they needed and hiked up the orange trail, looking for spots they could navigate to the gentler slope on the far side of the hill. All too quickly, they came to the slope and rocks they had ascended previously.

"*Verdammt!*" she groused. "I didn't see any way in. What do we do?"

He pondered. "Let's go down that way a bit and see if we can find a thin spot in the trees where we can get through."

They walked back down the trail and picked a point that appeared marginally more promising than any other spot they'd seen. The going soon got extremely tough when the underbrush became denser.

"Hold on," he finally said. "It was easier back near the rocky hill. We went straight up because we figured that was the easiest way to the top, but I remember looking down, and the trees thinned out once you got past the dense area near the trail, just like the other hill when we ran down. Maybe we should just walk along there."

Again, they backtracked. Sure enough, just at the edge of the slope, the trees thinned out beyond one fairly dense area of thicket. Relatively speaking, it seemed to be a clear path forward. The terrain would be rough, but this beat slashing through thick underbrush while carrying the cases. The two probed along the base of the hill until the slope started to smooth out, and the forest gave way to scrubby grass.

The hill towered to the right above them, almost a cliff-face here under the ridge from which they'd originally observed the valley and the magnetic anomaly centered on the double hillock. As they approached the stream, the grassy incline they'd descended before unfolded to their right. Aside from being uphill, it would be easier from this point forward. They had their route to the top.

"Great!" she happily said. "Why don't you start collecting some wood for the fires. I'll go up and try to scout for a good location to set everything up."

"Cool." He began to leave to get the wood, but then thought better of it.

Jeez! I almost forgot Horror Movies 101: never separate. Idiot!

He grabbed her, and together they went to collect the firewood. Once they'd gathered all they could carry, they ascended the grassy slope. When they reached a spot she found suitable, he scanned the double hillock in the distance with the binoculars. All seemed quiet, but Charun could have slipped out while they weren't looking.

They set up the fire at the top of a small rise, behind which they planned to assemble the portal, where it would be out of sight. He stacked the wood while she rolled up some old newspapers and stuffed them into various gaps. Then she sprayed on a bit of lighter fluid, lit a match, and tossed it into the pile. Soon, a small fire blazed under the morning sun.

To their surprise, the Afrit almost instantly rose from the trees below. It flew to the top of the hill, circled a few times, then flapped its wings in tight, short bursts, and gently lowered itself to the ground. Neither of them had seen the creature in broad daylight. It both glistened like a charcoal crystal, and simultaneously seemed to absorb light. The monstrosity loomed in front of them like a living statue.

It looks like some gruesome Disney attraction that tourists in shorts and sandals pose with for demonic selfies.

Lotte stepped forth. "Thank you for coming to us, great one. Do you sense the one we seek in the hills there?"

The creature didn't have to turn its head to see where she pointed. *'He is there. He slumbers in his den. We dare not move upon him in such a defensible position. We will wait, surprise him when he emerges.'*

"Is this close enough to him for us to set up the fire you requested, and your gateway? We fear getting too much closer."

'It shall suffice. We must lure him to this area to be close to the flame, but this we can do. Make ready. We will watch for him while you do so.'

Satisfied they'd have at least some protection if Charun appeared, they quickly returned to the van.

"You take a box of bowls," Eric said, "or two if you can manage. I'll take the marble slab. I think I can carry that. We'll start with those, figure out the best way up, and then come back for the case with the un-mirror and the other stuff."

Despite the somewhat easier route they'd identified, the trek still proved to be treacherous. They both slipped frequently on the uneven terrain, and the case he thought he could carry soon strained his hands, arms, and shoulders. He frequently switched sides, especially since his right hand still hurt badly, but he still had to stop often.

I didn't think I'd ever hate lugging something around more than my stupid clarinet case!

The seemingly gentle slope to the top turned into a grueling slog. In the end, Lotte temporarily abandoned her box in the scrubby grass and helped him carry the heavy burden the rest of the way.

The Afrit studied them as they dragged over the little rise and deposited the case on the ground. It squatted by the fire, which now smoldered, but the ashen beast still seemed to revel in the heat it produced. Its barbed tail periodically twitched from side to side, like a cat observing a bird.

Eric collapsed on his back, gasping for air. "Holy crap. This is gonna suck! Next time, we'll do the slab together from the start. What the hell am I saying? There isn't going to *be* a next time! Except getting the damn frame up here—ugh!—and then getting both of the damned things back down again. I think I might rather be dead."

"I know, it's awful. I just don't see another way. We'll do the frame now, together. Somehow, we have to do this. I know we can!"

Somehow, they did.

To their dismay, the wheels of the case got stuck in numerous ruts and were frequently blocked by rocks on the hill. Eventually, they became hopelessly entangled in the scrubby grass. It turned out to be easiest to temporarily discard the detachable hydraulic lift to make the whole thing lighter, and simply carry the gigantic box. They developed a pattern of, "heft, carry, walk, down, rest, repeat," all the way up. It took well over an hour, and when finished, both were exhausted and covered in sweat.

Fortunately, the other items were lighter. In two more trips, everything sat behind the little ridge near the top of the hill. Together, they maneuvered the frame into position with the reclaimed hydraulic, and attached its special stand. Then they set the marble slab in front.

He left her to place the bowls and prepare the candles while he went to gather more firewood for the large fire the Afrit desired. He figured she'd be safer with the glowering monster than she'd been with him, and he enjoyed having an excuse to get away from the nasty thing. He made many trips.

With the wood he collected, they prepared a larger fire near the first, which would be lit when Charun made his appearance. To placate the monster, Lotte kept the small fire burning low. If the beast appreciated the gesture, it gave no indication.

It was nearly 2:00 p.m. when they finally finished. The two were absolutely famished, but had wisely brought sandwiches, water, and Mason's trail mix of questionable vintage. They sat and ate, and periodically watched for signs of movement in the valley below.

Time passed, and nothing happened. As they faced west, the ever-lowering sun made it difficult to monitor the double hillock, but the Afrit seemed unfazed. The day dragged on. Supper time approached and they were forced to open the trail mix. It seemed fine.

This stuff will probably survive with the cockroaches and the Twinkies after the fall of humanity.

Eventually, the sun hung low in a brilliant pink and blue sky. Eric rarely looked at sunsets, but being here, it captivated him. In spite of his reticence, the brooding Afrit's presence enhanced the glory of the view. Its wings swayed gently in the light, evening breeze. While Eric admired the end of the day, the creature finally spoke.

'He stirs. Make ready.'

Lotte ran to the beast's side and prepared to light the large fire.

'Not yet,' it cautioned. 'Wait until we lure him closer. We need the flame at the peak of its power, roaring with energy. The small fire that burns here may be enough to attract his attention and draw him to this spot. Surprise, as always, will be our ally.'

With that, the Afrit rose, beat its mighty wings, and sailed into the sky. Immediately, the creature looped down and skirted along the treetops, almost impossible to follow. Eric tracked as long as he could, but the monster soon disappeared into the foliage across the stream, in the direction of the double hillock.

"I'm gonna go and watch through the binoculars," he said. "I'll let you know when they're close."

She waved in acknowledgment.

He ran down to the edge of the ridge overlooking the valley and crouched behind some rocks. He scanned back and forth through the binoculars and then zoomed out to get more of a panorama.

Suddenly, he saw movement in the trees on the double hillock. He zoomed back in and noticed more movement to the right, a disturbance in the leaves near the canopy on the forested mound nearer to their position, and then... something burst into the sky.

"It's Charun! I can see the hammer!"

"I can see him!" she called in response. "Keep your eye on him in case I lose him, and tell me when."

He returned the binoculars to his eyes and watched as the great Etruscan demi-god circled — once, twice, three times. Then, it started in their direction.

"Okay, he sees the fire. He's headed this way. Get ready!"

The beast approached in a zigzag fashion, seemingly cautious — wide to the left, and then to the right, and then to the left. Then, from the trees below, he saw the Afrit rocket upward. Charun didn't see it, had no idea. He was focused solely on the small fire that burned near Lotte on the little rise.

The creature's turn had just completed when the charging Afrit slammed into him from below. Charun was thrust upward, the sheer speed and power of the impact splaying his arms and wings helplessly against the Afrit's powerful surge. The sudden blow knocked the hammer from his grip, and Eric's eyes widened as he watched it fall toward the trees, until it shrunk and became impossible to follow.

As the locked beasts' momentum slowed, the larger Afrit grabbed the smaller being and attempted to wrestle him into submission. Charun writhed and frantically flapped his wings, but seemed to be contained. Then, in a move that surprised everyone, including the Afrit, Charun rotated his body, raked one great blue wing across the face of his captor, and then dropped straight down. The combination of moves loosened the Afrit's grip, and before it could regain its grasp, Charun pointed his head directly downward. Like a Stuka dive bomber, he plummeted straight toward the earth.

The Afrit wailed with rage and attempted to follow, but Charun had a head start, and his sleeker form made him impossible to catch as he plummeted almost suicidally into the thicket. Eric winced as he heard tree branches cracking and the ground resound with a tremendous thump. The Afrit briefly gave chase and circled above, but then arced downward toward the treetops and vanished in a forested area near the stream.

"Where are they?" Lotte shouted.

"I don't know. I lost them both in the trees." Long moments passed as they both frantically searched for any sign of the otherworldly beings. "Hold on. There!"

Charun slowly emerged from the green wash of the treetops. His great wings beat a slow rhythm, and he again clutched the imposing hammer in his mighty hands. He gained altitude, and his beak darted from side to side with lightning quick movements as he surveyed the area. Once again, he began to drift cautiously toward the small fire, but he kept a close watch on the ground beneath him.

Suddenly, Eric heard a shocking and mighty outcry. It came from the opposite side of the of the stream from the double hillock, far closer to their position on the ridge. The shimmering black creature had moved, unseen under the canopy of trees. The Afrit hovered just above the treetops and roared as if in challenge. Its horrible, raspy voice was unintelligible, though no creature could mistake its meaning.

Charun hovered hesitantly, and seemed to assess the opponent who had so recently surprised and nearly overtaken him. Then, with a snort of resolve, he brought his obsidian hammer to his chest and zigzagged guardedly toward the Afrit.

Eric's heart pounded as he watched the two hulking creatures close on one another. Each probed for an angle of attack or strategy that might give them an opening. They had come within barely ten yards of each other when Charun raised his hammer above his head and dove in for a massive strike.

It almost connected, but with dexterity that belied the creature's girth, the Afrit dropped at the last moment. As Charun sailed by, the ashen monster looped around, grabbed its surprised and disoriented foe from behind, and pushed him directly toward the hill.

Again, they became entwined as Charun thrashed and contorted against the Afrit's grasp in his attempt to get away. This time, however, the massive talons of the sparkling black beast had a secure grip, and the pair plummeted directly toward Eric, and Lotte behind him and farther up the slope.

He discarded his binoculars as the creatures now drew so close. "Light it! They're coming!"

She put her lighter to the large fire and it erupted into flame.

He turned back to the struggle above. Charun desperately lurched with all his strength and created just enough separation to beat his black-tipped wings. With Herculean effort, he redirected the intertwined pair. They trailed off to the right, almost directly over Eric's head, and with incredible force slammed into the grassy hillside beneath the ridge, which quivered from the impact.

He quickly ran to Lotte's side and looked down the slope. Both creatures writhed on the ground, seemingly in shock from the massive crash, which left a huge gash of upturned earth in its wake. With great effort, each beast fumbled on hands and knees, then rose woozily. Charun had again dropped his hammer, but with an extension of his palm, it flew to him and instantly grew to its gargantuan proportions.

Lotte fanned the flames, trying to stoke the fire to grow quickly. "We have to make sure it's big enough for the Afrit to use."

With reticence, the two monsters turned to face each other. Each shook their head in an attempt to regain focus. Eric wondered whether they couldn't summon the strength and coordination to fly away, or if neither were ready to back down now that the battle was locked. Warily, each creature circled the other, Charun with his hammer ready to sweep in front, the Afrit with its barbed tail at the ready.

When Charun's back faced their position, the Afrit struck. It launched itself at its opponent's midsection, intending to drive him back toward the flames of the fire. The ashen creature's clawed hand grasped toward Charun's ferocious hammer to stave off any counterattack.

Charun moved too quickly. He swung his hammer low and undercut the Afrit's outstretched arm. The massive head of the obsidian mallet drove into the creature's side with an incredible thud. The shining black beast howled in pain, and the two humans watched from the ridge in horror as dark and glittering ash spewed out from the area of impact. The Afrit tumbled wildly sideways and skidded to a halt face down in the grass. Its wings went limp and pathetically twitched at its sides.

Charun stepped cautiously forward. He seemed to sense his adversary's vulnerable position. Slowly, he raised his hammer and prepared for a devastating, and potentially killing, blow on the Afrit's unprotected back.

As if from nowhere, the prone creature's barbed tail shot forth and drove deeply into Charun's abdomen.

With a shriek of pain from his hooked beak, Charun lowered his fearsome weapon and staggered backward.

Then, like lightning, the Afrit removed the barb, jumped to its cloven hooves with the aid of its wings, and again hurled itself at its stumbling opponent. This time, it crashed directly into him. The impact forced the mighty hammer from Charun's grasp, and drove him upward, ever closer to the large fire.

"Clever," Eric said. "The Afrit played possum."

"More accelerant!" Lotte commanded, and he rapidly grabbed the can and squirted on some lighter fluid. The flames surged.

The Afrit looked up and appeared to see the blaze. It gave a mighty push, and Charun tumbled to the ground. As if sensing victory, the ashen monster spread its bony wings and raised its arms above its horned head. The flames in front of them swelled and grew, and when the Afrit pulled its arms back, an arcing column of fire shot forth down the slope, directly at Charun.

Still reeling from the gaping incision in his gut, the birdlike beast didn't see the strike coming. The twisting pillar of flame struck him full on. It seared his back and wings, and drove him headfirst into the dirt at the feet of the Afrit.

The energy quickly exhausted itself, and the large fire extinguished as smoke wafted upward from Charun's singed feathers and charred flesh. The Afrit reached down, grabbed its stunned opponent by his thick beard, and dragged him roughly to his knees. Then it tightened its grip around his neck, and began to squeeze.

Charun's vulture-like beak opened as if gasping for breath.

Weird. Maybe these things breathe after all.

The Afrit's tail twisted menacingly above its head. The lethal barb took aim at one of Charun's fiery eyes. It seemed about to strike when the bird-like creature's hand twitched.

In the blink of an eye, the obsidian T-shaped stone swirled up the slope and slashed through the back of the Afrit's left knee. The joint shattered with a massive crack, and more dark ash spewed into the air.

The sparkling black monster collapsed, roared in pain, and clutched at its buckled and broken knee. Released from his adversary's sharp talons, Charun stumbled to regain his balance, then turned to retrieve the T-shaped stone that had landed nearby.

Eric saw deep incisions in his shoulders where the Afrit's claws had raked and penetrated his flesh. He realized the beard likely covered equally gruesome wounds on his neck as well.

All too soon, the gargantuan hammer had reappeared in his hands, and he turned again to face the wounded Afrit.

"We have to do something!" Lotte cried. "More fire! It's the Afrit's only chance! The wood here is still good, but the paper and lighter fluid have been incinerated. Let's set more and light it quickly."

They both reached for the bag in which she'd stuffed old newspapers to stoke the fire. They madly tore at the paper and frantically stuffed it under the wood. Then he grabbed the can of lighter fluid and drenched the entire pile. She ignited it with her lighter, and jumped back as it burst into flame before her.

He turned again to the battle below.

Still woozy and unstable, Charun took great downward strikes with his hammer at the crippled Afrit.

The ashen beast acrobatically avoided the blows as it scooted along the ground, propelled by its one functional leg. It tried to lift itself into the air, but seemed unable to take flight. Its wings dug helplessly into the dirt as it repeatedly tried to gain upward momentum.

"Flame!" Lotte yelled, trying to attract the injured monster's attention.

It seemed to notice, and when Charun's next strike landed heavily in the dirt, the Afrit raised its arms and pulled its talons toward its shoulders. Again, the pillar of fire arced out and raced toward Charun, not as imposing as the previous burst, but still potent.

This time the blast hit him in the side with a great explosion. The massive hammer fell from his grasp as he tumbled to the ground, stunned.

The Afrit crawled as fast as it could toward its foe, dragging its body on massive, muscular arms, while its great talons ripped and tore at the soil.

Before Charun could regain his bearings, the ashen monster fell heavily on top of him, using its greater bulk to pin him to the ground. With claw tightly clinched, the Afrit struck downward with its brawny arm and repeatedly bashed at the face of its helpless foe. Shards of the vulture-like beak flaked and flew off, leaving pocked indentations like chisel marks on stone. Charun's head rolled ever more loosely with each forceful blow.

Charun appeared on the verge of unconsciousness when, somehow, he unexpectedly managed to extend his hand. The small T-shaped obsidian stone skittered awkwardly across the ground and into his palm. There, it seemed to stutter, and didn't grow with its usual speed and smoothness.

The Afrit saw the weapon as it began to appear. The brief delay gave the ashen creature the moment it needed to avoid the ensuing blow. It rolled away just as the hammer swung within mere inches of its head.

Eric couldn't believe it. "Get ready to run. If Charun finishes off the Afrit, we're in deep trouble."

"No!" she screamed in reply. "We have to light the fire again! We can't run!" In a frenzy, she began to rifle through the nearly empty bag for more newspaper. The can with the lighter fluid had likewise run perilously low.

Eric watched as Charun rose on wobbly legs and again began to move toward the Afrit, who appeared equally exhausted.

He's done for. We'll never be able to re-light that fire in time. Wait a minute!

He rushed over to the smaller fire, which still burned nearby, and squirted what was left of the can of lighter fluid on the smoldering embers. A flame roared up as the liquid ignited, and black smoke rose into the air. It wasn't much, but it was something.

Both Charun and the Afrit looked up the hill and saw the flames. As if sensing his opponent might be ready to unleash another explosive strike, Charun extended his now charred gray-blue wings and started to run down the hill. With a massive caw from his now disfigured beak, he lifted somewhat clumsily into the air and flew erratically back in the direction of the double hillock.

A streak of flame shot forth from the smaller fire, but dissipated well short of the fleeing Charun. The Afrit howled in frustration and pain, but it could not follow.

For now, the battle was over.

It seemed to be a draw.

CHAPTER 15

The sun set, and dusk enveloped the hill and the little valley below. Lotte and Eric stood by the Afrit.

The creature's rage had quieted. It sat in the upturned grass and dirt as it prodded woefully at its shattered leg. Finally, it gazed up at them with empty eyes.

"What can we do?" Lotte asked, her face blackened with soot from her proximity to the fire she'd started. "How can we help you?"

The beast looked down at its mangled leg. *'Flame,'* it intoned, with a weariness neither had heard in its voice before. *'We need flame.'*

They rushed back up the hill and gathered the wood from the large fire still fit for use, and what remained of their paper. Then they returned to the Afrit and built a fire in a gouge of earth formed by the recent battle of the otherworldly monsters.

When the flames roared, the creature scooted close and extended its useless limb. The bulk of the leg dissolved into a halo of shimmering, misty ash, like that which had emerged from the glass in the frame. The cloud rotated like a miniature hurricane. Slowly, the appendage re-formed. When complete, it appeared functional, but narrower, and likely not as strong.

The beast flapped its wings and attempted to stand.

Eric instinctively reached out to help it up, but then realized his assistance would be all but useless, and probably unwelcome.

After a wobbly rise, the Afrit gingerly tested its repaired joint. It took small, hesitant steps with its massive cloven hooves. The knee appeared solid, and soon the creature walked normally, though it still favored the repaired left leg.

"Great Afrit," Lotte said, her tone soft compared to the commanding voice she typically used with the beast. "What do we do now?"

The monster walked to her and crossed its mighty arms. *'We must leave. The one you seek is too strong, the risk too great. You must send us home to heal near the Eternal Flame. Our bargain cannot be fulfilled. We submit ourselves for judgment.'*

"Judgment?" she asked with shock. "Judgment from whom? Me? If so, I judge you to be in the wrong, and determine that you have to stay!"

'Not you,' the beast mildly replied. 'Those who judge. Those who are invoked by the power of the rings, and who come when a bargain is broken. Each side may state their case, and those who judge are the final arbiters. Rarely is their authority tested. Surely, we have never done so.'

"Great one, in all probability, these judges you're talking about are long gone. Even if they still exist, the knowledge of how to invoke their presence has been lost. Centuries have passed. These portals have been buried, forgotten."

'This is not our concern. If they come, let them come. We wish to return home. This task is too dangerous, too demanding. Our bargain is void.'

Eric could see panic on Lotte's face, and he shared her sense of dread. If the Afrit wasn't up to the task, he wondered if they'd have to get the authorities involved — mortal authorities, that is.

We'll call the Army. Hell, bring out the Air Force and the Navy too. And Marines could never hurt. Can't have too many Marines!

"Great one," she pleaded, "isn't there anything that can be done? What if we assisted you? We can light more fires for you to command, maybe find some way to distract your opponent."

The beast wavered above her and beat its wings while it rocked gently from side to side.

I hope that's a sign the thing is thinking it over.

Before the monster could utter an incomprehensible word from its jagged mouth, she spoke again. "The one we seek is rich in spoils. His would be a great power to take back to your Eternal Flame. We can help you! We can work together to formulate a plan. What do you have to lose from at least talking with us?"

The Afrit turned from her and looked out into the darkness toward the hills where Charun made his lair. 'Speak,' it finally said. 'We will listen to your words.'

"Thank you, great one," she said with relief. "Please, give us a moment to contemplate all this and try to make a plan. Then, we'll talk."

'We have nowhere to go,' the brooding monster replied, not taking its eyes from the enfolding darkness.

She turned to Eric. "We have to think fast. What are our options?"

"Lotte, this is more your department than mine, but I know one thing: we have to get that damned hammer out Charun's hands, and keep it out! That's the source of his power. Without it, he's no match for our boy Chuckles over there."

"You're right. The Afrit can knock it out of his hands, especially with surprise. The issue is keeping him from retrieving it. The hammer's obviously magnetic, and in some way, Charun must be as well. What could interfere with his ability to recall the weapon?"

"Well, when he dropped the hammer the first time, it fell down into the trees. He couldn't call it back from the air, probably because it was too far away. So, distance maybe?"

"Yes, that's probably right, but that would likely mean the Afrit would have to unseat the weapon when they're both airborne, and then secure Charun so completely he couldn't fight back. That's already proven to be difficult, and when they're in the air, we can't help."

He thought about that. What she said was true, and it left really only one option. "I guess one of us would have to grab the thing. Do you think we'd be strong enough to hold it long enough for the Afrit to finish him off?"

"There's no way to know, but I don't see any other way either. I just can't think—wait a minute! The hammer is magnetic. Charun can call it, but what if there were a stronger magnet pulling it away, or keeping it in place? Couple that with one of us holding it, maybe that could keep it from him."

"Great idea, but where exactly are we gonna get a stronger magnet? Can you order them with next day shipping from Amazon?"

She flashed a playfully scornful look. "No, *Dummkopf*, we already *have* one. The magnetic portal! When it's active, it generates a *huge* magnetic field. We should measure it with our magnetometer. I'll bet it's incredible. If we can get the Afrit to knock the weapon loose, and if we can get it into the field around the portal, we might be able to hold onto it."

"Are you kidding? It's Charun's freakin' portal. You don't think he can call the hammer out of that magnetic field?"

"Well, of course anything's possible, but something tells me the properties of the portal might be different. Think about it. Why did Charun establish his lair here? Why does he bring his victims to this spot to kill them and drain their energy?"

"I don't know. He likes the view?"

She rolled her eyes. "Really, like a six-year-old. No, silly, it probably has something to do with the magnetic readings we're getting from that double hillock. He's using that magnetism to further his own power, just like the Afrit uses fire."

"Except he's killing his victims on that other hill."

"We don't know that. Maybe he's just dropping the bodies there so they're not right near his lair, but that's beside the point. The critical thing is that he didn't use the energy of the portal after he took Emilia. He brought her here. Why? The only answer I can come up with is that he wanted to stay in our world, and if he'd been inside the portal's magnetic field, that wouldn't have been possible. It's almost like how the Afrit dissolves and returns to the glass with the 'spoils' it's consumed. Within the portal's field, Charun may completely absorb his victim in a similar way, but his structure may be similarly compromised, and he has to return to his plane, at least for a time. This may be why he was perceived by the Etruscans as escorting the dead into the afterlife. Feeding near the portal, there's nothing left when he's finished, just like with the Afrit."

Eric shuddered. "Why would Charun want to stay here?"

"I have no idea, but it's pretty obvious that he did. So, I think he needed to be outside the portal's magnetic field when he took Emilia, and he needed to find another source of magnetism to help power the process. The key is, he couldn't draw energy from the portal and do it there. Maybe that field is literally an extension of the plane, or realm, where Charun comes from. It's just too powerful to draw on unless you're in the middle of it. This is why I'm hoping he won't be able to extract the hammer from a distance, if we can get it into that area. It's true, he might be able to do it, but it would probably be much harder. That's the point. We'd still want to try and hold it, but I think this would give us our best chance."

"Okay, assuming that works, which is a pretty big assumption, there are still multiple problems with this plan. First, where and how are we gonna set up the magnetic portal? Second, how will we get the oh-so-cooperative Charun near enough for it to be useful?"

"Yes, all good points. Somewhere in all this, though, are the roots of a plan. As far as location, we really have no choice. We'll have to set the magnetic gateway up here, near the fire portal. The Afrit will need Charun close by to absorb his energy."

"There's no issue getting the stones up here, or even the equipment we need to carve the recessed doorway, but Charun is bound to the hear the noise. You don't think he's gonna come calling when he hears a freakin' air hammer chiseling rock for an entire afternoon?"

'He will not come,' the Afrit interjected, surprising them both. 'As long as we are here, he will not risk leaving his den.'

"What are you saying?" Lotte tentatively asked. "Can Charun sense you... feel your presence as you can feel his?"

'Charun, as you call him, has now seen us, and like us, only an image is necessary to form a bond. We track each other even as we speak. As long as we stay here, Charun will not dare venture forth.'

"What does that mean? Doesn't he need sustenance? Can we simply wait here for him to starve to death, or become so weak that he can't fight as effectively?"

In the darkness, the pair could hear the swish of the creature's barbed tail as if flicked across the scrubby grass of the hill. *'Waiting is not an option. This... Charun... needs to feed on the energy of the creatures of your world to remain here, as do we. If we wait, we both will eventually starve. Already we have expended much valuable energy.'*

"Is there something you can... well... *feed* on? An animal, perhaps? Something that would give you strength to outlast Charun?"

The beast chortled. *'Give us the one who accompanies you. That one would last us nicely!'*

"Hey!" Eric cried. "Fine thanks for saving your miserable life with the fire I stoked at the last minute. Yes, you're welcome. No problem. Any time. Please come again."

"Eric, enough!" Lotte sternly said, then turned back to the Afrit. "No humans can be taken! That's not part of the bargain. In fact, it's expressly prohibited by our deal. Why would an animal not suffice?"

The creature stood silent for a time. When it replied, its voice seemed distant, as if it recalled memories more ancient than any human could comprehend. *'Once, we fed on those beasts given to us as spoils. From them, we learned, and we grew. Those creatures live on in us, in our form, in our structure. Once we consumed the likes of your kind, however, we expanded beyond the capacity to gain from the meagre power of those lesser beings. Something in your nature is strong. As the life drains from your weak, mortal bodies, that strength, that power, flows from you. It is now the sole reason we venture here. Nothing else in this dour world can nourish us. There is no longer a substitute.'*

"This is why Charun is killing our kind. The more he takes, the more powerful he becomes."

'Not quite. As you surmised, for us, once the power is taken, our material form is compromised. We need at least some time to absorb the energy, and this is best done by the Eternal Flame. If we do it elsewhere, much energy is lost. Long ago, we were forced to feed in this manner. In this way, we maintained our form, but at that time there were many creatures to which we had not been exposed, including your kind, that could provide us far more energy. So, with time, and exposure to these beasts, we grew, but even that reached a certain limit. Now, we could at best survive, even by feasting on those of your ilk. Your Charun is likely similar.'

"So it may be that he wants to return home, after all. Maybe if we set up the portal, we can convince him to go away?"

'Perhaps. *We know not what motivates this one. All we know is that we will starve if the one you seek is not confronted soon.*'

"All right, I understand. We have to lure Charun out, and we have to get him to come back here... back to the fires, and the portals. It'll also have to be done soon so you don't starve. If he can sense you, though, then you'll have to be far away, or he won't come out at all. And if you're far away, then you can't help us. So, that won't work."

All went silent while they contemplated the dilemma. To Eric, it seemed hopeless now that he knew Charun could track the Afrit as it could track him. Charun would simply stay in hiding until the Afrit left, and when he came out, they'd have no way to wrest the weapon from his hands, and would be as good as dead.

He looked up at the sky. Here, the stars seemed larger and far brighter, with so little light to block them out. He wished he could lie back in the grass, relax, and simply gaze up at them, forget this entire mess. He remembered reclining on the floor in the huge living room at 246 Holton Hill Road, when he and Lotte studied together. Periodically, he would look up. She smiled down at him from the couch where she lay on her stomach, chin rested in her folded fingers, feet in the air, as she read a book or worked on her laptop. Light streamed in from the great glass wall, soothing and warm. In those rare moments, he remembered his mind being at peace.

The great glass wall... hmmm....

Disregarding the consequences of offending the beast, because the alternatives all seemed far more terrible, he shot out a question. "What if you were mist? I saw you once, or a part of you, anyway. You were a shiny black cloud, grasping for the last sunlight of the day near the big glass wall in the house where we first... well... *met* you. You needed fire to assemble yourself. But as mist, you just billowed around. You seemed harmless."

"Eric!" Lotte said with awe. "That's brilliant!" She turned to the Afrit. "Are you conscious when you're in that form? Can you spread yourself so thin that Charun can't find you, can't track you? If so, you can be here! When Charun is close, we just need to light a powerful fire, like the burner on the gas stove. It didn't take long for at least that little part of you to form over the flame. Maybe we can hold out long enough, and when you've formed, you'll have the surprise you need."

The beast stood perfectly still. Even the swish of its tail in the grass ceased. The light of the stars and the thin moon caused its back and wings to sparkle, and outlined the monster's form as it stared into the abyss beyond.

'This is possible,' it finally said. 'In this state, our thoughts will become... vague, scattered. Thus, your Charun may not sense us. The doorway will still center us. Around it, we will cluster, and from its proximity we will not venture far. A large flame will allow us to re-assemble, and he may not notice we are there if his attention is on you. It could work.'

Eric did the simple math. "So, essentially, we're bait. The magnetism of the portal will probably get Charun's attention when you're out of the picture, but he'll be hungry. In the end, that's what will get him over here. Unless he really just feels like going home, which I somehow doubt."

Lotte nodded. "I agree. Maybe we can give him that option, step aside and hope he just... well... leaves. But I think you're right. I think we're the bait. So, it will be up to us to fend Charun off long enough that the Afrit can re-form and come to save us. It's a massive risk, but I don't see any great alternatives."

She turned to the Afrit. "It will take us most of the day to prepare the magnetic portal. Can you hold out that long, basically until around this time tomorrow? We'd send you back, but you need to guard us while we do the chiseling."

'We will survive for that period, but longer than this we shall not wait. It ends at the time you stated, no later — one way, or the other.'

On the last point, all seemed to be in complete agreement.

The pair rambled back to the house in the dilapidated, and now mortally wounded, white cargo van. Hunger, exhaustion, and anxiety all battled for supremacy in their minds. They had much to do, but could do little of it now. So, they ate, and they planned... Lotte in her particularly energetic and obsessive way.

"We need more starter fluid for the fires," she said, her mouth full of spaghetti, "and more paper as well. We might just want to bring wood from here rather than gather it. Mason had quite a stack chopped for the fireplace."

Saying Mason's name quieted her for a time.

"What do you make of this 'ones who judge' thing the Afrit mentioned?" Eric asked, trying to get her mind off all the details they'd have time to deal with tomorrow.

"It just keeps getting more unbelievable. This ties in nicely with my suspicion that at one time, someone, or something, was behind all of these portals. Same design, and now we discover the rings might have some power in enforcing the bargains. Were the originators the judges, or some other being they summoned or controlled? We simply don't know, but this is far more involved than I'd ever imagined."

"I guess this will keep you pretty busy, huh? Trying to hunt all these things down, figuring out all the mysteries behind them."

"It's hard to know. It may be these are the only two that I'll ever see. It was nothing short of a miracle that Mason and Emilia stumbled onto this one, or that it came to *my* attention. I have no idea if Werner Institut technology, or other technologies, could help locate these items. Many may be utterly destroyed. I just feel compelled to try. None of what I'll be learning can't be applied to other wonderful things. I'll do my hunting on the side, if necessary, come what may."

Compelled.

He wondered what it might be like to feel that way about something. The only thing that had ever come close to a compulsion in his life was his desire to be with Lotte, but even that seemed to have its limits... practicalities that, when confronted head on, always seemed to make him back down.

Intense attraction to a person, though, seemed different to him than having a sense of "calling" for some kind of career, some purpose so great, so interesting, so lucrative, so... whatever... that he'd pursue it despite the challenges or the obstacles. He'd simply never felt that passion. He usually found himself basically satisfied with whatever happened to come his way, like Schneider Industrial Flooring.

Maybe that's what I'm suited for. Maybe that's where I belong.

In that sense, Lotte's seemingly irresistible fixation with these artifacts posed an additional challenge to having any sort of relationship with her. As his dad had asked, even if he won her over, was that the life he really wanted? He'd be chasing these portals around all over the world, to countries with different customs, different languages, constantly dealing with new things, not to mention potentially risking his life if another one of these otherworldly monstrosities got free.

Being with Lotte would never be like it had been when they first met, back when things seemed simple and safe — once they'd been rid of the Afrit, of course. Those unusual circumstances brought them together, and they found common ground despite their different temperaments. Life had become far more complex now, and headstrong Lotte would do as she wished, seemingly to the exclusion of romantic entanglements, were Eric to believe what Mason had said.

Where do I fit into all of this? Where do I want to fit?

Despite the recent days with her, he still didn't know. She still made his heart leap. Just stirring a pot of soup, or making coffee, or talking with her mouth full of spaghetti, she captivated him. There were just so many obstacles, so many practicalities. There was such a wide gap in their approaches to life. He wanted her to want him, wholly, but she hadn't said anything about what might happen with their relationship when all this reached a conclusion—assuming they survived, that is. These concerns caused him to hold back, and he found himself, as always, stymied and paralyzed.

"In any case," she went on, mouth still full of food. "We should get extra propane as well, for the generator, and make sure we bring more food. We'll need to go to the store...."

So much for distracting her from the details.

He listened quietly as they finished their spaghetti.

With the Afrit's portal and its various cases gone, they reorganized the living room after dinner to its former order. Together, they made a fire, then she hopped into a big chair, threw the nice, thick blanket Eric had been using at night over her legs, and drank her herbal tea.

He lay on the couch and watched the flames.

They were quiet, as if knowing this might be the last moment of peace either would ever know. Periodically, he looked at her, and she flashed him her patented Lotte's Almost Kind-Of Smile. It looked like she felt happy, and sad, and comfortable, and nervous, all at the same time.

Just like old times.

With a calm that surprised him, he closed his eyes.

He woke to darkness. The fire had burned low, and the blanket lay across his outstretched form.

She no longer sat in the chair. He must have fallen asleep, and she'd slipped away.

Morning brought an instant bustle of activity. They had far too much to do to wait for the stores to open. After a rushed breakfast of oatmeal, they loaded the van and transported the magnetic portal, the generator, the propane tank, the air hammer, the drill, and as much firewood as they could load and transport, up the hill.

By 9 a.m., all the equipment lay strewn behind the small rise near the top of the mountain. They saw nothing of the Afrit, but both trusted that it lurked nearby. No one would benefit from Charun escaping to feed.

They picked a spot about thirty yards from the fire portal to set up the magnetic gateway, a bit down-slope from the little ridge where they'd set the fires. Here, a natural cairn of rock gave them the palette to carve out the recessed area for the doorway. Lotte made measurements and Eric marked the stones with the drill. The noise echoed in the small valley nestled between the three hills below. The police tape had still been draped across the entrance to the trails when they entered, so they hoped no one was around to hear. They'd just have to deal with that problem if it materialized.

After an hour or so of work, Eric had made some progress. A natural indentation in the stone face helped tremendously, and he estimated that by mid-afternoon the chiseling would be complete. They decided to hit the stores, which were likely open by now, and get the provisions they needed.

The Bailey Market wasn't particularly crowded on a Wednesday morning. They stocked up on lighter fluid and food for the long day ahead. When they got to the checkout lane, he noticed the woman behind the register had a name tag that read, "Trudie."

"Going on a picnic?" she asked, noticing all the food.

He smiled and tried to appear normal. "Oh, yeah. Picnic, hiking... we're on vacation."

Trudie shot a half-glance at Lotte. "Trails are closed for hiking. Some people have disappeared, and one's turned up *dead*!"

Don't we know it.

He nervously improvised. "Oh, we're not staying in this area. We're just passing through on our way to Maine. We like to shop local, and weren't sure we'd hit any more stores. So, we stopped here."

She smiled, "Well, we appreciate your business."

Knowing Trudie's association with the local police, and now that he felt that he'd kind of won her over, he decided to fish for a little information. "I noticed all the missing persons posters. Do the police have any clues?"

"Not many. They just found that one hiker. He was... well... it was a mess, let's just put it that way. They had all kinds of folks up there with dogs and stuff, but they couldn't find anything. They're trying to get a helicopter to come by, but it's such a huge area, and they have so little idea where to look, so the State is holding out. I think they're looking down by the old quarry now. Lots of shady folks hang out there."

Yeesh, a helicopter would be the last thing we need. "Well, I hope it gets resolved soon," he said as they bagged the groceries.

"Us too! The whole mountain is shut down. They're not even letting people up on the peak right now. Disaster for tourism during high season, but what are you gonna do? You all have a great day."

"We'll try."

Lotte surreptitiously grabbed an armful of local fliers on the way out. "Great starter material!" She smiled slyly.

A trip to the general store earned them a fresh cannister of propane for the generator, and soon they were back in their beaten vehicle on their way up to the trails.

They had just rounded the corner on New Speck Lane when Eric spotted a car coming in the opposite direction. As it got closer, he saw lights on the top. "That's a police car, probably Vern. He may have been up checking the police tape, maybe even the trail. Just keep your head down, and don't look at the car. I'm gonna pull into the dirt road toward the house so he doesn't know where we're going."

Incrementally, the two vehicles closed. Each slid toward the shoulder on the narrow street as they passed. A mustached man wearing sunglasses looked out from the police car. Eric plastered a smile on his face and forced his eyes to face forward. Once clear, he looked in the rearview mirror and watched as the police car slowed, then stopped by the side of the road.

"Shit!" He continued to drive at a gentle pace. The dirt road that led to Mason's house approached on the right. He made the turn and drove a short way in before he pulled over. "He's suspicious. This vehicle is out of place here. If he follows us, we're screwed. He might also stake out there for a while to see what we do. This is the last thing we need right now."

"What can we do?" she asked with growing alarm. "We can't stay here!"

"We'll have to go back to the house and hope Vern doesn't decide to investigate. If he does, we'll just have to tell him we're friends of Mason's and that he's out. His car isn't there, so at least that's plausible."

He drove the van the rest of the way to the cabin and parked.

They both went inside and sat at the dining room table alongside all of Mason's computer equipment, and apprehensively monitored the road from behind the curtains of the front window.

"What I don't understand," he said as they waited, "is why those dogs didn't find the bodies. They weren't *that* far from the trail. I mean, maybe that wasn't where the hiker was found. We certainly didn't see any sign of where the cops had been when we walked around, but don't dead bodies start to smell?"

She considered for a moment. "Normally, yes, they do, but do you recall smelling anything when we were up there?"

"I can't say I do. It's all kind of a blur, but you'd think that a body that had been dead so long would reek."

"Exactly. Those bodies didn't smell at all. It's almost as if they were... like... petrified. All the liquid had been drained out, like a mummy. That must be a side-effect of how Charun absorbs their energy. The Afrit burns, but Charun somehow drains them."

Eric's spine tingled. "If a helicopter comes, it may spot them. They're not exactly hidden. I'm not sure we want those bodies discovered, especially in that condition."

"We'll have to deal with that later, which will be even more difficult with this damned delay. When do you think we can go?"

"When Vern leaves," he replied, pointing his thumb out the window at the police car that had just pulled up near the end of the driveway. They watched anxiously as the car made a slow right, then pulled up behind the dirty and beaten white cargo van.

"*Verdammt!* Exactly what we *didn't* need. Come on, let's go outside and see what he wants. He can't possibly have any knowledge of what we've done. He's probably just fishing."

Eric opened the door, and Lotte led the way down the stone steps to where Vern, presumably, examined the van. It wasn't clear he saw the damage to the roof, as there were no windows anywhere but toward the front.

"Can we help you?" she called as she descended the stone stairs toward him, her frustration hidden behind a manufactured veil of geniality.

"Well, maybe," Vern replied, for now also maintaining what seemed to be a façade of politeness. "Saw your van here pass by on New Speck just now. Hadn't seen you folks before. We've had some disappearances around here, and to be honest, what looks like a murder. Just doing my job to check on anything unusual. You all visiting this house?"

"Yes, I'm a friend of Mason's from college. This is my friend. We were invited up to do some hiking and enjoy some time away from the city."

"And what city would that be?"

"Berlin."

"Berlin? That's just down the road."

"Berlin, Germany. I met Mason when he studied at Oxford. We worked in Italy together as well. Briefly."

Eric contained a snort of contempt.

"You folks have names?"

"I'm Lotte Schwarz. This is Eric Schneider." Eric waved and smiled, even though he felt like killing himself.

"Well, I'm Vern Deckard. I'm the deputy for Bailey and the surrounding area. I'm pleased to meet you. Can you tell me where Mason is?"

"Mason had to go to Berlin. Berlin near here, not Berlin, Germany. He's applying for an important position in Greece and needed a cell signal to be in contact with them. He may decide to just stay down there, and he could be gone for a couple of days."

"He's okay with you staying here?"

"He is. We're quite good friends. We have the week. We'll see him when he's, umm, back." Eric heard the strain in her voice as she lied. It wasn't so much that she lied to Vern, but rather that she knew Mason would never be coming back.

"This your van?"

"It's a rental," Eric responded. "I got it in Massachusetts, where I live. My car was too small to fit all the camping gear and what not. So, we got this. It was cheap."

Vern laughed. "Yeah, this thing has seen better days, that's for sure. Can you explain what happened to the roof?"

Shit!

"Yeah, the roof. Well, so, what happened was... it kind of started when... uh—"

"It was the storm," Lotte abruptly interrupted. "Two nights ago, that tremendous storm. A great tree branch fell right on the roof."

"That must have been some branch. Where the hell is it?"

"The boys dragged it off the roof of the car," she coolly replied. "Then they took it out back and chopped it up for firewood. That's what left of it, there." She pointed at the large tree limb that had landed on the windshield of Mason's SUV.

Vern examined the branch. It had marks and scratches which hopefully made it appear as if it had damaged the van. He looked back and forth a few times, trying to size up how such a strike to the vehicle might have occurred.

"That's some damn bad luck," he finally said, shaking his head. "You sure this didn't happen on the trails? Somebody's been joy riding up there. Looks like they blew right through our police tape and then tied it back together. Know anything about that?"

"We only know the trails are closed. Three days ago, on Monday, Mason took us up to go hiking there, but he saw your cars. I know he got out and talked with someone. Wasn't it you? He came back and told us the trails were shut down because of the investigation. Mason was quite upset about it because he knows Larry Henderson. He said we'd have to find another place to go because he didn't want to interfere with what the police were doing. That's as much as we know."

Vern sucked at his lower lip as he circled around. "Yeah, it was me Mason talked to. I saw him pull off. You were in his car, right?"

She nodded.

"Where'd you all wind up going?"

"We went to Maine," she lied with utter ease. "I really wanted to see Old Speck Mountain. I know that New Speck is a spur of that range, but Old Speck is larger. I heard the views from there were fantastic, and they were."

Where does she come up with this stuff? How can she just rattle off falsehoods that sound so utterly convincing? As always, he found himself equally impressed and jealous of her quick intelligence.

"What about Tuesday," Vern casually continued, seeming to test her credibility, or perhaps trying to wear her down.

"Actually, we wound up going to Berlin. We had some things to do in town and we had a nice dinner."

He rubbed his chin. "Hmmm, and what about yesterday?" This he asked with a bit more of an accusatory tone.

"Yesterday?"

"That's what I asked. Can you tell me where you were yesterday?"

"We went fishing with Ethan McCarthy. Then we came back here and cooked up what we caught. It was a lovely day."

"Yeah? Ethan drive you all up there in his car?"

"No, we followed him there. Ethan has a truck. It couldn't fit us all."

"Right! That old blue Dodge. How could I forget?"

"Actually, it was red, and it had the letters, G-M-C on the front. I don't know what that means, but I don't think it spells, 'Dodge.'"

"That's right," Eric added. "General Motors Corporation. Not a Dodge at all."

Vern stared at them. They couldn't see his eyes for the big, dark aviator sunglasses he wore, but he seemed to be squinting, sizing them up. "You're right," he finally said. "That's Bill Dickinson's blue Dodge. I get them confused. My bad. What'd you make of old Ethan?"

She carefully chose her words. "Well, he has some most *interesting* ideas. I heard things from him that... well... how can I say it... I've never heard before. He certainly gave us a fascinating experience."

He smiled. "Give me an example."

She stammered as she tried to make a show of being polite. "Well, it sounds so odd out of context, but there was something about spaceships and magnetic ray guns, botched experiments with contrails and weather, government conspiracies. I don't think he cares much for the Chinese, either. I'm sorry if he's your friend. I really mean no offense."

He turned his back to the pair and put his hands on his lower back. Then he tilted his head into the sky and began to laugh before he returned his attention to them with a huge grin on his face.

"No offense taken, young lady! Ethan must have liked you. Magnetic ray guns? Never heard shit like that before. Listen you two, I'm sorry for bustin' your chops. These missing people have everybody on edge. I saw you, and I had to check it out, especially with that damage to your roof I saw in the street back there. Mason's a buddy of mine. He told me about that Greek job thing when he applied a while back. Tell him I hope he gets it. He's a sharp kid, when he's not being an asshole. Just please stay off those trails for a few more days while this investigation wraps up, okay?"

Both of them nodded sincerely.

"So, I gotta run. I have to go help the Staties down by the quarry for the rest of the day. You all have a wonderful time here, and I hope we see you back again some time."

With that, he strode happily back to his car and drove off. Once he'd departed, they stood at the base of the stone steps and stared at the empty road.

"We are fucked!' Eric said with dismay and anger. "He has our names, he knows what state I live in, where you live. We lied to him about Ethan. Shit, we lied to him about *everything*! When Mason comes up missing, we'll be on America's Most Wanted. What the hell are we gonna do now, Lotte?"

"We'll finish what we started," she boldly replied as she turned toward the steps. "The consequences will be what they'll be. I simply won't let Charun take another soul, and if I have to rot in prison for that, so be it! We've lost precious time. Let's focus on what we need to do. We'll figure the rest out later."

He fumed. He hated this plan—really this *non-plan*—but now, like it or not, he knew his neck was on the line.

I guess I wanted a taste of what it means to be with Lotte, and here it is. Is this what I really want? Is this how I want my life to unfold? In the unlikely event we get out of this, is this really the future I'd choose... a life in prison to save the skins of a bunch of low-life drug dealers, or those hikers, or Larry Henderson, or Mason? Fuck! I hate you, Lotte Schwarz. I hate you, and I love you, and I hate you, and I love you. And I don't know what to do. I don't know what to do.

When they returned to the hill, Eric immediately resumed chiseling. He ate while he worked, and tried to vent his pent-up anger and frustration on the rock in front of him. Lotte spent time preparing a series of woodpiles along the little ridge, each a bit smaller than the large fire of yesterday, but still theoretically sufficient for the Afrit to send out a mighty blast when needed. She placed one of the fires near the Afrit's portal and positioned the bottle of lighter fluid nearby. The creature would have to re-form quickly.

While Eric worked on the lower portion of the indentation with the air hammer, Lotte used the drill to create holes for the marble-like pieces of smooth, black material that would create the actual doorway within Charun's frame. This saved time, and by late afternoon, the two had completed the recessed area where the portal would be assembled.

They placed the interlocking black stones around the perimeter. As before, iron in the rock caused them to snap into place. Carefully, the pair used the small spike that jutted out of each of the circular pieces to hook them into the drilled holes. These also held firm as they coupled magnetically with the stone.

"That just leaves the three pieces on the ground," she said. "I want to try something. Let's place the two outer pieces farther apart. If this works, it'll create a greater area for the magnetic field, and give us more room to work. If it fails, we'll just move them in until it activates. That way we'll know it's as big as it can be. It should form a large triangular area, or a semicircle if the field radiates slightly outward. We couldn't see it before in that crowded tent, but I think it will look almost exactly like the marble board at the base of the fire portal, just bigger. This cannot be a coincidence."

They placed the outer stones on their ceramic pedestals near the rock face. When ready, they would position the middle piece a short distance out, directly in front of the doorway, embedded in the stone cairn.

They sat together on a rock near the edge of the slope and surveyed their work. The portals were ready. The fires were prepared. It only remained to summon the Afrit and transform the creature into a thin cloud of misty, and hopefully undetectable, ash. Then they would activate the magnetic portal and hope it attracted Charun, and that he would come.

Then, they would pray that nothing went wrong.

CHAPTER 16

The exhausted duo ate a couple of power bars to sustain their energy, and took some time to rest in the wake of the afternoon's exertion.

Neither spoke, but Eric felt comfort from his estranged friend's presence. Naturally, her instincts had been right. With few other options, they'd needed to focus on the task at hand. With that realization, most of his anger and confusion had faded.

We'll deal with Vern and the police if and when that problem comes. It will all be moot anyway if we don't survive, and given that we're essentially bait, that's a pretty realistic possibility.

Whatever happened, he wanted what might be his last moments with her to be peaceful. He felt calm and oddly happy, when she got up close to 6:00 p.m. and lit one of the fires on the ridge to summon the Afrit. The creature again rose promptly out of the trees below, swooped in, and settled gently near them. It still hobbled slightly on its weakened leg, but otherwise appeared ready for the task ahead.

"We've prepared the magnetic portal," she said. "Once you've assumed your cloud-like form, we'll activate it. When Charun comes, one of us will distract him while the other lights the fire near your portal for you to re-assemble, and those in the bowls so they're ready for you to absorb his energy and return to your home. Assuming he doesn't detect you, you'll likely have the advantage of surprise. With luck, we can hold out long enough that we also survive. Understood?"

'*We understand,*' the Afrit confidently replied. With that, the ashen creature walked to the fire and straddled it. After a few moments, wisps of black, mist-like ash began to trail from the monster's form. With exposure to the flame, more and more of the beast soon swept into what rapidly became a shimmering cloud.

As the last of the creature dissolved into mist, the cloud spread in all directions, blown on the mild wind. Eventually, all that remained visible were stray, shining particles, hardly noticeable in the diminishing light of the sun as it lowered to the west.

The two kicked at the fire and poured on dirt to douse the flames.

After about five minutes, Lotte looked in the air. "I think it's spread out as much as it can be. It's time to activate the magnetic portal and see if Charun comes out. Are you ready?"

No, I'm not really ready, but how do you actually get ready for something like this? Guess I'm as ready as I'll ever be.

To his surprise, he still felt calm. He simply nodded.

They walked downslope to the magnetic portal set in its cairn of stone. She lifted the final piece on its ceramic stand and transported it to the central point of the triangle, or the arc, depending on how one perceived it. She set the base in the ground and slowly rotated it toward the doorway embedded in the rock.

Just as the curved rectangular object came to directly face the obsidian frame of the passageway, the low humming noise they'd heard before again commenced. The ground vibrated, and sound echoed slightly in the little valley below.

"Louder than I remembered," she remarked. "Not so much louder than the air hammer, though. I just hope nobody's around to hear it. I think this valley sort of sucks up a lot of the noise. At least I hope it does."

The portal began to glow. Its blue-white light emanated from the circular pieces set within the frame and radiated in an arc-like pattern between the doorway and the three stones on the ground. The luminous pattern in the area between all the components of the gateway exactly mirrored the black marble slab of the fire portal.

Shocker, Lotte was right again.

The two waited anxiously on the grassy slope. Their attention alternated between the portal, which had now become a blaze of white light on the rock face behind the bluish hue of the magnetic arc, and the double hillock where they hoped Charun would emerge from his lair.

Fifteen minutes passed, then thirty. Finally, Lotte thought she saw something over her shoulder. "Eric, grab the binoculars! I think's he coming."

He quickly complied and scanned the double hillock. It didn't take long before he spotted movement in the trees not far from where he'd observed Charun previously emerge. "There! That's got to be him. Go check on the bowls near the fire portal. Make sure everything's good and that nothing fell over while we were waiting. We won't have a second chance to get this right."

She scurried over the small rise that separated the two portals from view of each other. He continued to monitor the horizon and detected more movement in the trees, slightly closer.

He's being cautious.

He hoped Charun couldn't detect the Afrit, but doubted he would have emerged from his lair if he could. He kept his eyes peeled for any sign of the beast.

"Eric," Lotte softly called from behind him.

"What? Everything good back there?"

"Eric, please turn around."

"I can't! I'm watching for Charun. I don't want him surprising us."

"Eric, really, I insist. You have to turn around."

"I insist too, Eric. Turn the fuck around!"

Eric's blood ran cold as he recognized Vern's voice. Slowly and reluctantly, he lowered the binoculars and turned to face him. The deputy stood behind Lotte, gun drawn. He still wore his sunglasses, but Eric could tell his disposition was far uglier than it had been this morning.

"You two little fucking liars!" he spat. "I took a photo this morning of that police tape on the trees. I got done with the Staties a couple of hours ago, came to check if anybody had messed with it, and, sure enough! Tied differently on one side. Came in to see what I could see, followed some fresh-looking tire tracks up the slope, and dammed if I didn't run smack into your fucking piece of shit white van."

Eric sort of took offense at that. Yeah, it was a piece of shit, but it was *their* piece of shit. Plus, it was where Mason had met his end. He'd oddly come to appreciate the dirty old thing, which had served them well on what would most likely turn out to be its final journey. At the moment, he feared the van might not be alone in facing the end.

"I was looking around for you two when I heard that noise." Vern nodded back at the magnetic portal that still hummed low and loud.

Eric guessed he'd come up the way Mason had taken them the first time they climbed this hill. He must have come up behind Lotte and surprised her as she inspected the bowls and candles.

This is not in the plan.

Vern motioned with his hand. "Get away from the edge and come over here! You too, missy. What in the Sam Hell is this contraption, and what is that big glass frame back there?" He pointed over his shoulder, past the rise leading to the fire portal, as he backed both of them up to the magnetic doorway.

Eric frantically looked past the deputy to the horizon, in search of Charun, but saw nothing.

"I could tell you," Lotte said with resignation, "but you'd never believe us. We'd sound like Ethan McCarthy, completely out of our minds."

"Try me!" he shouted as he waved his gun at the pair. "It better be good, though, 'cause right now, you two are the prime suspects in two murders and at least two disappearances."

Two murders. They must have found the body in the quarry building this afternoon. Lucky them. Bet it smelled awful.

"Vern," she said, with as soothing a tone as she could manufacture. "Calm down and listen. Time is incredibly short. I know how this looks, so I'm not going to lie to you. The device you see behind us is a portal to another world. It's summoned an ancient being who's responsible for the murders and disappearances. The people who've disappeared are dead, as are others you know nothing about."

"Jesus, Ethan would love this shit! So, who let this thing out? You two?"

"No, it was Mason. Actually, Mason's girlfriend. She did it by accident. She didn't know what she was doing. Now she's dead as well. Mason called me to help him figure out what was going on. We realized we needed to find the creature and send it home, and that's what we're trying to do right now."

"If that's true, where the fuck is Mason? Did he just leave you to do his dirty work?"

"Mason is dead too. The beast took him the day after you saw him, like the others who've disappeared. Their bodies are on one of the hills behind you. The monster drained them and ate their energy. He has a lair somewhere in that double hillock on the other side of the stream. But at this moment, he's coming our way. We're all in incredible danger. You have to let us act to stop the thing before he arrives. Please, believe us!"

Vern took a few steps back, quickly glanced behind him, then returned his focus on the pair where they stood before the magnetic portal. "I don't see shit! I think you're lying. I think that glowing thing behind you is some kind of weapon, and if I take my eyes off of you or let you do anything, you'll use it on me! We're gonna walk back to my car, and I'm taking you two in. Get marching!" He directed with his gun back up the hill.

He doesn't realize the grassy slope would be easier, but I don't think it's gonna matter now.

Eric watched in horror as Charun silently ascended behind Vern from the steep slope below.

He must have gone through the trees. I might have spotted the movement with the binoculars if I'd been near the ledge. Now he's right on top of us. Damn!

Charun still bore the marks of the battle the day before: a deep gouge in his abdomen, shoulders horribly scarred, beak cracked and broken, like a slab of marble violently struck with a hammer and chisel. The bird-like being's wings flapped slowly and silently as he hovered and cautiously surveyed the scene. As always, he held his massive obsidian hammer tightly to his chest.

He seemed curious, but wary. Surely, the magnetic portal had attracted his attention, but he didn't get any nearer to it. Most likely, he also feared the return of the Afrit. Little did he know the creature billowed nearby in its mist-like form. In this sense, their plan appeared to have worked. Unfortunately, neither of them were in a position to light the fire that would allow the ashen monster to reassemble and come to their aid.

Lotte finally found her voice. "No, Vern, we're not going anywhere. Walk slowly toward us. Don't turn around."

He laughed. "Yeah, that old trick. Don't turn around, he's right behind you! Sure. You think I'm a goddamned idiot? I said, move! Now! Stop dilly-dallying and... and... what the fuck?"

A great shadow cast across the grassy slope. Charun had drifted forward, attracted in all likelihood by Vern's angry words. The confused deputy started to turn, but before he could look behind, Charun grabbed him with one powerful arm. Vern screamed as the beast held him aloft and touched the head of his hammer lightly to his victim's skull.

The mighty weapon began to glow. Its blue-white radiance echoed that of the portal which shone brightly behind them. Eric watched in horror as the light from the hammer enveloped the deputy's head. His screams intensified, but then abruptly ceased as his upper body became rigid. His fingers splayed in agony, and his feet kicked uselessly in the air as Charun absorbed the life force from his paralyzed body.

"He's feeding!" Lotte screamed. "We have to stop him!"

"It's too late! He's had it. Go light the fire and the candles in the bowls. Maybe Charun will be distracted while he eats, and won't notice. The Afrit said it takes time to absorb energy. It's the only thing we can do!"

She took a fraction of a second to assess the situation, then seemed to decide he was right. She ran back to the fire portal and disappeared over the little ridge. Charun seemed oblivious to all but his intake of sustenance. Vern began to look like the corpses they'd seen on the hill. His skin turned grayish white, and his body became skeletal.

The glow from the hammer now enveloped him from the waist up. The wounds on Charun's beak, shoulders, and stomach began to heal. As more energy flowed in, the cracks and deep gashes smoothed over, as if being magically caulked.

Finally, the monster emitted a triumphant screech from its hooked beak, and the radiance from the hammer ceased. He then raised Vern's desiccated body into the air and tossed him casually aside to the dirt below.

The former deputy lay in grisly repose, his empty eyes staring blindly at Eric and the portal behind him.

For a time, the fearsome being hovered meditatively, wings softly beating to keep him aloft. His flesh and feathers rippled and surged, alive with replenished energy that now coursed throughout the structure that sustained him in this alien realm.

Eric watched. *He's absorbing Vern, just like the Afrit said. He's getting more powerful every second. I have to do something.*

He stepped forward.

With a lightning-fast flick of his neck, Charun turned his head and focused his fiery, hawk-like eyes directly at Eric. Slowly, the ancient Etruscan demi-god lowered himself to the earth. His wings twitched before he settled them gracefully on his shoulders.

Eric returned Charun's gaze. He stood his ground, hands behind his back. He dared the monster to come to him, come to where he stood, now just a few feet from the glowing perimeter of the magnetic portal.

If I'm the bait, then the portal is the hook, and the Afrit's the fisherman who's gonna have to time his pull perfectly, or else our prize fish here will slip the line. I just have to hold out long enough for the fisherman to show up.

It might have been only seconds, but to Eric, it felt like an eternity as the two locked eyes.

Finally, Charun stepped toward him. Eric didn't move, and the beast took another step, then another. The gap closed, and the mighty avian monster raised his hammer.

Uh oh. Looks like he's full and just wants to smash my head in. Hopefully, he's eaten his last meal. If this is it for me, then mine might have been a power bar. Peanut butter. That's a weird-ass last meal. It wasn't actually that bad, though.

Charun came upon him and began to swing the terrible black hammer over his shoulder.

If the blow connected, Eric knew his head would be imbedded deep into his chest with a single ferocious strike. From behind his back, he pulled out one of the guns he'd taken from the shed where Mason had left it, in a box on the shelf next to the old volleyball that had deflated to a sad, sagging mass of dirty white rubber. He'd hidden it in his belt, under his trusty Celtics t-shirt, so thankfully Vern hadn't seen it.

He aimed, and then fired. It was point blank range. He couldn't miss, even though he'd never fired a gun before. The recoil surprised him, as did the result of his strike.

Charun stumbled backward and grasped at his throat. The bullet had found its way into the beast's beard, and then to his neck. He didn't drop his hammer, but the head of the weapon plunged into the dirt as he staggered.

Eric fired again. This time he aimed for the face. His aim was a bit high, but the bullet found its mark. Splinters flew from the monster's snakelike crest.

Charun howled in pain and confusion and again lurched backward, wildly shaking his head.

Once more, Eric stepped forward and took aim.

Despite the creature's agony, he acted with speed and cunning. He dropped to his knees, grabbed the head of his hammer, and swept out with the handle.

It took Eric by surprise, and the powerful strike cracked painfully against his left calf. The blow toppled him, and the gun discharged into the air as he landed hard on his back. A sharp rock jabbed agonizingly into his left shoulder blade as it tore into his flesh.

Charun still reeled from the bullet wounds, but seemed to rapidly regain his bearings.

With sheer force of will, Eric lifted his upper body on his elbows and scooted backward toward the magnetic portal. Pain shot maddeningly through his shoulder and leg. He feared he wouldn't be able to stand.

Just as he began to try to get to his feet, Charun stepped forth, massive hammer-head thrust forth as it led the way.

Having no other real option, Eric aimed and fired again.

Charun flinched, and a loud *clank* sounded as metal seemed to hit metal. The beast paused and inspected the head of the hammer, on which a flattened bullet now clung. With a slight twitch of the weapon, the missile slipped harmlessly from where it had struck and fell to the ground. Charun then extended the hammer once more and menaced forward.

Eric fired again, but his gun made only a clicking sound, its chamber and cartridge empty.

Charun now loomed above him. The beast's hawk-like eyes stared down, void of emotion, like those of a bird of prey. With one clawed foot, he stepped down and locked his iron-hard talons around Eric's right leg and pinned him to the ground.

Again, the mighty Etruscan demi-god raised his hammer. This time, Eric knew he had no escape from the brutal blow that would pulp his skull and drive it deep into the earth where he lay.

"Charun!" Lotte suddenly shouted from the little rise near the fire portal. "I'm here, Charun! I know who you are. I know all about you, you who escort the dead. Come for me, Charun. This one is nothing. I burn with great power. Come taste of me. I dare you!"

The monster hesitated. His hammer wavered in the air, raised above his snakelike crest. The thick fibers of his muscled biceps flexed and pulsated, and the crooked, vulture-like wings quivered as he pondered what she'd said.

Can he even understand us?

Eric had never felt any thoughts emanating from the enigmatic monstrosity. He began to understand this creature bore little resemblance to the Afrit, incomprehensible and supremely terrible.

Lotte's gambit had been well played, but it wasn't enough to sway Charun. With a flick of his head, he returned his fiery gaze to Eric, who still lay on his back, locked in the beast's inescapable grip. With deliberation, the monster hoisted his terrible hammer into striking position. Then, he reached back, as if to add momentum to his blow, as if he wanted this swing to not simply pulp, but utterly pulverize and obliterate whatever dared stand in his way.

He swung.

The hammer reached high noon above his frightful head, with its snake-like crest, vulture-like beak, and murderous gaze.

Eric shut his eyes.

He felt an impact... a terrible impact.

Something slammed into his chin, and he painfully bit into his tongue and gums. The taste of blood assailed him, but with the torturous sting came the assurance that he still lived.

He noticed his foot had been freed of the monster's muscular talons, and heard a massive commotion above where his head lay, back toward the portal. He put aside the throbbing in his mouth, as well as the sharp contusion on his chin, and lifted himself onto his elbows. His shoulder screamed in agonizing protest, yet still he turned his head to see what had happened.

Charun lay prone on the ground. His wings flapped feebly as he rocked from side to side, apparently stunned. The blow must have come from behind, some sort of great collision that drove the monster over Eric's immobilized body and toward the portal.

Eric raised himself a bit more and, with wide eyes, saw the hammer.

It had been thrown into the portal's glowing magnetic field by the impact, no longer the gargantuan weapon it had been. Rather, the small, T-shaped, black rock floated in the dead center of the arced area of radiance. It hovered about twenty inches from the ground, rotating and incrementally picking up speed.

He suddenly felt Lotte crouch by him where he lay.

She put her hand on his shoulder. "*Alter!* Are you hurt? Can you move?"

He spat blood, and tried to speak clearly over the wound on his tongue "I'm definitely hurt. Help me up and I'll test my leg. That's the only thing that will keep me from moving."

She reached under his shoulder and started to lift.

"*Ahhhh*, damn!" he yelled. "Not that side! A rock cut me bad. The other side."

She shifted to his right and repeated the maneuver. This time they had more success, and he struggled up to his feet. He gingerly tested his left leg. Fortunately, the blow seemed to have hit him in the fleshy part of the calf. It would bruise, and it hurt like hell, but it wouldn't keep him from walking.

"Okay, let's go get the hammer," he breathlessly said.

They turned to face the portal.

In front of them, Charun had risen to his hands and knees. He beat his wings, trying to right his body, as he furtively and frantically looked to his left.

The Afrit approached, fully formed and seemingly ready for battle. The ashen creature still limped slightly, but that didn't slow the beast as it closed on its flagging opponent.

"We'll have to get around Charun to get to the hammer and hold it in place," Eric said, as he started to make his way to the left, where the Afrit might offer some protection. They proceeded cautiously, and Lotte still supported him under his right arm. Both kept an eye on the semi-prone monster, should he recover and attack.

"Look!" She pointed at the struggling demi-god.

He held his clawed hand outstretched. His palm faced the portal, and the hammer, which rotated ever faster in the center of the magnetic field. He jerked his wrist back in a quick motion, and expectantly waited for the T-shaped stone to fly to him as it had before, but the obsidian hammer didn't budge or stop spinning.

"He can't call it out of the magnetic field!" Lotte shouted joyously. "It's too strong for him! Eric, I think we have him. Let's stand back and see what the Afrit does." With that, they simply backed up toward the ledge, near where Vern's ruined form still lay.

The Afrit saw that Charun intended to retrieve his weapon, and the ashen monster surged toward its foe where he floundered, and tried to secure him in its muscular talons.

Charun used his wings to help him hop to safety a short distance away.

Undeterred, the Afrit again approached. It lurched once more, but the move proved to be a feint. When Charun tried to dance away, the beast quickly adjusted the direction of its strike, propelled itself forward with a huge sweep of its wings, and rammed into its adversary's side. After the violent crash, they both struggled and grasped at one another as they tumbled in the rocky soil.

Charun emerged victorious and gained the upper position. He brought his forearm down hard on the Afrit's neck and ground the beast into the ground. With the thick claws on his free hand, he repeatedly raked at his opponent's exposed abdomen.

The Afrit vigorously thrashed against the onslaught as black soot flew from the compound wounds and clouded the air. Then, seeming to gain its wits, the ashen monster extended its arms wide and, with a tremendous crash, brought its clawed hands together on either side of its foe's skull. The Afrit's talons embedded themselves in Charun's deathly blue flesh. One of them cut perilously close to his left eye, and the Etruscan monster shrieked in pain and terror.

Using his superior weight and strength, the Afrit threw the bird-like creature aside, and without hesitation began to repeatedly slam Charun's head into the rocky soil with all its might. Each impact sounded a forceful and ghastly thump. Large hunks of the snakelike strands on the monster's crest flew off as if shot from a catapult, and landed in a spray of debris. The tip of the monster's beak broke off with a sickening crack that sounded like a thigh bone being broken cleanly in two.

No howl of pain accompanied that frightful and merciless blow. Charun lay limp, face down in the dirt and rocks, now littered with the dislocated and unhinged parts of his own skull and face. The Afrit rolled its barely conscious opponent onto his back and the gruesome damage revealed itself fully. The once mighty being cast his gaze sightlessly into the rapidly darkening sky. His hand still twitched impulsively, palm outward, as it groped toward his weapon — the epicenter of his power.

It would not come to him. The T-shaped stone now spun in a haze at the center of the magnetic arc. The portal hummed even more loudly, and the blue-white glow had further brightened. The doorway looked like a tiny sun, hard to view directly for its intense radiance.

The Afrit rose and bellowed in triumph. The mighty cry echoed in the valley. The jet-black monster then looked down, and almost tenderly lifted its stunned and listless foe in its massive, muscular arms.

Charun weakly protested, pressing his hands uselessly against the Afrit's enormous chest.

This posed no obstacle. The Afrit soon had Charun's limp body in its grasp. It turned toward the fire portal and strode victoriously forward to claim its well-deserved spoils.

Lotte and Eric followed behind, and watched as Charun continued to weakly flail and push in futility against his captor. Without his hammer, he seemed powerless to fight back. The beating the Afrit dealt him appeared to have drained more energy than he'd previously absorbed from the hapless Vern. The battle had come to an end. The Afrit, with their assistance, had won.

The ashen monster strode over the little ridge and made for its doorway. Eric saw that the candles already burned, five strong in each bowl. Lotte had likely lit them after she'd ignited the flame that the Afrit used to reconstitute itself. With little wind, all still brightly flickered, and the *Alkuartiz Alnaar* glowed with glorious warmth. The portal stood ready to receive the Afrit, once the creature had absorbed the energy of the dying Charun and returned to ashen mist.

The exhausted and overwhelmed duo gathered at the apex of the black marble board. They watched in reverent silence as the Afrit carried the body of its victim toward the frame bearing the glass, then turned and held him over the flames.

Slowly, the monster guided Charun's weakened body forth. His disfigured beak opened in a grotesque pantomime of the formerly glorious and terrifying visage he'd once projected. Falteringly, his hands fell from the Afrit's mighty chest. He continued to paw uselessly in the air, but then....

He stopped.

He examined his palms.

"Oh, *Scheiße!*" Lotte whispered in horror. "They're black!"

For a moment, Eric couldn't tell what she was talking about, but then he saw it too. Charun's palms were black where they had pressed against the Afrit's body.

"So what?" he asked, not understanding her concern. "What does that mean?"

She turned to him with a look of panic. "It means the ash of the Afrit is magnetic!"

With a final and desperate burst of energy, Charun plunged his hands back at his captor. One touched the Afrit's arm, the other caught one of the goat-like horns. Then, he pulled... not with his strength, but with a force within him. It was like the force that called the hammer, a powerful magnetic force.

It rippled visibly through the Afrit's body, and had an instantaneous effect. The ashen beast froze in place, and then began to shake. Its pumice-like skin pulsated and boiled. Soon, the hazy black mist again appeared around the monster, but unlike before, when the particles had taken lightly to the sky, the ash now sputtered and gushed lifelessly toward the ground. It reminded Eric of the imp Afrit they'd dispatched all those years ago.

The powerful magnetic force that Charun exerted held his adversary frozen in place as it disrupted and destroyed the creature's inner structure. The Afrit couldn't reach out to the flame that might bring it salvation.

They watched with dread as the beast dismantled into dust.

Its weakened left leg collapsed first, and both beings tumbled to the ground, but Charun clung firm. Without removing his hands, he repositioned himself above his supine and immobilized enemy, grasping it by the shoulders.

The Afrit rocked and quavered as more parts disintegrated before their disbelieving eyes. The creature's wings withered to dust, as did its legs. Likewise, the one goat horn that Charun had originally grasped, one complete arm, and the lower part of another, all fell to bits—save a thin strand that connected to the talon that still bore the bent golden bracelet. Black ash gathered in a great heap where the Afrit had once stood triumphant.

To their surprise, just as it seemed the ancient and mysterious creature would disappear into the dust from whence it came, Charun let go and shakily rose to his feet.

What remained of the Afrit's mutilated head and torso wriggled grotesquely on the ground.

Charun swayed unsteadily over the body, obviously still horribly dazed. He yet bore the terrible wounds of the immense thrashing he'd received. With a flick of his neck, he looked at the rise, and back in the direction of the magnetic portal. Ignoring the panic-stricken mortals who had scooted back from the scene of destruction, he slowly and painfully took one step forward, then another, then another.

"He's going after his hammer!" Lotte said with alarm. "I think he wants to absorb what's left of the Afrit. Come on, we have to stop him! I have an idea."

Eric felt her grab his hand and pull him to him to his feet, then back toward the still humming and glowing magnetic portal. Pain shot through his leg as they dashed, and his shoulder burned agonizingly with every stride.

Even at a slow run, they easily beat the tottering Charun to the gateway. She fumbled in her pocket, and finally produced the two silver spiral rings, each tipped at both ends with a small round stone of the same black magnetic material from which the portal was constructed. She stood behind the central of the three stones on the ground and slipped the smaller of the two rings onto her finger, next to the gold ring that bound her pact with the Afrit.

Wow, one more and she'll be just like Tom Brady. Unless he wins more Super Bowls, that is.

"Stand over there," she pointed to her left, "out of the way. Let me handle this. I think I can bargain with him, send him home."

He did as she asked, but hovered near the rim of the magnetic arc so he'd be nearby in case of trouble.

Soon, the grievously wounded Charun laboriously staggered over the little rise and down the hill. If he noticed them, he gave no indication. His attention appeared to have locked in on the T-shaped stone that now whirred in a blur of motion in front of the intense glow of the doorway.

The moment he crossed the perimeter of the magnetic arc, Lotte spoke. "Charun, stop! You have to bargain with me! If you don't, one of us will destroy this portal, and you'll never get home. Don't you want to return to your world? You must be tired of constantly having to feed. We can bargain, and you can go back. That's the way of things, isn't it?"

Astonishingly, Charun did stop. He flicked his neck and turned his decimated face toward her. His shoulders slumped, and his eyes no longer burned with hawk-like intensity. Slowly, he opened his broken beak, and a song more beautiful than any earthbound bird issued forth. His message was incomprehensible, but like the Afrit's horrid tongue, the pair heard his words clearly in their minds, his psychic tone as beautiful and demure as his audible call.

'Bargain? I do not need to bargain with you. You did not summon me. That one, I took. She did not understand. You? You understand, but why would I now need to bargain? I am free.'

"You *are* free, but at what cost? You feed constantly, simply to maintain your form in our world. What kind of existence is that? Until this moment, you couldn't have returned to your world. You need us. We can operate and maintain the portal. Go through it now. Return to your world. Rest. Recover. We'll talk again in the future."

His head flitted from left to right before he again opened his beak and spoke, his song even more beautiful and compelling. *'Return? Recover? Positive. Negative. The poles do not align any longer. Once we were complete opposites who completed each other, attracted and perfectly harmonized. Now we fight for the scraps of our Zone, which can barely sustain one, let alone two. She is almost dead. My departure saved her. I cannot return. I will not return!'*

Eric watched as Lotte wracked her brain, trying to parse the creature's words. Just as she seemed about to give up hope, realization appeared to dawn on her.

"Vanth! The one you speak of is Vanth."

'You know her as Vanth, yes. Once, we inhabited The Zone in complete balance. Positive. Negative. Our attraction made us inseparable, but then, we were summoned. We each grew fat from the power we extracted from your kind, but like the wings of the birds of this world, whose form we first assumed, The Zone is a fragile and delicate realm. It could no longer sustain two of that size. Then, you ceased to call for us. Why? Over millennia, we had to battle for supremacy, fight for the scraps of what power remained to feed us. I emerged the victor, but I could not let her dissolve into nothingness. She is positive. I am negative. Once, we completed each other's circles. So, I nourished her as I could... kept her alive, if you can call the state of weakness and misery in which she exists living. I waited to be summoned again. Now, after countless cycles, it has happened, and with no bargain, I am free! The hunting here is good. I can survive. She whom I love can rule The Zone. It is the only way.'

"I can't believe you don't want to go back and see her, even for a just short time. We can help you. We can send you back, then recall you, so each of you can live, but still be in each other's presence."

'A compelling offer, but tell me, raven-haired mortal, where have your kind been for such a great time? While we battled and suffered because of the curse that your ancestors inflicted upon us, where were you? Even if your word is good, your life is so short. Time seems to take turns that no mortal can predict. To be locked away again is impossible. Even if I believed you, which I am not certain I do, it is unthinkable to take such a risk. Things change. Vanth has been dead to me for countless mortal lifetimes, a husk of her once vibrant and awe-inspiring form. Letting her live is the final gift I can offer. I will make my way in this world, until my time is done.'

With that, the mighty Etruscan demi-god turned toward the whirring hammer and stepped deeper into the magnetic field. He still stumbled from fatigue, exhaustion, and damage from the battle. He likely hadn't had time to fully assimilate Vern's energy, and without his hammer, had clearly received nothing from the Afrit. Now, however, his weapon was almost in his clutches. If he retrieved it, Eric knew that he and Lotte, and whatever might be left of the Afrit, were surely history, and that was intolerable.

With all his might, Eric ran straight at Lotte.

She looked to her left and saw him coming, and their eyes locked, hers with a look of shock and uncertainty.

He smiled and looked at her, and saw a girl dressed all in black, sitting on a low stone wall, reading a book and intentionally ignoring him while he examined her darkness. From that moment, her black sun had been a constant presence in his life.

When they almost touched, when they almost saw beyond the fleeting moment they so fleetingly experienced, when they nearly looked straight through each other's eyes and directly into each other's souls, he turned away.

Hard left. He had the momentum he needed.

She screamed behind him.

He didn't care.

Charun was just about to pick up the spinning hammer when Eric looped around and crashed full force into him. It felt like slamming into a bag of rocks, but in his target's weakened state, Eric drove the tottering avian toward the now sun-bright doorway of the portal.

It stood open. All he had to do was force Charun through.

I can do it. He's weak. He can barely stand, let alone resist, and I have surprise on my side. He pushed with all his might, and they both plunged toward the intense blue-white light.

It almost worked.

At the last possible second, Charun reached out and braced his hands on the interlocked obsidian stones of the door frame.

Try as he might, Eric couldn't push him through. Finally, in frustration, he grabbed the weakened beast by the waist and threw him to the ground. Desperately, he looked for a rock with which he could continue to bash-in the miserable creature's disfigured head, and finish the job the Afrit had started.

However, with superhuman speed and quickness, Charun grabbed his leg.

Despite the monster's weakness, he was still faster and stronger, and Eric again found himself immobilized. He remembered his encounter with the biker and elbowed the beast in the eye as he rose to strike.

Remarkably, that caused Charun to let go.

Eric plunged past the monster and nearly reached the perimeter of the arced field. He thought he'd broken free, but there, Charun tripped him and spilled him headfirst onto the dirt. He grabbed a rock and turned just in time to avoid a blow from the angry monster. He threw the stone, but it glanced uselessly off Charun's shoulder.

Then, behind the menacing creature, something moved.

Lotte had jumped with both feet on the small, spinning hammer. It now sat motionless under her Euro-style black Adidas sneaker with red stripes. She grabbed the T-shaped stone and ran full speed at the portal.

Charun didn't see her. He focused on Eric, and prepared the killing strike as he raised his claw-like foot over his erstwhile challenger's chest.

Eric braced for the impact, but it wasn't the impact he expected.

Lotte dove for the portal. She shielded her beautiful dark eyes from the dazzling glow with her free hand, and with a primal scream drove the obsidian stone directly into the center of the radiance.

The low hum began to vacillate.

Distracted by the change in sound, Charun turned his head.

It gave Eric a millisecond to roll to his side before the beast's talons came crashing down. One claw still scratched painfully across his back, but he avoided the full brunt of the blow.

The frequency of the hum quickly ranged from a high squeal to a sub-sonic and inaudible vibration. The luminous glow oscillated: bright, dark, bright, dark, white, blue, white, blue. Charun suddenly winced and writhed in pain as the magnetic field in the arced area began to collapse. The creature tried to move to the perimeter, but like the Afrit, he found himself frozen in place.

As the intensity of the field's oscillation increased, Charun began to literally come apart in the competing poles of the magnetic maelstrom. His legs swept to the left as his upper body tore toward the right. The two halves of the beast were ripped apart and began to disintegrate into the fluctuating magnetic glow. Rapidly, he dissolved into energy as he screamed in terror and pain through his disfigured beak, the last part of Charun that Eric could make out. The great Etruscan demi-god had been lost in the alternating light of the field.

Then, without warning, the portal exploded outward.

Eric saw Lotte, who still held onto the T-shaped hammer within the shining light of the magnetic doorway, until the blast violently threw her backward. She landed hard near the central stone on its ceramic stand, and her head bounced unnaturally on the rocky ground. The obsidian block in its clay stand shattered like black glass into a million pieces, and the other parts of the portal quickly followed suit. They created a crashing cacophony that left no stone intact, and ended only when the infernal hum finally ceased.

The concussion of the collapsing magnetic field flattened Eric's body sharply against the ground. His ears rang, and for a time he lay still, only semi-conscious. He fought to open his eyes, but the world spun around him, and his stomach lurched.

He tilted his head to the left, to Lotte, who lay sprawled on her back, hands wide at her sides. Blood streamed from her nose and dripped from her cheeks into the dirt, and into the scattered remnants of the shattered portal stones. The T-shaped object had disappeared, vanished into the portal, and likely had caused its destruction.

He tried to roll onto his side, tried to drag himself to her, but he couldn't move. The ringing in his ears intensified.

He realized that he looked into two suns: one orange as it set in the western sky, one black, yet eternally radiant as she lay unconscious, or perhaps dead.

His eyes closed, and everything went dark.

CHAPTER 17

Central Etruria, 539 BC

Rika cupped her hand around the lamp that sat on the windowsill and blew out the flame. Darkness enveloped their chamber in the great tower, punctuated only by the dim light of the moon and stars. She hardly needed the illumination. She could navigate this space with eyes closed, having lived here since its construction, first alone, and then for nearly forty summers with Abirami and their children.

Her heart raced with thoughts of her offspring. She heard little from Arnza, who had chosen the life of a soldier, now stationed far to the south in Campeva, where he lived with his family. Surely, she prayed for his safety, but her greatest concern at this moment was for her daughter, Ramuthia. Like Sethra's son Rasce, she had demonstrated aptitude for the priestly calling, and had recently transported the gateway under her charge to Fufluna, where she'd intended to use it in advance of a naval assault against a settlement of Phocaeans on the island of Corse.

That battle had ended in disastrous defeat of the combined fleet of the League of Twelve and their Carthaginian allies. Rumors circulated that Ramuthia had not supplied the agreed-upon aid, and the ship on which she'd secretly sailed west in advance of the flotilla never returned to port. Some feared the worst had happened, while others concluded that treachery was involved, possibly on the part of the House of Zalthu and its priests.

Rika had her own suspicions about what was afoot, which she had harbored for some time. What had occurred earlier in the day only confirmed her deepest fears....

―――― ⟨⟩ ――――

A troop of soldiers escorted the two-wheeled cart, drawn by two stately black steeds, as it entered the compound through the eastern gate. The box this wagon bore, and its tender, Rasce, had not returned home for a great while. In truth, the object's home might well be considered the secret location Rika's ever-loyal nephew had found for it to the southeast, where for several years it had helped to guard a sensitive border between the Rasenna, the Latini, and the increasingly quarrelsome Umbri.

Today, however, it arrived in answer to Arathia Zalthu's summons, to defend the great house on the plateau against an anticipated assault by their former benefactors and trading partners from Cisra, the powerful Paithna family. Despite Arathia's pleas of innocence, the Paithnas claimed that House Zalthu had withheld the agreed-upon support for the ships that sailed against the Phocaeans of Alalia. This represented the final blow to their once-dominant but increasingly strained partnership. Long walls and a second guard tower were already under construction along the southern ridge of the plateau, and new wells had been dug to ensure a stable water supply in case of a siege. The support of one of the creatures, however, would increase their chances of survival tremendously.

Everyone in the compound left their chores to witness the arrival of the mysterious relic. Even Rika had finally been allowed to leave her chambers for the first time in nearly three weeks; it would have been difficult for Arathia to explain the absence of the High Priestess on such an occasion. All watched in reverent silence as four elite household guards lifted the box, wrapped carefully in brightly colored, padded woolen quilts, placed it on a bier, and transported the container into the temple in the northern wing of the building.

Sensing a fleeting opportunity to gain information, Rika trailed after Arathia before she could retreat back to her quarters in the eastern wing. As she passed the wagon, the driver lowered the scarf from his nose and mouth, which he wore to fend off the dust kicked up by the horses. His eyes met hers, and she briefly froze. It had been years since she'd last seen Ahumm. Like her, he had aged, but appeared sharp as ever, just as he had all those years ago, when she'd spied on him as he spoke angrily with Abirami.

She'd seen him since then, once briefly on a trip to Fufluna, and once when he again made the trek to visit House Zalthu, at that time on more pleasurable business. His surreptitious presence here now told Rika almost everything she needed to know. Still, she pursued Arathia, and caught her just as she was about to go inside. If anything could be salvaged at this penultimate moment, Rika felt determined to try.

"Noble one, a word, if you would."

Arathia's head tossed with unsuppressed annoyance, but she turned in response to the request. Her beauty had diminished little, even as a woman in her early-fifties, and despite the omnipresent scowl she wore that kept all in a near constant state of agitation. "High Priestess, how can I help you this fine day?"

"Have you heard news of my daughter? The battle near Alalia is long over. I know many ships were lost, though hers sailed alone, and in advance of the battle to find a suitable spot on Corse to establish the gateway. I fear for her, and for the artifact in her charge."

"I've received no updated report. When I do, you'll be the first to know. Speaking of your kindred, where is your nephew, Rasce? I expected to see him arrive today."

So had I, and my heart weeps at what his absence implies.

Rika took a breath to calm herself before she replied. "Still in the east, I presume, aiding those who protect our borders. His presence here is not required. You know I can perform the summoning, if necessary."

"Hmmm... quite. I merely wish to avoid taxing you unnecessarily during this time of mourning. I know what it is to lose a loved one. With age, both of us have seen much. So bittersweet, that your husband would die hunting, an activity that brought him such pleasure. My sympathies to you."

It took every ounce of Rika's will to avoid striking the disingenuous and duplicitous woman. "Yes, I still grieve Abirami's loss. I've spoken with my mason, who informed me that the carving of my husband's tomb is complete. I wish to visit and bring gifts and food, that he should want for nothing in the afterlife."

"You need to return to your quarters, High Priestess. The box is secure in the inner temple. You will be called upon if, and when, your services are required."

"I've been confined in my chamber since the battle. Do you hold me prisoner?"

"Of course not! The precautions we take are for your own safety. The necropolis is far too distant and exposed to risk a journey there now, even under guard. As we just discussed, with Rasce absent, you will almost certainly be needed, and we cannot afford your loss. Even though it appears the Phocaeans will quit Alalia despite their victory, there is much uncertainty in the wake of the conflict. It's not clear which faction will prevail or what dangers we might face. This is why we now fortify our southern flank and dig new wells. Trouble may find us if certain parties determine that we've been deceitful."

"Why would anyone think that? We did exactly as the majority in the League of Twelve asked of us."

"So you say, but it's not clear your daughter summoned the creature to aid our fleet. Her ship sailed out secretly in calm waters with an experienced crew. The chances of discovery, or her boat sinking, were impossibly slim. It makes the Paithnas suspect that we betrayed them."

"Did we?"

"How dare you! Were you not the High Priestess, I'd see to it that you were stoned to death for such slander, like they did in Cisra to the poor Hellenic prisoners after the battle!"

"Oh, Arathia, spare me. It's common knowledge that you supported the nobles in Tarchuna who voted against aggressive action to deter the increased Phocaean settlement of Alalia. This is hardly anything new. Like your father, you've chafed for decades at the Paithna's monopoly on the mining of ore, and the power they wield in the League."

"Well do you know, Rika Matuna, that it goes far beyond that! It was their policy of appeasement and inaction with Lukius Priscus that led to the rebellion and the near destruction of my family."

"Nonsense. I wish not to speak ill of your grandfather, or my mentor, Thana, but in the end, it was their insular and shortsighted approach to the situation that precipitated the revolt. Our true enemies, the Hellenes, were there all along. We simply needed to be more inventive and aggressive, and that solved our problems. Eventually, even Lukius Priscus became a problem for us, as Thana knew he would, but the Hellenes still pose the true threat."

"This time, it's my turn to claim *nonsense*. The true problem is the Paithna's continued insistence on alliance with Carthage, a partnership which each year further erodes the fortunes of our people, as we long ago predicted it would. The nobles of Tarchuna see far greater benefit in allying with the Hellenes, and like my father, I agree with them."

"My point exactly. Would logic not dictate, then, that treachery against the assault on Alalia would serve your purposes? How convenient for you that Ramuthia's and the gateway's mysterious disappearance on the eve of the battle precipitated our defeat, though I still can't comprehend what benefit you'll ultimately derive from provoking the Paithnas to violence."

"If you have no evidence to support these spurious accusations, I suggest you stay your tongue."

"Arathia, I didn't come here to accuse you of anything. I've spent my life embroiled in the political turmoil of our people. I understand there are different sides, differing perspectives. At this point, I care only for the whereabouts and safety of my daughter. Despite our differences, you and

I have always been united by the power entrusted to your family generations ago. I call upon this bond between us now. Forego all other considerations and simply tell me true. Do you know anything about my daughter's disappearance? If you do, speak now, and all else for me will be as water under a bridge."

A look of sadness briefly replaced Arathia's interminable grimace, but then she stiffened. "I have many tasks that demand my attention. Return to your quarters as instructed, and prepare yourself to carry out your duties to my family, and to our people. I cannot help you any further, High Priestess."

With that, her guards interceded between the two women, and Arathia turned and went inside.

It is not I that need help, noble but foolish princess. Not now. Now, things are in motion, and like a spinning toy, events will wind around, and eventually down, until all is again completely and oh-so-perfectly still.

A thin wisp of smoke tickled Rika's nose as it trailed from the lamp.

They will have seen my signal by now, or not. I leave that in the lap of the gods.

Wearily, she rose from her stool by the window and groped toward the center of the chamber. There, a thick wooden beam rose from the temple below and provided support for the floor of her living space, the barracks above, and eventually the tower's roof. Unquestionably, it could bear the weight of far more than one additional 66-year-old woman, but it remained to be seen whether she still possessed the strength to complete the necessary climb.

Once, it would have been easy, but she was no longer the girl who frolicked on the thatched roof of their old abode, or even the woman who had ridden prized steeds and shimmied up the rickety ladders to the roof of the tower. Still, she had remained active as she aged, and she retained one other powerful resource: her unconquerable will. The singularity and urgency of her purpose would drive her, as it had through her whole life, to accomplish things which others could only dream of achieving.

She had coiled the long rope discretely amongst a pile of woolen blankets and balls of yarn. Even now, none would dare enter, let alone search, the chamber of the High Priestess, so it had gone unnoticed. She wrapped one end thrice around the great beam, tied it securely, and brought the other end to the middle window of her chamber on the northern wall. A heavy wooden doorway sat directly beneath this spot on the structure's second story, but it was barred from the inside. She intended to descend all the way to the ground.

Rather than toss the coil out the window, she lowered the rope carefully, so the guards on the roof or in the barracks above wouldn't hear any noise. Once the end lay in the grass, she removed her fine leather shoes with their upturned, pointed tips, as well as her cloak, richly decorated with the colorful hems she once unhappily wove on her loom. Her simple tunic would suffice in the still warm fall weather, and would create no encumbrance.

She grasped the rope and squeezed into the narrow windowsill, then slowly backed out and walked herself downward. No light or noise emanated from the roof of the tower, but she knew guards monitored the area, especially during this time of disquiet and unrest. Any noise would draw their attention, so she descended gently and deliberately.

A smile crossed her lips when her bare feet touched the wooden frame of the doorway that hovered a full story above the ground. On occasion, when the proximity of their target permitted, she had commanded this unusual portal be opened into midnight skies identical to tonight's, and watched as one or another of her otherworldly associates flew away on their assigned task. These beings, so opposite in every way from the other, yet still intimately entwined, had found contentment under her oversight, and that of her kin. They ate well, and often, to their benefit, and to the benefit of the Rasenna.

My success or failure now will determine whether that pattern shall continue.

A sturdy bar secured the door from the inside, so it didn't creak or sway as she deftly rappelled down its surface. Her arms and hands began to ache from the unfamiliar effort, but once she'd cleared the portal, the ground lay just a few cubits farther.

Soon, her heel found the soft, grassy turf. She took a brief moment to stretch her stiffened and burning joints, then scampered for the shelter of the northern outbuilding.

After the great fire, this had been the first building constructed on the plateau, and had served as a makeshift royal residence. Rika had stayed here as well, fiercely watching over the boxes that contained the artifacts to which the remainder of her life would be devoted. Now, the humble structure had been converted into a stable for the Zalthu's prize steeds, though most of them were currently in the service of soldiers, who patrolled the areas west of the hill in anticipation of the assault.

The quiet of the building served her purposes. She tensely rounded the corner to the northern face, then looked back to the tower. To her relief, no silhouettes of guards were visible. They hadn't heard or seen her, and probably still monitored the southern skyline for signs of campfires.

Wasting no time, she hurried northward toward the tree line, where the ground dropped precipitously. Once there, she slipped into the underbrush, then crawled eastward along the ridge.

"*Rika!*"

The whisper both startled and relieved her. She eased down the slope a bit before she felt a hand on her shoulder.

"By the beard of Melquart, you made it!"

The Canaanite accent of Ahumm's words brought almost unbearable memories of Abirami to her mind.

"Ramuthia got word to us when she reached Fufluna. Is it true, about your husband... my cousin? Is he indeed dead?"

"Before I answer, tell me about Ramuthia! Is she safe?"

"We believe she is alive. Her ship was intercepted and boarded once it left port in Fufluna, then escorted to Pyrgi, where our associates tell us they saw her disembark. Likely, they hold her captive there rather than take her to Tarchuna. Many nobles from Cisra have recently fled to that city due to the increasing troubles with Rome, and through loose talk might easily catch wind of her whereabouts. We doubt her captors would kill her until they see how events unfold. She is said to hold information related to the great power of House Zalthu, mysterious even to me."

"After all this time, you still don't know? Abirami never told you?"

"No. My cousin is... well... *was*, a man of his word, and he swore an oath of secrecy to you."

"A man of his word, save once, long ago. You came for him, but he wouldn't go. He wouldn't leave me or our children. You asked him for something instead, and he gave it to you. What was it?"

"You spied on us."

"I spied on my husband, only to see with my own eyes if he might leave me, and whether he had any choice in the matter."

"Well, he did not leave. As far as what he gave me, I too am a man of my word. I swore to cut out my tongue before speaking about that item to anyone."

"I understand. If an oath such as that was required of you, perhaps it's best I never know."

"In truth, Rika, my family sent me to bring Abirami home when the siege of our city ended. They knew of you, and of your children together, and feared he might remain, but they told me to demand the return of the amulet should it come to that. I suspect I know as little as he did about the nature of the item itself. We are a family of merchants, and that was our business together. Neither of us spoke of it again, and now I sense we never will. Is he truly gone?"

Rika felt her heart lurch. "Sadly, Ahumm, Abirami is dead, and his passing nearly broke me. Only the highly suspicious circumstances of the incident, and its timing, having been just two days before he was to have accompanied Ramuthia to Fufluna, kept me from cascading into complete despair. Inconceivably, it appears Arathia and her co-conspirators in Tarchuna have finally decided to act, and Abirami, whom they had always despised, constituted their first target. He always knew the risks, going against the Zalthu's wishes, but neither of us ever imagined it would come to this. I still didn't believe it, until my daughter disappeared."

"So her message indicated. She told me of your suspicions, and precisely what actions I must take should anything untoward happen to her. By your signal in the tower, I knew you would come to meet us in this spot."

"How many are with you now?"

"Only two. More would pose too great a risk of being noticed. What is our plan?"

"We must get inside the inner temple. That's where the box has been placed, but it's under heavy guard. When we have what I'm after, you and your men can exit through the outer door. A rope hangs there so you don't have to jump."

"What about you?"

"Worry not for me. Aid me in the completion of this task and see my daughter safe, and you will have your revenge for the death of your beloved cousin, along with my eternal gratitude. Are we agreed?"

Ahumm tightened his grip on her shoulder in reply, then turned his head and called quietly into the darkness. The underbrush rustled as they were joined by two soldiers, likely among those who accompanied the cart earlier in the day.

The party of four stealthily retraced Rika's route back past the outbuilding to the base of the guard tower, then crept toward the eastern face of the compound.

As they rounded the corner, torchlight near the main gate became visible. Two guards stood watch there. They could use the cover of darkness and the scraggly foliage that grew near the wall to get close, but the perimeter of illumination meant they could not take these men by surprise. The alarm would soon be raised.

I hope all are in their appointed places and that Laran favors us this night.

She and Ahumm fell in behind the two soldiers as they inched silently toward their quarry, conscious that the guards of the tower now loomed directly above them.

When they had gotten as close as they could without being seen, she whispered in their ears. "Focus on the one closest. Strike him down, and the other will retreat inside for aid."

Despite their skeptical looks in the flickering torchlight, they silently nodded. They gestured briefly to one another, then one of the men ran away from the wall into the dirt road in front of the gate.

The guards cried out in challenge, but as they did, the remaining soldier near Rika abruptly launched himself directly at the nearest sentry.

The distraction had given him near total surprise. Only at the last moment did the sentry swing his shield to block the thrust of his attacker's short sword. The hollow knock of metal on wood rang in the night air, and startled shouts erupted from the top of the guard tower. The soldier who stood in the road didn't hesitate, and descended on the sentry's unprotected right flank.

The bronze tip of his spear drove into the pit of the guard's arm as the man raised his own spear to fend off his first attacker. With a grotesque crunch, the weapon ripped through his shoulder, then into his neck, just beneath the ear. He screamed in agony and collapsed in a shivering heap.

Rika suppressed a sob at the fate of a man who had once guarded her very life, and likely slept at times in the barracks above her own quarters, but bloodshed at this stage seemed unavoidable.

As anticipated, when he saw his companion slain, the other sentry made for the gateway.

Rika grabbed Ahumm's arm and dashed forward. "Come, quickly! This is our sole chance!"

The victorious soldier abandoned his spear in the corpse of his victim, as all four darted through the gate in pursuit.

Neither the outer or inner doors were closed, as many deliveries of food and other items arrived during the night. The close pursuit prevented the sentry from securing them now. Instead, he ran into the courtyard and shouted frantically for help. Equally agitated cries came from the guard tower. The soldiers there loudly proclaimed they were trapped, so the sentry ran toward the southern wing of the building.

"Should we follow?" one of Ahumm's men queried.

"No," she answered. "Let him go. We must get to the tower!" They sprinted under the loggia toward the temple in the northern wing. Its doors stood closed, but she prayed they would not long remain so.

Just as they passed by, three guards staggered out of a doorway in the east wing. They wielded spears and shields, but had no other armor, having clearly just tumbled out of bed.

Rika and Ahumm turned left and ran up to test the door to the temple, but it was still barred shut. They would have to hold out until it could be opened.

The two soldiers who accompanied them squared for combat. They were outnumbered, and each carried only a sword, which put them at a deficit compared to the spears of their challengers.

Ahumm drew a curved dagger and stepped protectively in front of Rika as the attackers closed.

Sensing their advantage, the guards came full-on. Those on the outer flanks slammed their shields into the bodies of the defenders.

Deftly, each of Ahumm's soldiers avoided the pursuant spear thrusts by keeping their center of gravity low and pressing close to their aggressor's shields. One even swung his sword and scored a strike to his attacker's leg.

The man howled in pain, but somehow willed himself to maintain his feet.

The other soldier, meanwhile, did not fare as well. As he locked with his assailant's shield, the two rotated to his right. This exposed his back to a strike by the third guard, who chose to avoid his target's protective bronze cuirass, and instead drove his spear directly into the unfortunate man's neck. Rika gasped as the bloodied bronze point of the weapon ripped through her protector's flesh and emerged from just under his chin. He instantly dropped his sword and collapsed to his knees, as he choked and violently spat a torrent of blood.

Her shock doubled when Ahumm tore away from her and dove on the first guard. The revolving motion of the two combatants had turned his back toward them, and this man wore no armor. Ahumm drove his curved dagger upward into the unsuspecting warrior's kidney, then savagely twisted the blade.

The guard's body tensed and spasmed before he too plummeted to the ground.

Ahumm stumbled as he extracted his deeply embedded blade from the incision in his victim's lower back. This gave the guard who had lost his spear to the other soldier's neck a chance to grab his companion's dropped weapon. Even having retrieved his blood-soaked dagger, Ahumm stood no chance. The guard fiercely thrust his spear directly into the Canaanite's shoulder, and the old man dropped his knife and fell backward.

Rika screamed and recoiled in terror, but suddenly felt the temple door against which she pressed her back give way. She stumbled slightly, until strong hands steadied her and drew her aside. Several men shot past her into the courtyard and set upon the two guards who remained standing. Each gave a brief but dispirited defense before throwing down their weapons.

"Traitors!" the man with the gash in his leg shouted. "You will be stoned for your duplicity, or sent to feed the Gatekeeper!"

"It's the High Priestess herself who we serve!" one of the men shot back. "We would give ourselves to any fate she commands. Run now! You are our brothers in arms and we have no wish to spill your blood."

The two defeated guards looked dubiously at one another, but then began to back away, the healthy man aiding the injured. As they realized they wouldn't be pursued, they turned and made what haste they could toward the eastern gateway.

The men from inside the temple brought Ahumm to his feet, then escorted him and the other soldier through the door. As they closed the heavy portal, Rika saw men streaming through the southern gateway, likely from the encampment that had been established there behind the new wall to guard the southwestern perimeter of the compound.

Once shut, the men reset the bar in the great temple door.

"They come," she said, with as much calm as she could summon. "Barring this door will force them to cut through the workshop and kitchens on the west side, then come through the great hall. This should delay them enough for you to escape. What's the situation in the tower?"

One of the men stepped forward and bowed. "Priestess, we've jammed the door to the barracks and removed the ladder to the roof. Two men stand guard with spears to hold the hallway. There are only two lookouts. They're poorly armed and unlikely to jump down, but if our barrier into the barracks gives way, our men will have to flee."

"I understand. They know to run to my chambers and get out the window, yes?"

He curtly nodded.

"Very well. All of you, right now, into the inner temple! Open the doorway to the outside and use the rope to get to the ground. You know where to go after that. Make haste!"

"Rika, I can't make it." Ahumm's voice sounded weak. Blood stained the left side of his tunic from shoulder to waist.

She rushed to his side and stroked his cheek. The feel of his light beard again brought Abirami to her mind, but she pushed the painful memory away. "Get him into the temple. He'll stay with me."

The men appeared distressed by her words, but did as she commanded. Two of them lifted Ahumm and walked through the decorated curtain that separated the main temple in the northern wing from the annex in the northeastern corner. The royal family used this room for private worship, but it also served as the entryway to the various portions of the fortified tower that had been built adjacent to the north wall.

Rika followed them into the annex. Two dead bodies lay in pools of their own blood, while a prisoner cowered and wept in the corner under the watchful eye of a guard.

"We tried to spare them all, as you requested," one of the soldiers who carried Ahumm said, "but they wouldn't let us leave the annex."

"You did what you had to," she replied. "Take this one into the inner temple with us. If he cooperates, you can take him out with you."

They passed the small door that led to the narrow ladders to her chambers on the third floor, the barracks on the fourth floor, and finally the roof. Next to this sat a large double door, each side painted with the fearsome images of gorgons. As she had many times, Rika strode to the doors and pushed. They creaked like the wails of the dying as they gave way before her. Torchlight from the annex spilled into the massive chamber that dominated the first two stories of the mighty tower.

Dead ahead, on the northern wall, a ladder led up a wooden scaffolding that provided access to the outer doorway. With Rika's permission, two guards sprinted across the room, shimmied up the ladder, and began to remove the heavy, bronze-reinforced bar. Other men lit torches, while those who carried Ahumm set him gently down to the left. He faced the eastern wall, and stared groggily at the one remaining block of iron-rich rock, carved with the recessed doorway, which had graced the old tripartite temple. The other had been lost all those years ago in the great fire when it toppled over and shattered irreparably.

"Priestess, do you wish us to bar this door? They will be here soon."

"No. All of you, climb out and get to your positions. You'll be needed."

"We are needed here, to protect you! Unless you've changed your mind and now plan to come with us?"

"As I said, I shall remain. It appears Ahumm will as well. He clearly can't climb down. Worry not. Follow my instructions and all will be well... in this life, or the next."

The man reluctantly bowed and signaled for those with him to proceed up the ladder, prisoner in tow. Already the soldiers on the wooden platform had shimmied down the rope to relative safety.

All too quickly, Rika could hear shouts and stomping feet in the main temple. Above, she heard a crash, and guessed that guards in the barracks had finally broken through the barrier that had kept them in check. She whispered a brief prayer to Athrpa to not cut short the strands of the lives of those in the hallway who had turned on their fellows to aid her cause.

Would that I could do more to help them, but my own fate now hangs in the balance. May my actions speak for themselves before the judgment of the gods.

Men streamed into the annex, their shadows flickering like angry crows across the blood-stained floor. A soldier ran to the open double doors, and froze in place as he met the stony gaze of the High Priestess. Others joined him and gaped in awe and confusion at the lone woman who stood defiantly before them. Soon, the room became crowded as guards from the barracks and more from the southern garrison filled the room. They muttered amongst themselves, but none dared cross the threshold of the inner temple without permission.

Like the cry of a Siren, one voice pierced the hubbub. "Why are you all standing here? Get out of my way. Let me pass! You fool, be careful with that spear!" The throng of guards by the door parted, and Arathia strode into the inner temple with two elite warriors by her side.

Rika gave a slight curtsey. "Noble one."

"What's the meaning of this! What are you doing here? You were ordered to stay in your chambers!"

"My apologies. I've never been especially good at following the rules, especially when I see no sense in them."

"This transgression will spell your end, High Priestess. Violating an order is one thing, but fomenting rebellion is another. Men are dead. *My* men! There is no justification for this treachery. Like the last revolt, you will all be rounded up and left to feed the vultures!"

"No justification, Arathia? I think not. I know you and your friends from Tarchuna have my daughter captive in Pyrgi."

"How can you know this, or be certain that what you think you know is indeed true?"

"Because we watched it happen," Ahumm weakly interjected. "Ramuthia got a message to me in Fufluna before she sailed. We paid the fishermen to watch. They have small boats, very hard to see them on the horizon, but *they* see much. We know who took her, and where."

Rika went on. "I suspected something when Abirami died, or should I say, when you had him killed. He was to have escorted Ramuthia to Fufluna, and you knew he would have been able to contact his family there to provide greater oversight for the journey. Fortunately, you underestimated my resourceful daughter. You speak of treachery when you have assassinated my husband and taken prisoner my child. I gave you a chance today to tell me the truth. I could have called all of this off. Now, the truth will be revealed whether you like it or not."

Arathia scoffed. "Even if what you say is accurate, it matters little. The wheels are already in motion. When the Paithna's forces come, all we have to do is hold out for a few days. We have spies to identify their leaders. That's where you and the Gatekeeper will come in handy."

"What makes you think I'll cooperate?"

"Because if you don't, I'll send a man to Pyrgi to have your daughter killed, or we'll simply kill you and hope the threat of the creature deters them. In any case, when the Paithna's mercenaries come here to extract vengeance for Ramuthia's disloyalty for having disappeared before the battle, it will leave their palace in Cisra quite vulnerable. Already, they are stretched thin by increased pressure from Rome and the Latini. When the warriors here get wind of their employer's destruction in Cisra, they'll scatter like leaves in the wind."

"So, that's your plan. Now I understand. I'm so sorry to be the one to spoil it for you."

She gave a wicked laugh. "Spoil it? It seems too late for that now. Obviously, you came here to unleash the Gatekeeper. Was I to be his target? You are powerless, High Priestess. You haven't even had time to set up the gateway materials. They're still safe in their box."

"Are they?"

Arathia stiffened. "You men, come with me. You three, surround her and bring her as well. If she makes a move against me, slay her!"

A group of soldiers strode hesitantly into the room, took their positions, then followed as Arathia led the way toward the back wall. There, to the left and beyond the outcropping where the ladders led to the upper chambers, the box sat on a stone altar, still wrapped in its protective padded blankets. Another altar sat to its side, but this one stood empty.

"Open it!" Arathia ordered.

One of the soldiers cautiously untied the leather thongs that held the covering in place, and revealed the ceramic box. This one had been constructed about five summers ago to replace one that had aged and cracked beyond repair. Having not been transported frequently, it still seemed in excellent condition. Another guard joined the first, and together they lifted the thick lid. A final guard brought a torch close so Arathia could see inside.

She gasped. "It's empty! What have you done with the gateway materials, High Priestess? I remind you, they are not yours! They belong to *my* family, and I say where they go and how they are used!"

"This has always been your misunderstanding, Arathia. The gateways aren't yours, or mine. They belong to our people, fractious though they may be."

"History will justify my actions. The continued alliance with Carthage will spell our ruin, and our *people* will be swept asunder!"

Rika shook her head. "You may well be right. Never have I objected to your position in this matter, even though I personally disagree. It is the manner in which you impose your will that infuriates me! You failed to win the vote in the council, and now you attempt subvert the decision of the consensus. Our unity is the only thing that stands between us and our enemies. If we continue to fight amongst ourselves, the Rasenna are doomed. We learned this lesson long ago, when the League of Twelve was formed, but it seems it must be re-taught with each generation. This time, the message will ring clear through the centuries. This hill will become a place of ghosts... of legend that once a great and prosperous noble family lived here, but their hubris laid them low. They were obliterated, wiped away, smashed, and buried. And all that was ever known of them will be lost, like the fleeting memories of infancy."

A soldier rushed into the room. "Your pardon, Mistress. There is a disturbance along the southern wall. We are under assault, and most of our contingent are here. I fear we've been overrun. What do we do?"

Arathia went pale. "We've been tricked! Make haste to the southern and eastern gates and try to secure them. That's our only chance to defend the main building. Take everyone but three guards who will stay with me and bar this door. Go! Quickly!"

He scurried out of the room and the annex rapidly cleared. Two of the guards went after him, closed the double doors, and used the hammer nearby to secure the bar firmly into place.

"Take the hammer and seal that door as well," Arathia commanded, pointing at the outer exit. "They have a rope there. We don't want anyone getting in." She turned to Rika. "By my count, you have perhaps twenty warriors, between those who accompanied the cart this morning and those from the barracks who betrayed me. We still outnumber you. The battle is not over."

Rika shrugged. "What do you intend to do with me?"

"Let's wait and see how things turn out, shall we? I'd like to find out who gets to look on as the sword drives into one or the other of our bellies."

"I don't think that's how it will end."

"No? Pray tell, holy one, what do you foresee?"

The strike of a hammer resounded in the room as the soldiers on the scaffolding drove the bar to the outer door into place. After a pause, another blow rang out as the mallet contacted the bronze fitting.

"I cannot tell the future, noble one. My powers are limited to the present. Fate will always prevail. I do, however, try to look ahead as best as any person can. I find this the surest way to navigate the mortal realm, and my intuitions have generally proven sagacious. All I will say, for now, is that the sound of that hammer is as music to my ear."

CHAPTER 18

Eric opened his eyes. Dusk had passed. Another beautiful pink and blue sky had faded into the west, beyond the rocky ledge, beyond Vern's empty, dead eyes and desiccated husk.

Beyond Lotte.

He struggled to his hands and knees. His shoulder stung, but the ringing in his ears had subsided, as had the dizziness and the lurching in his stomach. He slowly crawled toward her. Dried blood caked her face, and she hadn't moved. He couldn't tell if she was breathing. She appeared dead, but then she often appeared dead, even when she was quite alive.

Well, that was a long time ago. Yet he still remembered.

He knelt by her and put his hand to her chest, but his own trembling made it impossible to tell if she took in breath, or if her heart pumped. He leaned close to her face. Her lips were closed. Could he hear air coming from her bloody nostrils?

"Lotte," he whispered.

Nothing. She lay utterly still.

"Lotte?" he asked, more loudly. He pressed close and prayed to detect some sign of life.

"Lotte!" he begged as he shook her shoulder.

A spout of bloody spittle shot from her mouth directly into his face as she gasped for air. The surprise made his heart leap, but then he laughed with relief as she coughed up more blood and cleared her throat.

"Lotte, are you okay? Man, I thought you were dead. Do you want to try to sit up? Let me get you some water."

He attempted to rise, but she clutched his arm. "The Afrit!" she gasped. "Where's the Afrit?"

"Uh, probably by the fire portal where we left it, assuming there's anything still there."

"Take me," she whispered. "Take me to it."

He tried to help her up, but found it hopeless. She'd borne the brunt of the blast full-on, and had been thrown practically twenty feet. She said her ears rang, and she felt dizzy, and had the same nausea from which he suffered, though it sounded vastly more severe.

He carried her in his arms, like the Afrit had carried Charun over the same ground a little more than an hour ago, according to his watch, whose crystal had cracked in the melee. His shoulder throbbed and began to bleed again, but he ignored it. They walked to the portal containing the great un-mirror, where the Afrit still writhed on the ground. Only its head, torso, and one feeble strand of arm connecting to the talon that bore the bent filigreed bracelet still remained.

"Put me next to it," she directed, her voice weak and unsteady.

He did as she requested.

The two creatures, one human and one not, lay on their backs, side by side. Each turned their heads weakly, and their eyes, both deep and black, and unknowable in their own way, locked.

"Charun is gone," she said softly. "Our plan both worked, and failed."

The Afrit barely opened its mouth to utter its sharp and gravely words. *'He was a worthy opponent. Powerful, we would have been, had we absorbed him. Now, we face the end in this dull and dour world. We risked all, and all is now lost.'*

"No!" she firmly insisted, coughing up more bloody spittle as a result. "We'll send you back... back to your Eternal Flame, to recover and heal. I can't make you whole, or replenish what you've lost, and you're in no position to do that either, but your time isn't done."

'We cannot move. We must be over the flame, over the sign to disassemble for the journey back.'

"The stone with the markings and the bowls? You have to be over that flame?" She gestured in the direction of the black marble slab which lay at their feet, or at least her feet, the Afrit's having become a pile of ashen dust.

'Yes. We cannot rise to reach it. We will end our time here.'

"No, we'll lift you. We'll hold you over the flame, and you can return to your home."

The creature seemed taken aback. *'You would do this? You cannot stand. How will you lift us? How can you hold us?'*

"Not me. Him." She pointed feebly and directly at Eric.

The Afrit emitted a low growl. *'We do not trust his kind. Traitorous they are. No honor. They lied to us early on, and in the end imprisoned us. Why would I trust one of his sort now?'*

"Because you have no choice, and because I'm giving you *my* word. This one can be trusted. He's with me, always. He's *mine*, and he'll do exactly as I ask."

The beast exhibited terrible consternation as it pondered its predicament. Had it possessed wings, they would have fluttered on its back as it rocked from side to side and twitched its barbed tail. Eric almost missed seeing that... seeing a creature from what might well be another universe just sit and think something over. Finally, the mortally wounded beast spoke.

'Very well. We trust your word. You speak the truth. We have little choice.'

She smiled. "I thank you, great Afrit. You honor me with your confidence. Eric, prepare the portal. The candles have burned down. Five candles per bowl. Light them all."

He did as he was told. Soon the frame and bowls emitted their signature warm glow, indicating the portal was ready for use. He returned to Lotte and started to pick her up. He intended to move her out of the way, but she stopped him.

She reached out her hand, which still bore the two rings, and laid it across the Afrit's chest. The small black stones on the spiraled silver ring had shattered, like the other components of Charun's gateway.

"Give me your hand," she said to the great but terribly diminished monster.

The beast lifted the fragile strand of its arm and placed its lone remaining talon in her outstretched palm.

She held it for a moment and smiled into the creature's black, pupilless eyes. Then, she slowly slipped the bracelet off the Afrit's pathetic and shaking claw.

"You're free to go. Our bargain is complete. May the Eternal Flame heal your body, and your soul."

The Afrit looked away as Eric lifted her and placed her, still on her back, at the apex of the black marble board. He then returned and considered how to lift the monstrous creature before him. Even without legs and wings, the Afrit's torso and head still seemed massive.

Surprisingly, the creature turned out to be remarkably light, like the ash that comprised its body, but it took effort. His shoulder emitted a sharp pain, and again, blood oozed through his shredded and now mostly crimson-colored Celtics t-shirt, but he lifted what remained of the otherworldly being and held it above flames on the marble board.

The Afrit looked him straight in the eye. Another low growl escaped from its clenched mouth, but as it began to dissolve, the creature seemed to calm. It wasn't until the features of its monstrous face had melted away, returned again to black misty ash, that it took its eyes from him.

As the shimmering cloud snaked its way back into the thick pane of ancient glass, Eric thought he heard a whisper of thanks somewhere in the wind.

Perhaps that was just his imagination.

The scent of blueberry pervaded his mouth.

There hadn't been any peanut butter energy bars left, so it had been blueberry or nothing. Turned out, blueberry tasted almost as good as peanut butter. In any case, he needed strength for what lay ahead.

Without regard to his already bruised and bleeding body, he methodically transported Lotte to the orange trail. He made frequent stops, sometimes propping her on his knees as he crouched, gulping for breath and fighting back tears of agony and exhaustion. Other times, he did his best to gently set her on the ground, then collapsed beside her.

It took well over an hour, and he could feel the pierced and torn muscles in his left shoulder giving way with each torturous step.

Lotte moaned the entire time in a sort of dazed misery.

It got worse when they reached the steep slope of the trail. He couldn't put her down here, because by this time, his arm had given out, and he'd never have been able to pick her back up. So, he hoisted her on his back and carried her piggyback.

This, she truly didn't like. She started to softly cry as her head bobbed from side to side.

"Sick!" she suddenly said. "Stop! Sick!"

He abruptly halted, and she leaned her head to the right and vomited over his shoulder.

She spat and gagged into his neck as they closed the last hundred yards to the van. Rather than put her down, he somehow managed to open the passenger door, then turned around and forced her up into the seat.

"Can you hoist yourself up just a little bit?" he asked, straining as he tried to press her the final few inches into the high seat of the chair.

She couldn't. She had no strength left.

He spent the last of his energy straining to lift her that small, but incredibly difficult, distance. The second she slumped into place, a loud pop emanated from his shoulder, and searing pain shot down his side and lower back. He started to black out, so he collapsed to the ground, and put his head between his knees until the waves of dizzying torment ceased.

Slowly and achingly, he stumbled to the driver's side and hauled himself in. She lay draped against the passenger door, head out the window in case she puked again. He couldn't fasten her seat belt in that position, so he just told her to hold onto the door, and started up the van.

He went slowly and tried his best to minimize jolts. Still, she whimpered with distress as her head shook from side to side. They reached the tape-tied trees, and in the van's lights he saw Vern's police car parked in the circle.

"Shit. What the hell are we gonna do about that?"

She didn't even seem to hear him.

He got out, untied the yellow tape, and just drove off. If someone found the police car, the displaced tape wouldn't matter for a hill of beans. He'd deal with all that later. Right now, he had to get Lotte home.

Though still rough, New Speck Lane represented a major relief after the potholes of the dirt road. Lotte seemed to calm a bit until they turned onto the gravely dirt road that led to Mason's house. This again caused the van to bounce erratically, but mercifully, they soon pulled into the driveway.

Eric tested his shoulder. Pain had given way to numbness that extended all the way down his side. He left her momentarily to open the front door of the cabin and turn on the lights, during which time he stretched and limbered his back and arm.

When he returned, she'd crumpled into the seat and tightly closed her eyes.

"Lotte, I'm gonna try to lift you out. You have to hold onto my neck if you can. It will make it easier. If you can't, I might have to put you on my back again. You hear me?"

She gave a tiny nod, and he stepped up and started to drag her out of the van. She did manage to throw her arms around his neck. This helped him carry her, despite the renewed discomfort to his shoulder.

Somehow, he managed to get her inside and up the stairs. He deposited her onto the flimsy double bed in the guest room, then immediately dropped to the floor, where he heaved for breath and waited for his muscles to stop screaming.

He had a million things to do, but he could barely move. They both needed to rest. He'd have to get up early and do what needed to be done. He removed her shoes and socks, and then her pants. She didn't resist or complain, so he maneuvered her under the covers.

She looked tense and miserable where she lay on her back, eyes still tightly clinched shut.

He walked to the far side of the room and turned on a small light on the old dresser whose drawers didn't open or close properly. Then he shut off the light on the nightstand near where she lay.

She seemed to relax slightly. The light clearly bothered her.

"You want any water, or anything?"

She barely shook her head.

Satisfied he'd done all her could for her, for now, he grabbed some fresh underwear and a t-shirt from his duffel, shuffled into the bathroom, and jumped into the shower. Blood flowed into the tub from the multiple cuts on his back. He looked down at the large red welt on his left calf, which still made it difficult to walk, and likely would for some time.

After his shower, he rummaged in the bathroom cabinet for Band-Aids. He used two large ones on his shoulder and tried to reach the ragged scratch on his back from Charun's claw, but could only cover tiny portions.

He put on his fresh clothes, went downstairs, grabbed two bottles of water, pounded some ibuprofen, and then returned to the guest room. He clicked off the light and carefully slipped into bed on the far side near the wall.

She didn't stir.

He could hear her breathing through nostrils stuffed with dried blood and whatever other gunk might be clogging them. Her shirt still smelled of vomit, but he didn't dare remove it for fear of jostling her head. She needed rest, and so did he.

It was pitch dark and who knew what time when she tapped him awake. "Eric, help me."

"What?" He shook sleep from his eyes. "What do you need?"

"Up. Sick. Need to get up."

"Oh, shit."

He jumped out of bed, which turned out to be an extremely bad move. Pain exploded through just about every portion of his body. His back seized up, and his leg nearly collapsed from the contusion on his calf. He stumbled to the dresser and turned on the light, then dragged himself to the side of the bed where she lay. She looked pale, even by her standards, and sweaty. He carefully tried to help her up, but the minute he lifted her head from the pillow, she lurched to the side and vomited on the floor. He barely got out of the way.

She moaned. "Sorry... sorry. Help me."

"More?"

She nodded.

He lifted her arms and pulled her toward the foot of the bed to try and avoid the mess. She still wobbled, so he supported her as they both teetered toward the bathroom.

She made it, but only just inside the door. There, she fell to her knees and puked again on the aged vinyl floor. He held her head, eyes shut because this kind of thing really made him gag. She spat and cried as she cleared the last of whatever remained inside her.

"Done?"

"Think so," she replied, still teary and trembling. "So sorry, Eric. So sorry... for everything... Eric... for everything."

"Don't worry about anything right now. Come on, we've got an emergency change of venue while I get all this cleaned up. Can you stand?"

With effort and his aid, she righted herself, and he guided her to Mason's room. He wasn't sure whether she even noticed or cared. He lay her in the bed and covered her shaking body with a blanket, then fetched a bottle of water from the guest room and helped her drink. She faded quickly, and soon fell fast asleep.

He had no idea how to clean up vomit. He'd never had the pleasure — *thanks, Mom!* He got the red plastic bucket from downstairs, the one Lotte had used to clean out the van, and filled it with soapy water, grabbed some old towels, and went at the mess. Fortuitously, he hadn't eaten much, because it made him retch and gag, but, like so many unpleasant things, it had to be done. He gritted his teeth and dry heaved through it.

He tossed the disgusting towels outside with his bloody shirt to deal with tomorrow, or maybe never. He rinsed out the bucket, and then dropped it by the side of the bed in the guest room, just in case. He grabbed some fresh towels and lay them on the floor of the bathroom, which made it feel a little cleaner, then sprayed some air freshener in both rooms. Things felt almost back to normal.

He went to retrieve Lotte from Mason's bed. He didn't want her waking up there and getting upset. Reluctantly, she let him lead her back to the guest room, where she sat on the flimsy bed.

Her shirt was a disaster: dirt, blood, vomit, Afrit ash. He figured she'd emptied her stomach, so he threw modesty aside and found a t-shirt from among her things.

THE CURE.

We can only hope.

He carefully lifted her upper body and distastefully removed her stinky shirt. As he was about to slip the new one over her head, she mumbled something.

"What?" he asked. "I didn't catch that. Can you say that again."

"The bra," she whispered. "Take that off too. Please?"

He gently turned her away from him and unfastened her sleek black bra, then slipped the shirt with the weird-looking dude with the punky goth haircut over her head. She fell back into his body, and for a brief moment, he wrapped his arms around her waist. Then he guided her carefully back to the pillow, where she lay on her side, looking far more comfortable than before.

He grabbed his phone and checked the time: just past 2:00 a.m. Another couple of hours, then he'd have to get up and get at it. He set his alarm, shut off the light, and got back into bed.

He'd almost fallen asleep when she again called his name. "Eric, I need you."

"Oh, shit, Lotte. Are you gonna be sick again? There's a bucket by the side of the bed. For the love of God, can you please try to aim for that?"

"No, I just have to pee."

Okay, that's not so bad.

He helped her to the bathroom. She refused to let him turn on the light above the mirror, which was too bright and bothered her eyes. They found their way by what little illumination trickled in from the window. He helped her get situated on the toilet, then made for the door, but she called him back.

"I'm really dizzy. Hold my hands so I don't fall over."

When she was done, she wrapped her arms around him and rested her head on his stomach. He ran his fingers through her raven hair, still caked with blood and dirt. He wasn't sure how long they stayed in that exceedingly awkward position, but in some irrational way, he wished it could have been forever.

CHAPTER 19

"Eric, tell me!"

He wished Lotte would just go to sleep. She still needed to rest. In fairness, it probably wasn't the easiest thing, sleeping in the back of the van as it bounced around while wind whipped in from the ragged gash in the roof.

He finally surrendered. "All right, what do you want to know?"

She screamed in frustration. "*Verdammt!* Eric, how many times do I have to ask? Everything! I want to know everything... how you did it! I've seen your shoulder, you poor thing, and your leg, not to mention your hand. I see you aren't moving right. Practically speaking, you should be in hospital. I want to know how you did all this. Most importantly, how did you get the frame down from the hill by yourself? That's impossible!"

He couldn't start there, at the end. He needed to start at the beginning: yesterday, at 4:30 a.m. on Friday, August 2, 2013, when his fucking iBlah 4's alarm went off. It woke him up after far too little sleep, and with far too much to do.

This is not gonna be fun. There isn't even time for coffee, and that's a recipe for a bad day.

Lotte stirred as he stiffly and painfully got out of bed, but soon breathed deeply again, lost in sleep. Despite his myriad injuries, he feared she might actually be worse off with a head trauma. He hoped she could pee or puke or whatever else she might need to do by herself for a while. He had little choice but to leave her. He scribbled a note on one of the strips of paper that clung magnetically to the fridge and left it on the nightstand by her bed.

Going out. Will be back. Don't worry. – E.

Nothing stirred in the chilly air of the pitch-black night. It felt like the silence of the dead. His footfalls on the twigs and pine needles made the only sound. His flashlight provided the only illumination, briefly interrupting the darkness with his jerky motions as he went to the shed.

He'd seen a lawn mower. There had to be a gas can. There it sat... remarkably, nearly full. A spot of luck. He grabbed it, along with the shoulder bag full of heroin, the knife, and the other gun they'd taken from the biker.

He laboriously climbed into the van and drove back to the trails. He didn't bother backing in. He'd only attempt that maneuver when the sun had risen, and he had light to see by. He had to guess where to enter, but they'd been in this area long enough that, by now, he basically knew. They'd been this way before — albeit in the opposite direction, while they ran for their very lives.

Not fast enough.

He found the way back up the hill — not *their* hill, the one he knew so well from the two surreal battles that had unfolded in front of his terrified eyes. He climbed the *other* hill. His flashlight lit the way. He also carried the gas can, and he'd slung the bag with the heroin and the weapons around his shoulder. It didn't take long to find them.

They wouldn't exactly be going anywhere. Although, I have to say, if they started walking around right now, I wouldn't be particularly shocked, given the other wacked-out crap I've seen.

There should be five in all. He knew the location of three. His already flagging spirit sank further when he discovered the fourth, near the first two they'd found, though perhaps this spot was appropriate. He looked down at Mason's disfigured form not twenty feet from where Emilia's corpse lay. He'd died horribly, as Vern had, drained to feed a monster that now too had expired.

What a waste.

He dragged the three corpses in this area together to a spot void of vegetation — he didn't want to start a forest fire. He fetched the other corpse he'd seen earlier from the slope. All were light, like papier-mâché casts of skeletons, left too long in the sun to dry and crack.

There had to be one more, probably Larry Henderson, who'd been among the first taken.

Where could he be?

He walked back up the slope to the point where he'd first observed Charun on the double hillock. He circled the area with his flashlight, but found nothing.

I think the woman hiker probably got taken around the same time. Larry's remains might be near where we found hers.

He went back to where her sad and twisted body had lain in the dirt near the edge of the ridge, and scanned the perimeter. He saw nothing, but took a chance and looked down the cliff face.

There it lay, having been tossed over the side.

He circled back down the slope, and approached from below to retrieve poor Larry's body from the little plateau where it had landed. The rigid and brittle corpse cracked and snapped as he hefted what remained of the old gentleman on his protesting back. He found it gruesome, but no worse than cleaning puke off the bathroom floor, or, for that matter, forcing himself to do thirty more minutes on the exercise bike as he tried to force the softness from his body, and Lotte from his heart.

He carried Larry back to where the others rested in a grisly heap. When they were gathered in the barren spot, he unzipped the bag and used the knife to slice open each little pouch of heroin. He poured the powder on and around the twisted bodies, then doused the area with gasoline from the can.

It didn't take much — the skeletal corpses were drier than kindling. They went up as if they'd released their very souls into the early morning sky.

A fitting end after such hideous deaths.

He went back down the hill and followed the streambed through the little valley. When he came to a suitable spot, he dropped the bag and again zipped it open. He buried the knife and the gun beneath the silt at the bottom of the stream. Later, when it was light, he'd need to locate Vern's gun, along with the one he'd used against Charun, and similarly dispose of those. For now, he picked up the bag and went on.

He easily found the familiar slope where the portals sat, one in shattered ruins, the other in majestic silence. He dragged Vern's body through the rocky soil, past the fire portal to a barren area largely out of sight. He rifled in the deceased deputy's pockets and found his car keys, then he doused the desiccated corpse with gasoline and surrendered it to the flames.

Sorry for lying to you, Vern. Talk about being in the wrong place at the wrong time....

He packed the bowls in their boxes and carried one box with him down the slope toward the van, along with the gas can. A hint of dawn now peeked over the mountain to the east. The light made it easier to navigate, especially with hands full and no flashlight, which he had stowed in the shoulder bag. He spied Vern's gun, along with the one he'd used, as he left, so he made another stop at the stream to dispose of the firearms.

When he arrived at the van, he secured his burdens in the cargo area, hopped in, backed out, and then bounced to the circular clearing where the police car waited in vain for its owner to return. He parked the van, walked to the car, opened the door, got out the keys, and started the engine.

He drove the police car back to New Speck Lane, then took the first right into a long driveway. If he'd understood Mason correctly, Larry Henderson lived here, or once did. So, in theory, no one would be home.

I hope to hell that's right.

He saw no lights on in the house, but it was only about 5:30 a.m. If anyone were home, he'd be screwed. He drove the car behind the building, where it couldn't readily be seen. He took the keys and wiped the steering wheel and door handles down with his Bruin's hoodie, which he then happily put back on to fend off the early morning chill.

With resignation, he began to walk back up the hill to retrieve the van.

"*Alter!* Eric! There wasn't any other way?"

"I don't think Uber picks up in Bailey yet. What was I supposed to do? Those were the two priorities. Dispose of the bodies before daylight so nobody would see the smoke, and hide Vern's car. How would you have done it?"

She lay silently for a time on the old air mattress that he'd found in a closet, which helped absorb the bumping of the van on the road. She wore her oversize sunglasses, as the light still bothered her eyes. They'd stolen a pillow from the guest room as well, along with a sheet, and the thick blanket from the plaid couch that had served him so well this past week.

After she'd absorbed what he'd told her, she continued her queries. "So, all you had to do now was get the fire portal down from the hill?"

"Well, that and the air hammer, the drill, the propane canisters, the generator, and the groceries we left up there. By the way, there's food and bottles of water in those bags, if you want anything. Water's not cold. Sorry. I also finished the last of the power bars."

"I'm not hungry. All right, I can see you getting some of that stuff down, but the generator? The marble slab? I doubt it—by yourself, especially in your condition—and what about the frame? That's out of the question. If you smashed it, and it's not in that case, I'll be furious!"

"Lotte, I'd never do that without your permission. Not that it would break my heart to never see Chuckles again, but it's there, and it's fine— a little dusty, but not a scratch on it."

"Then *how*, Eric? How did you get that and those other things down?"

Most of it, he'd just lugged—trip, after trip, after trip, after trip—but she had good instincts. The heavy generator and the case with the black marble slab were now well beyond his ability to carry, and moving the mirror by himself was never realistic. He and Lotte had barely gotten it up the hill together.

"Before I tell you, Lotte, I get to ask you something. Who the hell is *Vamp*, or *Vance*, or whatever her name was that you and Charun were talking about?"

"Ah, Vanth! She's another Etruscan chthonic figure, like Charun. They're often depicted together on funerary art, like tomb paintings and on sarcophagi. She's a winged female who carries a torch, a key, and a scroll... items associated with the transition from life to death, and also perhaps fate. She's usually portrayed as a benevolent figure, compared to Charun, who's more menacing. That was what made me realize who he was talking about. They're polar opposites, completing each other's circles."

"It sounded like the ancient Etruscans summoned both beings. Do you think they used the same portal?"

"I haven't had time to think it through, but my guess is no. The magnetic portal utilized an item to not only activate the gateway, but also to aid the creature summoned. In Charun's case, this was a hammer. There was no equivalent object in the ceramic box that Mason and Emilia found that would correspond to Vanth. That leads me to believe her portal was separate, perhaps in the same complex as Charun's. It may already have been destroyed by the ravages of time, but possibly it's still buried nearby. It could also be elsewhere. Regardless, I believe she probably had her own gateway, and when possible, I fully intend to look for it near Sarteano, where the first portal was found."

Marvelous. He imagined his head being pounded in by a giant obsidian torch. *I wonder what the scroll is for? Maybe she has an itemized list of all my sins that she reads while beating me to a bloody pulp. Fate, indeed. I can't wait.*

"Speaking of hammers," he asked, "how did you know shoving the T-shaped stone through the open gateway would destroy the portal?"

"Well, I didn't really. We'd wondered if solid items could pass through the portals, or only energy. Two things were in my mind when I did it. First, if the hammer could pass through, Charun might have gone to fetch it, and I could close the portal. Second, if the stone couldn't pass through, I thought it might be destroyed, depriving Charun of his true power and ability to feed."

"Umm, sounds like, in either case, I'd have probably been toast."

"We were out of options. If this didn't work, or had the hammer simply been destroyed, Charun would surely have killed us both. It's a risky game we play with these artifacts and the beasts they summon. Paying with your life isn't out of the question, as you well know."

Bitter and horrifying memories of Mason's death flashed through his mind. Some things you can't un-see, and he now had a carousel of terrible images that would haunt him, likely to the end of his days.

"In any case," she said, trying to redirect the conversation. "I've answered your question, now you answer mine. No more delays, you little shit!"

"Okay," he said, actually pleased to be distracted from his macabre recollections. "Here goes."

He exhausted himself as he lugged all the stuff he could actually carry down the hill. The cool of morning gave way to heat, and surprising humidity, for the mountains. The dog days of summer were upon them.

He drove back to the cabin close to noon, to eat and to rest. He hoped Lotte felt better and could possibly help him, but she was still fast asleep when he checked on her.

"Hey, how you doing?" he asked as he stroked her shoulder. "You need anything?"

"What time is it? God, my head hurts."

"It's about a quarter to twelve. I think you have a concussion. You seem a little better. Have you been able to get up?"

"I haven't tried. I do have to pee again, though. Maybe you can help me?"

He helped her to the bathroom. She seemed far steadier on her feet, and this time he waited for her outside.

"Actually, Eric," she called through the closed door, "I'm going to take a shower and brush my teeth. I'm absolutely disgusting! Can you get me a clean towel, and my sunglasses? The light is killing my eyes."

He did, and then crouched by the door as she washed, to make sure he'd be there in case she needed him. When she emerged, she looked, and smelled, far better. Unfortunately, she'd spent all of her energy, so he escorted her back to bed, then brought her some water and ibuprofen. Food was still out of the question.

He sat at the kitchen table and drank his coffee. For some reason, it didn't taste as good as when she made it. He also ate some soup, the only thing he had the energy to make.

Three things left on the hill, all too heavy to carry. I need to get them down off that mountain today. The risks are getting too high, and when Vern comes up missing, all hell is gonna break loose.

He looked at his watch: close to 2:00 p.m. He pulled himself together and went back to the van.

It was a short drive. He knew the way. He pulled in, parked, walked to the door, and knocked. A dog barked in the back yard as he waited. He knew it would take a moment. Soon, he heard footsteps, and the door cracked open.

"Who are you?" Ethan asked suspiciously. "You looking for a fishing trip?"

"Do you remember me? I'm Mason's friend."

"Oh, yeah. You were with that pretty little lady. I remember you two. Where's Mason?"

"I'm not gonna lie to you, Ethan. Mason is dead. He was killed by the same thing that's responsible for all the murders and disappearances that have been happening. He got mixed up with something he shouldn't have, and he called us to help him fix it. We fixed it, but before we did, it got him."

"What was it? Aliens?"

"Almost. Listen, I need your help. I've got $268.75 in cash. $250 is yours if you'll come help me move three heavy things down from a hill up near the trails. It's totally safe, unless the cops catch us, in which case we're screwed, but I think we have time. I'll explain everything on the way. If you want to bail, I'll give you half the money anyway. What do you say?"

Ethan stared coldly from the cracked doorway.

Eric met his icy gaze dead on.

"Show me the cash."

"Ethan McCarthy? Eric, what were you thinking? He's insane! There's no telling what he'll say to people!"

"Well, I didn't have a *lotta* options there, Lotte. Plus, you're right. He's insane! He talks about alien abductions, and government coverups, and contrails changing weather, and mind control experiments all the time. So, now he says some magnetic monster was running around bashing people's heads in with his magical hammer, and it finally got stopped by this Genie-thing that some dude and his hottie girlfriend summoned from the elemental plane of freaking fire! Who's gonna believe him? Plus, who's he gonna tell?

He's more mistrustful of the police and the government than he is of the bullshit he reads on the internet, or wherever he picks up all this crap. Some fishermen are gonna get some extremely interesting tall tales, but that's probably about it. This was the best I could do on short notice. I'm sorry if it's not up to your lofty standards, your royal highness."

She fell silent—*really* silent. Fifteen minutes of complete quiet passed, other than the sound of the wind howling through the jagged roof of the increasingly rickety white van.

"Eric?" she finally asked.

"What?"

"Do you really think I'm a *hottie*?"

Together, Ethan and Eric loaded the van with the final three items from the hill. He then returned the strange man to his shambolic abode with the admonishment to keep his mouth shut—which he likely wouldn't, but who really cared.

Eric shook with exhaustion by the time he got back to the cabin in the late afternoon. He'd had no sleep, and moving the heavy un-mirror had transformed the throbbing pain in his back and shoulder to a piercing agony. His badly bruised leg screamed in protest with every torturous step. Hunger and thirst assailed him, and he knew he looked and smelled absolutely disgusting.

Before he did anything else, he went to check on Lotte. She still lay in bed, curtains drawn, and covers pulled tightly to her face. Her eyes opened when she heard him shuffle into the room.

"Eric, my God! Where have you been?"

"I thought I needed some exercise. Maybe I overdid it." To his amazement, she rose, stumbled to him and fell into his arms, then dragged him to the bed.

"Lie down."

"I'm pretty gross. Maybe I should take a shower."

"You can't be any grosser than I was last night. Come on. I'm starting to feel a little better. Sleep with me for a while. It's always better when you're here. It makes me be still, and I need to be very still right now, or my head explodes." She helped him remove his dirty, sweaty, and blood-stained clothes. "Eric, your shoulder! This is awful!"

Yeah, awful pretty much covers it. What's done is done, though. I'll deal with it when we get back to Southby, assuming we do. We're not out of the woods yet. Literally.

In the end, exhaustion won the contest, and the promise of sleep next to her soft form called to him.

She helped him under the covers, then pressed close and gently stroked his chest. *"Schlafen,"* she whispered in his ear.

He slept.

The dawn light crept through the curtains as the sounds of birds woke him. He felt her close behind him. He turned to see if she still slept, but instead met her open eyes and smiling face.

"Moin! Sleep well?"

"You'd know better than me. I was asleep and missed the whole thing."

She giggled and gave him a playful tap. "Come on, then, we have a lot to do. I hope the police haven't been up on the hill, and that the helicopter hasn't come. We have to get everything down from there! I'm still so weak, and my head is killing me, but we don't have a lot of choice. Let's have something to eat, then maybe—"

"It's all done. We're ready to go. We just need to clean this place up and see if we can make a spot in the van for you to lie down while we drive home."

"Eric, it's impossible! How could you get all those things down from the hill?"

"Too complicated to explain right now. We really do have to get moving. Also, if you need anything off of Mason's computer, now's the time to grab it. All that stuff is gonna have to go. He has some USB drives down there. Can you do that? I'll rustle us up something to eat before we leave."

"But... but... Eric... how? How did you do it?"

So it went as they ate a rushed breakfast, as he cleaned their presence from the little cottage, as she took files from the computer then collapsed with exhaustion, as he packed all the computer equipment and their things—those they didn't burn in the barbecue grill for being too ripped, bloodied, or vomit-ridden.

So it went as she lay in the back of the dilapidated white van, as they drove for the final time down the gravely dirt road, then along New Speck Lane, then through Bailey, then back toward Berlin—the one close-by, not the one in Germany—and finally toward the interstate.

She didn't stop asking until he told her how he'd done it.

Then, finally, she slept.

Once again, they stopped in Concord.

They dropped the hefty trash bag full of Mason's valuable computer equipment into the familiar dumpster behind Market Basket. The USB drives contained what she wanted to keep.

He got some coffee and a small dish of vanilla soft serve at the dairy bar.

She still wasn't hungry.

He pulled the decaying white van into the parking lot of his apartment in Southby late in the afternoon on Saturday. There they stayed.

All Sunday, they rested. They lay together, legs intertwined on the futon couch, watching TV with the sound off, box fan pointed directly at them and blowing at full speed. Neither had the energy, or the inclination, for much else, other than sleep.

Hardly a moment passed in which they weren't touching. She cradled his swollen hand, and gently massaged his shredded shoulder. Together, they slept, sheltered in the warmth and comfort of each other's arms.

No one knew they'd returned to town, except the driver from the Bow Thai who delivered Lemongrass Chicken and Panang to Eric's door. The two ate together, straight out of the containers, periodically passing the little white boxes between them without removing their eyes from the mute images of violence in faraway places on the TV.

They hardly spoke. They hardly needed to.

By Monday afternoon, she seemed well enough to help unload the van. They drove to Eric's grandmother's building, and she again procured the keys. Slowly and agonizingly, they lifted and moved the flight cases. Each compensated for the other's current physical limitations.

Then they set off to return the wretched van. It had been a rough start with the venerable vehicle. In the parking lot of Vitis Brothers, they held hands and sat for a time in quiet reflection, still buckled into the pleather seats.

Reluctantly, Eric finally hopped out and went to find Ricky.

"Holy shit, man!" he said when he saw the extensive damage. "What did you do, take the thing to the goddamned Iraq invasion? What the hell happened to the fuckin' roof?"

"Ricky, I'm really sorry. Believe me, whatever it costs, I'll pay for it. Totally my bad. I'll tell you, though, for all the shit this thing saw, it never let us down."

Together, they drove back to the apartment in the little red Mazda. It felt strange and small to him after handling the big cargo van. He called Margot, and his dad. He'd go in tomorrow to see how things went, and to try and get reacclimated to a life that suddenly seemed remote.

Lotte asked for his laptop password, and she spent some time on the computer while he took their laundry to the coin-operated machines downstairs. After all that, they had another night of take-out and TV, this time with the sound on.

Baby steps.

As she rested her head on his shoulder — the right one, the left still being far too painful — he wondered if this might be it. Maybe the moment had arrived, the right time to take that next and ultimate step to consummate what appeared to be their rekindled romance. All the signs seemed to be there. It felt as if they were one touch, one glance, one word away. He knew in his heart that if he reached out to her right now, over the container with the Massaman Curry, and guided her lips to his, that she would offer no resistance.

But what would that mean?

Before he crossed that now seemingly nonexistent boundary, he needed to *know.* Had he won her heart, made himself irresistible, made her love him enough to want to be with him, wholly? She either needed to tell him, or he needed to ask.

Tomorrow, when I get home from work. One more day for wounds to heal, for the unspoken bond to strengthen.

He'd ask her tomorrow.

He got home early on Tuesday afternoon. It had been hard being back, almost confusing — too many stimuli and too much adaptation, even having only missed six days of work, and after a mere ten days away, albeit ten busy and incredibly strange days. Despite all that, he found himself in excellent spirits — excited. Life suddenly seemed full of *possibility.*

Lotte sat on the unfolded futon, *Cleopatra* closed by her side. It appeared she'd finally finished the book, not really having been able to read since last Thursday due to her head injury.

"How are you?" he cheerfully asked as he entered.

"Fine."

"What'd you do today?"

"I went to visit your grandmother."

"Great, bet she liked that! Listen, I was thinking maybe we could swing by my folks and get Langsam, maybe do dinner over there. They'd love to see you. You feeling up to it?"

She swung her head slowly toward him. "Eric, I have to go."

"Go? Go where?"

"Back to Berlin. Back to the Werner Institut."

His world started to collapse. "Oh. When?"

"I've booked a flight for tomorrow morning. That's what I was doing on your computer. Will you take me to the airport, or should I arrange for an Uber?"

Things started to spin. He sat at the kitchen table and stared at the worn linoleum floor. What was there to say? He had his answer.

"I'll take you. I'm gonna go get Langsam. I'll see you later."

He left without looking back.

He could already see the haze in the late morning August sky. It turned the blue to dusty gray, the gray to white, and the white to a vague ripple high in the atmosphere, like a giant contrail stretching beyond view over the horizon.

Eric saw the heat rise from the asphalt of the parking lot below. He could almost taste the humidity as it seasoned the air outside his window with the musky flavor of sweat that clogged and burned his nostrils as he inhaled. It was like a sauna, a steam bath. It felt as if he bathed in his own perspiration, as he'd done early that morning on his new hybrid bike. In a near baptism of exertion, he'd relinquished all the liquid his feeble body possessed into the dry and hungry winds that enveloped him like the arms of ghosts.

"What are you doing here?"

Margot's voice startled him. He jumped in shock and tore his feet from the little shelf under the window where he'd propped them, then swung swiftly in his chair to face the door. "Jeez! You scared the crap out of me!"

She didn't react. She just stared, arms crossed, as she leaned on the door frame.

I wonder how long she's been standing there? For that matter, I wonder how long I've actually been staring out this window?

"So," she said, obviously perturbed about something. "You gonna answer me?"

"Umm... yeah... I'm, uh... I'm doing payroll. I guess I should probably be showing you how to do that, huh? What time is it? Holy shit, 11:45? Wow. Hey, listen, maybe we could work on it after lunch. I'm happy to start showing you—"

With an angry expression, she strode directly to where he sat and forcefully punched him in the arm.

"*Ow!* Holy shit, that hurts like hell! I fucked my shoulder up on that side. What'd you do that for?"

She reached back to the door and, while not actually slamming it, slammed it shut. She then strutted with determination to the two-seater couch, plopped herself down, and stared at him. "Do I have your attention now?"

"Undivided," he meekly replied as he rubbed his arm to reduce the sting of her formidable right hook.

"Good. Now, what are you doing here?"

"Umm, I'm guessing *payroll* is the wrong answer? What do you want me to say? I'm... like... well, I'm... I don't know... working... on something. I guess."

She did a facepalm. "Eric, come off it! You've been sitting in this office for two weeks staring out that fucking window. I can see you, you moron! I sit right there! Your dad is starting to ask *me* what's going on. Things are piling up. So, what the fuck are you doing here?"

Has it really been two weeks?

It felt like yesterday when....

They stood at the entrance to security at Logan Airport's Terminal E. Lotte had already checked her suitcase, and now held only her duffle and her purse. She looked at him expectantly, like somehow, she thought he might have more to say. When nothing materialized from his ossified lips, she gave him an unreturned hug.

She backed away slightly, but still held his arms as she spoke sternly. "Eric, don't lose my cell number, and don't change yours again without letting me know! I'm serious! If you do, I'll be furious with you. But please, just don't. Can you promise you'll do this for me?"

He nodded.

She turned to leave.

He turned to leave... to walk back to his red Mazda 3, and his job that wasn't his calling, and his friend that wasn't his girlfriend, and his life that wasn't really a life, in his hometown that had never really been his home.

She called from behind.

He turned back to her.

"Eric." Her tone was pleading.

She probably wants to be forgiven for being so selfish, so headstrong, so... called. *Either that, or she wants acceptance... acceptance that this is how it's gonna be for us. In the end, her life is elsewhere, and her needs for me have their limits. So, forgiveness, acceptance, something else? I don't know, but it's clearly not something I can give her. I gave her my all, and it obviously wasn't enough.*

Finally, her shoulders slumped. "Just don't change your cell number."

With that, she hoisted her duffel and disappeared into the security line.

"I don't know, Margot. I'm not sure what you want me to say. I tried. I almost killed myself trying—physically, mentally, emotionally. I didn't leave anything on the table. I tried to win the hearts and minds of all girlfriends in a ten-mile radius. I tried to obey the First Law of Margot: make yourself irresistible. I wasn't perfect—I had my moments—but I really tried. I almost thought I had her."

Her visage softened... slightly. "Did you tell her how you felt? That you love her? That you want her?"

"How can I tell her that if I don't know it's true? I mean, I *do* love her, but Lotte and I are... like... almost polar opposites—positive and negative. There's a part of me that questions whether she really *is* what I want. Even if I had a place in her world, it would be a constant struggle for me. There'd be lots of changes, almost constant change, and that's not something I take easily. I'd feel a lot more confident if I knew *she* wanted it. In a sense, that would make the decision for me, but I can't deny it, things would still be difficult. She didn't give me any indication she wanted us to be together, and now she's gone back to Germany. Maybe she's just someone I love that I wasn't meant to be with, not because of who she is, but because of who I am."

She got up, maneuvered around him, and sat on his desk. Then she spun his chair around to face her, put her feet on the armrests, and grasped his shoulders.

She looked straight into his eyes. "Okay, here's the thing... you've gotta be who you are. You can talk all you want about choices and decisions and all that shit, but in the end, you've gotta be who you are. That's not always an easy pill to swallow. How do you think I felt? What do you think it would be like for Daddy's little angel to tell him he'll never have grandchildren, never have a son in law? He hasn't spoken with me in... shit... ten years? More? Who gives a fuck. It's his issue, not mine. I am who I am, Eric. I accept it. I embrace it. Because to fight against it is just impossible, unless you want to sleepwalk though some faked existence. Some do, but not me, and I don't think you can do it either. I think there's more going on in your head than you let on."

He suddenly felt that perhaps his problems weren't quite as monumental as he'd made them out to be. Whatever decision he made, or whoever he wanted or needed to be, he'd always have a family that loved him.

He sighed. "Okay, I hear you. So, you're saying I should just accept who I am and stay in Southby? Stay at Schneider? Stay with Erica?"

"I'm not saying that at all! I'm saying that before you make what you think is a choice, you need to *know* who you are, and who you aren't. Not *decide. Know!* I have no idea what you'll conclude. Only you can know that. But until you do, your choice is just an illusion, based on criteria that are temporary and transient, and prone to change as you come to realize who you *really* are. If you go against that, you'll find yourself right back in the situation you're in today, facing the same questions, over, and over, and over."

"I... I don't know if that's something I know yet. I don't even have any idea how to approach that question... issue... whatever."

"Yes, you do. You just have to free your mind enough to see the truth. Stop being so afraid of how others might see you, or how you do or don't fit all those roles and expectations you grew up with, even the ones you gave the middle finger and walked away from. You have to clear out all the voices in your head and hear *your* voice. And you need to have the courage and the freedom to embrace what you truly want. I free you, Eric Schneider! Go look at yourself in the mirror and see who you really are. No judgments. No recriminations. Look and see, and be who you see. Fuck the rest."

He sat in stunned silence. Aside from the really creepy mirror reference, he felt like she'd just dissected him. It was as if little pins held his flesh open, his insides on display for all to see.

Maybe I should take advantage and have a look. That seems to be what she's suggesting.

She climbed down from the desk and made for the door. "So, payroll after lunch, right? That's what you said, and I'm holding you to it. Sorry I hit you. You can file a grievance if you want."

"Yeah, sure. Payroll after lunch... and it didn't hurt that bad."

Yes, it did. It hurt a lot. In fact, I'm not sure I'll ever be the same.

CHAPTER 20

Central Etruria, 539 BC

An ominous noise filled the chamber, that of something very hard, very solid, as it struck the wood of the outer door. Both guards on the scaffolding jumped, and the hammer that one of them held fell with a clang to the ground. Briefly, each froze in terror, until another blow, this one mightier than the last, caused the bar to buckle and the doors to splinter. Neither bothered with the ladder. They each chose to jump before another blast might shatter the door open.

Arathia screamed. "No! I forbid this! You cannot! You must not!"

"I've done nothing, princess. As your own eyes beheld, the box lay empty. The Gatekeeper is not mine to command. Not now. It is my nephew, Rasce's, business where he chooses to send the creature. Surely, his actions on the borderlands these past years have been to the benefit of all. Do you not agree? When the full extent of your duplicity became apparent, he made his decision and availed himself of the recessed doorway I instructed my mason to carve in my beloved husband's tomb. The matter is entirely in his hands."

"Your self-righteous insolence has been the bane of my existence! I will bargain with the creature. He's rightfully mine to begin with. He'll listen to me, and I'll have him take *you* in my place!"

"It doesn't really work that way, my dear Arathia. You'd know this, had you, or any of your spoiled and decadent relatives, ever taken any interest in your family's legacy. But by all means, speak with him now. Try your best to convince him that it is I, not you, who should accompany him this night. Would that he could end the suffering I endure without the one I love."

The two guards who had jumped from the platform raced in a panic toward the door to the annex, and began to heft the heavy bar. The soldier near Arathia hesitated briefly, then dropped his weapon and ran to join them.

"You cowards!" Arathia screamed, but her words were lost when a final blow smashed through the outer door.

A deluge of debris spilled into the room and battered both women, who still stood near the wooden scaffolding. A plate of bronze sheared off of the bar and sliced into Rika's arm, while fragments of the doorway pummeled her back and head. She collapsed to the ground in agony.

For a time, all she could hear were the frantic prayers of the three guards near the inner door. They seemed to have abandoned their attempt to escape, and now lay prostrate at the threshold. With effort, she raised her head, only to meet Arathia's wild-eyed stare. The shower of rubble had left a nasty cut in the woman's forehead and bloodied her nose, yet still, she held the guard's abandoned sword, which she waved threateningly before her.

"Call him off! I command you! Do it, or I'll kill you myself!"

A stiff breeze from the beat of mighty wings tossed Arathia's hair and rippled across her robe, as the scratch of clawed feet on the wooden platform above heralded the arrival of a being from the realm of the gods. She spared a quick glance over her shoulder, then her body slumped. The sword slipped from her hand, and she dropped to her knees.

When she spoke again, all authority had drained from her voice. "Please, High Priestess. Please... Rika."

Rika.

In her mind, dizzied by the hail of debris and all that had happened this day, Rika saw the letters of her name float by, carved like a talisman on an object she hadn't held since she'd been a girl. The heart of that girl still beat inside her. Old as she now was, and having lost much, her bristling curiosity of what tomorrow might bring had never abandoned her, nor had her burning desire to lead a life beyond the ordinary.

Like those letters scratched into the ceramic, she had defied the humble background and paltry raw materials the gods had seen fit to bestow upon her, and carved the shape of her life into the intractable surface of a harsh and uncaring world. Due to the clandestine nature of her work, few would ever know. Her name would not ring through the ages like the great nobles and kings. Her power lurked in the shadows of night, and the deadly dealings with forces both terrifying and incomprehensible to most.

Yet, in truth, she knew, these forces were not wicked, and were not to be feared. They kept her people strong and safe, and her children would see to the protection of the next generation, and her children's children after that.

It would be a wondrous thing to see. How can this be bad? How can this be wrong?

She took Arathia's shaking hand in hers. "Fear not, noble princess. You won't be alone in the afterlife for long. All too soon, I will join you, accompanied by the Gatekeeper, just as you now shall be. I promise, I'll not abandon you to a solitary existence for eternity. Each day, we will visit, and we shall spin our wool and tend our looms. And we shall sing — oh, how we'll sing — and together, we'll watch throughout all of time as fate unfolds before us."

Berlin, Germany, Tuesday, August 27, 2013

It must be boring. Every day, the same thing. Locked behind a pane of glass. Examined and photographed like the victims of some horrific, but exquisitely beautiful and infinitely intriguing, crime scene.

History's remnants. Not history, but in Eric's mind, a proxy for the lives and loves, the passions and pains, the inspiration and idiocy of incalculable multitudes, faceless and unknowable. Those who had carved or sculpted, forged or molded, scribed or painted, served or ruled. All these lives, reduced to but a few objects that only a miniscule fraction of these ancient peoples had ever used, or even seen, as if all that remained of Eric himself was the Schneider Industrial Flooring sign outside his office, and a five-sentence letter he'd once written to a girl in exceedingly small print.

How can that sum up a person's existence? It can't.

These items *had* history, but they were not history itself. History is a story, a human story, and like all humans, it has a birth, and a death. These relics live on in half-life, sustained only by the interest that humans still have in the superficial elements they project: the stunning gold, the exotic and evocative images, the monumental edifices with enigmatic smiles and icy gazes that cut through their observers to the abyss beyond, or the abyss within themselves, pleading to be filled.

Once these items had been the stuff of life. Now, they served merely to entertain. Surely, the perfume bottles must yearn to be filled afresh with the sweet scents of old, and hear once more the gossip from the lips of their mistresses who formerly ruled the night. The combs must beg to brush their beautiful raven hair once again, and the cups must surely crave the watered wine that long ago slaked their owner's thirst, seemingly endless.

But everything ends.

So now, these artifacts languished in their cases, unused, untouched, save the delicate, rubber-gloved hands of those who posed them on little stands to smile for an eternity of "oohs" and "aahs," and pretty pictures.

They sat sequestered and isolated in the endless parade of uninvited visitors, there to steal a quick glance and get out before being sent off to the next attraction distraction.

It must be boring, but today, maybe they'll get a little treat.

He'd texted her after he paid his twenty Euros and got settled:

I'm downstairs. Pergamon room. Can U come?

He wasn't even sure if she were there until the reply came.

!

Now he waited on a bench at the back of the gigantic space as he gazed at the imposing and mighty frieze. The eighth wonder of the world. Gods and Titans, winged warriors engaged in heroic battles, horses, and exotic beasts, all surrounded and towered above him. He stared, as did the others who milled about in the massive enclosure. In his gaze, he thought he saw the marble stir.

They can feel it. Something different.

Maybe all these wondrous and ancient sculptures might turn to look and see an occurrence that didn't happen every day — not here, at least — not for them to experience.

Perhaps Nefertiti herself would crane her slender and beautiful neck to watch the proceedings with a regal, but now lopsided, gaze. Maybe she would think back to her mate, who spit in the eye of Amun and defied the priestly class to build a new city in the desert, where they worshiped the blazing disc of the Aten as it rose over the eastern hills.

Eric also worshiped the sun. A black sun. A sun with an event horizon beyond which gravity and mass gave way, where time and space lost their bearings, with the smell of gummy bears and morning coffee, mystical visions of squiggly black un-eyebrows, and the enticing sight of a girl wearing nothing but a t-shirt and her underwear.

He didn't have to look to feel her radiance, didn't have to turn his head to feel her gravitational pull. He knew the instant she walked into the room, and he got ever warmer as she approached and stood above him where he sat on the wooden bench.

"Eric," she said, with calm surprise. "What are you doing here?"

He reluctantly pried his gaze from the great frieze.

The marble figures now morphed from actors to audience, observed to observers. Briefly, they ceased their myriad activities to contemplate the strange little creatures below once more — those who had made them, and then imprisoned them for eternity in a cell of endless gawks and gazes, awe and artertainment, selfies and superficiality. There wasn't a real emotion to be found. The lively gait and thriving bustle of everyday life had been replaced by the drab and lonely existence of an animal in an especially opulent cage.

But not today. Today, they'll get a little glimpse of the real thing, of life actually being lived.

He wondered if they'd enjoy again bearing witness to the joy and the sadness, the risk and the struggle, the hiding and the revealing.

The expectant chatter of history's weary survivors faded as the curtain rose on this one-day-only exhibition, for which their price of admission had been so abominably high.

"Oh," he said, "I just happened to be in town, taking in the sights. I wanted to see if I could crash on your couch."

She gave an almost imperceptible little snort of laughter. It signaled her failure to deny humor in a decidedly unhumorous situation. "I don't think you'd like my roommates. Very noisy, always having boys over. You'd never get any sleep." She took a seat on the bench, just out of arms reach.

"Yeah, probably true. I was just kidding anyway. So, umm... listen... I've decided to move to Germany."

"Really?"

"Yeah, Berlin."

"What will you do?"

"That's a good question. I have some ideas. I'm thinking about teaching. Apparently, I'm good at that, which isn't surprising because I had a great example to learn from. Maybe I'll be a tutor for English, maybe teach history in an English-language school. They have them for embassy kids and stuff. I don't know, maybe I'll just clean bathrooms. I got pretty good at that recently too."

Another faint snort of laughter escaped from her nostrils.

"Truth is, Lotte, I don't really care that much. I want to be with you. Deep down, that's all that ultimately matters."

She took that in for a time, then finally spoke. "Are you sure? Are you certain this is what you want? My life is, well, really quite insane. Longer term, I don't know where I'll be. You know very well what I want to do, at a minimum quietly on the side, and you know very well the potential dangers involved."

She paused, perhaps expecting a response. He gave none, so she went on. "I don't know if I'll have a central point where I'd spend most of my time, or if I'd have to constantly travel. Even with a secure position, I imagine I'll be gone frequently with conferences and other sorts of trips, on-site digs, and the like. Is this something you can be comfortable with?"

"Yeah, I've thought about all that. It's not optimal for me, but it's a hell of a lot better than living without you. I just don't think I can do that, unless you make me. Then I guess I'll have to. I'm not really sure what that means, living without you. I guess I'd figure it out. Put it this way, though: if you go to the Sahara for six months, I'll go and set up tents. If you go to the arctic, then I'll go and... umm... I'll... jeez... I don't know what the heck they do in the arctic. I'll set up warmer tents. Whatever. Tell you what... don't go to the arctic. It's fucking freezing there, anyway. Where was I? Oh, yeah. In any case, when possible, I'll go where you go, but if you're gone for a while and I'm not with you, maybe if you could just try to stay in touch a little better, and then I wouldn't feel so... well... so... *abandoned*."

He clamped his lips and bit back tears. He didn't come here to cry. He came to state his case. It just hurt to admit this to her, and to himself. He closed his eyes and tried to regain his composure.

She sat silently, perhaps sensing he needed time. "What about Erica?" she finally asked, her voice barely above a whisper.

What about Erica?

It hadn't been pretty, if that's what she wanted to know. It had been as messy and ugly and disappointing and hurtful as one would have expected it to be. Eric had faced otherworldly monsters of fire and magnetism, been raked by demonic claws, almost killed by the hammer of a demi-god, but having to face Erica had truly scared him.

In a sense, as difficult as it had been, Erica had proven to be the key, the final point of inflection at which all the conflicting emotions, all the various opinions and possibilities that existed for him, either turned one way, or the other.

So, what about Erica? In every sense, she fit the bill for a life that seemed most suited to his sensibilities. Most would jump at the chance to be with a person who genuinely loved them, and wouldn't pressure them to be something they aren't, and to simply let them be what they were meant to be.

Therein, however, lay the problem, or rather, problems. First, could he truly love her and not secretly wish she were Lotte, or hold that glimmer of hope that somehow, someday, Lotte might return? He had to face the ugly fact that the answer to that question was simply no. True, people lived their entire lives with that sort of dissonance, and to an extent, he'd almost acquiesced to such an existence, and understood he may yet if Lotte rebuffed him.

Still, there was more to it.

In Erica, Eric saw his reflection, but as he knew from experience, a mirror isn't a doorway—it's a trap. The mirror didn't provide a path back to what he once had been, that boy who teetered on the sharp blade of Lotte's scalpel. Consciously or not, he'd made a choice back then, and like the otherworldly beasts they'd encountered, he'd passed through a portal, and the new world he'd entered had transformed him.

It made him larger. It changed his shape, his makeup, his being. Even if he found a gateway back, his essential form would never be the same, just like the Afrit and Charun. For better or for worse, he'd been remade, the product of a long-ago choice. That was now a part of him, and made him what, and who, he was.

In the end, the decision to be, or not to be, with Lotte hadn't been a matter of choice at all. It came down to recognition, and *acceptance*, just as Margot had said. He realized that life with Erica would, in truth, ask him to be something that no longer suited his makeup. Once he grasped this, it had been easy, and terrifyingly difficult.

He opened his eyes, and the wonder of their audience, the Pergamon Frieze, unfolded once more before him. "What about Erica? Yeah, well, we just couldn't agree on who would change their name. She wouldn't accept being called 'Lotte,' and she just couldn't live with the name I chose for myself."

"Which was?"

"Well, Lemmy, of course."

She hiccupped a little laugh.

He worked up the courage to face her. She had an odd expression. Something between wonder and happiness and sadness.

"So," she quietly said. "Germany. Berlin. Teaching, or tutoring. Are you certain this is what you want?"

"One hundred percent certain. I've never been more certain of anything in my life."

"Well, I think this would be marvelous for you, and that you'd be wonderful at it. Berlin will gain a fine instructor. I think this is a great idea."

"You do? Seriously?"

"I do. Sadly, I don't think I can be a part of it. I've—"

"What do you mean you can't be a part of it?" he shouted in a flash of anger, drawing the attention of several surprised museum patrons.

She recoiled slightly and brought her lips tightly together.

"Lotte, I... I don't understand. Or, maybe I do. I guess this means you don't love me, at least not in *that* way. You want me as a friend, sort of, when it's convenient for you — when you have some multi-dimensional monster you need my help to track down, or put back in its damn bottle, or a new portal you might have found, or when you just need a warm body to sleep next to, or put your head in their lap when you're having fucking nightmares! Otherwise, though, hey, you've got a busy life, things to do, places to see, Afrits to command! Okay, scratch that last one. I know that's not you, but can you sort of see my point? I can't do this anymore. I love you! I want you! No, actually, I don't want you. I need you! I need you to be in my life wholly, or out of my life, wholly. I can't do this middle-ground, up-and-down thing anymore, and if I have to choose one, though really choice has almost nothing to do with it, I choose to be with you, whatever that means. And believe me, nobody gets what that means better than I do."

Her eyes went wide and, remarkably, she smiled. She slid on the bench and put her hand on his shoulder.

He flinched slightly, as his wounds from nearly a month ago still ached, but he forced the pain from his mind.

"My timid little Eric Schneider. My little tortoise, finally poking his head out of his shell. No, Eric, I don't want you as a friend just when it's convenient for me. I can see why you say this. I failed you that first year in school. I took for granted that you'd always be there. If you're the tortoise, then I'm the hare. I run ahead. I get caught up in my own world — obsessed, really. Everything else just... well... fades. But then I woke up to what I'd done. When you cut me off, I called your father to find out what had happened. I was afraid you were sick, or dead. When he told me to back off and give you time, I got angry! First at you, but then at myself. How could I have been so selfish, so blind? I'll never get over what I did. When I realized I needed your help, I tried to show you I was sorry. What good is there, really, in saying it? In a sense, I tried to win you back. I tried to show you that I could be there for you, be aware of your needs. I tried to listen and not get angry, and I also tried to prove these things to myself, because I had to know if I really am that heartless, that selfish... that blind. I love you, Eric. I thought I did previously, but seeing you again and going through what we did together has made me understand it completely."

He felt dizzy. "Why didn't you tell me all this before? If I'd known what you wanted, I'd have come here a lot sooner."

"Exactly, my love. I lead, you follow. That's been our pattern as long as we've known each other. I know I have this power over you, like the power I have to attract boys, and I *hate* it! I hate the boys who grovel and grope and hope I'll throw them a bone... who think every touch is a 'come-on.' You're not like them. I've always felt safe with you, that we shared so much more. Yes, sometimes I just want to lie next to someone, or need to put my head in their lap, and sometimes I need it to be just that, and no more! Because hares get *tired*. They don't always want to satisfy a boy's urges at the end of a hard day, when their minds are racing with all the thoughts of what they want to accomplish. They want to sleep... *shhhh*. They've run themselves ragged and can't finish the race, unless some kindly tortoise puts them on his back as he waddles by. Umm... no offense intended by that last bit."

"None taken." *Actually, kind of an amusing image.*

"In any case," she continued. "I know I have this power. In some things, I'm happy to lead, but not *this*. I can't lead you here, Eric. It's too important. It's *your* life, and you and I are so incredibly different—the tortoise and the hare. I left the door open, but you had to walk through. You had to poke your head out of your shell, because it isn't going to be easy. Let alone almost dying twice at the hands of monsters, and possibly more in the future, it will be hard to be with me, especially for you. I needed *you* to make that choice. I had to hear from your lips that this is what *you* want!"

"But I did that! I told you what I wanted! I made the choice. As hard as it was, I did it, and you still say you can't be a part of my life. Why?"

She smiled wryly. "Well, Eric, you interrupted me. I was going to tell you, if you're teaching in Berlin, then I'll be far away. I just got accepted to graduate school."

"Graduate school? Okay, you're going to graduate school, very interesting. But if I interrupted you, why didn't you stop me? Why did you let me say all those things?"

"Because I wanted to hear them! I've wanted to hear those words from you for years! I wanted you to scream them in my ear, because sometimes, I'm deaf. I can't say what I'd have done, but if you'd told me that first semester the kind of troubles you were having, I might have gotten on a plane. Don't get me wrong, I'm not blaming you. I blame myself. But of all the things I'm good at, perhaps this is one I'm not. You have to tell me what you need if you're not getting it. Give me the chance to try. So, I didn't stop you because this is what I *want* from you. It's what I wanted every day we were in New Hampshire together, and even more when we got back to Southby, and when we were in the airport! This is what it means, Eric, to be with me. This is the struggle you have to accept. Is it still worth it? Is it still what you want?"

Of course, it wasn't really a matter of want, or choice. He knew that it came down to acceptance. He was who he was, the person who, in a sense, Lotte had made him. There was no path back. He accepted this struggle, and all that meant, and all that came with it.

"So," he asked. "Graduate school. For a PhD, I assume?"

"A Master's, then a PhD. Yes."

"Where?"

"Harvard."

"Harvard... like in Massachusetts, Harvard?"

"No, Eric, they opened a branch on Mars, but I'll have to be a commuter student because there aren't any dorms."

He smiled. "I didn't realize they had a college in Harvard, Mass."

She laughed... a full laugh, with teeth and everything.

"Were you ever gonna tell me this, or were you planning to just show up on my doorstep in Southby again?"

"I almost told you many times when we were together, but things were still up in the air. I only got the acceptance letter a couple of days ago. Very late in the game, but there were still details to work out about laboratory and computer access, support for travel to dig sites, conferences, and what-not. I was going to call you when all that got worked out, which is why I wanted you not to change your bloody cell number. I just didn't want it all to fall through and have you disappointed. I didn't want to hurt you again. Eric, I love you."

He basked in that for a time. For better or for worse, for richer or poorer, in sickness and in health, in battles of fire and magnetism, he'd gotten what he wanted.

Till death do us part.

He turned to her. She still tightly held his shoulder, but the pain didn't register. Her face again became his world, all that he could see, all he ever wanted to see. Gravity and mass gave way as he gazed straight into the black sun.

Nefertiti would be proud of me.

"That was pretty funny, actually... what you said about Mars. I think you've been hanging around with me too much."

"I agree completely," she replied. "You need to go back to the States now, Eric. Back to Boston, before you destroy my sense of humor entirely. Anyway, I have a task for you."

"Yes, Master. Your wish is my command!" He crossed his eyes and stuck his tongue out sideways.

Jeez, that's actually harder than I thought.

She giggled. "Stop it, little shit! I want you to find me an apartment near Harvard. A one-bedroom is fine. I can set up my study in the living room. But, umm, if you prefer, find one with two bedrooms or more. I can move my study into one of the other rooms. If you go with a larger apartment, though, make sure there's plenty of light in the place... for Langsam."

Together, they walked arm in arm out of the Pergamon Museum. It was nearly noon, and he figured he still owed her lunch. She could pick the place this time. As they ambled under the grand and majestic Ishtar Gate, he swore he saw the great golden lions, bulls, and dragons rise in front of their stunning azure backdrop. And somewhere in the echoes of the cavernous building, he thought he heard distant and indistinct applause.

Perhaps that was just his imagination.

THE END

(...although Eric's and Lotte's adventures will continue. To help ensure that happens, please consider leaving a review on whichever site you typically purchase books online. Your support is critical to the success of independent publishers like Evolved Publishing, and independent authors like William E. Noland. Reviews send a strong signal to potential readers and encourage online booksellers to promote the titles. If you'd like to see more books like this one, leaving an honest, heartfelt review is one of the best, and most sincerely appreciated, forms of support that any loyal reader can offer. Thank you so much.)

ACKNOWLEDGEMENTS

Once again, I'd like to express my sincere appreciation to the team at Evolved Publishing, especially my editor, Dave Lane (AKA Lane Diamond), who continues to help hone my thoughts and writing to make my books the best they can be. I'm also thrilled that *Hammer to Fall* features another fantastic cover by artist Kris Norris.

To all my friends and family who have read earlier versions of this and other books in the series, your feedback and support has been indispensable to me, and you have my deepest thanks. I'd like to give special mention to Professor Anthony Tuck, with whom my wife and I spent a magical day in Tuscany, and who shared with us his knowledge and passion of Poggio Civitate and Etruscan culture and history... including the thrill of holding the mysterious "Rika" bobbin. I can't thank you enough for your support and inspiration.

Finally, and as always, I can't give enough thanks to my wife and steadfast partner in all things, Madeleine, whose level head, and objective input keeps me on track when things threaten to go off the rails. With you by my side, anything seems... possible.

ABOUT THE AUTHOR

William Noland combines a lifelong love of speculative fiction with a passion for history, sociology, and psychology. Engaging and entertaining, Noland's stories carry his hallmark of strong character development that weaves through every book in this page-turner series. In addition to writing, William plays in multiple rock bands and loves international travel and reading. He lives in Massachusetts with his wife and two cats.

For more, please visit William E. Noland online at:
Website: www.WENoland.com
Goodreads: William E. Noland
Facebook: @WENoland.Author
LinkedIn: www.linkedin.com/in/william-noland-103804140/

WHAT'S NEXT?

William and his team at Evolved Publishing are fast at work on Books 3-6 of the "Uncommon Bonds" series. Stay tuned to the web page referenced below to keep up to date.

www.EvolvedPub.com/UB

MORE FROM WILLIAM E. NOLAND

PLAYING WITH FIRE
Uncommon Bonds - 1

FINALIST: Independent Author Network – Book of the Year 2022 –
FICTION: PARANORMAL/SUPERNATURAL

WINNER: Pinnacle Book Achievement Award, Fall 2022 –
BEST SUPERNATURAL THRILLER

An ancient entity, trapped and suffering; a girl who inexplicably hears cries of anguish in her dreams.... What's their connection?

~~~

"I just kept turning the pages and could not put it down... The story was fast-paced and very interesting and kept me on the edge of my seat."
~ *Readers' Favorite Book Reviews, Alma Boucher (5 STARS)*

~~~

"I seldom read a book and start laughing out loud, but with *Playing with Fire*... this happened more than once. ...Waiting for the next book is going to feel like an eternity. I can't wait to read more about these characters who later on felt like friends."
~ *Readers' Favorite Book Reviews, Antoinette Wessels (5 STARS)*

~~~

Lotte has moved from Germany, and is new to Southby High School, where Eric is trapped with her as his German tutor. Despite being somewhat dazzled by her unusual beauty and keen intelligence, he quickly realizes there may be more to her crabby demeanor and the scary black circles under her eyes than anyone realizes.

The unlikely couple must discover the mysterious source of Lotte's debilitating nightmares... before madness overtakes her.

MORE FROM EVOLVED PUBLISHING

We offer great books across multiple genres, featuring high-quality editing (which we believe is second-to-none) and fantastic covers.

As a hybrid small press, your support as loyal readers is so important to us, and we have strived, with tireless dedication and sheer determination, to deliver on the promise of our motto:
QUALITY IS PRIORITY #1!

Please check out all of our great books,
which you can find at this link:
www.EvolvedPub.com/Catalog/

Thank you!

www.ingramcontent.com/pod-product-compliance
Lightning Source LLC
Chambersburg PA
CBHW020544020726
47494CB00006B/1914